DO WHAT GODMOTHER SAYS

L.S. STRATTON

UNION SQUARE & CO.
NEW YORK

Union Square & Co., LLC, is a subsidiary of Sterling Publishing Co., Inc.

ISBN 978-1-4549-4748-6 (trade paperback)
ISBN 978-1-4549-4749-3 (e-book)

Library of Congress Cataloging-in-Publication Data

Names: Stratton, L. S., author.
Title: Do what Godmother says / by L.S. Stratton.
Description: New York, NY : Union Square & Co., 2024. | Includes bibliographical references. | Summary: "A dual-timeline psychological thriller about a sinister white patron of Harlem Renaissance artists known as "Godmother" and a contemporary young Black woman who has inherited what may be a cursed painting"— Provided by publisher.
Identifiers: LCCN 2023043114 (print) | LCCN 2023043115 (ebook) | ISBN 9781454947486 (paperback) | ISBN 9781454947493 (epub)
Subjects: LCGFT: Psychological fiction. | Thrillers (Fiction) | Novels.
Classification: LCC PS3605.L4695 D6 2024 (print) | LCC PS3605.L4695 (ebook) | DDC 813/.6—dc23/eng/20231017
LC record available at https://lccn.loc.gov/2023043114
LC ebook record available at https://lccn.loc.gov/2023043115

For information about custom editions, special sales, and premium purchases, please contact specialsales@unionsquareandco.com.

Printed in Canada

2 4 6 8 10 9 7 5 3 1

unionsquareandco.com

Cover design by Lisa Amoroso
Interior design by Igor Satanovsky
Cover art: Getty Images: Westend61 (girl); Shutterstock.com: antpkr (wall texture), ionut Dogaru (frame), PK55 (wallpaper), timquo (paint)

DO WHAT GODMOTHER SAYS

To Annie Estelle Stratton and Rachel Louise Barr. You wondered for years if you inspired any of my work. I wish you were still here so I can show you this novel and say, "Yes. Yes, you did."

I love you and I miss you. I hope I continue to make you proud.

PART I

CHAPTER 1

ESSIE

NEW YORK CITY

March 9, 1928

YOU COULD SEE HER IN THE CROWD, THE LONE FIGURE WALKING AT A fast clip down Lenox Avenue like she had the devil at her heels. She was in search of a taxi that could take her to Penn Station. She had no suitcase, just the clothes on her back and one painting in her arms—the last she would ever paint.

Gales coming off the Hudson River shoved at her like the rude pedestrians she passed along the way. Mostly boozehounds drunk on bathtub gin or giddy couples headed toward the drumbeats and the twinkling marquee of the Savoy Ballroom. She gave up trying to keep the panels of her mink coat close. Each gust of wind revealed a glimpse of the billowing silk nightgown she wore underneath, but thankfully, not the russet-red splatter.

"Hopped outta bed and didn't even grab your clothes, huh, Sugar? Was he *that* bad?" one catcaller had shouted to her from the front stoop of a row house as she walked by, making his companions cackle and slap their knees.

Her teeth were chattering. Her feet, which were clad in damp men's, white buck oxfords, were going numb. She longed to stop at one of the cabarets where jazz and ragtime music seeped through the doorways like cigarette smoke. She longed for just about anyplace that wasn't wet with melting snow or cold, where she could sit for a minute or two, but she didn't dare stop.

They'd probably discovered she was gone by now. They'd be coming after her.

Essie squinted, peering into the headlights of the passing cars. Among the Fords, Falcons, Packards, and Studebakers, she searched frantically for a flash of yellow. Finally, she spotted a taxi in the distance, coming toward her. She ran to meet it, watching as the driver approached the curb. She waved him down.

"Stop! I need to get to Penn Station! Please stop!" she yelled.

But he didn't. Whether it was because of her wild eyes, odd appearance, or her brown skin, she didn't know. But the taxi driver kept going, though they'd locked eyes through the taxi's glass. He continued down Lenox Avenue, his rear steel bumper receding into the night.

Essie dropped her hand.

"You need a ride to Penn Station?" a raspy voice called behind her.

She whipped around to find an old Negro man staring at her. His hands were shoved into the pockets of a wool jacket. A cigar was clenched between his yellow teeth. She watched as he adjusted the bill of his flat cap then gestured to the beat-up Ford Model T where he currently had one foot braced on the running board.

She nodded. "Y-y-yes."

"I can take ya' there," he said.

"You're a taxi driver?" Essie asked with disbelief, spotting no identification number on his vehicle or even a sign in the window that said he had a chauffeur's license.

"Sure am!" He tossed his cigar to the ground and walked to the car's rear door. He pried it open with a loud squeak. "Hop on in."

She hesitated.

She *did* need a ride, and she knew that not all taxi drivers in New York, especially the ones that ferried Negro passengers, drove the yellow cars that traversed the city. But she had also lived in Harlem long enough to know that not everyone was who they claimed to be. What if she had just escaped one hell and was running toward another?

The man cocked an eyebrow. "You comin' or not, honey?"

Essie started to walk away, shaking her head, but stopped short when she spotted another car at the end of the block, turning onto the street. Her heartbeat quickened when she saw the familiar sparkling grille and the white front fenders and hood. She began to tremble as the Rolls-Royce Phantom's emblem came into view. The Spirit of Ecstacy sailed ominously toward her with arms outstretched, as if riding on the wind.

She ran toward the Model T before tossing the painting onto the backseat and climbing inside. She grabbed the handle and slammed the door shut, catching the man by surprise.

"Go!" she shouted.

His easy smile disappeared.

"Go!" she shouted again. "We need to go now!"

He didn't ask any questions—to her great relief. He ran to the driver's side and climbed behind the wheel instead. They pulled off seconds later.

When they reached the intersection, Essie eased aside the rear flap and looked to see if the Rolls-Royce was following them, but true to its namesake, the car had disappeared like a phantom.

Had it really been there? she wondered as the taxi drove toward Midtown.

"You runnin' from somebody, sweetheart?" the driver asked, making her whip her gaze away from the rear flap to look at him. She stared at the back of his bald head, at the two rolls of fat over his shirt collar and his wide shoulders. "Your poppa comin' after you? Or maybe one of them card sharks? You owe somebody some money?"

"No," she answered softly.

The car fell silent as he waited for her to elaborate, but he would have to wait forever. How could she possibly explain to him—a total stranger—what had happened to her and not sound stark raving mad? She was still grappling with what had happened herself, second-guessing everything even now.

But the splatters on her gown were a reminder, along with her painting—and the other token she now carried.

"This is the closest I can get you," the driver suddenly announced several minutes later. He pulled to a stop along the curb and pointed to the granite building at the end of the block. "It ain't that much of a walk, though."

She swallowed, following the path of his finger. Penn Station may as well have been twenty miles away.

Essie dug into her coat pocket, pulled out a wad of crumpled dollar bills, and handed the driver his fare.

"Hey, thanks for the tip!" he shouted to her as she grabbed her things and leaped out of the taxi.

She walked swiftly to the entrance, keeping her eyes forward and stride long. But she could sense that she was being followed as she made her way to the main entrance. She stole a glance behind her.

Could she see white?

She turned her head completely and saw the Rolls-Royce Phantom again, gliding in her direction.

It's not real, she told herself. *It's not real.*

But it seemed real. She couldn't help but run, nearly bumping into an older white man as she made her way into the station.

"Watch it, jig!" he shouted after her.

She ignored the insult and zigzagged her way through the crowd.

Essie was nearly out of breath when she approached the line in front of one of the ticket booths.

She'd done it. Despite the odds, she'd made it this far. All she needed to do now was to buy a ticket and board a train that would take her out of New York. But where should she go?

She could go back to South Carolina, back to her family. She could grovel at Aunt Idalene's feet and ask her for sanctuary. But Essie wasn't eager to do that or return to the old homestead with its tobacco barns and dirt roads, to the land of Jim Crow. Back home, she'd had to endure a lot worse than white cab drivers ignoring her and being called a "jiggaboo." She couldn't see herself settling there again, not after living up here in Harlem.

Besides, they knew where she was from. They could easily find her down there.

Maybe she could take a train to Boston or Chicago. Change her name. She could disappear in another big city.

"Next!" the woman behind the gated ticket counter barked.

Essie stepped forward. "I . . . I need to buy a ticket."

The woman rolled her eyes. Her pouty mouth, painted to look like Clara Bow, puckered with distaste. "Yeah, it's a ticket window. You wanna buy a ticket *to where*?"

Essie hesitated, still unsure. She looked up at the departure board overhead. The train to Boston was exiting from Terminal 13. *Thirteen.* That was a bad sign, and she had ignored the signs before—to her own folly. But the train number for Chicago was 26668. That wouldn't do either.

"Hey!" the woman behind the counter snapped. "We've got other people in line. Either buy a ticket or—"

"Philadelphia," Essie blurted out. "I want to buy a ticket to Philadelphia. Broad Street Station, please."

The train to Philly was departing from Terminal 7. Lucky number seven. And Louise was in Philly.

They'd both left South Carolina to follow their dreams. Essie would become a painter and study in New York. Meanwhile, Louise would travel from city to city like a vagabond, taking jobs as a maid, a salesclerk, and even a nightclub coat check girl before finally settling in Philly five months ago, securing a spot as a hotel cleaner.

Louise wouldn't turn her away; Louise would help.

"That'll be $2.60," the woman behind the counter said.

While Essie sat in the waiting area, surrounded by people eating popcorn and peanuts, reading issues of the *New York Herald Tribune* and *Photoplay,* she knew that she was being watched.

They were watching and biding their time. They were laughing at her hubris.

She would never get away. Someone or something would stop her.

It'll happen now, she thought as she walked down the platform to board her train, taking cautious glances over her shoulder.

As Essie listened to the "all boarding" last call minutes later and then felt the train lurch forward as it pulled away from the station, she had a death grip on the armrests, still anticipating some force stopping her or the train. Maybe a massive snowstorm. Or a derailment. Maybe the ground would open and swallow her whole. But as the skyscrapers and lights of New York City gradually disappeared from her window view—nothing happened. The train continued into the night. She loosened her hold on the seat's wooden arms. She was both shocked and relieved that she'd regained her freedom. She'd escaped.

Essie realized this would probably be the last time she would ever see New York. She couldn't come back. She said a silent goodbye to her art studio, to Central Park, to the jazz clubs she'd frequented, to the rent parties where she'd danced the night away, to the lovers she'd had, and to the friends she'd made.

The fatigue that had been tugging at her for hours finally won out. With her painting resting safely on her knees, her eyes slowly drifted close. Essie moaned and whimpered as she slumbered though, making one of the Pullman porters stare down at her worriedly when he passed by. He wondered what she was dreaming about.

Blood. A face contorted in pain. Being chased in the dark.

By the time Essie woke up, her train would be ninety miles out of New York City, only minutes from Broad Street Station. Back on the Upper East Side, a housemaid would find Maude Bachmann—esteemed philanthropist and Essie's art patron—tangled in the bloody sheets on her four-poster bed.

The old woman's eyes would be open and she would be stabbed three times—a mystical number—twice in the chest, once in the stomach.

The maid would let out a scream that would wake the entire household, maybe even the dead.

CHAPTER 2
SHANICE

WASHINGTON, D.C.
Present day

THE PAINTING HAS BEEN HANGING ON THE WALL OF MY GRAND-mother's bedroom for as long as I can remember. I call it *The Portrait of the Defiant Woman*, though I don't think it has a name. I don't even know who painted it.

The color palette is dark. Lots of browns, grays, and blues. The woman in the portrait—ochre-skinned with short, curly hair—is cradling a bundle protectively against her chest, covering her naked torso. The bundle's fabric is made of intricate woven patterns. You can't tell what's in it; it could be bread or even clothes.

Her garb is a crude imitation of tribal. A crown of chicken feathers sits askew on her head. A necklace made of bones dons her neck. Probably not something someone from any real African tribe would wear, but the movie version circa 1940s Tarzan—a caricature of what tribal would be. But her face . . . her expression keeps the viewer from even thinking about laughing.

Her brown eyes are wide like she's been startled. Her face, which is partially hidden in the shadows, seems to dare the viewer to look at her.

The portrait vaguely reminds me of Johannes Vermeer's *Girl with a Pearl Earring*, but more intense. It used to scare me when I was little. I always felt like the woman's eyes followed me around the room, so I would avoid going in there.

Gotta clear out the house, Gram's text says. That old painting is yours if you want it.

I squint down at my cell screen, surprised that Gram is giving away something she's owned for so long.

Thanks, Gram, I type back quickly, not having time to ask her why she has to "clear out the house," let alone why she's giving up such a prized possession, because I'm too preoccupied with something more important at the moment.

Jason is leaving me.

For the past few months, I could see it coming, like one of the many signs and omens Gram always talks about.

"Your hand itchin'?" she asked me once as I absently scratched my palm. "Looks to me like some lucky girl is about to get some money!" she said in a singsong voice.

Or when I was ten, my allergies were so bad that I got a sinus infection, and I made the mistake of complaining in front of her that I had an earache.

"Ears ringin', huh?" Gram slowly shook her head and made a *tsk, tsk* sound. "Somebody must be talkin' about you."

I know I've inherited her superstitious nature because, like I said, I could see the breakup coming. The beard shavings left in the bathroom sink. The overflowing trash cans in our apartment. The nearly empty containers of ice cream and OJ I kept discovering in the fridge no matter how many times I threw the old ones away. They were signs of disrepair. Atrophy. Our relationship was slowly grinding to a halt like an old car engine.

And then, about a week ago, I returned home to find a stray cat asleep on our welcome mat. The black feline was curled into a ball with its eyes closed and its left ear flicking as it slept. It didn't stir until I was nearly two feet away. When I came close, it jumped to its feet with its back arched and tail puffy, like it was going to defend its new home or die trying, but then the cat seemed to think better of it and scampered off, disappearing down the corridor.

The next morning Jason told me we were done. Today, he is making it official.

I drop my cell into my purse and walk out of our kitchen to head to work after loitering and avoiding having to say goodbye to Jason all morning. I grab my keys and my thermal coffee mug from the counter and watch Jason close the lid of one of the many boxes he's amassed over the last week to move out of our apartment.

There are little cardboard mountains in every room now, and archipelagoes of garbage bags along the walls. They're filled with items he plans to throw away or donate to the Salvation Army. I watch as he leans down to grab packing tape from one of the end tables to seal the box he's just finished packing.

"I don't understand why you have to do all this now," I say, gesturing to the box.

Jason yanks a long wad of tape from the roll with a piercing screech, making me wince.

"Why can't you wait until I get home from work?" I ask over the noise.

I'm drumming my nails on the side of my mug as I talk. It's a nervous tick and it's annoying but I can't stop.

"Why do you have to be moved out before then?"

I don't think I can bear to come home to a dark, silent apartment. I imagine that all the boxes and our living room furniture will be gone save for a lone coffee table where Jason will leave his house key.

"Because the moving guys will be here in a couple of hours and who knows when you'll get home anyway. You're always working late." He glances over his shoulder at me as he tapes the lid close. "Besides, what's the point of me being here? What more is there to say?"

"What more is there to say? We were together for almost *five years*. You can't give me a decent goodbye? You at least owe me that."

Click, click, click, click. My nails drum to a steady beat.

I think about the early days and how much Jason pursued me. How he'd *just happen* to show up at our office building whenever I did every morning, or how we'd always end up at the same sandwich shops for lunch, standing in line only a few people apart.

I found out later that Jason had been stalking me for almost a month before he finally asked me out, trying to work up the nerve to talk to me. And our first date had been so over the top—a private rooftop dinner and a Ferris wheel ride overlooking the National Harbor.

Where had all that fervor gone? Shouldn't our ending match the beginning?

I want sobbing. Shouting. Maybe even some dishes to be thrown. Something melodramatic. Not this sad, unexceptional exit like two college roommates going their separate ways at the end of the semester.

Jason tosses aside the roll of tape. He turns away from the cardboard box to finally look at me. I hoped to find his expression apologetic. Maybe he's ashamed of how he's treating me. Treating *us*. Instead, his nutmeg-hued face remains impassive. His dark eyes are flat.

"I don't know what else you think I owe you at this point, Shanice. Considering how much I've been carrying the weight of our relationship . . . hell, carrying *you* for the past year, I don't really feel like I owe you a thing."

I stop drumming my nails. I'm shocked into silence.

It wasn't a shout or a dinner plate hurled at my head, but it hurts just as much.

"Fuck you," I say because I can't think of anything else.

I walk to our apartment door. My hand is shaking as I grab the doorknob and slam the door shut behind me.

CHAPTER 3

Inhale, exhale.

Inhale, exhale.

Inhale, exhale.

I've been taking slow, deep breaths the entire metro ride to work, but it's not helping. Every screech of the train wheel over the track has me on edge. The operator did a hard brake a few stations back, and I bit down so hard on the skin inside my mouth that I thought it might bleed.

"Dupont Circle," the automated voice says over the static-filled speaker. "Doors opening."

I hear the chime, rise from my seat, and join the dozen or so people waiting to be disgorged onto the even more crowded platform. It feels like I've just done this, but in reverse. I worked late last night, like I have many other nights, toiling at the office over page proofs—even though we'd had an office party that day and everyone else had taken off early. I rode the same train home after ten o'clock, almost nodding off to sleep in my chair.

Now as I walk to the escalators, I glance at my reflection in the plexiglass of a passing train.

My curly hair is tucked into place, pinned in a loose bun atop my head. I'm wearing makeup and a small heel. The red shirt I chose this morning brings out the warm undertones in my brown skin.

In the glass, I see the image of a twenty-nine-year-old woman who seems capable and stable, of the woman I have to be to get through the long, busy workday ahead of me. I don't have the luxury to think about the breakup or about Jason. I don't have the luxury of falling apart.

As I scan my metro card over the gate reader and see that I only have $3.65 left—*just* enough for my train ride back home—I try not to obsess about how I'm going to afford transportation and rent in a major city with my miniscule savings (exactly $437 total), a lack of real income, and no more financial support from my gainfully employed boyfriend.

I know that's what Jason meant when he said he'd been "carrying" me for the past year. But he agreed to do it. *We* agreed that this was the sacrifice we needed to make so I could take my editorial internship at *The Intersector* magazine.

"It's *unpaid*? You don't get a salary?" Jason choked after taking a bite of the lemon blueberry cake he'd picked up at Sprinkles in Georgetown on the way home so we could celebrate my getting the job. He grabbed a glass of water to swallow down the rest. "You never told me that."

"It's not unpaid. It has a five-hundred-dollar stipend."

"Five hundred dollars a week?"

"A month," I said, making him look like he was about to choke all over again.

"Shanice, you quit a job making eighty grand a year for this."

"A boring job that didn't fulfill me."

"Do they at least give you medical insurance?"

"I'm an intern, not an employee. Why would I get medical insurance?"

"Jesus, Shanice," he exhaled. "Someone with your . . . with your issues—"

"*Issues?*"

"Don't get defensive," he said tightly. "You know what I mean. You need medical coverage. What if you have a—"

"It's only temporary. I'll be an intern for a year or two, and then they'll bring me on full-time. I'll get a pay increase and insurance. Problem solved!"

He still didn't look convinced.

"Jason, I knew if I told you all this stuff what you would say, but . . . but I can't turn down this job. Do you know how many folks applied for this thing?"

The Intersector magazine was well respected. Plenty of its former editors had gone on to places like *The Economist*, *The Atlantic*, and *The New Yorker.* Maybe the same could happen to me if I worked there, worked hard, and moved up the ranks. This was my gateway.

"And you left your job at that firm three years ago to work at a startup. Nothing was guaranteed for you either, but now you're making six figures," I argued to Jason that night. "You're the friggin IT director!"

"That was different, Shanice. I—"

"No, it wasn't. It's the same thing. Your boss chose you because they saw your potential and the editors at *The Intersector* chose *me*, honey. Out of all of those folks, they chose me."

Jason hesitated before taking another bite of cake. "Okay," he said between chews, "as long as you aren't being taken advantage of. As long as this isn't just . . ." His voice faded.

"Isn't just . . . what?"

"A way for them to get cheap labor. I don't want you to waste your time and end up at a dead-end job."

"It's not! It's not that at all. It's gonna lead to big things, honey. I know it."

He didn't say it at the time, but I guess Jason didn't believe me. He never did.

I climb the last stair on the escalators and emerge out of the dark metro tunnels into a blazing bright morning and a street already teeming with foot and car traffic. I take a few steps and slow to a stop. Instead of running into my normal flock of pigeons fighting over bits of bagel or puttering down the sidewalk like morning commuters, I see a solitary crow near a parking meter.

Another bad omen.

It looks up and focuses its onyx eyes on me. I stare back at it until it lets out a squawk as loud as a car horn. I turn away and continue walking, telling myself to calm down, to not let my superstitions get the better of me.

I wasn't dumped because I saw a black cat on my welcome mat, but because Jason and I hadn't had a date night in six months. Because we'd lost our ability to communicate as a couple. And nothing will happen now that I've seen the crow. It's just a random coincidence. That's all.

But that doesn't mean I don't hesitate before stepping into every crosswalk, on the lookout for a speeding car or a runaway bus. It doesn't mean that I don't go to the other side of the street to avoid walking under the scaffolding where construction workers are hammering and buzzing away.

I manage to reach the magazine's office building a few minutes later. No catastrophes along the way. There, I see Priya, the editorial assistant, near the entrance. She's leaning her petite frame against the building's granite exterior. Like me, she's also nursing what looks like a cup of coffee.

She seems hungover. I'm not surprised. A few of the other staffers took her to a bar after her going-away party to celebrate her new job. As I draw closer, she looks up, lowers her cup, and waves at me before taking another sip.

"Hey," I say.

"Hi, Shanice," she answers weakly, pushing her sunglasses to her crown. Yeah, she is definitely hungover. There are bags under her eyes. "I guess I beat you to work today. You're later than usual this morning. What happened?"

Inhale, exhale.

Inhale, exhale.

Inhale, exhale.

"Just . . . uh . . . metro. You know how it is. So are you excited?" I ask, changing the subject from my lateness, not wanting to give the true reason behind it. "Just two more days, then off to *The Miscreant*."

It's a new online news venture that's been getting a lot of buzz. She's joining as one of the editors. Priya shrugs. "I'm more relieved than anything else."

"Well, I'm happy for you."

I start pivoting from one foot to the other, bouncing on the balls of my feet like I have to use the bathroom. More fidgeting. I force myself to stop so she doesn't notice that something is off. But my mask isn't as good today.

I watch as Priya wiggles her head. I'm not sure if it's indifference or thanks.

"Really. I mean it, Priya. If anyone deserves to move on, it's . . . it's you."

She was the intern before me—the lowest on the office totem pole before she was promoted to editorial assistant. Though she outranked me, she never made me feel that way.

Her face softens. "Thank you, Shanice. I appreciate that."

"Well, I better head upstairs since I'm already late." I turn toward the doors. "You comin'?" I ask, inclining my head toward the entrance.

"No, not yet, but I will be in the office soon. I just have to finish this first." She holds her cup aloft.

I nod and face the doors again. In the glass reflection, I notice over my shoulder a fuzzy object in one of the trees across the street.

Perched on one of the branches is another crow, or maybe it's the crow from earlier.

"Something wrong?" Priya calls.

"Huh? Uh, no," I say, adjusting my satchel. "No, I'm . . . I'm fine."

I push open the door and step inside. When I take a final glance over my shoulder, I see that the crow is gone.

CHAPTER 4

LISTENING TO THE SERIES OF PINGS AND SCREECHES, TO THE LABORED whine of decades-old cables, I close my eyes as I ride the building's rickety elevator to the fifth floor. Today, it feels like it's a flip of a coin whether this ride will be my last. Whether I make it to the magazine's offices—or go plunging back down to the floors below.

The Intersector is housed in one of the older buildings in Dupont Circle. It's six stories tall and nestled on Florida Avenue, not too far from Embassy Row.

A photo of the building is featured on the magazine's website. It's shot in black and white, highlighting the exterior's Beaux-Arts architecture with all its flourishes and shadows. The whitewashed granite and scalloped brass awning over the entrance. The arched windows with their fierce gargoyles perched at the corners of each ledge. Those shadows are even more pronounced at night when the streetlights hit the building at just the right angle. It looks almost forbidding from a distance.

Whatever rich, old white dude built it a hundred years ago obviously meant it to intimidate—and it does, but it's a false bravado. You realize that as soon as you step inside and make it past the ornate lobby. You see the 1980s, industrial offices with their drop ceilings, linoleum tile, and heavy-duty, nursery-school-style carpets. And you ride the deathtrap elevators that probably haven't been serviced since 1996.

My eyes pop open when I hear a loud buzz; it's my cell, not the elevator. I've got a new text. I dig through my purse, in search of my phone.

When are you gonna come to get it? I can wrap it up for you, the text from Gram says.

I stare at the screen, confused, but then I realize she's talking about *The Portrait of the Defiant Woman*. I get a flashback to the woman's haunting eyes that I once believed could actually see me. I shake my head.

No thanks, Gram, I start to type in reply. I don't want it, but I could–

I'm about to offer to take it to Goodwill for her, but stop typing as the elevator car I'm riding shudders to a stop. I tuck my phone back into my purse—I'll finish writing the text after I settle into the office. I turn the corner, surprised to find a few of the other staffers congregating in the hallway as if someone decided to hold an impromptu meeting there.

Ted, our managing editor, is leaning against the wall, chewing his nails. Connor, our designer, is sitting on the hallway floor with his legs crossed at the ankles. He looks worried. Meanwhile, Darcy, our associate editor, is pacing up and down the hall, shoving her glasses up the bridge of her nose as she excitedly talks into her cell.

"Yeah. Yeah, the police are here," she says, twirling a lock of curly hair around her finger. "They told us to stay out here and wait . . . No, I don't know . . . I said I don't know, Kendall! Maybe they're calling in CSI."

"Uh, what's going on?" I ask Connor. "Why is everyone out here?"

He slowly looks up at me. "Someone broke into the office last night and trashed the place. Stole equipment too."

"What?"

"They didn't break in," Ted says, though it sounds more like "*Zey didn't take in,*" because he's still chewing his nails. He finally lowers his hand from his mouth and shoves them into the pockets of his khakis. He purses his chapped lips. "The cops are saying there's no signs of forced entry. It looks like the door was left unlocked. Kinda makes you wish now this building actually had a security desk instead of part-time guards."

I was the last person to leave the office last night—or at least, I thought I was. I frantically try to remember if I locked the door behind me when I left, replaying the sequence of steps in my head. I remember placing the stack of corrected page proofs on our editor Gary's desk. I remember turning off my laptop. I even remember turning off the lights and shutting the door behind me, but I can't remember if I locked the door. My mind is drawing a blank.

Instead, I remember the crow. The one in the tree. It was a sign that something bad was about to happen, like I thought.

Inhale, exhale.

Inhale, exhale.

Inhale, exhale.

I turn away from Ted, walk over Connor's extended legs, and make my way farther down the hall. I peek through the doorway where Gary stands, shoving his hand into his graying hair, looking what could only be described as shell shocked while he talks to a uniformed police officer. As he talks, another cop walks around our offices, surveying what is now a crime scene.

Connor was right. Whoever was here trashed the place. Papers are everywhere. Drawers are hanging open carelessly. One is yanked out of Ted's desk completely and its contents now spill onto the floor. They (whoever *they* were) knocked over the water-cooler too, either purposely or in haste during the burglary, soaking the carpet and the sea of strewn papers. I can see that some of the laptops are missing, probably stolen. A few of the plaques from the Society of Professional Journalists and National Magazine Awards are ripped down, leaving rough gouges in the drywall.

"Had your office received any threats before this?" the officer standing closest to Gary asks. "Anything that might make you believe this was more than just a burglary."

Gary throws out his hands. He shrugs. "Uh, I guess. I mean . . . yeah, sure! But we're a political magazine. We're always getting emails and hate tweets telling us to die in a fire. But I don't know if . . ." His words drift off as his eyes shift and land on me. "Shanice, there you are! I've been looking for you."

I point at my chest. "For . . . *me*?"

"Yeah," he says, beckoning me into the room, "you were the last one here last night, right?"

I step into the office, listening to the crinkling of paper under my feet. "I think so."

"And who are you?" the cop asks, head cocked, now looking at me too.

I can feel the heavy weight of their gazes. My throat is dry, so I loudly clear it.

"I'm Shanice Pierce. I work here. I'm . . . uh . . . the . . . an intern."

"When did you leave last night, Ms. Pierce?" the cop asks.

Inhale, exhale.

Inhale, exhale.

Inhale, exhale.

"I left at ten o'clock. Maybe ten thirty," I say, clenching my hands in front of me while silently telling myself that if there is any time *not* to fidget, it's now; I don't want to look guilty.

"Do you remember hearing anything?" the cop asks. "Did you see anyone unfamiliar in the building as you left?"

I slowly shake my head. My armpits are getting damp under my red shirt. I imagine little sweaty semicircles forming there.

"Uh, no," I say. "I didn't . . . I didn't see anyone. I didn't hear anything unusual."

The cop nods and turns to face Gary again. "It sounds like a case of just a random burglary. Happens all the time. Maybe someone was roaming through the building late last night, looking for an unlocked door, and just happened to stumble upon yours."

"But we've been in this building for over twenty years and we've never had a burglary. Why did it happen now?"

"Don't know, sir. Neighborhoods change."

Gary and the cop are talking privately now; I'm no longer in the conversation. I guess I've been dismissed.

I slink out of the office and return to where the rest of the staff is huddled. Priya now stands with them. She's talking to Ted. I assume he's caught her up on the news.

When I draw close, they all stare at me.

"Did you talk to the police?" Darcy asks. Her blue eyes assess me eagerly behind the smudged lenses of her glasses.

I nod. "They asked me if I heard or saw anything."

"Well? *Did you?*" Ted asks.

I shake my head.

"Shit! We are so fucked," he mutters. "With our computers gone, there's no way we're gonna be able to finish the issue in time."

"We still have most of the files on the server," Connor begins, "but I didn't get the chance to . . ."

I stop listening to the rest of their conversation, now lost in my own thoughts.

I was the last one here, which meant I was most likely the one who left the door unlocked. This is all my fault. What does that mean for my job?

I've worked twelve-hour days, six days a week for less than minimum wage. I put on a cheerful facade while I did the office grunt work. So far, Gary has rejected all my pitches. He'd either seen it before, said it wasn't right for the magazine's readership, or didn't think I had the chops to pull it off.

"I liked your pitch about the long history of hip-hop and activism," Gary said at our last meeting. "It has potential, but it needs some refinement. I'd feel much more comfortable with something like that in our more senior editors' hands. Someone like Ted."

"Just got the new Drake album," Ted said with a grin and a nod. "It was fire! I'd *love* to tackle a topic like this."

"Sure," I said through gritted teeth, "I'll give you my notes."

I did it all to prove myself. This was supposed to be a new beginning. This was supposed to be my big chance—only to have it wiped out by one mistake.

That crow. That stupid crow! I knew when I saw it this morning that something was going to happen. I'm going to get fired. I probably won't even have the chance to—

"Are you okay?" Priya asks, snapping me back to the present.

Gradually, I nod again.

"Are you sure?"

"Yeah, I'm . . . I'm fine."

An hour later, we're back in the office, trying our best to clean up the mess the burglars left behind. I keep quiet, gathering handfuls of paper and shoving them into garbage bags.

"I can't believe this," Gary murmurs as he stands in the center of the office, still shaking his head and noticeably not lifting a finger to clean. "I just can't believe this! How the hell did this happen?"

No one answers him, continuing our tasks in silence.

"Who robs a magazine?" he laments.

"Maybe it was the maintenance staff," Ted volunteers. "I think they work with contractors. I bet they don't always do background checks. Maybe one of them came in, grabbed the equipment, and decided to pawn it to feed their drug habit or . . . or something."

Or something?

I can't decide if Ted's baseless accusations about the building's mostly black and Latino maintenance staff is racist or classist. Maybe both.

"We don't do background checks either," Gary says. "I just trusted that everyone in the office has been honest with me."

His words fall like an anvil in the room, making us all go silent again. I pause from my cleaning to look up at Gary. His green eyes are focused back on me.

"What are you saying, Gare?" Darcy asks.

"I'm saying that I've trusted everyone here to act professionally and responsibly, but maybe I shouldn't have."

I set down my trash bag. My face flushes with heat. My ears are starting to ring.

Inhale, exhale.

Inhale, exhale.

In—

"We've never had a break-in. This was our first time ever, and *you* were the last one in the office, Shanice, and you were one of the last people here this morning. You're never late," Gary says, striding across the office toward me. "Did you or did you not let someone in here last night? Do you know who did this?"

My stomach tightens into a painful knot.

I don't know how to respond to Gary's question.

I knew eventually I'd be held responsible for not locking the door behind me last night, but I never expected Gary to think I was in any way connected to the burglary. That I tried to *rob* the place.

"Are you serious?" I ask.

"Gary," Priya begins, a grimace marring her brown face, "you can't—"

"Yes, I'm serious!" he says, talking over her. "I want to know the truth. It's a simple question. Do you know who did this, Shanice? Do you know where our laptops went? Just tell me!"

I look around the room, waiting for someone besides Priya to come to my defense, but they don't say anything. Ted, Darcy, and Connor either stare at me like they were waiting for my answer or sheepishly look away.

I'm stunned. Stunned that they would think I was capable of such a thing. These people have known me for almost a year. Worked with me. They all signed a card for my birthday. And now this is happening.

Is it racist or classist? I wonder again. It could be all of it or none of it. The truth is it doesn't matter. The accusation stings all the same. It burns hot, making my skin tingle. My body temperature is skyrocketing. My heart is racing. The urge to flee is screaming inside my head.

I stumble to my desk and quickly gather my things, barely paying attention to what I'm shoving into my tote bag. My desk calendar. A stapler. A chipped coffee mug. I head to the office door to escape.

"What are you doing? You can't just leave! You didn't answer my question!" Gary calls after me.

I want to shout back at him, but I can't breathe, let alone speak.

"Shanice," Priya says. "Shanice, wait!"

But I won't wait. I can't. I'll die if I stay here.

I walk out the door and no one follows me or tries to stop me, which is good because I'm breathing like I've just run a marathon. I feel like I'm wearing a corset that's tightening around my rib cage.

By some miracle, I make it to the lobby. I can barely see because of the tears in my eyes. I push through the glass doors that deposit me back onto the curb. The vice grip around my ribs has only gotten tighter. I'm shaking all over and sobbing now. I lean forward with my hand on my stomach, choking as I gasp for air.

Inhale, exhale.

Inhale . . .

In—

"Yo, sis, you good?" a stranger asks, but I can't answer him.

I can't form a sentence because my mind is racing, and I'm getting sensory overload from the city traffic and people walking by. I hear the blare of a fire engine. The heavy bass of a car stereo. A woman talking loudly on her cell phone. I close my eyes to keep from feeling dizzy.

Calm down. Calm down. Slow, deep breaths, I tell myself.

"You need me to call somebody? You need a doctor or an ambulance or somethin'?" he shouts.

Inhale . . .

Inhale . . .

Inhale, exhale.

Inhale, exhale.

Inhale, exhale.

The dizziness wanes. Slowly, I can breathe again.

How long have I been standing here? Sixty seconds? Five minutes? I open my glassy eyes and finally, I nod, wiping the tears from my cheeks. "Yeah, umm . . . I'm . . . I'm fine. I'm okay," I say shakily. "You d-d-don't need to call anyone. Thank you."

The stranger—a guy with dreads who's probably my age, maybe younger—eyes me warily but keeps walking, joining the rest of the pedestrians.

I force myself to stand upright, wondering who else saw me. As if on cue, I hear the squawk overhead.

I see it perched near the building's entrance on the head of one of the gargoyles. The crow. It's staring down at me, like it's been waiting for me this whole time.

I glare back at it until it flaps its wings once, twice, then takes off.

CHAPTER 5

My cell phone buzzes, and I'm startled awake by the sound of it and my laptop falling to the hardwood floor. I rub my eyes with the heels of my hands and look around my bedroom.

There is no longer light outside my window and the bedroom is pitch black, making the glow of my cell seem even brighter. Where did all the sunlight go? I could feel the emptiness of the room, but now I can see it in the dim light coming from my phone screen. The open spaces on my dresser. The vacant pillow beside me.

It's all a reminder that Jason doesn't live here anymore. That I'm alone.

I haven't seen him since he moved out. The day I quit and had a full-blown panic attack, I went to a nearby sandwich shop and stayed locked in one of their bathroom stalls so long that one of the waitresses knocked on the stall door and asked if I was all right in there.

I stayed another hour, willing myself to regain control, until I got a text from Jason saying that he'd finished loading his things into the moving truck and the apartment was all mine. I finally left the restaurant and went home.

He and I have only "spoken" once since that day and briefly: it was by text five days ago when I reminded him that he left his apartment key, but forgot to leave the spare.

Away on business, his message said. Will bring it when I get back.

Either he still hasn't gotten back from wherever he went for his business trip, or he's completely forgotten about the spare key. I wouldn't be surprised if, like the spare key, he's gradually forgetting about me too.

My cell phone buzzes again. I reluctantly reach for it, prepared to press the button to send the call to voicemail. But when I see the name onscreen, I don't tap the little red button.

Damn. Gram is calling.

I remember it all at once. Her texts about cleaning out her house. Her offer of the painting in her bedroom. She left me a voicemail too.

"Just checkin' in on you, honey," her gravelly voice said. "I even called your father to see what's goin' on with you, and you know how much I just *love* talkin' to him. He claims you're goin' through a lot right now, but I said you're a strong girl. You'll be okay. Call me back!" she implored.

But I didn't call her back. Instead, I've stayed mostly in bed for almost a week, not seeing or speaking to anyone. Gram deserves better than that, better than being ghosted by her granddaughter.

I sit upright in bed and press the green button on the screen. "Hey, Gram," I say, forcing lightness into my voice.

"There she is!" my grandmother cries. "I figured if I kept callin' you, you'd pick up."

"Yeah, uh, sorry. I meant to call you back, but I . . . well, I—"

"Uh-hunh," she grunts, cutting me off, like she has less energy to hear my halfhearted excuse than I have to say it. "Your daddy said he hasn't heard from you in a while either. I was about to tell him to beat down your door and make sure you were still alive."

I choke back a laugh. "I'm still alive."

"Still walking too, I guess. Do your hands still work as well?"

"Yes," I say slowly, wondering where she's going with this.

"Good. Then you can come over and do a little favor for me."

"What little favor?"

"I started straightening up the house, like I said, but it didn't take me long to figure out that it's just too much for an old lady like me to do on my own."

I'm not surprised by this. That old painting isn't the only thing she's had forever.

Gram's home has been in our family for generations, and she seems to have inherited or collected furniture, knickknacks, and tchotchkes spanning more than a century. She's stuffed all that crap into every square inch of her little bungalow and her fenced-in yard. She isn't quite ready to be featured on an episode of *Hoarders*, but she's getting there.

"I thought you could help me," Gram continues, "since you probably ain't busy. Your daddy said you lost your job."

"I quit, actually," I whisper.

The phone line goes quiet. She waits for me to explain more, but I don't. I guess Dad didn't tell her everything. Of course, he didn't. Those two barely talk anyway, but I'm in no mood to rehash the story to her right now. I didn't even tell my bestie, Tati, the true reason why I quit. It's too . . . triggering.

I've heard people use the word before, usually casually, even flippantly.

I was so triggered.

Uh-oh, trigger warning!

But I'm not being hyperbolic. There's nothing else to accurately describe what it feels like to be put back in one of your lowest moments, in that bad place all over again. The rush of emotions. The sensations are replayed almost verbatim. Then you're reminded of even worse moments. You're dropped back into those heart-wrenching memories that you don't want to think about, and they all coalesce into one singular thought that threatens to crush you.

"Well, I'm . . . I'm sure you quit for a good reason," Gram says after a while in an unspoken understanding that I love her for, "and you'll find a new job. I know you will. Until then, you've got plenty of time to help your ol' Gram."

How the hell am I going to find the will or energy to clean the overflowing museum that she calls a house? I wasn't even able to get out of bed today. Then I remind myself that I can't talk to Gram about stuff like this, about dealing with heartbreak and loss.

This is a woman who would never allow herself to wallow in self-pity. She wouldn't even allow herself time to mourn after my mother died. I heard the morning after Mom's funeral, Gram was back at work, answering phones and getting coffee for the Fed chairman she used to work for before she retired.

And Gram is pretty old-fashioned; she doesn't believe in therapy. When I was diagnosed with generalized anxiety disorder back when I was a teenager, she couldn't be convinced I even had a disorder. She still can't.

"We didn't have any 'anxiety disorders' in my day," she told me once. "You'd tell the old folks you had a disorder, and they'd tell you to go pray, take a long walk, and get some fresh air."

"Maybe we can hire some people to help you clean up the house," I now suggest to her so I can get out of it. "Maybe a . . . uh . . . maid service."

"And just who has this maid service money? *You?* I can't ask your daddy for money. You know how much I hate to ask that man for anything, especially since he isn't even my son-in-law anymore now that he's remarried to that woman."

By "that woman" she means my stepmother, Dana, who my father has been married to for almost thirteen years.

But I guess her animosity is less directed toward Dana than it is to anything related to Dad. Gram and Dad have always had a reluctant relationship that only got worse after Mom, the peacemaker in the family, died.

"Plus, you're my blood, Shanice," Gram continues. "You're the only blood I've got left."

So she's pulling *that* card?

Yes, I'm her "blood." I'm her only grandchild and Mom was her only child. As far as I know, Gram has no other living relatives but me.

"Okay. Okay." I throw back my head and glare up at my ceiling fan in the dim light, stifling a groan. "I guess I can come Thursday."

"Tomorrow would be better, honey. I've already gotten started. No point in slowin' down now," she replies before hanging up.

I press the red button on my cell screen, not stifling my groan this time.

Tomorrow it is.

CHAPTER 6

I BORROW DAD'S VOLVO AND DRIVE TO GRAM'S WITH A BOX FILLED with garbage bags, rubber gloves, a bucket, a mop, a six-pack of sponges, and two bottles of lemon-scented Pine-Sol stowed in the back.

All of it cost about fifty bucks, bringing my already meager savings to a grand total of $385.48.

I have to battle lunchtime city traffic on the way there, almost getting sideswiped by a delivery truck, and then I circle the neighborhood a few times before I can find parking. By the time I do, I'm already exhausted.

I close my eyes and take a few deep breaths.

When I got my diagnosis over a decade ago, I was relieved. At least I finally had a name for what I was feeling, for the fidgeting, worrying, and avoidance due to irrational fears. For the monster that kept me from sleeping at night and filled my mind with the most random thoughts like what if a Boeing 737 fell out of the sky and came crashing through my ceiling? Is that how I was going to die?

This disorder can be a moody beast. A real bitch. Sometimes, I can go months with it sitting quietly in the background, and I'm perfectly fine, bright, and happy. And then something bad happens, like a fender bender or my credit card number gets stolen or my boyfriend of five years leaves me and my boss accuses me of burglary, and suddenly the beast taps me on the shoulder and says, "*Hey!* Remember me? It's been a while. I'm about to make your life miserable, girl."

Today, it isn't just tapping on my shoulder. It's practically sitting in the passenger seat beside me.

Inhale, exhale.

Inhale, exhale.

I finally climb out of the car. By the time I arrive at the bottom of the wooden stairs leading to Gram's house, I am reluctant but ready to work.

Gram lives on the outskirts of Anacostia in a neighborhood that's starting to gentrify. It's been a slow creep of rehabs and renovations, elaborate landscaping and the repaving of driveways. Now Gram's house is noticeably different from the others on her block; it stands out like an inflamed pimple on an otherwise unblemished face.

The other bungalows feature pristine lawns, artfully sculpted topiary, and flower boxes. Meanwhile, Gram's front lawn is overgrown and the paint is flaking along the front porch and window trim. The cedar siding is missing in some spots. A stack of mildewing, old newspapers sits near the door.

I take a quick glance at the sky and the trees overhead, on the lookout for a crow, but I don't see one. No bad omens. Just a normal day.

I slowly climb the warped stairs, shifting from side to side with the cumbersome weight of my load. Just when I'm about to knock on the door, I hear someone say behind me, "Excuse me! Hello! *Hello!* Do you live here? I don't think I've seen you before."

And just like that, I'm instantly yanked back to the office where I stand with a trash bag filled with wet papers, where Ted, Darcy, and Connor are either staring at me or looking away from me, shamefaced. I can hear Gary's words echoing in my head: *"Did you or did you not let someone in here last night? Do you know who did this?"*

My cheeks flush with heat. My ears are ringing.

I turn to find a woman standing on the sidewalk. A robotic grin is frozen on her pale, freckled face. She has a Whole Foods canvas bag in one hand and the other hand is around the wrist of an apple-cheeked toddler in denim overalls with curly red hair like her own. He isn't smiling; he's picking his nose.

What does this woman think? I'm about to break in using a mop and a bucket?

"Why are you even asking me that? Who are you?" I ask in return.

"Oh, I'm sorry! That's not . . . that's not what I meant," she insists, rushing forward, making the little boy lurch after her and dislodge the finger from his nostril. "I'm sure you could live here. I'm not insinuating that you don't."

My heartbeat starts to decelerate. The ear ringing disappears. My fight-or-flight mechanism eases its hold.

"I just meant we hadn't met before," she continues. "My name is Fawn, and this is my son, Wesley. We live five houses down. Moved in late last year. I'm the newly elected neighborhood block captain. Have you been to any of the meetings?"

I take a deep breath and force a smile. "Uh, no. Sorry. I misunderstood you. It's . . . It's nice to meet you." I wave awkwardly, still juggling my cleaning supplies. "My name's Shanice."

"It's great to meet you too! I've been trying to introduce myself to everyone and let them know I'm here to help. For instance," she says, inclining her head, "I don't know if you realize this, but you're supposed to separate your recyclables. The bin is for paper and the lidded can is for glass and plastic. It's labeled, but you may not have noticed."

"Oh, umm . . ." I pause to gesture to Gram's house. "Actually, I—"

"I just point that out," she says, interrupting again, "because I notice that you never separate them, and as neighborhood block captain, I wanted to make you aware. Just to be helpful! Also, I keep a slew of eco-friendly bags for lawn debris, if you ever need some. It's no problem."

"Mommy, I want merry-go-round," the little boy whines as he sucks his finger. The same one that was up his nose.

"We're going to head to the park soon, honey," she assures him, before turning back around to face me. Her wide grin never budges. "If you ever need any bags for grass clippings or leaves, just reach out. I could even recommend a lawn service, since I notice that you don't—"

"We got all the bags we need," Gram calls out.

I glance over my shoulder to find her standing behind me in the doorway.

"Oh, well that's great to hear!" Fawn says as I step through the door, past Gram. "I don't believe we've met either. I was just introducing myself to Shanice. I'm Fawn from five houses down the block. You must be—"

"Good to meet you," Gram murmurs dryly before slamming the door on Fawn and her booger-eating toddler. She then engages the dead bolt.

"One of the new neighbors, huh?"

Gram rolls her eyes at my question while I kiss her cheek. "She stops by here two to three days a week, knocking on the door or peeking through the blinds. She might as well wait around in the bushes for me to come out of the house. I don't know what the hell she wants."

"Maybe she just wants to say hi. You know, to be . . . well . . . friendly, but she has a *really* bad sense of personal boundaries?"

"Uh-hunh," Gram grunts, sounding incredulous.

Gram is wearing a Clinton-Gore T-shirt and denim capris with an elastic waistband today. Like her clothes, she seems frozen in time—from her wrinkle-free skin that makes her look like she's in her late forties though she turned seventy last year, to the way she wears her hair in the same Farrah Fawcett hairdo she's had since the '80s, though the teased curls have gotten thinner and grayer over the years.

I take a quick scan around me.

There is a maze of piles in the living and dining rooms. A few are sitting on the shag carpet. Another on the leather recliner. Even more are on the dining room table. I wonder if they are "keep" piles, or stuff she's planning to dump or give away.

"So why are you doing this?" I ask. "Why are you clearing out the house anyway?"

"I got a letter from another one of those real estate agents a couple of months ago. Those letters, cards, and postcards have just been piling up on my kitchen counter. All of them keep saying they wanna buy the house or know people who would want to buy my house." She walks across the living room and begins to add more papers and books to another pile. "I finally decided to call one of them back." She looks over her shoulder at me. "It's not like you want this place."

She's right. I want the house even less than I want that old painting she offered. I'd rather get a roommate or move back to the burbs to live with Dad and Dana than move here.

Not only are there so many things that need to be fixed around the bungalow, I wouldn't have the skill or the budget to do it. There are also too many memories here. Too many artifacts of Mom. Pictures on the walls and shelves. Her old cheerleading uniforms and homecoming dress are still in one of the upstairs closets in their dry cleaning bags with the receipts attached.

The truth is, even if we packed it all up and sent it to Goodwill, I'd still be able to tell Mom once lived here. I can feel it in the walls. It would be like living and sleeping in a tomb.

"So," Gram says, "I let the agent look around and give me an estimate for how much I could get, which is more than you'd think. It seems silly to keep holding on to the place, don't it? I could sell it and move into something smaller, but nicer. One of those senior communities with the pools and golf courses. Find me a rich ol' husband and make him take me on getaway vacations."

I snort before dropping everything to the floor that I've carried inside.

"And the neighborhood has changed so much," Gram goes on. "All the old folks are leavin' either in a U-Haul truck or a pine box, and these new folks like *her*," she pauses to glance with exasperation at the closed door, "just keep movin' in. Some of them are nice enough, but I feel like . . ."

Her voice drifts off as she does a double take. She looks horrified, like I've just spat on the carpet.

"Are you out of your *damn mind*, girl?" she cries before rushing toward me. I jump back when she reaches down and grabs my purse, which I've set next to my feet along with the bucket filled with Pine-Sol bottles. She picks up the purse and shoves it at me, catching me off guard, making me clasp it against my chest.

"Don't sit your purse on the floor, Shanice. It's bad luck!" She shakes her head, looking from me to the purse and back again. She points at it like it's a cursed object. "How long have you been doing that? Just dropping it anywhere?"

I stare at her, now speechless. I shrug. "I . . . I don't know."

"You don't know?" She sucks her teeth. "No wonder you've had it so hard lately." She returns her attention to her sorting, still shaking her head and muttering to herself.

I wonder if Gram realizes how crazy she sounds. But then I remind myself I was paranoid that a crow was stalking me, that a black cat made my boyfriend leave me. I had a panic attack on a busy sidewalk only a week ago. I don't have any room to judge.

I rest my purse on an empty spot of her coffee table and get to work.

CHAPTER 7

THE CLEANING PROCESS IS A SLOW AND DUSTY ONE, BUT AT LEAST IT is a mindless distraction.

I dump old issues of *Soap Opera Digest* going back to 1984 and organize Gram's vinyl records. I throw away old crossword puzzles and sort through a pile of photo albums. While digging, I stumble upon a stack of funeral bulletins that Gram has collected like baseball cards. In the pile, I spot a familiar face.

An image of Mom smiles up at me. It sits at the center of the bulletin above her name, Marissa Lynn Pierce, and the dates showing her birth and death.

In the photo, Mom's long hair falls around her shoulders in soft waves. Her head is cocked to the side. I look a lot like her—same brown eyes, button nose, and wide mouth, though her skin was a few shades lighter. I keep a picture of her and me on my night table at my apartment, from back when I was maybe four years old. She's a little older in this photo though.

I haven't seen this picture in years. I haven't read her bulletin probably since the day of her funeral. I open it to scan a few sentences and see that there's an old newspaper clipping tucked inside.

ONE DEAD, TWO INJURED IN RUSH HOUR COLLISION, H STREET CLOSED.

I drop the paper as soon as I read the headline, like it singed my fingertips. I lurch back as it flutters to the shag carpet and I bump into Gram's coffee table, sending two of my organized stacks of records clattering to the floor. Etta James and the Isley Brothers form a pile at my feet.

"What was that?" Gram calls from the neighboring room.

I don't answer.

"Shanice, did you hear me?"

I stumble out of the sitting room and head toward the stairs. My breath comes out in short, shallow bursts as I climb. I have to hold the handrail to steady myself. I rush down the hall to the house's only bathroom and feel my way around in the dark, in search of a light.

I can't make out the toilet or the sink in the dark. What I *do* see in the pitch black of the bathroom is a series of images in quick succession, like I'm clicking through the reel of an old View-Master. Broken glass. A blue mailbox that had once been on the sidewalk, now sitting inches away from my face. A limp, bloody hand. I hear shouts and the faraway wail of sirens.

My eyes blur with tears from a phantom searing hot pain in my leg, from the throbbing now in my hip. A dashboard is crushing my chest.

I finally find the switch to turn on the bathroom vanity. The grizzly images are replaced with pastel yellow tile and bathroom fixtures from the 1980s.

"Shanice?" I hear Gram call from downstairs.

She'll probably come up here to look for me if I continue not to answer her. She could be here any minute. I have to pull myself together. I don't want Gram to see me like this, but I'm starting to feel light-headed. I shut the door.

Take deep breaths, I tell myself, much like the woman EMT who placed the oxygen mask over my face in the ambulance that I rode in after the crash.

"Where's my mom?" My voice behind the mask sounded alien and distant to my own ears. "Is . . . Is she okay?"

I watched as the EMT locked eyes with her partner, a big guy with broad shoulders who was sitting on the other side of the stretcher, starting an IV. The look they exchanged made me go cold, like I had ice water in my veins.

She turned, focused her dark eyes on me again, and smiled.

"Just take deep breaths, honey," she urged, not answering my question. "Breathe in and breathe out for me."

I now lower the toilet lid and sit down on top of it.

You can breathe. It's all in your head. Just take deep breaths.

Inhale, exhale.

Inhale, exhale.

After what feels like an hour but was probably just five minutes, the tightness in my chest finally wanes. I can breathe again.

I raise my head and slowly stand. I still have to hold on to the counter because of my dizziness though; my feet feel unsteady underneath me.

I turn on the cold water and splash it on my face over and over again. One minute passes. Then two. The world is no longer topsy-turvy. I wipe the water on my face away with one of the hand towels, but stop when I think I hear the creak of a floorboard outside the bathroom door.

"Sorry, Gram. I'm okay now. Just started sneezing and tearing up from . . . uh . . . from all that dust," I lie, keeping my voice even. Hoping I sound normal.

I reach behind me and open the door, prepared to step back into the hallway.

I raise my reddened eyes to look in the bathroom mirror over the sink, expecting to find Gram in the reflection.

But I don't see her. Instead, I see the painting . . . *The Portrait of the Defiant Woman* . . . staring back at me through the crack in the bathroom door. The woman's eyes are almost iridescent in Gram's darkened bedroom. I turn and push the door open wider then walk across the hall.

The painting isn't huge. About twenty by twenty-four inches. It hangs over Gram's bed between two velvet oil paintings. One of a slumbering tiger. The other of a red rose.

I'm no art critic; I've taken only one art class in my entire life, back in college as an elective. But even with my layman's eyes, I know the execution of this painting is miles ahead of the cheesy velvet oil paintings beside it. A real artist made this. It's so lifelike, it's almost eerie, like the defiant woman could toss down her bundle and climb out of the painting at any moment.

"The Realtor told me I should take that stuff down," Gram suddenly says over my shoulder.

I turn to find her standing in the bedroom doorway with her arms crossed over her chest. I hadn't heard her come into the room or up the stairs.

"Paintings and pictures. He said it's easier to sell the house without any 'personal artifacts' around." She sucks her teeth. "I think he just don't want the people buyin' the house to know I'm old and black."

"Is that why you wanted to give the painting to me?" I ask, gesturing to the wall.

"That . . . and I think it's time I passed it on. My mama gave it to me. Her mama gave it to her. I would've given it to your mama if . . . well, if she was still here with us, but"—Gram pauses and purses her lips—"she isn't anymore, so it's yours. It's been with me long enough."

"I didn't know the painting was that old." I look back at it, feeling my dislike of it lessen now that I know the family connection. "I wonder who's it by."

"Estelle Johnson," Gram says without hesitation, making me blink in surprise.

"Who's Estelle Johnson? And how do you know that? It isn't signed."

"Yes, it is. Her name is written on the back."

Gram climbs on the bed, wincing at the crack of her knees, and takes the painting down from the wall to show me. It's been there for so long that an outline of the canvas is on the wallpaper, creating a rectangle in a slightly lighter shade than the existing pink stripes and red vine design. I rush forward to take it out of her hands and help her back down from the mattress to the floor.

It's odd to hold it. To have the woman staring at me up close. I flip it over and see the name scribbled on the canvas in pencil on the back. The writing is starting to fade a little, but you can clearly see the cursive letters spell out "Estelle Johnson" in the upper right-hand corner, along with "1928," showing the year I presume it was painted.

"Was she famous?" I ask as I flip it back over to gaze at the portrait again. "The painter, I mean."

"I don't think so. Just a friend of the family. I think she was good, *good* friends with Grandma Louise—your great-great-grandmother—and gave her the painting as a gift." Gram wrinkles her nose down at it. "Truth be told, I've always found it a little creepy myself. That woman looks like she'd cut you if you look at her sideways."

I laugh. So *she* was creeped out by the painting too? "Then why in the world did you keep it? Why not just give it to Goodwill with the rest of the stuff downstairs?"

Gram shrugs. "Because it's ours. It's *always* been ours. Plus, if I'm giving up the house to a stranger, I don't want to give this away to a stranger too. I want it to stay in the family."

I understand what she's saying, what she means. I run my hands over the canvas and feel the paint strokes—all the swirls and slashes—like braille underneath my fingertips.

"You like it?" Gram asks.

I tilt my head. "'Like' isn't the right word. It *is* a little creepy like you said, but it's also . . . interesting. It's not something you can find just anywhere."

"Then take it. It's yours."

She turns and walks out of the bedroom, leaving me alone with the painting. I listen to her footfalls as she walks back down the stairs to return to her cleaning.

Looking at the portrait, I have the same feeling I had when I saw the crow on the street my last day at the office, like it's the harbinger of something.

Whether good or bad, I do not know.

A few minutes later, I head downstairs and return to the sitting room with my new painting tucked under my arm, ready to get back to sorting.

I'm surprised to find the records are neatly stacked on the coffee table again; the floor is clean. Gram must have done it while I was in the bathroom. When I draw closer, I see that beside the stacks is Mom's funeral bulletin. I hesitate, pick up the bulletin, and open it to find the old newspaper clipping is gone.

CHAPTER 8

It's almost evening when I step out Gram's front door, and I can barely walk. My arms, shoulders, and back are sore. My eyes are red and my nose still runs from all the dust. My fatigue isn't just from the physical strain of cleaning; hyperventilating and crying in a bathroom can take a lot out of you.

I wince when I reach my dad's car and hear, "Shanice, hey!"

I turn and find Gram's neighbor Fawn waving me down like I've forgotten something.

Where did this woman come from? Maybe Gram was right and she does hide in the bushes.

"I wanted to give you the business card for the lawn service I mentioned earlier," Fawn says, holding out a laminated card.

I set down the portrait on the curb and take the card from her. "Oh, wow. Thanks so much. We'll definitely call them," I lie, tucking the card into the pocket of my shorts.

"What an interesting painting," Fawn says as she reaches down and picks up the portrait. She holds it up in the air. "I don't think I've ever seen anything like it. It's so arresting."

"Thanks," I murmur, taking it out of her hands and tucking it under my arm.

"Where did you get it?"

"Umm, Gram has had it forever." I shrug and unlock the car doors. "I took it off her hands."

"Really? Is your grandmother an art collector or was it given to her as a gift? Does she know what period it's from?" Her robotic smile is back. "You see, my husband and I are budding art collectors and—"

"You don't say? That is so cool," I say as I walk to the driver's side, not wanting to get sucked into a conversation. "Well, I really should get going. I'm exhausted from all the cleaning we did today. Great meeting you, Fawn. I'll tell Gram to give the lawn service a call." I start the car engine, give a quick wave, and then drive off.

When I arrive back at my apartment, I set down everything by the sofa and slowly make my way to my bedroom. The sun is starting to set outside my window as I peel off my sweaty clothes, and I let them fall to the floor and puddle at my feet.

I step into the bathroom and then the shower stall and turn on the water full blast, leaning my head against the glass tile as it sprays my back. I scrub off the sweat and dirt. As I run the sponge and soap over my body, I try not to let my gaze linger on the old jagged scar spanning from my hip to my thigh. After seeing the news clipping today, looking at it might trigger me again. All the memories will come flooding back.

I stay in the shower for I don't know how long. When I return from the steamy bathroom in my robe, I find the rest of the apartment dark and silent.

Any other time I would hear the neighbors above me stomping around upstairs like they're wearing wooden clogs, or I'd hear the passing cars or random voices of people on the street and sidewalks several stories below. But I hear nothing. Absolutely nothing. It's like the world outside my walls has evaporated.

All this quiet should be tranquil, but instead, it's unnerving.

I should have left the television on, or played something on the Bluetooth speakers in the living room. I'll have to remember to do that now that Jason is gone. He was the one who always had some football or basketball game playing on the flatscreen. The voices of the announcers and cheers of the crowd were the soundtrack of our apartment, but not anymore.

I head into the living room to grab my phone and find something to push away the silence. A song that's soothing and comforts me.

Mom used to do that. She would always play music on the stereo at our old house, like she couldn't stand silence either. On Saturdays, when she cleaned, the music would be playing all day. As she scrubbed and vacuumed, you could hear the soulful sounds of jazz and R&B ballads streaming between the rooms like water and vibrating through the walls and floors.

I smile at the memory of Mom dancing as she vacuumed while I walk down the hall and enter my living room, but freeze in my steps, startled to find a face in the dark.

For a second I think maybe someone broke in while I was showering. Then I realize that it's the painting leaning against the back of the sofa, right where I left it. It's waiting to be hung.

Why the hell did I ever agree to take this thing?

I flip the painting over so that the image faces the wall, so the defiant woman is no longer staring at me, and that's when I see the signature again.

Estelle Johnson.

That's why I took the painting. Estelle was a close family friend and possibly an unrecognized artist, which seems tragic with her level of talent. But then again, I don't know much about art movements. Neither does Gram. Maybe Estelle was famous during her time.

Instead of lying down in bed like I planned, I grab my laptop and fall back onto my sofa, tucking one leg underneath me.

Jason took the loveseat and the end tables, but thankfully, he left something for me to sit on.

I finally turn on music—a pop tune about sunny beaches and fast cars—and flip open my laptop. I pull up Google before typing in the words "Estelle Johnson artist."

I get about a hundred hits, finding artists of a similar name among the most popular links. All are living. One, according to her Instagram page, is a folk singer who will release an album in September—definitely not the artist I'm looking for. Finally, I land on a page about the Harlem Renaissance. That sounds more plausible. But when I click on the link, I don't find a page about Estelle Johnson, like I thought I would. Instead, I land on a Wikipedia page about someone named Maude Bachmann.

The sepia-toned picture of Bachmann is of an older woman dressed in a white toga, wearing a wreath of flowers and her white hair falling around her shoulders. Her arms are raised like she's about to break into a dance. She looks like an aging wood nymph or a pre-Raphaelite painting.

The 1928 murder of Maude Bachmann, Harlem Renaissance art patron and avid spiritualist, I read, *sent shockwaves through New York.*

I read on and see that this woman Bachmann, who funded and nurtured the careers of artists such as Zora Neale Hurston, Aaron Douglas, Langston Hughes, and our family friend, Estelle, was a controversial figure during her time. "Her death remains unsolved, but police at the time speculated that it might have been committed by Bachmann's long list of enemies that included a few of the artists she once patronized," the Wikipedia entry says. "It also may have been connected to the occult."

"Ooookay," I say slowly, in no mood to read about this tonight. I've had enough emotional upheaval for one day. "Good vibes only," I whisper.

I click on the name Estelle Johnson in the entry, deciding to get as far away from the story of Maude Bachmann as possible. When I do, all I see is a link to an art appraiser's website. Mark Vivaldi Antique Art Services.

I follow this link, which leads to a picture of a painting on a much larger canvas. One that takes up an entire wall. It shows tangled bodies with glowing limbs, lost in either dance or the throws of passion—I can't tell. But it is mesmerizing. The color scheme is different from *The Portrait of the Defiant Woman*, but the style is very similar. This has to be Estelle's. Beneath the photo, in smaller print, are the words "From a private collection."

The website doesn't give a lot of information about Estelle other than her being a Harlem Renaissance painter who grew up in the small town of Turnbridge, South Carolina, and moved to New York in 1925. She would later die in 1929 at the age of twenty-six in Philadelphia.

"Twenty-six?" I say, cringing.

So young. Three years younger than I am now.

"Underappreciated for her talent, Estelle Johnson had the potential to become one of the artistic greats, if given more time," the website says.

I click on the little icon that shows the appraiser's email address and quickly type a note to him, explaining that I have another painting by Estelle and would be interested in learning more about her and the painting itself. By the time I press send and close my laptop, I really am tired. I walk out of my living room and collapse onto my bed, still wearing my bathrobe. Within minutes, I'm out cold.

CHAPTER 9

ESSIE

NEW YORK CITY

April 5, 1927

A MAN WAS DANCING WITH A LAMPSHADE ON HIS HEAD, DOING A slow stroll to "I'm Coming, Virginia" as the band played, but he seemed to attract less attention than the woman who was currently performing a backbend on top of the baby grand piano.

Essie lowered her martini glass while the crowd circled the woman and cheered on her impromptu performance.

On any other night, at another party, Essie might hop up on the piano and join her to see who could hold their backbend the longest, but she had to be chaste tonight, to make a good impression. So, Essie watched and chewed her martini olive as the woman's blond hair dangled over the black, polished wood in golden waves, and the muscles in her pale arms jittered, straining to hold her weight. Her black, beaded gown rose several inches as she kicked up one leg, then the other, revealing the rolled-up stockings underneath, her rouged knees, and her silk bloomers. She did a handstand, wobbling slightly, making Essie hold her breath, making the crowd release a series of shouts and squeals. One man rushed forward to catch her if she fell, but there was no need. She executed her backflip and waved her hands triumphantly and the crowd of partygoers clapped and hooted even louder.

This isn't what Essie had expected when Mrs. Bachmann had invited her to one of her soirees at her Park Avenue penthouse apartment. She'd thought it would be something a lot more sedate, considering where she was.

Mrs. Bachmann herself seemed so refined with her three-string of pearls, elaborate ladies' hats, and wooden cane with its silver serpent handle.

"We have the party every year. You absolutely must come, my dear," Mrs. Bachmann had said in her clipped New England accent.

Between the hundred dollars Mrs. Bachmann had paid for one of her works—the first painting Essie had sold in months—and the rare chance to step into the sparkling world of the Upper East Side, there was no way Essie could resist the older woman's invitation.

She'd been so nervous, agonizing over what to wear. Even though she was short on funds, she'd spent almost twelve dollars on a new frock she'd spotted in the window of a shop on 137th Street: a golden yellow gown with spaghetti straps and a slim belt at the waist, made of tiers of silk that swayed gently as she walked. Essie resolved that if she was going to be the only Negro girl in the room, she was at least going to be a dazzling one. She would stand out like a vibrant sunflower in a field of white daisies.

She'd asked Dorothy West, one of her chums who had grown up among the upper-class Negroes in Boston, to give her a quick overview on proper etiquette so she wouldn't embarrass herself.

But now Essie wondered if she should have made such a fuss. This bunch of white folks who were running around barefoot and drinking champagne straight out of the bottle seemed just as wild as her friends and the other artists she knew back in Harlem.

But she mustn't forget the reason she was here. Essie decided to look for her host; she hadn't seen Mrs. Bachmann all evening. She turned away to start her search, bumping into someone instead.

"Pardon m—" she began, but couldn't finish once her eyes settled on the man in front of her.

He was stunning. That was the only word that she could use to describe him. It was as if Rudolph Valentino had stepped off the flickering movie screen and emerged in color to stand before her in real life in a trim tuxedo and white bow tie.

"Don't dawdle too long," he said, making Essie frown in confusion. "A crowd like this will start to get restless."

"What?"

He gestured across the room. "The music, luv. It stopped. You're on your break, aren't you?"

He thought she was with the band.

She supposed she shouldn't be surprised since the musicians and the servants were the only other brown faces in the room. But Essie was a little annoyed that this man automatically assumed she was here to do nothing more than entertain the crowd, to sing a jaunty ragtime ditty or the blues.

"I'm not the entertainment," she clarified. "I'm a guest of Mrs. Bachmann."

. . . *thank you very much*, she wanted to add, but didn't.

"A guest?" He sounded shocked. Even amused. "So you're the new artist I've been hearing so much about."

Now Essie was the one who was shocked. "Mrs. Bachmann has spoken about me?"

"Why, yes! Positively raving about your work. Well, well, well." He leaned against one of the Corinthian columns along the ballroom's entryway and slowly looked her up and down. "Her great new find—and a fetching one at that."

"Elias!" a voice called out.

They both turned to find a middle-aged woman standing in the corridor. Her dark hair was parted on the side. Marcel waves framed her narrow face, stopping at her chin. She was wearing a party dress, but it was much simpler than what the other women were wearing tonight. Its dull brown color, tunic style, and lack of embellishment made her look dowdy.

Unlike Essie, who had wanted to stand out, this was a woman who wanted to fade into the damask-patterned wallpaper, to stealthily disappear into a crowd.

Essie had seen this woman before though she couldn't remember her name. She'd been at Herr Reiss's art studio with Mrs. Bachmann that day the two women met, standing silently at Mrs. Bachmann's side while Bachmann prattled on and on about how much she loved Essie's work.

"I hope you're being cordial to our party guest," the woman now said to the man named Elias.

"As cordial as can be," he muttered dryly.

"Good. Your mother would be greatly disappointed if you weren't."

His mother? Maude Bachmann was his mother?

Elias rolled his hazel eyes before stepping out of Essie's way. "Don't worry, Agatha. You can tell mother I'm being a good little boy." He then looked at Essie again, giving her a wry smile. "It was a pleasure to meet you." He did a slight bow. "I hope that I see you again, Miss—err . . ."

"Johnson. Estelle Johnson. But everyone calls me Essie."

"Then I shall do the same." He nodded. "See you soon, Essie," he said before strolling into the ballroom. Essie watched as he walked away.

"Miss Johnson," the woman in the corridor said, snapping Essie's attention.

The woman's face now donned a tight smile. It seemed to hurt her to wear it, like uncomfortable garters.

"I'm Agatha Pickens, Mrs. Bachmann's social secretary. We're elated to have you in attendance tonight."

Essie nodded. "Yes, I'm so happy to be—"

"Mrs. Bachmann would like to speak with you privately," Mrs. Pickens said, cutting her off. "She's been waiting for you upstairs."

"She has? I'm sorry to have kept her waiting. I wasn't aware she knew I was here. I hadn't seen her tonight."

Mrs. Pickens narrowed her eyes. Her smile disappeared. "There isn't anything in her home that Mrs. Bachmann isn't aware of. Please follow me."

Essie trailed after her, following her down the hallway to a door then a winding staircase. Once again, like at the studio, Mrs. Pickens said nothing, refusing to engage in small talk.

They strolled down another corridor, passing several rooms. Behind more than one door Essie heard voices. She thought the ballroom was crowded but it seemed the entire penthouse was abuzz with activity. She paused at one of the doors that was only partly open, trying her best to nonchalantly peek at what was going on inside. Essie saw four people, all wearing tuxedos and gowns, sitting around a table with their eyes closed. Lit tea candles sat in front of each. They were holding hands and all seemed to be softly whispering something as if they were saying grace before a meal.

She leaned in closer to hear what they were saying.

"Miss Johnson," Mrs. Pickens said, making her jump back from the doorway. "As I said before, Mrs. Bachmann is waiting. Shall we hurry along?"

"Y-y-yes," Essie stuttered. "Sorry."

Mrs. Pickens quietly shut the door, turned, and resumed her swift strides down the corridor. Essie stared a beat longer at the closed door, listening to the sound of the hushed voices, but turned and followed. They finally stopped in front of another doorway and Essie found Mrs. Bachmann standing at the center of a gigantic room.

"Come! Come in, darling girl," Mrs. Bachmann's voice echoed to her over the sound of the music and laughter filtering from the floor below. The older woman wore a red-beaded gown and headband adorned with a giant plume of feathers. She looked like a bedazzled rooster.

She beckoned Essie forward with her free hand while the other clutched her cane. "I'd like to show you something. Thank you so much for bringing her to me. We're fine now, Agatha!" she said, waving off her secretary. "Go back and enjoy the party, dearest."

Mrs. Pickens's thin nostrils flared, like she wanted to insist on staying, but instead she simply nodded and stepped aside to let Essie walk over the threshold into a room that was almost as grand as the ballroom downstairs. Essie's eyes were drawn to multitiered crystal chandeliers and the coffered ceiling overhead inlaid with golden suns. Some small, some large. All were surrounded by fiery beams.

On the walls were paintings, mostly modernist works. Throughout the room were several podiums featuring sculptures and artifacts, some from the Natives of the Great Plains and others were tribal masks and wood carvings from Africa.

Essie drew closer to one of the podiums that featured what appeared to be a shrunken head on an iron spike. The skin looked as if it had been dyed indigo. The eyes were sewn shut. So were the head's distended lips. Long dark, matted hair hung from the head, sweeping the top of the podium. She stared at it, transfixed.

"I'm so glad you came tonight," Mrs. Bachmann said, making Essie turn to face her. "I do hope you're having a good time."

"I am," Essie lied.

Mrs. Bachmann nodded. "I generally find it much more enjoyable to throw parties nowadays than to attend them, which is why I usually am there only for an hour or so, then I disappear. But twenty or thirty years ago, I could go until dawn fueled by nothing but wine, dance, and absinthe." She inclined her head. "Have you tried it?"

"Why yes, I've been known to enjoy myself. To dance and drink at parties."

"No, my dear. Absinthe. Have you tried it?"

Essie blinked. "Afraid not."

"Oh, you simply must, my darling. Everyone should at least once, *especially* those who are artistically inclined. And when you do, report back and tell me the results."

Essie's mouth fell open, unsure of how to respond. The older woman wasn't at all what she'd expected.

"I see my little head has caught your attention. It's from the Shuar and Achuar people of Ecuador," Mrs. Bachmann said, strolling toward her. "It was given to me by a friend who knew I was once a member of the tribe."

"You . . . you *were*?" Essie asked.

"Indeed! It was in a past life, of course," Mrs. Bachmann clarified, leaving Essie still gaping. "As I was saying, the head was gift from a collector friend during a South American tour Mr. Bachmann and I took years ago, back when he was still able to travel. There are similar heads at the Pitt Rivers Museum at Oxford. Do you like it, Estelle?"

Essie hesitated. Not only was she getting whiplash from the shifts of this conversation, she didn't want to offend her host. She opened her mouth to lie again, but the expression on her face must have given her true feelings away. The older woman nodded knowingly.

"Some find the heads grotesque, even frightening," Mrs. Bachmann answered for her. "But they are no more grotesque than this," she said, gesturing to a Vincent van Gogh on one side of the gallery. "Or this." She pointed at a cubist work by Pablo Picasso, the Spanish painter that Essie had been hearing so much about. "*All* of this!" Mrs. Bachmann exclaimed, making a sweeping gesture to all the paintings on the wall before returning to the shrunken head. "This is truth in its most primal form. It isn't bloated with pretension. It is honest in its beauty. An average individual cannot withstand such honesty. *That* is what makes it so frightening to the onlooker, Estelle."

She reached out and clutched one of Essie's hands, catching the young woman by surprise.

Her hand was cooler than Essie had expected. The surface was wrinkled and warped by veins, but the skin and palm was smooth as a baby's—much smoother than Essie's hands, which were made rough and calloused from years of toiling in the fields in South Carolina.

"And there is honesty and beauty in your work as well," Mrs. Bachmann assured, gazing up into Essie's eyes.

Mrs. Bachmann's own eyes, wide and eager behind her spectacles, were hard to describe. Not quite green or blue. Essie wondered what colors she would choose if she were to replicate them on a canvas.

"I knew it the moment I stepped into Herr Reiss's studio and saw your painting," the older woman continued. "It *spoke* to me. It shouted, 'Stop! Tread no farther because you have found what you are looking for!' It's a modern version of the Dutch painters, of Rembrandt and Vermeer, but the choices you made showed much more than a crude imitation or adaptation of their work. How you placed the Negro singer to the foreground and the White figures to the background and in shadow. How subversive, you naughty girl."

"You noticed?" Essie asked, gazing at Bachmann in awe.

"Of course, I did! It is positively revolutionary. There is truth in your art, and that is not easy to come by. It comes from your people, Estelle. You know that, don't you? From your music. Your connection to the spiritual. I just had to have it." She released Essie's hand and looped an arm through hers, guiding her past the podium to the other side of the room. "I'm getting the painting framed now, but I plan to put it right over there. It will look perfect between the Gaugin and the Cézanne, don't you think?"

Essie's chest swelled.

To think, the number of times Essie had considered quitting. How many times had she'd worried that she'd deluded herself into believing she could ever become a respected painter? She'd left the university and her home. She'd alienated her Aunt Idalene and everyone who thought she was a fool to walk away from a career in education and head to Harlem to pursue her art.

Now Essie had something to prove Aunt Idalene wrong. She had validation, and not just from anyone, but from Maude Bachmann, who saw merit in her art. Someone who regularly appeared in the New York society pages. Someone who Essie's peers would sell their souls to get her attention. Someone even Aunt Idalene could respect.

"Thank you, Mrs. Bachmann. What you're saying . . . ma'am, you . . ." Her voice trembled with emotion. Estelle struggled to say the words. "You have no idea what this means to me. That you understood my work."

"Oh, none of that 'Mrs. Bachmann' nonsense any longer," Bachmann playfully chided. "Please, call me Godmother. All my artists do."

"All your artists?" Essie whispered, now confused.

Calling Mrs. Bachmann "Godmother" seemed apt. Essie felt like she had suddenly been dropped into a fairy tale. She was Cinderella in Charles Perrault's *The Little Glass Slipper,* and now she was at a dizzying ball filled with jazz music and champagne thanks to her Godmother and her magic.

"Yes, you understand that I don't want just one painting from you, Estelle? I believe in your vision. I believe in *you.* I want to facilitate your career. I would be honored to become your patron."

Essie felt like her heart stuttered to a stop then started up again. "My . . . my patron?"

The older woman nodded.

"No, the honor would be mine, ma'am . . . I—I mean, Godmother!"

"Wonderful!" her newly minted Godmother exclaimed. "Then tonight is a double celebration! I am your Godmother from now on, and I solemnly vow to take care of you. Tell me what you need." She let go of Estelle and faced her. "Just say the word, and you will have it."

"I would like a ride home," Essie said timidly. "It was a challenge getting a taxi cab here."

And even if she could by some chance hail a taxi on Park Avenue, she doubted she'd find a driver who was willing to take her back to Harlem.

Godmother burst into laughter. "Is that all, darling girl? Well, I'm sure we can arrange that. Agatha! Agatha!"

"Yes, ma'am," her secretary answered a second later, startling Essie.

She turned to find Agatha standing in the doorway. She'd thought Agatha had left to head back to the party, but there she was, eagerly awaiting Godmother's command.

Had she been hovering near the doorway this entire time, listening?

"Have Harold bring the car around and take home our lovely guest."

"Oh, I . . . I didn't mean right now," Estelle rushed out. "You don't have to—"

"You don't have to feel obligated to stay, my dear," Godmother said, patting her hand.

Essie supposed she hadn't been very convincing that she was having a good time tonight.

"You've done your duty for Godmother, and it is appreciated," she assured Essie before kissing her cheek. "You are now released."

Essie took another step toward the room's doorway, where Mrs. Pickens stood waiting. She then made a hesitant glance over her shoulder at Godmother.

"See you in a few days, dearest," Godmother assured.

Essie nodded then walked out of the room.

Essie tightened her wool coat around her to ward off the chill and the rain as she stepped underneath an awning. A car waited for her at the curb.

But "car" didn't seem to be a proper word to describe such a magnificent vehicle. Essie's eyes scanned over the limousine's white front fenders and hood, at the black hardtop. Her gaze lingered on the rims and fender. They seemed to sparkle in the falling rain. The driver walked out of the Rolls-Royce Phantom and held open the rear door, revealing the sumptuous leather interior.

Essie felt like Cinderella climbing into her crystal carriage. She settled onto the backseat and looked up at the driver.

"Thank you, sir," she said. "Could you please take me to—"

"I have the address, ma'am," the driver said curtly before closing the door behind her.

"You do? But how—" she began to ask but stopped herself, thinking better of it.

He'd probably gotten the information from Godmother. How the older woman had found out where Essie lived, Essie did not know, but she supposed Godmother had her ways.

Before the Rolls-Royce pulled off, Essie let out a delighted squeal and looked over her shoulder again at the building behind her, wanting to encapsulate one final picture of such a memorable night.

She couldn't wait to get home and write Louise, her childhood friend, to tell her about all that had happened tonight. Louise wouldn't believe it.

But instead of seeing the exterior of the 925 Park Avenue, Essie saw a ghostly pair of dark eyes staring back at her through the glass.

Essie did a double take, wondering if it was a trick of the light, making her own face, now distorted, reflect in the Phantom's glass. But she realized she wasn't mistaken. There was a Negro woman outside standing on the curb in the rain wearing a wool coat as well.

Her cloche was soaked to the brim. Water dripped off the tip of her nose and her bottom lip. But the young Negro woman, who didn't look much older than Essie, didn't seem to mind the cold or the wet. Her focus was solely on Essie, like she recognized her. But her expression wasn't that of a friend who she once knew from down home, or one of the acquaintances she'd met at some other party here in New York. Her expression wasn't friendly at all.

Essie watched uneasily as the woman walked closer to the edge of the sidewalk and approached the Rolls-Royce's rear door. The woman's eyes never shifted from Essie as she reached for the handle.

"Stop! What are you doing?" Essie shouted, just as the car pulled off.

"Is everything alright, ma'am?" the driver asked, glancing behind him. "Did you leave something?"

"No, there was a . . . a woman. She was trying to get inside."

"What woman, ma'am?"

Essie turned around. The woman was gone. She glared out the back window and saw a figure—the woman, maybe—disappear into the shadows of another Park Avenue building.

Essie turned back around to face the driver. "Nothing. I'm sorry. My . . . my mistake." Essie forced a laugh. "Please ignore me."

As the car continued down the road, Essie remembered the hollow look in the young woman's eyes and her wet hand reaching for the door.

Who was she?

CHAPTER 10
SHANICE

BETHESDA, MARYLAND
Present day

"I REMEMBERED TO BRING IT BACK WITH GAS THIS TIME," I SAY proudly, dangling the car keys to my dad's Volvo in the air just as he opens the door to his house. "The tank is full."

The gas cost me twenty-two dollars, but it felt right to do it. I had to prove I'm still capable of doing things that competent adults do like filling a car with gas.

Dad pushes his glasses up the bridge of his nose and leans against the doorframe.

He's wearing a flannel shirt and gray sweatpants. It's his new retirement uniform, unlike the tie and dress shirts he used to wear as a civil engineer for thirty-five years.

"Much appreciated," Dad says before taking the keys from me. He clutches them in his fist. "Come inside and take a load off. Dana just made some bacon and cheese paninis and tomato soup. Have lunch with us. We've got enough for three."

I shove my hands into the pockets of my jeans. "Actually, Dad, I was about to walk to the metro and head back home. I have to—"

"It'll just be a couple of hours, Shanice." He gestures at me, ushering me through the doorway. "Come on. We haven't hung out in a while. Have lunch with us. I can drive you to the metro after."

I want to make another excuse to leave. Maybe say that I already have plans with friends or that I have to run errands, but Dad will know I'm lying. My mask isn't that good today.

"Okay," I mutter. "Thanks."

I step into the lemon-scented foyer, and Dad shuts the door behind me.

Dad's home is the opposite of Gram's. Her house seems to burst with furniture, household disarray, and dust, but Dana keeps a tight ship. Their house is airy, bright, and clean.

"So how's the old lady?" Dad asks, adjusting his glasses as we walk out the foyer and down the hall that leads to their eat-in kitchen. "Did she make you burn sage and hose her house down with holy water? Did you slaughter a chicken?"

"Dad," I say warningly.

"Fine, fine." He holds up his hands in exaggerated surrender. "Let me rephrase that. How is your grandmother, Shanice?"

"She's okay. Just demanding, surly, and bossy as ever."

Dad laughs before going somber. "And what about you? We didn't get to talk when you got the car yesterday. You rushed outta here like your feet were on fire. Before that, we hadn't heard from you since . . . well, since that last day at your office." He places a hand on my shoulder. "How have you been holding up?"

"Besides being unemployed with no current job prospects and dumped by the man I thought I was gonna one day marry?" I shrug again. "I'm okay, I guess."

"Just okay?" He squints at me. "You're not feeling . . . anything?"

"What should I be feeling?"

"Shanice," he says impatiently as he drops his hand from my shoulder. "You know what I—"

He stops when we both hear, "Shanice, I didn't know you were stopping by today, kiddo!"

Dana walks out of the kitchen, wiping her hands on a dish towel.

She's middle-aged and plump with peachy skin that burns easily in the sun. She lightened her hair to a platinum blond a few years ago to cover the gray. It suits her.

She gives me a hug and a kiss on the cheek, something she does without hesitation now, but Dana didn't know how to approach me . . . We didn't know how to approach each other when Dad introduced her to me almost two decades ago.

"Shanice, this is Dana Wozniak, my friend that I was telling you about," he had said back then, sounding and looking nervous. "Dana, this is my daughter, Shanice."

Dana had smiled and offered me her hand, an unusually formal gesture when meeting a thirteen-year-old girl. "Pleased to meet you, Shanice. That's a pretty dress you're wearing! Yellow looks lovely on you."

I'd mumbled, "Thanks," before giving her a stiff handshake.

I didn't know what to make of this perky white lady full of compliments, this interloper that my dad brought home less than a year after Mom died. He said he and Dana had bonded during sessions of their grief recovery group held once a week at a local church and then over cups of coffee and long talks thereafter. Dad had gone to the group for Mom. Dana, a divorced mother, was there for her only son, Zachary, who'd died of a painkiller overdose.

Dad had asked me to go to counseling with him, but I'd turned him down. By then I'd already started my one-on-one therapy sessions after the car accident; I didn't see the point of going to even *more* therapy, sitting around sobbing with a bunch of strangers.

But seeing Dana sitting on our living room sofa, sipping sweet tea and holding my father's hand, I'd inwardly kicked myself for not going with Dad to those meetings. Obviously, he had been seduced and would be taken advantage of by this conniving woman, I told myself the first night Dana and I met. But I was wrong.

Not only was Dana truly in love with Dad, but she'd helped usher him through the other side of his crippling grief. She'd made him happy again. And she's always been kind to me. She took me shopping for my prom dress. She always came to my defense whenever Dad lost patience with me.

Dana has been a good stepmom. The best, actually.

We all sit down at the dinette table near the bay window overlooking their garden where a bushel of hyacinths are coming into bloom. Their powerful fragrance filters through the windows, overwhelming the smell of fried bacon.

"So," Dad begins, before taking a bite of the sandwich Dana sits on the plate in front of him, "how much of a dent did you and your grandmother make yesterday in all that mess?"

"Not much," I confide, nodding my thanks to Dana as she hands me a plate and takes the chair across from me. "We cleared out the living room and dining room. Ended up with about a half-dozen trash bags worth of stuff, but I didn't get to the kitchen, let alone get to do any scrubbing."

"I'm shocked that she's doing it at all," Dad mumbles between chews.

"I was too." I pause to blow on a spoonful of soup before sampling it. "Gram says she talked to a real estate agent and wants to sell the house."

Dana frowns. "She doesn't want to give the house to you?"

"Your grandmother and I don't talk about much, but even I know she wanted to leave that house to you when she died," Dad says.

"But I don't want it."

"You sure?" Dad lowers his sandwich back to his plate. "It could be a good property investment, especially now that you and Jason have gone your separate ways. I know that apartment of yours in Northwest ain't cheap. Can you afford to live there all by yourself?"

"*Why?* Worried that I'm gonna ask to move back in with you guys?" I ask with a sly smile, only half joking.

I have about another month that I can stay in my apartment before I get threatened with eviction.

"You know you always can live with us if you need to, kiddo," Dana says, just as my Dad begins to shift uncomfortably in his chair and grumble.

Dana reaches across the tabletop and grabs Dad's hand, giving it a silencing squeeze.

I'm not offended by Dad's response. Their front door may as well be one of those revolving glass doors in department stores from how many times I've moved in and out of here. And since I started my internship, I've borrowed money from Dad a few times to cover my expenses.

I know Dad cares about me, but worrying about me has made him tired. Not knowing whether to coddle me more or give me more independence exhausts him. He knows I'm broken in many ways, but he doesn't know how to fix me.

Frankly, I don't either.

"You can move back in if you need to, Shanice," Dana repeats firmly, "but your father and I have wondered what plans you have now for your living situation. For your job situation too."

"Shanice, can you stop doing that and listen to what she's saying?" Dad asks.

"Stop doing what?"

"That."

I follow the path of Dad's gaze, look down, and realize that I've been tapping my spoon on the side of my bowl of tomato soup. I was fidgeting while Dana was talking, without even realizing it. I set down my spoon on the table mat and clench my hands in my lap.

"Sorry," I mumble.

"You can't let one bigot scare you out of the job market, honey," he says. "You *are* looking for another job, aren't you?"

They both stare at me expectantly, and I don't know what to say.

I try to imagine myself applying for jobs again, maybe at a magazine or media company, and getting the call to come in for an interview. But then I see myself sitting in an office with the interviewer.

Someone from HR or the editor herself. I see the moment when they politely ask, "So why did you leave your last position?" and the beast will make itself known.

That's when my face will flush and my ears will ring and my heart will start pounding 200 beats per minute.

I'll open my mouth to answer the question, but nothing will come out.

But I can't tell Dad and Dana this. They'll both suggest that I go back into therapy, even though I have no idea how I would pay for it unless I borrow money from them again. Dad will float the idea of trying meds. Maybe Paxil, Prozac, or Lexapro, even though none of those worked the last time. Maybe hydroxyzine. Or if it seems like it's getting *really* bad, I can go back on benzos. Those worked, but I'm too scared to try them again.

I can't even deflect and make a joke about how I want to wait it out and not make any big decisions until my run of bad luck is over, because I know Dad won't find it remotely funny.

So what do I say? What kind of performance do I put on this time?

Lucky for me, I don't have to answer them at all because my cell phone chimes. It couldn't have happened at a more perfect moment.

I glance down at the screen, seeing an unfamiliar number with a New York area code. I decide to take the call anyway.

"Sorry, guys. I'll be right back," I whisper before rising from the dinette table and walking out of the kitchen.

"Hello?" I answer after pressing the green button on the screen and strolling into the foyer.

"Hello, is this Shanice Pierce?" a man replies.

He sounds like a telemarketer, but rather than hang up, I decide to play along to stall. "Yes, this is she."

I can already hear Dana and Dad talking in the kitchen about the grout work in the upstairs bathroom, and arguing over whether Dad or a contractor should fix it. Good. They've moved on to another subject—*thank God*.

"Ms. Pierce, this is Mark Vivaldi," the voice on the other end of the line says. "You contacted me about a painting you inherited. The piece by Estelle Johnson."

"Oh! Oh, hey! I mean . . . umm . . . hi!"

I sound surprised because I am; I wasn't expecting a call from him. Not this soon anyway.

I emailed Mark Vivaldi Antique Art Services yesterday and got a formulaic autoreply he probably sends to every art collection inquiry, asking for a photo attachment of the artwork along with as much I knew about the painting's provenance and my contact information so that he could reach me at a later date.

I'd done as the email requested before heading out to give Dad back his car, and hadn't given it a second thought. I assumed it might be weeks, maybe even *months* before I heard back from Mark Vivaldi. Or maybe I wouldn't hear back from him at all.

I guess I was wrong.

"So to be clear, the painting is now in your possession? *Correct?*" he asks. "You are the sole owner?"

"Uh, yeah. My grandmother's owned it for years, but she gave it to me just this week," I say as I lazily pace around Dad and Dana's foyer. "It's kinda a family heirloom. She said my great-great-grandmother was a friend of Estelle's and—"

"Yes, I read your email, Ms. Pierce," he interrupts impatiently. "You received the painting from your grandmother, Joyce Sumner. It has been in your family for almost a hundred years. Would it be possible to see this painting in person? To examine it more closely? I could come to you. You're located in Washington, D.C. Correct?"

"Umm, yeah. Yes, I am," I say, a little put off by his tone, but I can hear the buzz of voices in the background. Laughter. The plodding of footsteps. It sounds like he's in a very busy place. Maybe he's rushing somewhere and doesn't mean to come off so abrupt. "And sure, you can see the painting. That shouldn't be a problem."

"How about tomorrow?"

I stop pacing. *"Tomorrow?"*

That soon?

"Yes, we can meet at one of my partner galleries in D.C. You can show me the painting there. Could you meet me at three o'clock?"

"Uh, yeah. Sure."

"I'll send you the address. I look forward to seeing you," he says, then hangs up, leaving me staring down at my phone screen.

CHAPTER 11

I ARRIVE AT THE GALLERY ON NEW YORK AVENUE AT THREE P.M. ON the dot, and I feel underdressed in my Pumas, though they are my favs.

I saw part of the cavernous showroom through the floor-to-ceiling windows as I walked along the sidewalk, but it looks even grander now that I'm inside. The floor is crowded with antique furniture. I spot a nineteenth-century federal sideboard, a Queen Anne–style mirror, and even a desk that looks like it could have come out of the Palace of Versailles. There are also paintings hanging on the walls that look a few hundred years old. Japanese signed woodblock prints. A gold-embossed Jesus. Watercolors of reclining, coquettish maidens and harbored boats.

I glance down at *The Portrait of the Defiant Woman*, which I wrapped in garbage bags to protect it during my metro ride, and I wonder if maybe she's underdressed too.

Do we even belong here?

"Can I help you?" the Asian woman behind the varnished wood counter asks.

She looks as polished as the showroom in her understated white blouse and asymmetrical bob.

"I'm here to meet Mr. Vivaldi," I say. "My name is Shanice Pierce. He and I have a three o'clock appointment."

"Ah, yes!" She nods before reaching for a desk phone and raising the receiver to her ear. "I'll tell him that you're here."

A few minutes later, I turn to find a short, balding man in an expensive-looking pin-striped suit walking toward me.

He looks me up and down. His eyes linger on my tennis shoes for a beat. "Ms. Pierce, I presume. I'm Mark Vivaldi."

I shift the portrait to offer him my hand, hoping my palms aren't too clammy. "Yes, it's good to meet you, Mr. Vivaldi."

He gives me a quick shake and I glance at his hand and see a large gold ring on his index finger. The gem is a smooth oval that's deep crimson with hints of orange, brown, and maroon.

"That's really nice," I say, pointing at the ring. "I've never seen something like that before."

"Ah! Why, thank you. The stone is the red tiger's eye. Some ancient cultures believed it was a source of strength and protection," he says.

"Protection against what?"

He shrugs. "Whatever they believed they needed protecting from, I suppose." Mr. Vivaldi rubs his hands together and stares down at the painting. "What an interesting storing method." He narrows his eyes. "Are those . . . *Hefty bags*?"

"Yes, umm, I . . . I grabbed what I could."

He nods, turns, and heads across the showroom. "Follow me."

I have to rush to keep up with him. He takes us to a long, dark corridor that makes me pause. I see nothing but empty, silent rooms down its length. No one else is down there. Where are we going?

Mr. Vivaldi stops when he realizes I'm no longer following him. "This way, Ms. Pierce," he says, gesturing to me. I can hear the impatience in his voice again.

I hesitate then resume walking.

"You happened upon quite the artistic find. Are you an art collector?" he asks as we walk.

"No, not really. I'm not really an art person, per se."

He glances back at me and chuckles softly, but doesn't comment. The look in his eyes tells me he isn't surprised by that admission.

We stop in front of one of the open doors and I look inside. In the dim light coming through the blinds of a solitary window, I can see that there is a desk and a large table at the center, covered with a sheet of vellum.

"You can set it there," he says, before turning on the overhead lights and shutting the door behind us.

I place the portrait on the table and begin to remove it from the trash bags as he walks toward the desk and rummages around in the drawers. I struggle with one of the bag knots.

"What are you doing?" he shouts, making me halt.

"Huh?" I ask, looking up at him.

"Don't *jostle* it around like that! Are you out of your mind?" he says, tugging on white gloves and reaching for the portrait.

I glare at him and pull the canvas out of his grasp.

His tight expression relaxes. He forces a smile. "I just mean that we should be careful. This painting is one of a kind, Ms. Pierce. We don't wish to damage it, do we?"

Don't wish to damage it?

The painting has been with my family for almost a hundred years and we've done fine with it so far. I don't need a lesson on handling it from him.

I now know for sure that Mr. Vivaldi's rudeness over the phone wasn't because he was just in a hurry and distracted; this guy practically has a glowing neon sign over him that spells "PRETENTIOUS DICKHEAD." I swear that I'm five seconds away from leaving and taking the portrait with me, but I want to learn more about the painting and about Estelle Johnson. I've come all this way. I might as well stay.

I place the painting back on the table, watching as Mr. Vivaldi painstakingly removes it from its bag.

"Your photo didn't do it justice," he whispers as his smile widens. "The poor resolution hid the details."

I try not to roll my eyes as he lowers the metal visor that is now perched on his head. It has a pair of magnified lenses. He leans in closer to inspect the painting.

"Has it been altered in any way?" Mr. Vivaldi asks. He's gnawing on his lower lip eagerly. "Any touch-ups?"

"Not that I know of," I say, looking over his shoulder.

The room falls into silence that stretches on for an achingly long time as he hovers over the canvas.

"So, umm, did Estelle Johnson paint a lot? Are there more pieces like this one?" I ask.

"About seven," he murmurs. "Mostly portraiture. This one was a self-portrait."

"Really? This is what she looked like?" I whisper, now in awe.

He nods. "It's so lifelike, isn't it? She had a marvelous understanding of the human form. I would have loved to see what other works she could have done after this. I'm sure Johnson would have been a much more prolific painter if she'd have stayed in New York. It provided her with stability, but she left New York and met her death soon after."

"How did she die?"

"In a house fire in Philadelphia. A freak accident."

Poor Estelle. I let that knowledge settle into me.

"Almost all of the paintings she did in her Harlem studio," Vivaldi rambles on, oblivious to my mood change, "but she was working on another painting while living with her then patron during her last months in New York."

"You mean Maude Bachmann?"

He turns his head so quickly to look at me, I wouldn't be surprised if I heard a tendon snap. I see his green eyes through the magnified lenses. They are larger now, almost twice their size.

"You know about Bachmann?"

I nod. "I read about her on Wikipedia."

"Wikipedia." He stares at me a bit longer with a weird expression. He then wipes it away. "Why yes, of course. So, then you know the story of Mrs. Bachmann's murder as well? That Johnson was rumored to be a prime suspect?"

I gape, making him chuckle.

"Well, I suppose not everything is available on the web."

"Why did they think she did it?"

"Circumstantial evidence, mostly. Johnson was living with Bachmann at the time, disappeared the night of the murder, and never returned. But Johnson died before the police were able to question her. I suppose she made this portrait either while she was still in New York or after she fled. Perhaps this was the last painting she owed Bachmann."

"Owed her? What do you mean?"

"All of her paintings were owned by Mrs. Bachmann. In exchange for room and board and for Mrs. Bachmann's patronage, which provided steady income, Johnson agreed to give her all of her work."

"But ownership would revert back to Estelle after a while, right? She could eventually sell her own stuff?"

"No, Mrs. Bachmann owned Johnson's work in perpetuity. That was their contract."

I gaze at him, once again stunned. Who in their right mind would sign a devil's bargain like that?

"But Mrs. Bachmann wasn't just her patron. Their relationship was a partnership. Bachmann guided the direction of Estelle Johnson's art so that she created works like this." He looks down at the portrait again, hovering his hand over it almost reverently. "You have to understand that Johnson was an unsophisticated young woman from the rural South who grew up in a sharecropper shack. Bachmann was a highly educated, cultured woman who had traveled the world. She spoke five languages. She was a scholar of Hinduism. Native American spiritualism. Voodoo. Johnson's tribal period, the almost visceral nature of her later work—it *all* came from Bachmann," Mr. Vivaldi gushes. "She never could have done it without her. Bachmann used to say that she was the gardener, but all her artists were her flowers. It was her job to enrich them and help them grow. She was their nurturer, much like a mother."

"I don't know if I would describe someone like Bachmann as 'nurturing,'" I mutter. "It sounds like she took advantage of vulnerable artists."

To be honest, if I were one of those artists and had to hand over everything I'd ever written to Bachmann and let her own my work wholesale just to have a place to live and food to eat, I'm not sure if I would be very fond of her either.

Mr. Vivaldi's serene smile disappears. His brow lowers. "Many of them would have starved without her, Ms. Pierce. And in the end, Bachmann was likely murdered for her misplaced trust and kindness." He returns his attention to the painting. "I'd argue that *she* was the obvious victim, not the—"

His voice suddenly fades and he leans in closer to the canvas.

"Is everything okay?" I ask him. "The painting isn't damaged, is it?"

Mr. Vivaldi doesn't answer me right away. He seems to go silent for a full minute before he stands upright and raises his visor, blinking rapidly. He clasps his hands together. "It's uh . . . fine. The painting is perfectly fine. This really is an exquisite work that you have here, Ms. Pierce. One that should be showcased."

"I haven't really thought about what I'm going to do with it, but my grandmother wants to—"

"I'll offer you fifteen thousand for it," he says, just as I finish saying, ". . . keep it in the family."

"I'm . . . I'm sorry. Did you say fifteen thousand dollars?"

He nods.

I open my mouth then close it. "Uh, thank you, but I hadn't planned to sell this. I was just trying to get more information about the work."

"Twenty thousand," he says like he didn't hear me. He removes his gloves.

My frown is back. "Mr. Vivaldi, that is a *very* nice offer, but like I said, my grandmother was adamant that she wanted to keep the painting in our family. She *just* gave me the painting a few days ago. It wouldn't feel right to—"

"Forty thousand. I can offer you forty thousand dollars, Ms. Pierce." He yanks off his visor. "I will go no higher."

But I can tell from the look in his eyes that he will go *a lot* higher if I keep saying no.

Part of me wants to take his offer. My poor bank account could use an extra forty thousand dollars. I could stay in my apartment. I could pay for therapy. I could support myself until I found another job. It would solve a lot of my problems.

But then I remember Gram's wish. Even though it creeped her out, she kept that portrait on her bedroom wall for decades. What would she think if I told her the painting had stayed in our family for four generations, and I couldn't wait a full week before selling it off to a stranger?

And Estelle was never able to own any of her work; Bachmann controlled it all. This was the one piece she had left, and she'd given it to her friend, Louise—my great-great-grandmother. Would *she* want me to sell it? I didn't know Estelle, but I feel a kinship to her now, realizing that she died young and tragically, just like Mom.

And finally, there's Mr. Vivaldi. I don't trust him. I think there's something about this painting that he isn't telling me, that wasn't in his story about Bachmann, Estelle, and all the other artists.

"Look, I appreciate your time and everything you've shared with me today, but this painting isn't for sale. I'm going to have to stick to my grandmother's wishes. Sorry."

I reach for the portrait and put it back into the trash bag. I turn toward the door, but stop short when he walks around the table, blocking my path.

"My offer is more than generous, Ms. Pierce."

"Yes, I heard your offer, and I'd like to go now," I say, enunciating every word since he obviously isn't hearing me. I attempt to walk around him but he wraps his hand around the door handle, barring my exit.

My eyes lock onto his hand. My heart rate increases. I start to sweat.

"Why won't you accept my offer? You said you weren't a collector. You know nothing about art. You know nothing about Johnson."

"I told you why," I say tightly.

"To 'keep it in the family'? And what purpose would that serve?" he asks, sounding angry now. "There's a tremendous amount of history surrounding this painting! It deserves better than to be imprisoned in someone's living room next to a flatscreen TV or shut away in some . . . some *garage*. It is too important."

"Get out of m-m-my way!" I say, hating that I stuttered, that I gave this man any inkling that he's starting to scare me.

But he doesn't budge. Instead, he fixes me with a stare that's so intense, I take a step back. I swear his eyes have swelled as large as they'd been under the magnified lenses.

"Don't be stupid, Ms. Pierce," Vivaldi says through clenched teeth. "Accept my offer. That would be a wise decision on your part."

My heart is pounding now. The stress is making me breathe harder. I have to get out of here.

I shove him aside with all my might. I'm taller than him and I guess a little stronger, and he lets go of the doorknob and slams back against the desk beside him. Vivaldi quickly gets his bearings though and lunges with his hands outstretched—for either me or the painting—but I yank the door open and rush out of the room before he can grab either of us. I run down the darkened hallway into the bright lights of the gallery.

"Ma'am?" the woman behind the gallery's desk calls to me and rises to her feet just as I sprint past her and out the showroom. I keep running until I reach the metro, until I see that he isn't there.

CHAPTER 12

"I TOLD HIM NO AND HE *WOULDN'T LET ME LEAVE*. I THOUGHT HE WAS going to lock me in there," I say over my shoulder to my grandmother, recounting the story five days later. I tell her what happened in the gallery while I toss a pile of toaster cozies she's been hoarding for decades into the garbage.

"Oh, no, he didn't!" she cries from the galley kitchen's doorway with her hands on her hips. "He must have lost his damn mind! Did you use your pepper spray?"

"No." I pause to wipe sweat from my brow. "I guess I was too . . . stunned. I didn't even think about using it."

But I thought about it later that night and the day after, obsessing over what I should've done differently. How could I have avoided the situation?

But how the hell was I supposed to know he would react that way? Even the beast, which usually creates dozens of catastrophic scenarios in my head, couldn't have predicted that. The whole situation was so bizarre.

"You should've called the cops on his ass. You still can! You want me to do it? What's that bastard's name again?"

"I don't want to call the cops. I just want to forget about it and let it go, Gram," I mutter, tying off the trash bag.

I decide not to tell Gram about the voicemail Vivaldi left me the next day, apologizing for his "unprofessional and unbecoming behavior."

"I let my eagerness get the better of me, and I am deeply sorry for that," his message said. "I honestly don't know what came over me."

I almost felt bad for him until he ended the voicemail with "I'm willing to raise my offer price by another ten thousand dollars. I can assure you the piece will be well taken care of in my own private collection. Please contact me if you change your mind."

I deleted the message.

"I swear you just can't get a break, girl," Gram now mutters, shaking her head. "You aren't leaving your purse on the floor anymore, are you? Because I told you about—"

"No, I'm not. And will you please stop going on about the purse? This has nothing to do with some superstition."

"No, I will not," Gram says firmly. "Not leaving your purse on the floor is not just 'some superstition.' It's words of wisdom given to me by my mama and her mama before her. Words to guide you and keep you safe in this crazy world. One of the few things you can control, when you can't control much else. You ain't gotta listen if you don't want to, but I'm gonna keep saying it."

"Fine, Gram, but this has nothing to do with bad luck. That guy was just an entitled ass who can't accept someone telling him no. But I know one thing . . ." I pause to turn to face her again. "For him to act like that and offer that much money, the painting must be a big deal. Estelle Johnson must be a big deal. A lot bigger than we thought."

I decided to not tell Gram about the other part of the story that Vivaldi shared, the part about Estelle being a murder suspect. At least not for now. I don't want to make an allegation like that against a close friend of her grandmother's based only on the word of a guy I don't trust. And even Vivaldi said all the evidence against Estelle was circumstantial.

"I tried to find out more stuff about her online, but there's nothing," I say to Gram. "Just a few lines here and there from books. I thought . . . if it's okay with you . . . maybe I'd leave here a little early to head to the library to find out more. Can you finish the rest of this without me?"

Gram nods. "I'll be fine, honey. You go on. We can do more cleaning another day. And while you're there at the library, I think I'll have a look around here."

I furrow my brows. "What are you looking for?"

"I remember Mama keeping some things from Grandma Louise."

"Were they pictures? Maybe she had some of her and Essie together."

Gram shakes her head. "No pictures, I don't think. I don't even know what Grandma Louise looked like. I never met her. She died before I was born, honey, and Mama didn't talk about her much. I think Grandma Louise was real sickly," Gram continues. "In and out of hospitals most of her life, from what little I heard about her. Even went to a sanitarium once. I guess not many memories of her mama were good ones for her. You know how people were back then. Especially old black folk. If they had painful memories, they never wanted to talk about it."

It's not just "old black folk" back then, I note. Gram rarely if ever shares her memories of Mom.

"But I know I've seen some of her things around here," Gram says. "I just can't remember where. Maybe she kept some letters from Estelle."

"Maybe," I say before kissing her cheek. "See you later."

"See you," she says before kissing me back.

I grab the bulbous trash bag and tug it toward the kitchen door. "I'll put this in the trash bin outside, and I'll make sure I put it in the *right* bin this time. We don't want any more visits from the block captain, do we?" I say with an innocent smile.

Gram sucks her teeth. "Go, chile."

CHAPTER 13

When I arrive at the library not far from my apartment—a one-story, greenhouse-like building with high ceilings and lots of light—I beeline over the polished concrete floors to the book stacks.

I already checked the catalog online back at my apartment this morning and have a list on my phone of what I'm looking for.

I pass the children's section where a half-dozen preschoolers sit on the rug in a semicircle around a librarian who is reading a book with a dancing giraffe on the cover. She recites a line in the book then turns it around so all the children can see the page. She points to the illustration and the kids erupt into giggles.

I smile at the sound of their little voices.

Mom used to take me to storytime at our local library when I was little. I'd sit with the other kids "crisscross applesauce" on the rainbow-colored rug and listen to the misadventures of Curious George and the Cat in the Hat and the folks in Whoville while Mom searched among the adult paperbacks. When I got older, I would head to the tiered children's display that showed *The Baby-Sitters Club* or the latest *Harry Potter*, and Mom and I would meet at the circulation desk with our finds.

After she died, I stopped going to the library for a long time. Dad offered to go with me, but I refused. The library was for me and Mom; it was our special place, no one else's.

I think about those days as I start my search. I move to one of the stacks toward the back of the library, by the reading nooks. All the seats are empty and the hushed voices of other patrons are muffled. The laughter from the children's reading hour has evaporated.

Back in my college days, this would've been the perfect place to study; it's so quiet that there's just the sound of my footfalls and my purse thumping against my hip.

Though the building is mostly glass, it suddenly becomes darker in the library as the sun disappears behind fluffy, cumulus clouds overhead, yanking away most of the light and creating stark shadows on the floor. I have to squint to read some of the titles on the book spines because the lighting is so bad. The clouds have also taken away all the heat from the natural light. I shiver a little. Goosebumps sprout on my arms and bare legs.

I bend down to reach for one of the books on the lower shelves, but stop short when I feel someone standing behind me. I didn't hear anyone approach but I ease forward anyway, closer to the shelf to let them pass when I realize I'm taking up the whole aisle.

"I'm sorry. I'm in your way, aren't I?"

No one answers, but the feeling of someone standing there, hovering behind me doesn't leave either.

They don't leave.

They just loom over me. I can practically hear them breathing.

I wait another few seconds, not moving an inch.

I'm overwhelmed by the unnerving sensation. The one you feel when a stranger stands too close in an elevator or when a car is riding your rear bumper on the highway. I feel like I'm being boxed in.

I shoot to my feet and turn around to see who's there, but there's no one. It's just me alone in the book aisle.

I give myself a little shake before grabbing the book on my list and returning to the more populated part of the library. I continue my search. After about a half hour, I assemble a sizable pile, but then realize one book is missing even though the catalog said it wasn't checked out. It should be here.

I make my way to the checkout counter.

"Whoa!" the librarian behind the desk says. She laughs. "You've got quite the tower there!"

She looks to be around my age and is wearing bright purple cat-eye glasses with a messy bun of dark hair piled atop her head. As she takes one of the books off the stack and reads the cover, her glasses slide down the bridge of her nose. She has to push them up again.

"I noticed you walking around," she says.

She noticed me? Do I stand out that much?

"We generally get two kinds of patrons at this branch: the grazers that get one book or none and the gatherers, and you, my friend, are a *mega* gatherer." She pauses after she scans another book. "Harlem Renaissance art movement, huh? Are you working on a thesis or something?"

"No, umm, I'm a writer."

That's true—sort of. Just because I'm unemployed doesn't mean I stopped being a writer.

"Oh, are you writing a book about the Harlem Renaissance?"

"No, I'm writing about a painting I inherited."

The words are out of my mouth before I realize what I'm saying. Since when did I decide to write about Estelle's portrait?

I gradually nod to myself.

I guess I decided it right now.

"It's a painting by the Harlem Renaissance artist Estelle Johnson," I explain. "I'm trying to find out more about her."

"Who?" The librarian frowns. "I've never heard of her before. Should I know her?"

I grab one of the books the librarian has already scanned and flip to one of the pages that has a small paragraph about her.

"Oh, wow!" she says, looking genuinely impressed. "And you said you inherited one of her paintings?"

"A self-portrait. It may have been her last work."

"That is fascinating!"

Someone loudly clears their throat behind me. I turn to find an older woman clutching a stack of self help books. She inclines her head and widens her eyes in a *"Are you going to be done soon?"* silent expression.

The librarian nods at the woman, scans my last three books, and shoves the heavy hardbacks back across the counter toward me. "Well, good luck on your research. I'm interested in hearing what you find out."

"Actually, there's one last book that I was looking for that wasn't in the stacks, and I looked all over." I slide my cell toward her to show her the title.

"That's odd." She stares down at the screen and frowns again. She then takes a few steps to the left and begins to type on a nearby computer.

The woman behind me in line loudly sighs and begins to grumble. I want to tell her to read whatever chapter in those self-help books she has on "finding your inner peace" and chill the hell out.

"You're right," the librarian murmurs as her brow crinkles. "It should be there. That's so strange. I wonder if it's on one of our shelving carts or there's a mistake in the database." She looks at me again. "You know what? Let me do some research and get back to you."

"*Really?* Would you?"

She nods. "The piece you're writing sounds awesome! I'd hate for us to slow you down. Can you give me your number and I'll let you know when I find it?"

"Sure! That would be perfect. Thanks so much!" I scribble my name and cell number on a sheet of paper before handing it to her.

CHAPTER 14

I DIDN'T BRING ANYTHING WITH ME TO HELP CARRY MY BOOKS, which was a mistake. Now I'm battling a leaning Tower of Pisa that I can barely hold or see around as I leave the library, and I have to walk about four blocks before I get to my apartment building.

I carefully make my way down the library stairs and then to the sidewalk. But as I near the crosswalk, I have an unwelcome sense of déjà vu. I can feel someone behind me.

I'm being followed.

I know what this is. I have now arrived at another symptom of the beast: paranoia.

I bet I have Vivaldi to thank for this. I decide to focus on the heaviness of the books in my arms, on my breathing.

Inhale, exhale.

Inhale, exhale.

The sense of someone behind me, of being followed, starts to wane.

I'm about to step off the sidewalk when a guy walks by, bumping my arm as he passes. My books go flying and tumble to the ground.

"Shoot, I'm so, *so* sorry," he says.

I scramble to grab the library books before they fall into the street and get run over.

"I should've looked where I was going. I was scrolling on my phone and not paying attention. I'm such an ass. Let me help you."

As I reassemble my pile, I see tan hands and slender fingers reach for one of my hardbacks. Hairy knuckles. A smattering of hair peeks around the shirt cuff. I glance up to find two, bright blue eyes staring down at me. The eyes crinkle at their edges as he smiles, revealing one crooked incisor.

"Again, I am *really* sorry," he says, blushing. "I didn't mean to startle you."

He's now assembling his own stack a couple of feet away.

"It's . . . It's okay," I say shakily.

I pick up the last book in front of me and see there's a penny underneath, making me pause. I slowly pick it up.

"There you go! It's not all bad. Some good luck is comin' your way, huh?" He hands me his half of the stack and grabs his phone from the sidewalk. He rubs it against the side of his pants to remove the smudges and the dirt. We both slowly rise back to our feet.

I can see that he's tall. Over six feet. I can also see that he's cute in a sweet, wholesome sort of way. He has sandy blond hair that would look even better longer, but he probably keeps it short to look professional. A suit jacket is thrown over his forearm.

I'm trying to balance my tower again just as he takes a sharp intake of breath then slowly lets out a gust of air. I crane my neck around my library books and gaze down at his phone. There's a huge crack in it.

"Oh, man! Did that just happen?" I ask.

His phone doesn't look cheap.

Wholesome guy closes his eyes, grimaces, and opens them again. He dismisses my concern with a shake of his head. "It's fine. It's my fault for walking and being on my cell," he says. He then tucks the phone into his back pocket and looks at me. "Do you need help with those? I can carry some for you."

I step back, clutching my books against me.

There are some things . . . behaviors I can blame on the beast; others are just the byproduct of living and growing up in the city. It's conditioned me to a lot of things that might seem odd to other people, like walking alone late at night with my Mace strategically hidden in one hand and my cell in the other with my finger hovering over the emergency call button. Avoiding parking on city streets whenever I can because the parking signs are harder to decipher than the Rosetta Stone. And always, *always* being suspicious of offers from strangers. They're trying to either sell you something or steal something from you.

But I hear a twang in this guy's voice. He doesn't sound like he's from around here. No one's given him the primer yet.

"No, I've got it. Thanks," I say and attempt to walk away, but I only take a few steps before dropping a book again from my stack.

He reaches down and picks up the book. He cocks an eyebrow at me. "You sure?"

I hesitate for what feels like a full minute, feeling the weight of the books increase in my arms with each passing second. Finally . . . reluctantly, I nod.

"Thank you. I appreciate it. It's just . . . it's only a few blocks."

"It's not a problem." He takes most of the books, leaving me with only two hardbacks to carry. "My name is Noah, by the way. Noah Kelly."

"Shanice Pierce. It's nice to meet you."

"Same!" He then gestures to the crosswalk. His smile widens. "After you."

He quietly walks one step behind me, carrying my book stack. After about half a block in mutual silence, I start to feel a bit ridiculous. I glance back at him.

"So do you work or live around here?" I ask him.

"Neither. I was on my way to get dinner at the Thai place up the street before I took a train home. Do you work or live around here?" Noah asks in turn.

"Live."

"Oh, really? Where? Is that where we're headed?" he asks as we reach another busy intersection.

I open my mouth and close it. It dawns on me that I'm about to show a guy who I met five minutes ago where I live. A definite no-no. I'm willing to bend my "taking an offer from a stranger" rule, but I'm not giving him my address.

My apartment building doesn't have a doorman. There's no front desk security guard either. Once, when I forgot the code to get inside, I managed to sneak in behind another resident without them knowing. Anyone else could do the same, including this guy—no matter how nice he seems.

"Uh, yeah. I live at the corner of Connecticut and Belmont. It's not too far from here."

I actually live a block away from that address, but Noah doesn't need to know that.

"That's cool! I was thinking of gettin' a place around here, but the apartments are crazy expensive," he says as the light turns green and we walk again. "I'd practically have to sell a kidney to afford it. I moved up here to Washington ten months ago for work."

"Yeah, I could tell you weren't from around here. From the accent, I mean. You're from Texas, right?"

"Is my accent that strong?" Noah chuckles.

"No, I just have a friend . . . her name's Tatiana . . . she's from Texas. The accent sounded similar."

I hadn't heard it before she and I became college roommates at Howard. We've been friends ever since.

I now point to the building in front of us. "This is me. Thanks so much again for doing this. And I'm really sorry about your phone."

"It's fine." He shrugs. "The warranty will cover it." He hands me back my books. "And if you really feel that bad, you can make up for it by buying me a cup of coffee sometime. Maybe later this week?"

I pause, once again caught off guard. Is Mr. Wholesome Texan asking me out?

My expression must look more alarmed than surprised, because he takes a step back.

"I mean if you want to, but . . ." He stares down at me. His cheeks are going pink again. ". . . you don't look like you do though. Man, this is embarrassing." He lets out another gust of air and rakes his fingers through his hair. "I called this wrong, huh?"

"No! No, you didn't. I'm just . . ." I purse my lips. "Look, I've just had a bad breakup and I definitely haven't been asked out by anyone in a while."

"So that's a no then?" Noah asks, inclining his head. "Too soon after a breakup?"

Is it too soon? It's been less than a month since Jason moved out, but then I think about how things ended between us. He seemed certain it was over and was ready to move out and move on without any misgivings. Why shouldn't I try to do the same?

Because you're currently battling anxiety disorder.

Because you're unemployed.

Because you're in desperate need of money and a new place to live.

All true, but it's not like this guy is asking me to marry him. It's not even a real date; it's just coffee.

"Uh, no . . . I mean yes. I mean it's a yes! I can meet you for coffee. How about Saturday at the bistro up the street? The one with the striped blue-and-white awning. They make a pretty good espresso. But let's meet later in the afternoon. It's usually a lot less crowded then."

His smile is back. Noah nods. "Sure! Sounds good."

He and I exchange numbers and say goodbye. I pretend to walk into the building as he walks away, and I watch him through the tinted glass. He politely steps aside to let a UPS delivery guy with a dolly truck pass in front of him, then waves as if to say, "You have a good day, my friend," and continues down the block. He's practically whistling as he walks.

I shake my head at him in exasperation. Poor guy. This city is going to eat him alive.

When he's out of sight, I continue to my apartment building, dropping my books a few more times along the way and even at the door as I dial my code into the metal wall panel. But I don't mind.

By the time I reach my floor, I'm still thinking about Noah and our coffee date this weekend.

I have a date. I'm no longer buried under my weighted blanket in the dark, losing myself in YouTube videos until I fall asleep. I'm going to write about Estelle Johnson and her work. Tati would be proud of me. Maybe I should finally give her a call back and meet her this week for lunch, like she's been asking.

It's strange to actually be looking forward to things again. Maybe, the beast is starting to lose its chokehold on me; my luck could be changing.

I walk down the hall and turn the corner. That's when I see a white envelope taped to my door. As I draw closer, I see my name printed neatly on the front. I slow my steps. It's probably a letter from the leasing office downstairs. I'm two weeks behind on rent. I expected a note or an email from them eventually.

I guess even a penny on a street can't work a miracle.

I set my stack of books on the floor and take down the envelope. I open it and find out that it isn't a note from the leasing office. It isn't signed either, but I know instantly who sent it as I unfold the paper and hundred-dollar bills flutter to the hallway floor and my welcome mat like green confetti.

ACCEPT THE OFFER! Consider this a gift for now, the note says.

I gather the bills by the fistful, scrambling to get them all before anyone else can see. I then shove them into my purse, grab the note and envelope, and take my books inside.

CHAPTER 15

FIVE THOUSAND DOLLARS. I COUNTED IT ALL. VIVALDI GAVE ME FIVE thousand dollars in cash.

I rest my elbows on my knees and hold my chin in my hands as I stare at the neat rows of hundred-dollar bills now assembled on my living room sofa cushions.

I didn't even know Vivaldi knew where I lived until I remembered the contact form I filled out when I answered his request for more information about Estelle's painting. I'd included my address among other details about me. But I never thought he would come here. I never thought he would do something so desperate as leave five thousand dollars taped to my apartment door.

Is he stalking me now? How many times do I have to tell him he can't buy the painting? That *I* can't be bought?

And what was with the "Consider this a gift for now"? What did he mean by *for now*? It sounds ominous.

Fawn, Gram's neighbor, was instantly drawn to the portrait. Now Vivaldi is practically salivating over it.

"What is it about you, Estelle?" I whisper, looking at the painting.

I don't call it *The Portrait of the Defiant Woman* anymore because now that I know who the woman is, it doesn't seem right to be so formal; I feel like she and I are on a first-name basis. She's a family friend, after all.

I still haven't hung the painting on the wall though. It's leaning against the vertical blinds of my sliding glass doors that lead to my deck where I keep a few ferns and succulents that I keep forgetting to water.

Every time I grab a hammer and nails to hang it and see those big, dark eyes, I get a chill like I did back at the library today. I just can't bring myself to put it up. I guess I will eventually.

I turn away from the painting to look at the money again.

What do I do with all of this?

It worries me that he's this obsessed, that he just won't let the portrait go. What will he do next? Try to steal it?

I guess I could go to the police like Gram said, but what do I tell them? He wouldn't let me out of a room and then tried to make up for it with a bribe of five thousand in cash?

I pick up the money and run my thumb over the consolidated stack of bills, listening as they flap rhythmically like a deck of cards.

Maybe I'm seeing this from the wrong angle. This could just be the result of my newfound good luck. Maybe this *is* a gift like the note said—one that's unexpected, but useful right now in my time of need.

I glance at the painting again. My shoulders slump.

"A gift like this with no strings attached. I'm delusional, right?" I ask it.

Of course she doesn't respond, but she doesn't have to. I already know the answer. No gift like this comes without a ribbon of tangled strings.

I swear I'm on the verge of opening the glass door, tossing the money from my balcony, and watching the people below scramble and fight for it like they're in some demented game show just to get it off my hands. Only fifteen minutes ago, I was starting to feel better, and now I'm stuck in the same worry loop like before.

"I can't deal with this right now." I shoot to my feet. "And I don't have to."

I walk into my kitchen and shove the money into the envelope, and the envelope into the junk drawer by the sink.

I wanted to research the painting and Estelle and reheat some bolognese I made last week, not to be burdened with the weight of what to do with five thousand dollars from some pompous asshole.

Fuck Vivaldi. Fuck him *and* his money.

I slam the drawer shut and open the fridge to get my last bottle of wine. Less than five minutes later, my microwave beeps. I press the button to open the door and take out my steaming bowl, burning my fingertips in the process. I blow on them and my dinner, letting the bowl cool down as I open the wine bottle and pour myself a glass.

By the time I return to the sofa, I'm slurping spaghetti while trying not to spill red wine on myself. I set down both the bowl and the glass on the coffee table and crack open one of my library books. I read a few pages then open another book and read some more. After a while, the surface of the coffee table is covered with books.

I forget about my wine. My spaghetti slowly goes cold. I'm lost in the world of Estelle and her days in Harlem.

It turns out, according to the books, Estelle was a member of "The Niggerati," a clique of Harlem Renaissance artists and intellectuals who dominated that scene in New York at that time. They didn't all like the name, but after the black novelists Zora Neale Hurston and Wallace Thurman used it (no one can decide who said it first), the name stuck.

Some called themselves Niggerati as an act of self-mockery and irony. Others as a way to thumb their noses at the uppity black elites who looked down on the free-loving, brandy and gin-drinking, weed-smoking artists they believed were bringing shame to the families, in particular, and their race, in general.

Estelle was one of the wild ones, showing up at salon parties at "Niggerati Manor"—Langston Hughes's abode on E. 127th Street—to laugh and dance the night away or talk about art, politics, or the meaning of life, I'd like to imagine. It was around this time that she'd crossed paths with her patron, Maude Bachmann.

It annoys me that there's a lot more about Maude in these books than there is about Estelle. Almost every reference to Estelle leads back to her. Even pictures. There are about a half dozen of Maude as an old woman, as a young woman, her posing in profile, her posing head on, but *none* of Estelle. It's bad enough that Maude owned all her work outright. Did she have to take over her life story too?

But the more I read about Maude in my books and online, the more I realize why she casts such a big shadow.

She was rich, *really* rich. So rich that her descendants created a charitable foundation and they're opening a new exhibit this year at MoMA in her honor. The money came from her family—the Chapmans of Connecticut—and her husband, Klaus Bachmann, a German doctor and viscount. Maude and Klaus had one son named Elias. She used her family money to help artists, paying what would now be the equivalent of more than a million dollars to fund their work and careers.

But the woman was also odd, to put it mildly. Vivaldi forgot to mention that Maude liked to talk to dead people. She regularly held séances at her Park Avenue apartment. She also believed in divination and consulting shamans and clairvoyants.

Yes, I'm a superstitious person, and I check my horoscope on occasion. I even accepted a gift of healing crystals from a friend once, though I have no idea where the crystals are now. Probably in my closet somewhere. But I'm a Little League player in the world of the occult compared to a pro like Maude.

She and her husband were members of an old-school spiritualist society, The Bridge of Light, which believed there was an ancient path to enlightenment hidden among the more "primitive cultures" of the world. They had several members from New York high society. They even held ceremonies.

Curious, I looked them up online. The group no longer exists as far as I can tell, but I found their old insignia—a blazing sun with two intertwined serpents at its center—on a website.

Maude and Klaus Bachmann traveled the world trying to find this golden ticket to enlightenment, hopping from India to Turkey to Mexico before finally settling back in the US when Dr. Bachmann fell ill. It was back in the States that Maude's interest in the Harlem Renaissance started. It's also in Harlem that she believed she was finally on the path to enlightenment that she'd spent so long searching for.

"Wonder if ol' Maude found the end of the rainbow before she was murdered," I mumble, though I don't find out much more about her murder than what I already read online. Nothing to corroborate anything Vivaldi told me about Estelle being a prime suspect, which makes me curious as to where he got *his* information.

I slam my book shut, yawn, and rub my tired eyes before tossing the book onto the table and glancing at the steno pad beside me on the sofa. It's covered in notes I plan to use for my essay on Estelle. What I'm going to do with the essay after I write it, I have no idea, but it feels good to be inspired and have a plan for once. And there's no Gary telling me that my idea is unoriginal or that the execution is way off. I can write whatever I want, however I want.

I rise to my feet and stretch, taking my empty bowl and wineglass to the kitchen. After putting them both in the dishwasher, I head down the hall to get ready for bed. I'm standing in front of the bathroom mirror, brushing my teeth, when I hear the knock at my front door.

Well, "knock" isn't an accurate description. It's a series of thumps that causes the wall to shake and makes me almost drop my toothbrush into the sink. It sounds like someone's punching or ramming the door over and over, trying to pry it off its hinges.

"What the . . . Who the hell is that?" I mumble.

I quickly walk back down the hall, wiping away the minty toothpaste from my mouth with a hand towel.

"*Yeah?*" I call out. "Who is it?"

When I reach my front door, I stare out the peephole, but don't see anyone. I unlock the door and cautiously open it, prepared to slam it shut if anyone sketchy is standing out there waiting.

I search up and down the corridor. No one's there. It's the same sterile hallway as always with white walls, recess lighting, and gray carpets. I don't even hear footsteps. There's just the vague sound of someone playing their television too loud in one of the other apartments.

I step back inside and close the door behind me.

I definitely heard someone knocking. That wasn't my imagination.

It's like back at the library when I was sure I felt someone standing behind me, but no one was there.

The paranoia. It's starting again.

I try to think of possible explanations for that noise to calm myself down.

Maybe the knock was on someone else's door. The apartment above?

Or maybe *I am* imagining things. I'm tired, after all. And I was drinking. Not a lot—just a glass or two, but perhaps enough to alter my perception.

I'm a single woman living alone for the first time in years, and I've been reading about Maude Bachmann's murder, séances, and The Bridge of Light for hours. It's bound to mess with my head.

Or . . . *or* someone really is screwing with me. It couldn't be Vivaldi, could it?

"That doesn't make any sense," I whisper. "Why would he just bang on my door and run away?"

To harass me. Maybe even to scare me.

Inhale, exhale.

Inhale, exhale.

Inhale, exhale.

I look at the portrait and gnaw the inside of my cheek. I take a few quick steps and grab the painting, tucking it under my arm.

"I'd feel better if you weren't just sitting out in the open anymore," I say to the portrait.

I check the lock on my front door once . . . twice, then head back to my bathroom and turn off the light.

I walk to my bedroom and look around me, searching for somewhere to hide the painting like a wall safe or a secret crawl space will suddenly manifest themselves. I eventually decide to tuck the painting in my bedroom closet for now, stowing it behind a pile of boots. I shut the door, then climb into bed, and try my best to go to sleep.

CHAPTER 16

"I FOUND IT!" GRAM CRIES ACROSS THE HALL IN HER BEDROOM THE next day. "I knew it was here."

"Found what?" I ask, distracted by a giant box of Kotex hidden in all the debris of the cabinet underneath the upstairs bathroom sink.

"Why is this even here?" I mutter under my breath, before tossing it into a trash bag. It's probably been decades since anyone living in this damn house has even *had* a period.

Gram and I have made enough progress on the first floor of the bungalow that it's relatively presentable for a real estate agent to do a house tour. We've decided to move onto the top floor—the bedrooms and the bathroom—which is even more cluttered.

Later this afternoon, I'm supposed to meet Noah for our coffee date. I'd almost forgotten about it until he sent a text this morning.

See you at 4, the text said, followed by a steaming cup emoji.

"What do you mean, 'found what?'" Gram now asks in exasperation, making me turn around to look up at her. She's standing in the bathroom doorway, holding an old shoebox while I kneel on the floor. "I found the letters, girl! The ones from Estelle and Grandma Louise."

"What?" I rise from the pastel yellow tile and see that the torn lid on the shoebox sits up a little because it's filled to the brim with envelopes.

"Are *all* those letters really from Estelle?" I ask breathlessly, taking the box from her.

"Well, not all of the letters are from her. Some of them are from your great-great-grandmother and a few other people, but there's plenty of 'em in there," Gram says, gesturing to the box in my hands. "Mama really did keep them all. I don't know why though."

I remove the lid and look at the pile. Oxidation has turned the papers yellow over time. The sealing glue of the envelopes along the edges has browned. The ink has started to fade too, but the name and address for Estelle Johnson, Harlem, NY, is still readable.

"This is just . . . I'm so . . ."

I can't find the words. I'm speechless. Gram actually found her letters. Estelle's own words. Staring at them, I don't know why I'm so emotional. Maybe because the discovery of Estelle has been one of the few bright lights in my life right now, or maybe she offers me the distraction that I desperately need.

"Thanks so much, Gram," I say, giving her a quick kiss on the cheek before I lower the toilet seat and sit on top of it. I set the box on my lap and take out one of the letters, not wanting to waste a minute before I dive in.

"I'm not gonna get any more work out of you today, am I?" she asks.

"Huh?" I reply, barely listening.

"Uh-hunh," Gram grunts, then chuckles. She walks out of the bathroom.

I read letter after letter, leaping back in time to Estelle's years as a diligent though bored student at Claflin University in South Carolina where she was learning to become a teacher, until she took her first art class and a world opened up to her. I read about her first year in New York as a broke border who made what little money she could transcribing lectures and research papers for professors at NYU. Estelle, or "Essie," as she always signed her letters, was one of the few black artists accepted at the famous Winold Reiss Art School and it is there that she met Bachmann.

I'm just about to read about the lavish apartment on W. 134th Street that Bachmann moved her into when I feel an insistent tap on my shoulder.

"You *still* readin'? I thought you said you had somewhere to be at four o'clock," Gram says with a frown as she stands in the bathroom doorway.

I slowly lower one of the letters back to my lap and look up at her, dazed. "Huh?"

"It's already after three thirty, Shanice."

"After three thirty?" I grab my cell phone from the sink counter and see the time on screen. "Damnit," I mutter before quickly folding the letter and stuffing it back into the box with the rest of them.

CHAPTER 17

I ARRIVE AT THE CAFÉ FOR MY DATE WITH NOAH SWEATY AND ALMOST thirty minutes late. I'm still clutching the old shoebox of letters as I come to a stop near the café entrance. I search through the window for Noah at one of the bistro tables, then the counter, then the leather lounge chairs dotting the room. Instead of seeing him, I catch my reflection.

"Damnit," I say under my breath again.

I didn't get a chance to take a shower to scrub away the grime and dust from cleaning or to change my clothes. My T-shirt has a big blue spot on it, near the shoulder. I'm hoping it's only Windex. I'm not wearing any makeup. I try to finger-comb my hair into place and then give up when I realize it's pointless.

I want to turn around and head to my apartment, but I have to go in there; I texted Noah that I was running late, that I was on my way.

I open the café door, and I'm instantly hit with the aroma of coffee, baked bread, and chocolate, with the cacophony of voices, the gurgling blast of the espresso machine, and the generic pop rock band playing on the background speakers. I glance around the room, on the lookout for Noah again among all the controlled chaos.

"Shanice?" I hear a voice call behind me.

I turn to find Noah rising from a chair at one of the two-seater tables on the other side of the room. He beckons me toward him.

"Over here!" he says.

I wave and walk across the café.

Noah is as cute as I remembered, maybe more so. He's in a dress shirt and slacks again, but he skipped the tie and rolled his sleeves up to his forearms. You can tell he made an effort to look nice, that he wanted to make a good impression for our date. As I draw closer, I notice that he smells nice too, like minty bodywash. Meanwhile, I'm worried that I smell like a heady mix of bleach and body odor.

"Glad you texted me," he drawls before walking around the table and pulling out a chair for me. I nod in thanks before sitting down and setting the box at the center of the table. "I thought you were gonna stand me up and I'd have to pay for my own cappuccino."

"Yeah, sorry about that." I fidget in my chair as he sits down. "I was helping my grandmother with something, and I uh . . . I just . . . I'm sorry, but time got away from me. I didn't mean to be late or to . . . well, to come looking like this," I say, gesturing to myself.

"What d'you mean? You look fine." He takes a drink from his cup.

I eye him and I can't help but bark out a laugh. "That's sweet, but I don't look fine. I look terrible!"

Noah shakes his head. "You couldn't look terrible, even if you tried. But you do look like you've had a pretty busy day. At least you spent it helping your grandmother. I can't fault you for that. I can't even think of the last time I talked to my grandmother." He glances down at the box. "I'm guessing that's not a gift for me."

"Oh, uh, no," I say, placing my hand on the lid. "It's just a . . . a project I'm working on."

"Really?" He braces his elbows on the table. "What kind of project?"

I hesitate.

It's on the tip of my tongue to info dump, to tell him about Essie's painting and all my research. I'm bursting at the seams to share what I've found. After reading her letters, I'm solidly addicted to Essie's story; I know now that I *have* to write about her.

Essie was a young woman with hopes and dreams much like my own, who struggled in her life much like I am struggling now.

Vivaldi had described her as "unsophisticated," but that description was not only unfair, it was also inaccurate. Essie may have grown up in a sharecropper shack, but she was also college educated, articulate, and inquisitive. I lost my mother when I was twelve, but from what I've read, Essie lost hers in infancy. She was searching for something back then, just like I am.

I want to know what happened to her. What took her from that bright-eyed, eager girl in her letters to the startled, intense woman in the painting who Gram said looks like "she'd cut you if you look at her sideways." What could have happened that possibly made her commit murder?

But that's a lot to tell Noah. It's a lot to explain to *anyone*, especially someone I've just met.

"Just a writing project," I say instead, rubbing my hand over the lid affectionately. "I needed these letters . . . the info in them for background."

He nods. "Sounds interesting. So you're a writer, huh? Have I seen your work anywhere?"

"No, not yet. I'm working on it though." I shift the box aside and bounce my feet restlessly underneath the table, forcing myself to stay still above the waist. "So tell me about yourself, Noah. Besides the fact that you're from Texas."

"Not much to tell," he says before taking another sip of coffee. "I grew up in a town just out of Galveston. My father worked on oil rigs. My mother was a stay-at-home mom who took care of me and my brother and sister. I got a soccer scholarship to Baylor University and majored in economics. I'm not playing for the San Antonio FC like I hoped, but now I work as a labor economist." He shrugs. "You take what you can get. What about you? What are your highlights that I couldn't get from Twitter or Instagram?"

"You stalked me online?" I lean back and laugh again.

"Doesn't everybody before the first date?" he asks over the lip of his cup. He takes another sip.

Noah has a point. Before Jason and I got together, whenever I went on a first date, I usually did a search of all the guy's social media accounts, if I could find them. I'd comb through his posts and even what accounts he followed. It's been a while since I've done that kind of sleuthing though. I guess I'm out of practice.

"Why don't you tell me what you already know about me?" I say. "Then I'll fill in the rest."

"Well, you turn thirty in a couple of months and you're kinda freaking out about it."

I nod. "Fair assessment."

"You used to retweet a lot of articles from this online magazine called *The Interceptor.* I guess you're really into politics."

"It's *The Intersector,* and I used to work there." I shift uncomfortably in my chair again. "I don't . . . umm . . . anymore though."

"You used to post on Instagram lots of photos of places and restaurants that you liked too, but that stopped about a month ago. I kinda wondered why."

"Just really busy lately," I lie.

"So, fill in the blanks for me. Where'd you grow up, Shanice?"

"Well, I lived here in D.C. until I was about fourteen. Then we moved to the suburbs. Then I moved back after I graduated from college and got a job in town."

"Wow, you're one of the few people I know who live in Washington that actually grew up here."

I nod. "Yeah, we're pretty rare."

"So why'd your family leave the city? Didn't like it?"

"No, they loved it. Always have. Especially my mom. But my dad remarried and he and my stepmom bought a house in Bethesda."

"So did your mom stay in the city then? Did you have to hop back and forth between houses? I had a friend who did that after his parents got divorced too." Noah takes another sip of his cappuccino and shakes his head ruefully. "He hated it."

"No, my parents aren't divorced. My . . . my mom died."

Noah lowers his ceramic cup back to the table. "Damn, I'm sorry."

"It's okay. It was *years* ago. She was in a car crash. I mean *we* were in a car crash. She and I. I was pretty badly beaten up. Broke my leg in two places. And Mom died at the hospital from her injuries. They tried to save her, but . . . well, they couldn't."

"Shit, I didn't know." His face goes ashen. "I'm such a dumbass for bringing that up."

"No, like I said . . . it's okay. How could you have known? I wouldn't put something like that on Instagram," I insist, trying to make a joke, but it doesn't land. He still looks flustered.

"Look, uh, I should get you something," he says, rising from the table. "I'm just sitting here making an ass of myself. I'm messing this up. Can I get you a cappuccino or an espresso, maybe?"

"You aren't messing up anything, and an espresso is fine," I say as he nods and heads toward the counter. "But I'm supposed to be the one treating you!" I call after him, but Noah doesn't hear me. He's already standing in line, waiting to make an order.

I slump back into my chair. This date is not going well. I look awful. I'm still sweaty, and now I've managed to freak out Noah by mentioning the car crash that killed Mom—and it's only been ten minutes.

"I should not be here," I mumble.

But I can't just walk out while he's ordering my espresso. I have to make the best of it, so while I wait for Noah to come back, I people-watch.

I see an elderly woman in a floppy, wide-brimmed hat and oversized Chanel sunglasses pushing two dogs in a pink two-seater baby carriage.

I see a couple having an intense argument as they walk past the café storefront.

A few seconds later, a guy wearing a baseball cap and oversized reflective aviator sunglasses walks into the café. Even though it's almost 80 degrees outside, he's wearing a black hoodie. The only part of his face that's visible is his mouth and blond goatee. Like me, he seems to jitter with nervous energy and is only able to manage it by shoving his hands into the hoodie pockets. He looks around the café like he's searching for someone.

The door to the café opens again, yanking my attention, and my breath catches in my throat.

It's Jason.

"You've got to be kidding me," I whisper. What are the chances of him coming here today? Why *now*?

Jason is wearing a T-shirt and basketball shorts. Maybe he's just come from the gym. He's started growing a beard since I've last seen him. I watch as he searches through his side satchel for something. He takes out his phone, looks up, and drifts toward the counter.

I guess he's back in town from his "business trip." I wonder when he got back—or if he even left at all. Maybe it was just an excuse not to text or call me back. Either way, I sink farther down in my seat, relieved that he hasn't noticed me. I hope it stays that way.

Noah takes the cup of espresso from the barista, pays, and nods his thanks before turning around and heading back to our table. As he does, he bumps shoulders with Jason and I let out an "oomph," like he bumped me instead.

"Excuse me, buddy," Noah says to him and walks toward me. "Here you go."

"Thanks," I whisper as Noah hands me my coffee. I blow on it and take a few sips, telling myself to drink slowly. Running into my ex shouldn't be this big of a deal.

Noah sits down and I start to feel what has now become a familiar sensation. Like I'm under a spotlight. Like I'm being watched.

I look up and discover that Jason is now staring at our table. I accidentally lock eyes with him and almost choke on my coffee.

"What's the matter?" Noah asks. "Too hot?"

"No." I shake my head, tearing my gaze away from Jason.

Noah glances over his shoulder just as Jason pretends to look away. Noah frowns. "Do you know that guy?"

"Yeah." I gradually nod. "He's . . . he's my ex."

"*Your ex?* Oh, wow!" He looks at Jason again. "Now that you mention it, he does seem kinda familiar. I guess I saw him on your Instagram."

My fidgeting is getting worse. My heart is starting to pound and not because of the espresso. This whole situation feels wrong. Just *seeing* Jason has messed with me this badly. I knew it was too soon to start dating. This was a mistake.

I set down my cup and push back my chair, making it scrape loudly over the café's terra-cotta tile. "Look, Noah, you seem like a . . . a really nice guy. But based on everything happening in my life overall, I'm going to say this maybe wasn't a good idea."

"*Why?* Because your ex is here?"

"No." I grab Essie's box of letters. "It's not just that."

His blue eyes search my face with concern. "It's because I mentioned your mother, right? I knew I screwed up when I did that."

"No, I told you that you didn't do anything wrong—and I meant it."

"Then what is it? Why are you running out of here without even finishing a cup of coffee? I'm confused."

I close my eyes, take a deep breath, and open them again. "The truth is, I quit my job only three weeks ago, the *same* day my boyfriend dumped me. I don't know where I'm going to live a month from now because I can't afford my apartment anymore. I'm going through a lot and . . . I'm . . . I'm not in a good headspace, and I don't want to subject anyone else to that right now. Okay? So thank you for the coffee, but I think . . ." I rise to my feet, clutching the box against my chest. "I think I'm gonna head home now."

I then walk toward the coffee shop door.

"Shanice, come on. Wait up!" Noah calls after me, but I don't wait.

I keep walking out of the café and down the sidewalk in the direction of my apartment building, my refuge. But I stop short when I reach the end of the block and I hear him jogging up behind me.

"Shanice, slow down!" he shouts.

I pause and he skids to a stop. I turn to find him gulping for air. His face is flushed.

"You're not . . . you're not the only one who's had a . . . a bad break, all right?" he says between gasps.

"What?" I can barely understand him, he's huffing so badly.

I hear a crack of thunder overhead even though the sun is out. I glance up at the sky as Noah takes a deep breath and tries again.

"I said you're not the only one who's had a bad break! You're not the only one who's gone through stuff. I have too with my ex-fiancée," he explains. "Laurie. She's the reason why I left Texas and came here last year. She cheated on me with a guy I've known since Little League, and I got in a bad headspace too."

"I don't just mean heartbreak, Noah. I mean a real diagnosis. I . . ." I pause, not wanting to say the rest, but I might as well just tell him. "I have anxiety disorder. It doesn't take much to make me worry. To make me tense. Sometimes, it gets so bad that I'm scared to head out the front door in the morning because I don't know what the hell will be waiting for me on the other side. I—"

"And I was diagnosed with depression. I lost my job. I couldn't stand anything or to be around anyone. It got really bad, Shanice. I saw a doctor for a while. He advised that a change of scenery might help, so I took a job offer and came up here to Washington."

Depression? I find it hard to believe that Noah was diagnosed with depression; he always seems so cheerful. He was practically whistling as he walked away a few days ago. I can't imagine him sad, let alone depressed.

I guess looks can be deceiving.

"Did you get any better?" I ask softly as I feel the first sprinkle of rain.

He nods. "After a while. I still have rough days sometimes though, but they're further and further apart." He takes a step toward me, blinking through the drizzle. "I'm just saying I get it. I understand. I've been through my . . . well, through my rough patches too. It doesn't mean you should close yourself off." He looks up at the sky, licking his lips. "Sunshine while it's raining. That's weird."

I laugh. "Actually, it's good luck."

He grins. He has a nice smile, even with the crooked tooth. "Maybe it's a sign that we should get a do-over. Maybe dinner instead of coffee? Not today," he rushes out, "but maybe . . . maybe next week. What do you think?"

I hear another crack of thunder and feel the warmth of the sunshine on my face. It's a good sign. Just like the penny on the day he and I met.

"Okay, but you choose the place next time," I say.

Maybe then there will be less of a chance of us running into someone I know.

Noah nods. "Sure. I can do that."

PART II

CHAPTER 18

ESSIE

NEW YORK CITY

June 25, 1927

Essie walked to her new apartment with her groceries cradled in her arms. This stretch of block was still fresh to her, as sparkling new as the gramophone now on display in one of the store windows. She'd only moved into her current abode two months ago. It was nestled inside one of the many grand brownstones on Sugar Hill.

She dabbed at her sweaty brow with a handkerchief as she walked, eager to get indoors and out of the smog-filled, stifling hot Manhattan summer. It would be one of the hottest on record, a headline in *The Evening World* had said just yesterday.

Just six more blocks, she silently assured herself. *Only six more.*

When she got home, she planned to strip naked as the day she was born and walk around her apartment with all the Westinghouse fans sitting on the floor, turned on high. She'd then recline on her bed while sipping a glass of fresh squeezed lemonade and bask in all the cool air.

Well, after she finished writing the itemized list of everything she'd purchased today so that it could be reviewed by Agatha.

"With *all* prices as well," Agatha had told her when she'd forgotten to include the prices in her last list which she'd submitted for review only two weeks ago.

When she'd inquired to Godmother about the request, her patron had laughed. "Yes, it does seem frightfully strict, but I trust Agatha as my secretary. Even I provide her with lists of my purchases every month. It's how we keep full accounting of all my expenses."

Hearing Godmother's explanation made Essie chafe less at writing the lists. Besides, Essie supposed it was a small price to pay for the life she was leading, for the freedom she had in many other ways.

A car beeped its horn, catching her attention, making Essie slow her pace. The cherry red Duesenberg glided to a stop along the curb. She recognized the driver who was partially hidden under the shadow of the hardtop. He leaned over the black leather seat to gaze at her, revealing the rest of his handsome face.

"Why, hello there, Ms. Johnson," Elias Bachmann said, tipping his straw boater hat and giving her a charming smile that made her stomach flutter.

"Hello, Mr. Bachmann. And I told you that you can call me Essie."

"That you did." He nodded and inclined his head. "How rude of me to forget."

"Are you going on an afternoon drive?" she asked him over the steady chug of the automobile's engine, wondering why he was here in Harlem and not the Upper East Side, his neck of the woods.

"No, I just happened to have business near here today and noticed the stunning young lady walking with her groceries. I just had to stop and introduce myself and I realized, belatedly, that I already knew her. Can you believe that?"

She laughed and shook her head at him. "No, not a word of it."

He grinned. "Fine, maybe I just wanted to stop by to see how you were settling into your new home. Mother told me you lived here now." He took off his hat and waved it in front of him. "It's hot as Dante's inferno out there. Would you like a ride?"

She hesitated. Unsure how to answer, she pursed her lips.

"Oh, come now, Essie! It's just a car ride." He held up one of his hands from the steering wheel. "I solemnly swear that I will behave."

Maybe she didn't want him to behave—and that's what she was worried about.

After the Park Avenue soiree in April, she'd asked around about Elias among her friends and the other artists she knew.

"Why do you want to know about Elias Bachmann?" her friend, sculptor, and sometimes lover Sylvia Bonner had asked her. They were at a party at the townhouse of A'Lelia Walker, the late Madam C. J. Walker's daughter, almost a month ago.

"No particular reason," Essie had said before plopping onto Sylvia's lap and plucking the lit cigarette from her mouth. She'd taken a drag from the cigarette before puffing smoke into the air. "I met him at one of Godmother's parties on Park Avenue and was just wondering."

"Well, he's a shameless playboy," Sylvia had said, snatching her cigarette back.

"Who's a shameless playboy?" A'Lelia had called out, striding across the salon's parquet floor, champagne flute in hand.

Sylvia had given a droll eye roll. "Elias Bachmann. Essie here was askin' about him."

"Was she now? Well, I heard he's bedded more artists, actresses, and singers than the pearls around my neck," A'Lelia had said, gesturing to her choker. "He collects them like trinkets. I heard he secretly has a thing for *Negro girls*. Why do you want to know about him?"

"Humph, probably because she wants to be next in line to have a go with him," Sylvia had answered for Essie before she took her own drag from the cigarette and adjusted her ascot. "She's a glutton for punishment, if you ask me."

"Aww, are you jealous, sweetheart?" Essie had asked with a mischievous pout. She let out a squeal and a giggle as Sylvia slapped her rear end.

"All jokes aside, Essie, even if you do have a roll in the sheets with Elias, don't let his mama find out," A'Lelia had warned.

"Oh, she's not prejudiced," Essie had insisted. "She's the most open-minded person I know."

"Sure," Sylvia had murmured dryly. "But even the most open-minded white rich folks don't want their sons fraternizing around town with a Negro girl on their arms. You'd have to be his *dark* secret, or that Godmother of yours could cut you off and toss you out on your ass."

Essie had frowned. "Godmother wouldn't do that."

"Are you willing to take the risk to see if she would?" A'Lelia had asked.

A'Lelia was right. Elias was handsome and enthralling, but she didn't come this far to risk alienating her patron for a fleeting romance with him.

"You're positively melting out there, Essie," Elias now continued playfully. "Please let me rescue you."

Essie clutched her paper bag of groceries tighter against her chest. "All right. Thank you kindly."

It's just a car ride. Nothing more, she told herself.

When she climbed inside, she placed her grocery bag firmly between them like a barrier, making him chuckle. They were silent most of the drive though there was a palpable tension between them. It grew stronger when she glanced his way and they briefly locked eyes.

"This is me," she said, pointing to her building when it came into view. "You can stop here."

Elias pulled up along the curb. Essie opened the passenger door and turned to reach for her bag. As she did, Elias suddenly leaned forward and extended his arm along the back of the seat, drawing so close to her that their noses nearly touched.

"I would be happy to carry that in for you. You could show me around the place."

Her eyes locked with his again, making her breath catch in her throat. It was like staring into two amber pools of honey that she wanted to dive into, but she knew if she did, she'd likely drown.

So, Essie licked her lips and forced herself to utter, "Maybe some other time."

"But I'm sailing to Europe next week. I won't be back for months," he lamented.

She felt a slight pang at his words. "Really? For months?"

He nodded.

"Then . . . then when you get back."

"Do you promise?"

She nodded.

"I'll hold you to that," he said, just as she climbed out of the vehicle. She bumped the door closed with her hip. "I assure you, I will, Essie!"

He then winked again, shifted gears, and pulled off.

The butterflies in her stomach finally stopped fluttering. Essie hoped she could hold her resolve with Elias, but it would be hard if he kept fixing those heavy-lidded eyes on her the way he did. At least he would be in Europe for a while. Maybe she could build up more willpower with time and distance.

She turned away from the busy road and spotted a vagrant standing near her front stoop.

The woman was wearing a gray cotton dress stained with dirt and perspiration. A straw cloche with a frayed gingham ribbon was pulled low on her head, covering the top half of her brown face. The woman clutched a battered knitted handbag against her chest, like she feared someone taking it away from her.

Essie drew closer to her as she rounded the corner of the stoop and neared the stairs.

"Excuse me?" the woman called out to Essie.

"Sorry, I don't have any change on me," Essie answered distractedly with a polite smile as she passed. She placed one foot on the concrete stairs but stopped short when she felt a sweaty hand clamp around her forearm.

"I don't want your damn change," the woman said.

CHAPTER 19

Essie's gaze shot up from the hand on her arm to the woman's face. Under the shadow of her cloche, Essie could see her eyes. Big, dark eyes.

If Elias's eyes were pools she wanted to dive into, these eyes were two deep whirlpools she'd fight to escape.

Essie instantly remembered where she had seen this woman before. It had been months ago outside of the Godmother's Park Avenue home. She'd been standing in the pouring rain watching as Essie walked to Godmother's Rolls-Royce Phantom. She'd stared at her through the Phantom's glass like she knew her, but hadn't said a word. She'd grabbed for the door handle instead.

"I want my things," the woman now said. "I want what was taken from me."

"I . . . I d-don't know w-w-what you're talking about," Essie stuttered, attempting to pull away from her, but she stopped short when the woman pulled a knife from her knitted pocketbook and jammed it into Essie's side. Not deep enough to break the skin, but enough so that Essie could feel the pointed end of the blade through the fabric of her dress.

"I don't wanna hurt you, but I will if I have to," the woman hissed into Essie's ear. "Open the door and let me inside. All I want are my things."

Essie glanced over her shoulder. Elias's Duesenberg had disappeared around the corner; he was long gone and couldn't help. She looked at those passing by, wondering if she shouted, maybe one of them would aid her. Or maybe the opposite would happen: no one would help and the woman would panic, stab her, and run off.

"Don't even think about it," the woman said, reading her mind and resting a hand on her shoulder. She squeezed her there, holding her in place. "Just walk up those stairs and open that door, if you know what's good for you."

Essie followed her command, putting one unsteady foot in front of the other and climbing the stairs to her brownstone. She halted in front of the two oak doors.

"I . . . I have to s-s-set down my b-bag to get my . . . my k-k-key."

The woman nodded, but didn't lower her knife. "Go on, then."

Essie slowly stooped down and set the brown paper bag of groceries in front of the ornate wooden doors, keeping a wary eye on the blade all the while. Her hands shook as she took out the key to open the lock.

"Go right down the hall to the apartment, Estelle, and open the door," the woman ordered as Essie picked up her bag. "Don't try anything funny. You hear me?"

How did the woman know her name? How did she know that Essie's apartment was the one on the first floor? Had she been watching and following her all this time?

Less than a minute later, they were inside the apartment. As soon as they crossed the threshold, the woman headed straight to Essie's bedroom.

"Take whatever you want!" Essie called to her from the doorway as she set down her bag again. She could hear rummaging around in there, drawers and doors being opened and slammed shut. "Jewelry. Whatever! Just take it and leave. Please!"

Most of it wasn't even hers; it had been gifted to her by Godmother.

"Where are they?" the woman shouted from the other room. "Where the hell are they?"

The woman came rushing out of Essie's bedroom. She walked straight toward her with the knife firmly in her hand, jabbing it at her again. "Where are all my goddamn papers? What did you do with them?"

Essie shrunk back, shaking her head. "I—I don't know what you're talking about."

"My manuscript!" the woman screamed. "All of my writings! What did she do with them? Did she throw them away? That bitch didn't burn them, did she?"

When Essie continued to gaze at her blankly, the woman sucked her teeth. "Of course she did. Of course she burned every single one. I kept them in the desk drawer in the corner. Something told me to hide them. I should've kept them with me, but I didn't think about it. I didn't think!"

"Wait. You . . . you lived *here*?"

Godmother had told her that other artists she'd patronized in the past had lived in the furnished apartment before Essie.

"I find that when artists are freed from everyday worries of having to keep a roof over their heads, they are also freed to create at will," Godmother confided to Essie as she handed her the keys. "That is why I have kept this lovely home. It fosters beauty in this world. Now it is yours as long as you need it. As long as you wish, Estelle."

Essie had always been under the impression that the other artists had moved on to bigger and better things once they didn't need Godmother's assistance anymore.

She didn't know that one of them had been forced to leave.

The woman finally lowered the knife and nodded. "Yeah, I lived here, until she threw me out on the street. Came home one night and she had changed the locks. Didn't even give me a chance to grab my things." She gazed around the living room. Her eyes, alert and bright with fury a few seconds ago, now looked vacant.

"You got any hooch around here, Estelle? You aren't dry, are you? You don't seem like the type."

"Uh, I've got some brandy. It's with the glasses in the cabinet over—"

"I *know* where the cabinet is," the woman muttered before striding across the living room to the teak cabinet by the sofa. She put the knife back in her purse. "I lived here. Remember?"

Essie watched as the woman took out a bottle of brandy and a tumbler. She filled the glass almost halfway and took a swig. She then narrowed her eyes and turned in a circle, looking around the room.

"She added new curtains." She then pointed to the settee. "That used to be on the other side of the room. She changed the wallpaper in the bedroom too." She took another drink. "The one she had when I was living here was better though."

"What's your name?" Essie ventured.

"Why do you wanna know?" the woman asked, eyeing her suspiciously.

"Well, you know mine, but . . . but I don't know yours."

"Doris," she said. "Doris Bingham."

The name sounded vaguely familiar. Essie tried to recall where she might have heard it. Had someone said it at one of the parties at the Manor? Had she met her when she first arrived in New York and forgotten? Those early days had been such a blur.

"I'm sorry, but . . . have we met before?" Essie asked.

"No, we've never met. I've seen you though. I saw you at her place. I saw you move in last month and I found out your name. This place sat empty for a while after she kicked me out, so I was curious who she moved in here to replace me."

"Why did she kick you out?"

Doris gave a bleak laugh. "Because I wouldn't follow orders. That bitch let me live here while I worked on my novel, but she didn't like the direction it was going. It didn't have enough 'truth of my people.' It wasn't authentic enough and full of pretension, she said. She kept telling me I had to change it. Finally, I told her it was my name on the manuscript, not hers. She said if I didn't do what she said, she couldn't be my patron anymore. Then one day, she just upped and threw me out on the street. Didn't even let me pack my bags. Just tossed me out with the clothes on my back!"

Essie was frowning again. The part about truth, authenticity, and pretension sounded like Godmother, but the rest didn't. She knew Godmother to be kind, to be supportive of her and her art.

But Godmother did have opinions and had no problem expressing them. When she visited Essie at her studio, she never said outright that Essie had to alter her paintings, but she didn't hesitate with her critiques.

"This is lovely, Estelle, but wouldn't it be so much lovelier if there were more shadows there?" she'd said just last week, pointing at the canvas. "It would add so much more emotion and duality . . . depth, don't you think?"

And after Godmother left, Essie added the shadows, not because she felt she had to do it, but because she respected Godmother's opinion.

"One time, she had one of her friends who said she was clairvoyant read my palm, to tell me about my future. You know what the woman said? She saw nothing. She said my future was like standing in an empty room in the dark. I should've known then that Godmother had cursed me," Doris went on. "That bitch cursed me! Everything I had . . . everything I was doing fell apart. Lost my man. None of the journals would print my work anymore. I heard news that my mama died back in Mobile. All my old friends disappeared. I just became nothing overnight." She walked toward Essie again. "She has the power to do it, you know. She and those friends of hers. They can curse you. They did it to me!"

Essie's frown deepened. She looked down and for the first time noticed the purple bruises on Doris's arms, just beneath the cuff of her quarter-length sleeves. She knew those bruises . . . the familiar tracks showing injection points. She'd spotted them on the arms of a few fellow artists and jazz musicians she'd met.

Doris was a heroin addict. That would explain the ranting and paranoia. It all made sense now. Had that been the *real* reason why Godmother had tossed her out? Godmother couldn't very well house and continue to enable a volatile drug addict. No wonder she'd made her leave.

"You'll watch out for her, if you're smart," Doris went on, finishing the last of the brandy in her glass. "She wants your power. She wants what's in here." She leaned forward to tap Essie's temple, making her wince. "And what's in here," she said, pointing to her chest. "She feeds on it until it's all used up. Until *you're* all used up." She then reached into the collar of her dress and pulled out a twine necklace with a small leather sack attached to it. "I had a witch doctor in East Harlem make me this medicine bag to stop it. But I think I got it too late. Do you have one?"

Essie slowly shook her head.

"But you need somethin' to protect you! You really don't have anything?"

Essie shook her head again.

Doris stared down at the medicine bag then slowly removed it from around her neck. She handed it to Essie. "Take it. Go on! It didn't work for me. But maybe it'll work for you."

Essie took the bag, feeling the coarse string and soft leather against her fingertips. She caught a mix of smells emanating from the bag—earth, spices, and the vague stench of dirty hair. "Th-thank you."

Doris nodded. "Keep it close. It'll protect you."

"I will," Essie assured.

She was willing to say anything to make this crazy woman go away.

Doris staggered backward. "She told me I was a literary genius. That they'd be reading my work for decades to come. And I was so gullible I believed her. Then she took everything from me. Everything! Now I'm nothing. I'd kill her dead if I could." She looked helplessly around her again. Tears filled her big eyes. "She cursed me, Estelle," she whispered. "They did this to me."

"Who . . . who's they?" Essie asked, though she felt silly as soon as she asked it. Why play into the woman's hallucinations?

"They have ceremonies at the penthouse. They make sacrifices so they can bargain with the devil. Get out while you still can," Doris said, not answering her question, "or what happened to me could happen to you. Or it could be a helluva lot worse. You hear me? It won't just be a curse. They'll sacrifice you too."

Essie nodded again, but Doris gave another hollow laugh as she shook her head.

"You don't believe me, do you? I can see it on your face. But you'll learn, just like I did."

At her words, Essie felt a chill. She watched as Doris dropped the tumbler to the floor and tucked the bottle of brandy under her arm.

"Mind if I take this?" Doris asked, gesturing to the bottle.

"Go ahead," Essie said.

When Doris stepped past her into the hall, Essie rushed to close the door behind her and locked it.

She looked down at the leather medicine bag clutched in her hands and walked to the waste bin on the other side of the room to toss it. She dangled it over the bin for several seconds by its coarse twine, but couldn't let it go. Even though she knew it was nonsense. Even though she suspected Doris was deranged. Instead, she sat it on one of the end tables.

I'll toss it later, she told herself before heading to the bedroom to clean up the mess Doris had made in there.

CHAPTER 20
SHANICE

WASHINGTON, D.C.
Present day

I HATE MY CELL RECEPTION, BUT IT'S THE PRICE I PAY FOR HAVING A cheap phone plan. It's probably why I don't notice my cell buzz while riding back from Gram's house this evening after another day of cleaning and only see the notification saying I have a new voicemail as I walk from the train station back to my apartment.

I'd hoped it was a message from Noah. We've talked a few times since our first date and are even supposed to meet tomorrow night for dinner—our official do-over. But the message is from an unfamiliar number.

I reach my apartment building and dial the code into the wall panel to get inside. I walk through the door and down the hall toward the bank of elevators and play the voicemail.

"Hi, Shanice. This is Isabel from the D.C. Library," the voice on the line says just as the elevator doors open and I step inside before pressing the button to take me to the ninth floor. "I wanted to let you know that I found the book about the artist that you were looking for. As it turns out, it was on one of our shelving carts, like I thought. We've been a little understaffed lately and fell behind on returning books to the stacks. I'll leave the book for you in our reserve pile whenever you want to pick it up."

"Cool," I whisper.

I guess I can pick it up sometime this week. Hopefully, it can add to my research. I haven't gotten through all of Essie's letters yet, and, so far, I've already cranked out almost three thousand words.

I lower my phone from my ear to delete Isabel's message, but pause when I hear she's still talking. There's another twenty-seven seconds left of her voice message, so I raise the phone back to my ear to listen to the rest of it.

". . . he asked about you. He asked me what you were looking for. I told him that I don't give out information about our patrons, but I thought you should know something like that. Anyway, the book will be waiting for you at the front desk. Any of the librarians can give it to you. Hope that helps!"

The message runs out and I frown. What was she talking about at the end?

As the elevator doors open, I run my finger over the cell phone screen to rewind the message to the part I missed. I step out of the elevator compartment and slowly walk down the hall, listening to the message again and my thumping footsteps on the hallway's industrial carpet.

"I'll leave the book for you in our reserve pile whenever you want to pick it up. By the way, while you were here, there was this guy following you around the library," Isabel says on the voicemail. "I don't think you noticed him, but I did. He came back later that day and he asked about you. He asked me what you were looking for. I told him that I don't give out information about our patrons, but I thought you should know something like that. Anyway, the book will be waiting for you at the front desk. Any of the librarians can give it to you. Hope that helps!"

I halt in my steps.

So I wasn't being paranoid that day. Someone *was* standing behind me in those deserted book stacks. Not only that . . . they were following me around the library. But who could it have been?

My mind immediately goes to Vivaldi, but I don't want to jump to conclusions. I call back the number to the library as I dig through my purse for my house keys, trying not to panic, though I can feel the beast chomping at the bit.

"Belmont Branch D.C. Library. How can I help you?" a man on the other end answers.

"Hi, I wanted to talk to one of your librarians," I say into the phone as I near my apartment door and take my keys out of my purse. "Her name is Isabel. My name is Shanice Pierce. She . . . uh . . . she left me a message about thirty minutes ago."

"I'm sorry but Isabel is gone for the day. Can one of our other librarians help you?"

"Uh, no . . . no, I need to speak to her. Umm, I'll just call back tomorrow."

"She's off tomorrow, ma'am," the man says.

"Off?" I raise my key to insert it into the lock. "Well, when will she be . . ."

My voice fades when my front door creaks open. I stare at it in amazement.

It was already unlocked and I know for a fact that unlike back at *The Intersector*'s offices, I locked the door behind me this time.

I lean toward the open door. I can hear rustling inside my apartment and the sound of footsteps over hardwood.

Someone is in there.

"Ma'am," the voice on the other end of the phone line continues, "I'm sure that we can—"

I hang up, unsure of what to do next. My heart is racing. I'm starting to breathe hard, to feel my throat tightening, so I take slow breaths.

Inhale, exhale.

Inhale, exhale.

The last thing I need right now is another panic attack.

"Fuck," I whisper. "Shit."

Calling the police is my best bet. But I can't sound hysterical. They won't understand me. I have to stay calm.

I ease back from my door and quickly dial 9-1-1. I cup my hand around my mouth just as I hear the dispatcher answer on the other end.

"*Hello?*" I whisper into my cell while I keep an eye on my doorway. "Someone has broken into my apartment. I live at—"

I stop talking and nearly drop my phone when the door creaks open wider. Jason stands in the door frame, backlit from the light of my living room. He stares down at me quizzically.

"I thought I heard you out here," he says, like it's the most normal thing in the world for him to be standing in my apartment in his suit and tie, just like old times. "Why didn't you come inside?"

"*Why didn't I come inside?* What the hell do you mean, why didn't I come inside?" I yell. "Why the hell are you even here?"

I hang up my cell, shove him aside, and stride past him.

"I called the police, Jason! You scared the crap out of me. I thought someone had broken in. You should've told me you were coming. You should've asked. You can't just . . . just *barge* into my apartment."

What was he even doing in here? Moving out more of his things? I take off my purse and scan the living room and the kitchen, but nothing seems out of place.

"Why would you call the police? And what do you mean *your* apartment?" He shuts the front door. "Since when?"

"Since you packed all your stuff and moved out more than a month ago!"

"That may be the case, but my name is still on the lease. Remember? I still have a key to get inside," he says, holding it up in the air like its evidence in a trial.

"That's the spare I asked you to bring back *weeks* ago, which you didn't."

"I'm here now though, aren't I? I was having dinner with friends a few blocks away and decided, why not stop by and bring it to you?

You weren't home when I got here so I let myself in. That's all! I thought I was doing you yet another favor."

From the smell of him, he and his friends had a lot more than just dinner; Jason reeks of alcohol.

"Fine," I snap, "you brought it back. Thank you for finally doing the bare minimum that I asked of you. You can give me the key and then you can leave." I hold out a hand to take the key. I point the other toward the front door.

Jason turns in a slow circle then shakes his head, having the gall to look aggravated—like he wasn't the one who entered my apartment without my permission.

"You are a piece of work," he mutters. "You were practically begging my ass not to move out of here, and now you're in a rush to see me go? Is it because of the new guy?"

"What are you talking about? What new guy?"

"You know what I'm talking about. Don't play dumb. That white guy you were with at Bread and Grounds last week. Is he stopping by later? Is that the *real* reason why you're rushing me out of here?"

I close my eyes and pinch the bridge of my nose, trying my best to retain what little calm I have left.

"Is he the new sucker you've recruited to pay all your bills since I won't do it anymore?" Jason persists.

"Who I'm dating now is none of your business."

"So he *is* the new sucker then?"

"Why do you keep acting like I'm some manipulative gold digger? I never asked you to . . ." I stop myself when I realize I'm yelling again.

I can't believe I wanted this. I wanted these fireworks when Jason and I broke up. Words lobbed at each other like hand grenades. Plates thrown. But I was wrong. I don't have the energy or tolerance for this kind of nonsense. I don't have the patience for this whole bitter, jealous ex routine.

"Jason, please just . . . just leave. I'm going to assume it's the alcohol talking right now."

"I'm not drunk!"

"You smell like a distillery! Go home and sober up, because you're making a fool of yourself."

"No," he says, taking a step toward me, "I was making a fool of myself when I let you use me for as long as I did. I was making a fool of myself when I let you float around in this . . . this *delusion* that you were discovering your life's purpose when I was really carrying your ass the entire time. I paid the bills and the rent. *Everything* was on my back! Including our relationship. You were never here. You were always at the office. The magazine was your priority. It wasn't us. And now you don't even have the magazine. So, I guess you have no alternative than to look for a new job now, huh, since that fell apart too?"

"Wait, how . . . how did you know I quit the magazine?"

He rolls his eyes. "How the hell do you think? And you had the nerve to just drop on me the fact that you quit your fed job, that you accepted an *internship* that was going to pay you basically nothing and threw in that detail like it was an afterthought. You put me in a position of being the bad guy if I said no!"

"For the last time, I wasn't trying to take advantage of you. All I was asking was for you to be patient. I was asking for you to believe in me. I thought it was going to lead to something bigger. I thought I was going to—"

"And where did it get you? Nowhere! That job led to nothing."

I don't know what hurts more: that he would say something like this to me, or that he's right.

"You want to hear the truth? You're a user, Shanice. You're selfish. You used me. You use your dad. You've used your mom's death and your goddamn anxiety disorder as an excuse to just float along and not be responsible for *your* life! Just grow the hell up!"

I glare at him, no longer recognizing the man standing in front of me. Had he been this belittling and cruel during our entire relationship and I'm just noticing, or is our breakup bringing out the worst in him?

I don't know and I don't care. I just want him to leave.

"Yeah, well, then I guess it's a good thing we aren't together anymore and you don't have to deal with me or my *delusions*." I hold out my hand again. "I'll take that key now."

Jason's face hardens. He narrows his dark eyes and opens his mouth to say something, but doesn't. He doesn't give me back the spare key either. We're in some bizarre standoff.

"The key, Jason," I repeat.

Inside, I'm shaking, but I force myself to keep my hand steady.

The muscles ripple along his jawline. He's actually gritting his teeth. He's that pissed. Instead of dropping the spare into my open palm, he tosses it onto the kitchen's granite ledge where it skids across and clatters to the floor.

"Really, Jason?" I slowly shake my head. "What are you? Twelve?" I bend down to pick up the key, and hear the door to my apartment slam shut behind him.

"Asshole," I mutter before slapping the key back onto the counter.

CHAPTER 21

"BACK UP! JASON BROKE INTO YOUR APARTMENT?" TATI CRIES, WHIPping her head around so fast to face me that her braids almost hit me in the eye.

"No," I huff as I jog beside her, pausing to wipe at the sweat on my brow. "He had a key. And that's not the important part of the story. The important part is what the librarian said. The part about the guy who was following me."

This morning, Tati and I are running along the Tidal Basin, not too far from the United States Holocaust Memorial Museum. The cherry blossoms that D.C. is famous for blossomed earlier this month but their pink petals still litter the sidewalk and pavement, coating the bottom of our tennis shoes. The view is amazing. I can see the ducks swimming along the waterfront and the seagulls flying overhead.

So far no crows, but the day is young.

I decided that my personal life was getting to be way too much drama to work through on my own and told Tati what's been going on with me. If there's anyone to confess all this to it's Tati; she's good in a crisis. She even does it professionally. Her job is handling crisis PR for clients. So, I told her about Essie's painting. About Vivaldi and his offer of five thousand dollars. About the stalking. I suggested that we finally have that long-delayed lunch date, but she offered to meet and talk some more during one of her morning runs instead. She mentioned something about endorphins from cardio exercise.

"It can help, just in case you're feeling . . . you know . . . off with everything that's been going on," she said.

I didn't object. In lieu of therapy sessions and medication, I've been doing meditation exercises and yoga routines from YouTube videos. I figured some cardio couldn't hurt. And if Vivaldi is stalking me, I should make him work for it by keeping a ten-minute-mile pace.

Tati slows down as we approach the paddle boats. She peers down at her watch, jogs in place, and taps a few buttons on screen. "Four and a half miles, three hundred forty-seven calories." She wiggles her head and wrinkles her nose. "I guess that's good enough for today."

"Thank God," I say between gasps while adjusting the straps of my sports bra underneath my soaked T-shirt. "Because I was about to ask if we could . . . you know . . . take a break."

Tati props her foot on the rusted metal railing along the waterfront and starts to do her stretches. Meanwhile, I sit down on the concrete wall overlooking the water and lean forward with my hands braced on my knees and fight to regain my breath.

I turn to Tati when my heartbeat feels like it's back to a normal pace and find that she's barely breathing hard. I don't even see sweat on her color-coordinated tank and stretch pants.

"So, I was planning to go to the library tomorrow or later this week talk to Isabel so she can give me a description of the guy she said was following me around the library since she's apparently out today," I say, continuing my story. "Maybe she can let me know if it was Vivaldi."

Tati hops down and raises her left foot to the metal bars to stretch her other leg. "And Vivaldi is the art appraiser?"

I nod. "He left me the money too, back at my apartment."

"What are you going to do if you *do* find out it was him following you around?"

"I don't know." I shrug. "Get a restraining order? Or maybe find out who his boss is at the gallery and tell them what he's been doing."

Tati loudly sighs and shakes her head.

"*What?* You don't think that's the right move?"

"It's not that." Tati lowers her leg and seems to consider my question. "I'm just not . . . well . . . I'm not convinced it's that Vivaldi guy."

"Why wouldn't it be him? He's the one that's obsessed with the painting. He gave me thousands in cash for it."

She purses her lips as she twists at the waist, doing torso stretches. "Shanice, let me tell you a story about a client I had once. It was a CEO of a big coffee company who shall remain nameless."

I frown. "Coffee company? Wait. You're not talking about St—"

"Who *shall remain nameless*," Tati says over me, before giving me a look that tells me I'd have a greater chance of finding the Holy Grail than getting the truth out of her about the company's name or the name of the CEO. "Anyway, he was bracing for a PR disaster due to some chick he met online. I don't even know how it started, but they had been exchanging DMs for months. It got pretty hot and heavy. He even sent her a few pics."

I raise my brows.

"Yeah, the kind of pics you wouldn't send home to the kiddies. *Anyway*, soon after, the mystery girl flipped out on him and told him she'd send the pics to the media if he didn't immediately come clean to his wife about what was going on between them."

I nod as I listen, though I don't know what her story has to do with me or Vivaldi.

"He was having investigators track down her Instagram account and identify this woman so they could charge her with extortion or whatever, but in the meantime, we were on standby to brace for the fallout. We were developing this whole PR strategy when the investigators finally figured out the source of the account. It was his wife. His *wife*, Shanice!" Tati stops twisting her torso. "She was catfishing this man the whole damn time. She owned up to everything. She said she suspected the CEO was cheating on her and wanted to test him, and he failed. This online affair he had with the fake woman she created pushed her over the edge. It set the whole crazy ball rolling."

"Oh, wow," I murmur, then stare at Tati blankly, still waiting for her to connect this back to my dilemma.

"What I'm saying is that when it comes to love and relationships, people don't act logically. They make irrational decisions and do stupid things. Your stalker probably isn't Vivaldi. I bet it's Jason."

I go silent. My mouth opens and closes. I shake my head. "No. No, it can't be Jason. Why would it be Jason?"

"You said he broke into your apartment and smelled like alcohol, and when you questioned him about being there, he acted jealous and just unloaded all this emotional shit on you."

"No, you weren't listening." I shoot to my feet. "I said he *didn't* break in. He used his spare key, which he was returning yesterday because he was nearby."

"Maybe—*or* maybe it was an excuse he made up only because you caught him in your apartment."

I stop shaking my head. I hadn't considered that.

Why would Jason make up a lie for being there last night? But I had heard him walking around in the living room. He could've left the spare, a note, and shut the door behind him. Why had he stayed? And I still don't know how long he'd been there before I returned home, or what he was doing the entire time.

"Remember when you said before you started dating, he low-key stalked you?" Tati prods. "The man followed you to lunch. He made sure he arrived in the office parking garage at the same time you did during the week. He did it for *weeks* before he finally asked you out."

"But that wasn't stalking."

She rolls her big brown eyes to the oak trees overhead.

"I mean, I used that word at the time, but I didn't mean it in *that* way. I meant it as a joke! Jason was just trying to work up the nerve to talk to me. And besides, he has no reason to stalk me now even if he did back then. He broke up with me. Remember? He's the one who ended our relationship and moved out."

"And obviously he has misgivings about it or he wouldn't have gone on his little rant last night. He wouldn't have asked you about the new guy you're dating now."

I go silent again, at a loss for words. She's raising good points. I knew Tati would, or I wouldn't have come to her for advice in the first place. But I still find it hard to believe that Jason is the one who followed me around the library, who banged on my door last week, scaring the hell out of me. It's so out of character for him.

But he did look like he was in bad shape yesterday. And he was so angry. Jason didn't seem like himself. And he knew I'd quit the magazine and didn't tell me how he knew. Then there was that day that he showed up at the coffee shop at the same time Noah and I did. Has he been following me, and for how long?

"But what about the money?" I say. "What about the note?"

"Now that was likely the art appraiser. Frankly, girl, you've got a lot of weird shit going on. But everything that's happened since . . ." She shrugs. "I'm just saying," Tati murmurs as we begin to walk back to her car that's parked in a lot not too far from the running trail, "keep an eye on that ex of yours. And while you're doing that, get your locks changed, even if Jason gave back your spare key. I wouldn't be surprised if he had an extra one made."

"You're right. You're right," I say as I nod and walk beside her. "It's all good advice. Thanks, Tati."

Though I feel more unsure and confused now than I did before our talk.

CHAPTER 22

I ARRIVE FOR MY DATE WITH NOAH A LITTLE AFTER SEVEN. IT'S AT A restaurant on a busy stretch of F Street.

I'm relatively on time and not sweaty, which is an improvement over our last date. The humidity is minimal, so my curls are behaving. I'm wearing a blue maxi dress and gold hoop earrings and bangle bracelets I borrowed from Tati. I wanted to look more put together this time around, not like someone who's teetering on having a breakdown even if that's what I feel like on the inside.

Before I open the restaurant's door, I take a cautious glance over my shoulder at the people walking along the sidewalk behind me. I'm on the lookout for . . . who? I'm not sure. *Vivaldi? Jason?* Maybe some random guy I don't know.

I shove open the front door and paste on a smile. The restaurant is warm. There's a brick pizza oven on the other side of the restaurant, and the color scheme is in earth tones of reds, browns, and yellows, with lots of wood and stone. The lights are set low, bringing an orange glow to the space.

The atmosphere is definitely romantic. Noah made a good choice.

I find him waiting for me at the maître d' desk.

"Perfect timing! I was just about to check in," he says, shoving away from the desk's wooden counter. He then gives me a slow, assessing gaze. "You look . . . you look . . ."

"*Clean?*" I finish for him with a laugh. "Not covered in questionable stains?"

"I was gonna say beautiful," he drawls. "But yeah, that too."

I tilt my head, reach out and smooth a wrinkle in his jacket. "Well, you don't look so bad yourself, Mr. Kelly."

The gesture seems to catch him by surprise. His smile widens into a grin. "Thanks."

He really does look good in his black sport coat that he's paired with dark, low-rise jeans. He looks casual yet charming. I'm reminded why I keep saying yes every time he asks me out.

"Your table is ready," the hostess says. She grabs a couple of leather-encased menus from behind the desk and we follow her across the dining room to a table in one of the dimly lit corners. Noah holds out my chair for me and I sit down. He takes the other seat.

After the hostess leaves, I glance around the restaurant and return my gaze to Noah. "This is a nice place."

"I'm glad you like it." He shakes open a dinner napkin and tosses it over his lap. "A buddy recommended it and I checked out the reviews before I booked a reservation. I figured we might not get a third chance at this, so I should make it count."

"I appreciate the effort. Thanks for doing this, by the way. For giving this another try."

"You don't have to thank me. I *wanted* to see you again, Shanice."

"*Really?*" I want to say but don't because it sounds so desperate. But in the age of simply swiping left or right, most guys would've given up by now. There are much easier ways of getting a date. There's probably women he could date with a lot less baggage. I marvel that Noah keeps trying.

The waiter arrives a few minutes later, taking our orders. As we share a bottle of white wine, I try my best to settle in, to "make it count." I try to get to know more about Noah and tell him more about myself. I stay away from the touchy topics; I don't mention Mom, Essie, or my stalker. I try to stay engaged and keep the fidgeting to a minimum.

He offers me some of his hors d'oeuvres and I take a bite. Noah laughs when I frantically wave my hand in front of my face, cough, and grab for a glass of water.

"Oh my God, that was spicy! Whoever said white people only like bland food lied. Jesus," I say as my eyes water, and he laughs even harder.

Noah tells me the story of the time he wiped out on a motorbike when he was sixteen. "I dislocated my shoulder," he says, making me cringe.

I tell him about when I decided to use my dad's workout bench as a balance beam when I was five years old and attempted a double full twist I saw a gymnast do on television.

"Ten stitches here," I say, pointing to my brow.

We talk about our favorite movies and our favorite albums.

After the waiter clears the table and we wait for our main course, Noah places his hand over mine on the tabletop. I don't pull away and instead enjoy the warmth of his touch.

"I really am glad you came tonight," he says, gazing into my eyes.

"I am too," I whisper. "I'm having a surprisingly good time."

He raises an eyebrow. "Why is it surprising?"

"Well, considering our last date, I wasn't sure what to expect."

"Ah-ah-ah, we will not speak of the bad coffee date," he joked. "Besides, we both agreed to a do-over. Clean slate, right?"

I nod. "Clean slate."

And then someone grabs my shoulder. I startle in my chair, yank my hand away from Noah's, and whip around, expecting to see Vivaldi or even Jason. Instead, it's a woman in a business suit.

"Pardon me," she says with a smile. "I just needed to get by." She then walks around our table.

"You okay?" Noah asks.

I nod and slowly drink some of my wine. "Yeah," I say, clearing my throat, "I'm . . . I'm fine."

After that, I can't stay focused on him, on our date. My eyes keep darting to the floor-to-ceiling windows. I can't help but search for a familiar face on the other side of the glass—and not a friendly one.

"Shanice?" Noah says, grabbing my attention.

I turn away from the windows and face him again. "Yeah?"

"I was asking how was your food? Do you like the salmon?"

"Oh." I glance down at my fork. It's been hovering near my mouth for the past thirty seconds. I finally take another bite. "It's good," I say between chews then lower my fork back to my plate and wipe my mouth with my dinner napkin. "Sorry. I drifted off for a second there."

He slices into his steak. "Yeah, I could tell. You seemed a little distracted. Everything okay?"

"Uh-huh."

"Are you sure?"

I could continue pretending that I'm not struggling right now, that my mind isn't being pulled in a hundred different directions. Or . . . *or* I can own up to everything because I'm obviously doing a poor job of hiding what's going on. I don't want Noah to think it's him, that I don't want to be here. But this is a lot to drop on someone you're just getting to know.

I loudly exhale, unsure of what to do, making him frown.

"Okay," he murmurs, lowering his steak knife and fork, "that doesn't sound good."

"I . . . I probably shouldn't do this. It's a major first-date faux pas," I begin.

"Technically, this is our second date."

"I thought we were pretending the first one didn't happen."

"You are right," he says.

"Anyway, can I ask you something?"

"Sure. Go ahead." He reaches for his glass of Chardonnay.

"When you and your ex broke up, how did she take it?"

He stops mid-motion with his fingers only centimeters away from the wineglass. "What?"

"*Your ex?* Laurie? How did she respond when you guys broke up?" I pause. "Wait. Did you break up with her, or was it the other way around?"

He sits back in his chair, looking uncomfortable now.

"Oh, I'm sorry. I didn't mean to trigger you with that question," I say, holding up my hand, realizing what I've done.

I should've known better considering how often it happens to me. Their ugly breakup was the catalyst to his depressive episode. He probably doesn't want to do a recount of what happened.

"You didn't trigger me." He grimaces. "It's just an awkward question to answer on a date."

"Like I said, I know this is a first-date faux pas, discussing exes, but I think I might be having a . . . uh, issue with my ex and I wondered if . . . well, if maybe you've experienced something similar to help put it in perspective."

"Well," Noah says, taking that sip of wine, "if you really want to know, *I* broke up with *her.* I did it after I found out she cheated on me. She didn't like it. She even begged me to forgive her and take her back, but I didn't. I couldn't. I couldn't trust her anymore."

"So did she harass you?"

"Harass me?"

"I mean was she persistent in trying to get you to change your mind and take her back?"

He thinks for a few seconds. "I guess. She called and messaged me a lot and showed up at my apartment once, but that was about it. *Why?*" He narrows his eyes at me again. "Is your ex harassing you? Is that what you're saying?"

"Not harassing me. More like stalking." I take another deep breath. "But the truth is, I don't know if it's even him. It could be someone else."

I give Noah a quick rundown of what's been happening to me for the past couple of weeks, including the phone call from Isabel, the librarian, and Tati's suggestion that Jason could be the culprit.

"I'm trying to get in touch with Isabel. That's how I'll know for sure if it's him. I was going to ask her what the guy following me looked like."

Noah slowly nods, not saying a word. His expression is blank; I can't read him.

"You're ready to hop off the crazy train now, right?" I ask him. "You want to finish your meal, say it was nice knowing me, and not ever call me again? I wouldn't blame you. It's a lot to take in."

He shakes his head. "No, actually the opposite. I was thinking there's no way I can let you walk or take the metro home by yourself. If you're okay with it, I'd like to come with you. I'd like to escort you home tonight, Shanice."

I stare at him in shock, pleasantly surprised by his offer. "No, I wouldn't mind. Not at all."

We get an Uber to my place. The driver—a part-time college student who smells suspiciously like weed—is talkative, peppering us with questions as he takes us from the restaurant to my apartment building. It's like he's the host of a talk show and is getting paid to keep the conversation going. I mostly give one-word answers, but Noah, being the friendly guy that he is, indulges him.

When we arrive at my building, Noah leans forward just as the driver pulls up to the curb. He looks out the window at the stone and glass exterior of my building.

"Hey," he says to the driver, "I think you took us to the wrong address. This isn't right."

"No, it's the right place," I say, making him frown.

Noah glances over his shoulder out the sedan's rear window. "But I thought you lived back—"

"I know," I say sheepishly. "I just told you that I lived there."

He stares at me in shock. "You *lied*?"

"We'd just met on the street. I barely knew you! I didn't know if you were going to . . . if you were going to—"

"Stalk you?"

I nod, my cheeks warming with embarrassment. "Kinda. Yeah."

He shakes his head and laughs. "Well, turns out someone already beat me to the punch." He opens the rear door and inclines his head to the building's entrance. "Let's get you upstairs."

A few minutes later, the elevator doors open, revealing my floor. I step into the hall, and Noah trails after me.

"I can cover my eyes and follow your voice if you don't want me to see your apartment," he deadpans. "I won't be offended."

I playfully nudge his shoulder as we walk. "You can keep your eyes open, funny guy."

When we arrive at my door, I hesitate. During the car ride there, I was distracted by Noah and our driver, but now alarm bells are going off again.

"What's wrong?" he asks.

"I'm half expecting someone to be waiting for me in there."

"I'm sure it's okay, but do you want me to wait here while you look around?"

"Would you?"

"Of course."

"Thank you," I whisper, more than just a little relieved that I won't have to walk in there alone.

I unlock my door. It opens with a slow creak that seems to echo down the corridor. I poke my head inside to find my living room and kitchen blazing bright. Noah steps through the doorway and into my foyer.

"I'll stay here," he says.

I walk down the hall that leads to my bathroom and bedroom, pushing open doors as I go. My apartment is much like I left it hours ago when I headed out for our date. My bed is a mess, covered with the clothes I discarded while trying to choose what to wear. I catch a glimpse of my bathroom counter, which is in the same state of disarray with open compacts, eyeliner, and bobby pins strewn around the sink.

All is quiet. Nothing seems amiss.

I push open my closet door and turn on the overhead light. My walk-in closet is as junky as my bedroom, maybe more so. The painting isn't visible now that it's buried in the corner behind a mound of shoes. No one, not even my stalker, could be hiding in here.

I walk back to my front door to find Noah still standing in the foyer.

"Everything looks good?" he asks.

"Yeah, thank you again for coming up here with me."

"I told you I didn't mind."

We both fall silent. I twist the leather strap of my purse anxiously in my hands, unsure of what to do or say next. I want to offer him a drink and to sit down on the sofa so we can talk a little more. I like Noah's company. His sense of humor. His smile. I can feel a budding chemistry between us. But considering the circumstances—stalker and all—the offer of a nightcap seems like a bit much.

"I had a good time tonight," I say. "And despite everything, I hope . . . I hope I see you again, Noah."

"Oh, you will," he assures me. "Don't worry."

"Well, good night."

I climb to the balls of my feet to kiss his cheek. But he leans down, and instead of my lips landing on his cheek, they collide with his.

The chemistry I thought we had is confirmed as we kiss. And he's a good kisser. Gentle yet skilled. He wraps his arms around me and pulls me closer, and I feel butterflies that I haven't felt in years. My heart starts to pound again but for reasons a lot more pleasurable than what I was feeling hours ago. When he steps back and releases me, we're both smiling.

"I'll give you a call later this week so we can set up another date if you want," he says.

"I *do*. And text me when you get home to let me know you got there safely."

"I will." He gives me a quick peck on the brow, thinks a second, and then gives me a peck on the lips. He steps through the door and back into the hall. "Lock the door behind me."

I watch his receding back until he turns the corner and heads to the elevators. I close the door, lock it, and fall against it, pressing my fingers to my lips, savoring the memory of our kiss.

Before I drift off to sleep, I hear a buzz on my cell. I read the text on screen.

Made it home. No stalkers in sight, Noah's text says. **I'll check in with you tomorrow. Sleep tight.**

I set down my cell phone and walk across my bedroom to take one last look out my window. I gaze at the streets below. There are several cars parked along the curb. Other cars make their way down the street. I can see some pedestrians, but for the most part, the sidewalks are deserted at this late hour.

Nothing happened tonight, but I can't help but wonder if he's down there. My stalker. Whoever he is.

I pull the curtains close and turn off the lights.

CHAPTER 23

That night, I dream not about Noah or my stalker, but about Mom.

I'm in my apartment, walking down the hall to my living room, following the sound of music. It is a sad tune by Anita Baker about broken hearts and fairy tales that don't come true—one of my mother's favs. Under the music, I can hear the steady drone of a vacuum cleaner.

I enter the living room and find Mom there, humming and dancing along with the song like she did in the old days. She's vacuuming the floor rug with my Dyson and twirling the cord. The light streaming through windows is bright, but the air in the living room feels cold for some reason, making me close my robe and knot the belt around my waist.

I look at the sliding glass doors leading to my balcony, expecting to see big, fat snowflakes falling to the concrete and asphalt several stories below, but the leaves on the trees outside are green. The sky is cloudless and sparkling blue.

Why is it so *cold* in here?

Mom doesn't seem to mind the chill as she cleans. She's just as I remembered her, petite with her long, curly hair in a ponytail, wearing her favorite pink velvet tracksuit and fluffy white slippers.

I look over the top of her head to find Essie's painting is no longer buried in my closet, hidden under several pairs of boots.

It now hangs on the wall in an ornate, gilded frame.

Mom pauses from her vacuuming to turn off the Dyson and look up at me. She glances at the painting too, following my gaze.

"I know you didn't want to put it up yet, but she told me to hang it there. I had to, honey."

"Who told you to put it there, Mom?"

I then hear a banging at my front door that makes us both jump.

"Who the hell is that?" I ask as the person on the other side keeps pounding. "Who is it?" I call out before turning back to her. "Mom, do you know who it is?"

Her easy smile disappears. Her lips fall open. I wait for her to answer me, but she doesn't.

She's too scared to speak.

The banging only gets louder. Like a dozen fists are pounding on the wooden slab, making the door rattle on its hinges. Making me clap my hands over my ears. It's so cold in my living room now that I expect to see a mist sprout from my lips into the air.

"Stop it!" I shout through chattering teeth. "Stop knocking!"

"I'm sorry," Mom calls to me over the noise and the incessant pounding. "A lock isn't going to keep her out—or the rest of 'em. I'm sorry."

"Who?" I choke as the pressure around my rib cage increases and the air fights to get out of my lungs.

"I'm sorry," Mom says, just as my front door bursts open with the explosive sound of crashing glass and crunching metal. I vaguely hear screams and the far-off wail of a siren. Everything in my apartment—the coffee table, the sofa, even the painting on the wall—goes flying.

I startle awake, fighting tangled bedsheets, gulping for air. I scramble to sit upright and quickly turn on my night table lamp, flooding my bedroom with light.

I look at my alarm clock; it's a little after three a.m. I don't hear anything.

No knocking. No screams.

I walk out of the bedroom and down the hallway with my heart still racing, turning on lights along the way. The living room wall is vacant; Essie's painting isn't there. I stare at my front door, half expecting to find it open and hanging from one of its hinges with splinters of wood littering the hardwood floor, but the door is closed and locked.

No one got in. I'm safe.

I close my eyes. Relieved. I know it was a dream: the vision of Mom, the painting, and the door exploding. The beast does that; it causes nightmares. But I can't shake the feeling that it wasn't just a dream. In the world of omens, bad dreams rank pretty high, especially ones so vivid.

I take a few tentative steps toward the door and press my hand flat against it, making sure it's stable, that it's real. I then go to my kitchen and grab one of the kitchen chairs and wedge it underneath the handle for added security.

I stare at the door a few more minutes before turning off the lights and heading back to bed.

CHAPTER 24

My cell buzzes, yanking me awake. I feel around blindly for it on my night table. My fingers brush the cool glass of the old photo of me and Mom then finally my phone. I open my bleary eyes to look at the screen.

Hope you slept OK, the text from Noah says. Was worried about you.

After that nightmare, it took me hours to get back to sleep. I kept seeing the terrified look on Mom's face every time I closed my eyes. I kept hearing a phantom pounding at my front door. I didn't nod off until the sun started to rise behind my linen curtains.

Above the text Noah sent is the time. It's 11:56 a.m. Almost noon.

I'd told Gram two days ago that I would be back at her house today by ten o'clock at the latest to help clean the bedrooms upstairs.

"Damnit," I murmur as I throw my legs over the side of the bed and climb to my feet.

I take a quick shower, brush my teeth, throw on some clothes, and head out. I jog down the escalators to the metro to hop on the train to take me across town. Almost an hour later, I arrive at Gram's block. I'm a few feet away from her walkway when I hear, "Shan-ice! Hi!"

I turn to find Fawn, the neighbor from down the street who I met weeks earlier, waving at me. She's wearing a black bathing suit, white peasant skirt, and straw sunhat. Her son, Wesley, sits in a red wagon behind her wearing blue swim trunks.

"Hey," I say breathlessly, waving back, not eager to get caught in a conversation with Fawn. I know Gram is waiting for me.

Fawn pulls the wagon and walks toward me anyway. She's grinning again. I'm starting to suspect that it may be permanently plastered to her face.

"I thought that was you!" she gushes. "We were on our way to the pool and I saw someone jogging down the block and thought, 'She looks familiar.'"

"Yeah, I was just in a hurry. I told Gram I would visit her today and I'm running late," I say, hoping she'll take the hint.

"I think it's so sweet that you're so close to your grandmother." She draws closer to me. "I notice that she doesn't get out much. I read studies on how senior citizens can get lonely. I sent her an invite to a barbecue I'm throwing next month. I hope you can convince her to come. We'd love to have her there! She can even meet the rest of the neighborhood board."

I remember seeing the invitation. It was gingham patterned and brightly colored in yellow, white, and green.

"Grill 'n' Chill with us!" Gram read aloud before rolling her eyes and chucking the invite into the trash.

"I'll try my best," I lie to Fawn. "She might be busy, but I'm sure she'll come if she can."

"And you don't have to worry about your grandmother when you're not here. I'll make sure to keep an eye on her and stop by. Just to be neighborly and see if she needs anything."

"That is *so* thoughtful of you, Fawn. Thank you," I say before patting Fawn's freckled arm.

"No problem. Oh, and I wondered if you had a chance to reach out to that lawn service I recommended? I know sometimes they can be super booked this time of year, but if you need me to—"

"Not yet, but I really have to go now, Fawn. You and Wesley have a great time at the pool!" I say with a wave.

She opens her mouth to say something else, but I turn away and race up the stairs before she can. I knock on Gram's front door and hear the squeak of wagon wheels as Fawn walks away. I wipe my eyes with the heels of my hands, hoping I don't look too exhausted.

Gram doesn't answer, so I knock again and finally hear her shuffling around on the other side. The door opens a few seconds later and Gram stands in the doorway with her hands on her hips, looking indignant.

"You were supposed to be here four hours ago," she says.

"I know," I mumble while easing through the doorway past her. I kiss her cheek. "And I'm sorry. I overslept."

"Uh-hunh." She closes the door behind me and gestures across the sitting room toward the stairs. "Well, you can head on up and get started. I have to finish down here first, and then I'll help."

"Finish what down here?" I ask, taking off my purse. I catch myself before I lower it to the floor; I set it on the coffee table, instead. "I thought we were done with the first floor."

"I'm not cleaning. I'm talking to a man who stopped by about a half hour ago. I think he's another real estate agent." She glances at the kitchen doorway. "I've already got one, but he said he has a proposition for me that could be 'very lucrative.' I figured I'd hear him out. I invited him inside and made him some coffee. We'd just got to talking when you knocked on the door."

I frown. "A real estate agent? What's his name?"

"I don't know. Pringle? *Piker?* One of those." Gram waves her hands, dismissing my question. "Chile, I can't remember! Come in the kitchen and ask him yourself."

I follow her across the room through the kitchen entryway, interested in hearing what this real estate agent has to say. If Gram is going to sell the house, she should get the best deal she can, especially after all the work we've done. But I stop in my tracks when I see who is sitting alone at her kitchen dinette table.

Mark Vivaldi is sipping Folgers from one of Gram's chipped coffee mugs. He gazes at her backyard through the many potted plants hanging around the bay window.

He looks severely out of place here in his tailored suit and Gucci slippers. It's like finding one of his gallery's eighteenth-century vases sitting on her yellow laminate countertop between Gram's toaster and Ninja smoothie blender.

I'm too furious to even feel panic. How dare he come here?

"What the hell are you doing?" I shout, making him turn from the window and look up at me. "Why are you here?"

Vivaldi lowers his coffee mug to the tabletop and rises to his feet. His face reddens. His lips form into a grim, white line.

"Shanice, why are you yellin'?" Gram asks. "I told you he's my guest. Have you lost your mind?"

"He's not a real estate agent, Gram! He's Mark Vivaldi. The art appraiser who looked at Essie's painting. The one I told you about who wouldn't let me out of his office. He must have followed me here then lied and gave you a fake name to get in!"

"I did no such thing," Vivaldi insists, raising his chin into the air.

"You're serious?" I turn to face him again. This man has gall. "Now you're about to lie *right in front of me*?"

"I did not follow you; I looked up your grandmother's address. And I didn't give a false name. Vivaldi is my married name. I took it when I married my partner, Luciano Vivaldi, who is no longer with us. He died three years ago. I provided my maiden name, which is Pickens. Mark Pickens. I did not lie."

"I don't care! You made her think you were a real estate agent. You knew I'd probably told her about you. About what you'd done. About what you *have* been doing! He's been stalking me, Gram, and now it looks like he's stalking you too."

"I don't know what she's talking about." He has the nerve to look outraged. "Mrs. Sumner, I can assure you I have stalked no one. Her allegations are not only wrong, they are ludicrous."

"Bullshit!"

"Shanice!" Gram says, slapping my arm.

"I'm sorry. I didn't mean to curse in front of you, but he's full of it, Gram. He went to my apartment and taped money to my door for the painting. He's been following me around town. He even followed me to the library that day when I went to research more about Estelle, and he asked the librarian what I was looking for. She called me and told me."

"None . . . *none* of that is true!" Vivaldi argues. "I may have called you to follow up with another offer, but that is all that I have done since that day at the gallery. I've had no interaction with you thereafter. For the past two weeks, I've been in London. You can ask my colleagues. Besides, I live and work in Manhattan. I'm rarely in D.C. I made an exception to see your painting. I wouldn't have the time to stalk you, nor do I have the desire. I mean you no ill will, Ms. Pierce. I swear."

He looks and sounds so earnest and his story is very convincing. I'll give him that. I'd probably believe him if he hadn't been so sketchy before this. But I know he's lying. Just like he lied to Gram. Something is truly off with this guy.

"So why are you here?" Gram asks. "If you ain't stalking her or me, why'd you come to my damn house?"

Vivaldi takes a deep breath. "Because I do have a lucrative offer for you, like I said earlier, Mrs. Sumner. For you *and* your granddaughter if you agree to sell the painting by Estelle Johnson to me. I thought perhaps I could sway you to my way of thinking."

"Oh, good God!" I throw back my head. "You are seriously obsessed. Let it go! You made your offer. I get it. You'll pay fifty thousand dollars. We're still not selling."

"No," he says softly, "I am willing to offer ten times that. A half-million dollars if you agree to sell me the painting."

A silence falls over the kitchen. Gram and I stare at him in amazement.

"A . . . a *half-million* dollars?" Gram repeats. "You're jokin'."

He gravely shakes his head. "I am not. Your painting is very valuable and worth the investment."

Gram looks up at me. Our eyes meet.

An offer like this is not only unbelievable, it's also hard to dismiss. It's too good to reject, too, and Vivaldi knows it. He knew a number that big could sway Gram to "his way of thinking," and that it might even sway me too. But something still doesn't feel right. I have the same sensation now that I had back at Vivaldi's gallery. I feel not only his hunger, but also a sense that there's something he isn't telling me, that he isn't telling us.

"Why is the painting so valuable?" I ask, crossing my arms over my chest. "You said Essie was basically an unknown artist. Why are you offering a half-million dollars for her work?"

He hesitates. "I cannot divulge that information, but I can assure you it is worth the price."

So Vivaldi is not only a liar, but he also likes to keep secrets. A half-million-dollar secret.

"We'll think about it," I say.

Gram opens her mouth to speak, like she's going to argue differently, but she abruptly closes it. If she disagrees, she won't say it in front of Vivaldi.

Now Vivaldi is the one who looks shocked. "What is there to think about, Ms. Pierce? It's five hundred thousand dollars! You won't—"

"I said we'll think about it and get back to you. I have your number."

Vivaldi turns to Gram. "Mrs. Sumner, surely you can be reasoned with. You know how good of a deal this is. What it could mean for you and your family. It could—"

"You heard what my granddaughter said," Gram replies firmly. "We have to think about it. We won't give you our answer right away. Not now. So thank you for stopping by, Mr. Whatever-your-name-is, but we have things we have to do today. I'd like you to leave my home." She gestures toward the kitchen door, shooing him away like a housefly.

Vivaldi is biting his lips again; that thin white line is back. His face has gone even redder. He looks like a cartoon teapot that's about to explode. But what he tried with me at the gallery, he won't try here with Gram—if he's smart.

He gradually nods. I guess he's decided it's better to back down.

"Well, I'll await your call," he says, though I know it pains him to utter the words. "And I'll . . ." He clears his throat. "I can see my way out. Thank you for the coffee, Mrs. Sumner. Enjoy the rest of your afternoon."

We follow him to the door anyway, watching as he walks down the porch stairs to the sidewalk below.

"Oh, and Mr. Vivaldi," I call to him from Gram's doorway, making him halt in his steps and turn around to face me. "I'll contact you. Don't contact me. No more surprise visits. No more following me around. If you do, I'm calling the police."

Anger erupts on his face again, but he doesn't comment. Instead, he turns back around and walks down the block to where he parked his car, which turns out to be a silver Tesla.

"A half-million dollars," Gram says in awe over my shoulder as Vivaldi drives off. "And to just think, I had that thing hanging on my wall for all this time, paying it no mind, letting it collect dust. A *half-million* dollars! Who'd have figured?"

"It might be worth more," I say, facing her and closing her front door behind us. I fall back onto her sofa in the sitting room and clasp my hands in front of me. "But we can't sell it to him, Gram. I don't like him. I don't trust him, either."

"Well, you don't have to like somebody to take money from them, honey, especially *that* much money." She slumps into the leather recliner on the other side of the coffee table. "But you should've told me that man was following you around."

"I didn't want to worry you."

She shakes her head ruefully. “I swear you sound so much like your mama. More and more everyday. But you shouldn’t keep big stuff like that from me. I told your mama her whole life, and she only ever told me anything when she had to.”

“That’s the other thing,” I begin. “About Mom.”

“What about her?”

“I had . . . I had a dream about Mom last night. About her and the portrait. It wasn’t a good dream, Gram.”

Her face changes. She sits upright in her chair, now alert. “What do you mean? You had a nightmare?”

I nod. “And I haven’t dreamed about Mom in years. I didn’t understand the dream or what she was saying, but she seemed worried. She was scared of something.”

Or someone. I close my eyes and see Mom’s face. I remember her words: “*I’m sorry. A lock isn’t going to keep her out—or the rest of ’em. I’m sorry.*”

Then my apartment door exploded.

“Your nightmares are just manifestations of your fears, worries, and stimuli from the daytime, Shanice,” one of my therapists explained years ago. “It’s like a little movie reel. It doesn’t mean anything.”

But is that true? Could last night’s dream be something more?

“Then Vivaldi shows up here the very next day, making another offer to buy the portrait,” I say. “An offer for an absolutely insane amount of money this time. It just seems like more than just a coincidence. Like Mom was trying to warn me he was coming.”

I open my eyes again to find Gram staring at me. Her usually wrinkle-free face is etched with concern.

I sit back on the sofa. “I sound crazy, don’t I?”

“You know I would never say that. And I think you’re right. The dream and him showing up the same day ain’t a good sign,” Gram admits.

“It’s another reason why I don’t want to sell him the painting. I can’t.”

"Okay, so what do you wanna do with it? *Keep it?* Sell it to someone else?"

I think for a few seconds. "I don't know, but I guess I'll have to figure it out," I say with a shrug.

"Well, figure it out soon, because I don't like that dream. I don't like what's happening to you. You don't ignore stuff like this. I'm worried."

So am I, I think, but don't say it aloud.

CHAPTER 25

I STOP READING ESSIE'S LETTERS WHEN I HEAR A KNOCK AT MY DOOR.

"Who is it?" I call out.

"It's me, Shanice," Dad calls back.

I set down the letter and climb to my feet.

I've been nestled on the sofa, researching and writing my essay for the past four hours. I've been lost in Essie's words and my own. I haven't even stopped to eat. But I think I'm almost finished writing the first essay, and yes, I mean "first."

I've decided that this is going to have to be a series since there's so much ground to cover and I'm still plowing through the letters. This one will cover how I came upon her portrait, her connection to my family, and the backstory of how Essie became a painter. The second will be about her relationship with Bachmann, her patron, and Bachmann's impact on her art and career. The third, I hope, will give an answer to the big questions I still have: Why did Essie leave her cushy apartment, studio, and all of New York when everything seemed to be going so well? Why did she walk away from her art wholesale, only to meet her death a year or so later in Philly? Did it have anything to do with Bachmann's murder? Did Essie kill Bachmann?

I hope the answers lie in these letters and books.

I still haven't decided what to do with the essays when I'm done. I'm thinking about sending this one to Priya to get her feedback. We've exchanged a few emails since she started her new job. She wanted to know how I was doing, especially in light of how I left *The Intersector.* She's offered to meet up for lunch or coffee a few times. I've been considering it. Maybe Priya can give me her honest opinion on my essay and tell me where I should submit something like this.

I walk into the foyer and look through the peephole.

Dad glances down at his watch and knocks again.

I unlock the door and whip it open. "Hey, Dad. Thanks for comin' over."

"No problem! Would've been here sooner, but I had to drop Dana off at her Zumba class." Dad looks at my apartment. "You might try cleaning up this place once in a while."

"Dad," I groan, "*seriously*?"

"Okay." He throws up his hands. "No lectures. What did you need? Why were you all secretive on the phone?"

I wave Dad inside and shut the door behind him. I then walk him out of the foyer and across my living room where a cardboard box now sits by the sofa with a pile of clothes on top.

I may not know what to do with the essays about Essie, but I know what I have to do with her painting. I'm not going to sell it to Vivaldi, even for a half million. But I can't keep art as precious as this hidden at the bottom of my closet anymore either. I have to get it somewhere safe, so I packed it yesterday in one of the empty boxes Jason left behind. I did it after I left Gram's house, after Vivaldi showed up with his latest offer. I called Dad soon after, making him promise to come to my apartment as soon as he could.

"That big fireproof security safe in your basement . . . the one that you keep your birth certificate and other important stuff in, is it full?" I now ask Dad. "Do you think it could fit a painting that's about the size of a small wall poster?"

"I guess," Dad says. He adjusts his glasses then frowns down at the box. "What's this? You're finally packing up and moving? Did you find another apartment?"

"No. There's a painting inside of it. It's something Gram gave me, but I can't keep it here anymore."

"Why not?"

"Because it's worth a lot of money, Dad."

He laughs. "Shanice, if it's something your grandmother owned, trust me . . . it ain't worth much. No matter what she says. The most expensive thing your grandmother has in that old house of hers is probably her TV, and I bet that thing is about twenty years old."

"No, I got the painting appraised and someone made an offer for it. It's worth . . . it's worth half a million dollars."

He chokes out another laugh then stares at me. "What?"

"Yeah, a half million and the person who wants to buy it, wants it *bad*."

"Then why aren't you selling it to them? Get their offer in writing. Get it today! I have a friend who's a lawyer. He can draw up a contract." Dad pulls out his cell phone from his back pocket and starts to type on the screen. "I think I have his number in here. I can give him a call for you and tell him—"

I place my hand over Dad's, making him stop typing. He tears his eyes away from the phone screen to look at me.

"I'm not signing any contract, Dad. I can't sell it to him."

"*Well, why the hell not?*" he exclaims. "That's a lot of money, sweetheart. Live off it! Get a good investment planner to handle it for you and you could be set for life."

"Because the person who wants the painting has been really . . . well, persistent. He's been very aggressive and I don't—"

"That's even more of a reason to strike up a deal with him. Rich people are just like that, honey. They don't like to be told no. Maybe you can get him to up the price. The best way to get him to leave you alone is to give him what he's asking for, right?"

I think for a few seconds, unsure of just how to explain this to Dad.

When I told Gram about my worries and my dream, she immediately got it; she understood why entertaining Vivaldi's offer was out of the question.

Dad is a very different person. He's the quintessential engineer. He sees a problem and he tries to solve it logically and methodically. He wants empirical evidence. Data that can be plugged into equations.

Dad won't understand the attachment I've developed for a painting that I've owned for only a few weeks, for a painting that I've disliked most of my life.

He won't understand that I couldn't protect Essie from her sad fate, but I *can* protect her portrait—or I can damn well try.

"I . . . umm . . . I think other parties might be interested," I say instead. "They might offer more. I just want to do a little more research before I make a decision."

Dad finally lowers his cell phone and tucks it back into his jean pocket.

"Okay," he says, "I'll take the painting and store it in the safe for you." He pauses. "But don't take forever to make your decision on whether to accept this offer, Shanice. I know how you are about these things. It's like how you're waiting around to apply for another job, like one is gonna plop into your lap. It's like how you won't decide what to do with this apartment that you can't afford anymore. You can't just wait around."

"I know, Dad."

I don't need him to tell me this. In addition to getting the notice about overdue rent, I've also gotten emails about my electric and cell phone bills being overdue and credit card statements with minimum payments I can't afford. My refrigerator shelves are alarmingly empty. I checked my account balance this morning. It was $162.57. I may not be willing to take half a million dollars from Vivaldi, but I'll have to use that five grand still sitting in the kitchen drawer that he gave me. I hate the idea, but I don't know what other choice I have besides begging Dad for money, and I can't do that. Not after the little speech he just gave me.

"I'll get a new job soon and find a new place. I will. Don't worry."

"*Don't worry?* Easier said than done! How can I not worry? You've been like this before, Shanice."

"Like what?"

"Erratic. Unfocused. There's always a calm before the storm. You know you're supposed to look for the signs. You're supposed to keep an eye out for—"

"Dad, you don't have to explain my own mental health to me."

"But I do," he says with a nod, "because when you fall apart, it doesn't just happen to you. It happens to all of us."

"The panic attacks don't happen to you," I begin tightly. "The night terrors don't happen to you. The racing thoughts don't happen to you. You don't have those flashbacks. *You* weren't there that day!"

I regret the words even as I say them, but I can't take them back. I watch as Dad slowly shakes his head.

"No, I wasn't. And you don't know how many times I wish I'd been there. That I was the one behind the wheel. That I had been the one driving, not your mama. Maybe it could've changed things. Maybe our lives would be different." He exhales, making his nostrils flare. "But I can't change the past. Neither can you, honey. We can only deal with the here and now. And I think it's time you go back on your meds."

"You know that's not gonna happen, Dad. I'm going to become dependent on them like I almost did before, and then I'll trade one disorder for another."

I knew I was becoming addicted to benzos or, more specifically, Klonopin, long before Dana called it, before she saw the signs that she'd seen with her son, Zachary. But I didn't want to admit it. I didn't feel like I could face each day without my pills.

I didn't stop using them, even after Dana's tear-filled confrontation when she told me she didn't want to lose another kid to addiction. It took another car accident to do it instead. The police officer who showed up at the scene claimed I was so out of it that he gave me a breathalyzer test. After that, I asked my doctor to shift me to a different drug that I wouldn't be as tempted to abuse, that I could use "as needed." After a while, I felt like I didn't need even that anymore; I stopped using my meds completely.

"I know. I know it was rough," Dad says. "But maybe there's a new drug you can try that's less addictive but it works. Dana and I know money is very tight for you right now. We're willing to pay for any medication you need." He sighs. "Just promise me, you won't rule it out. If it gets worse, if you feel yourself losing . . . losing control of the situation, you will consider exploring medication again. That's all I'm asking, Shanice."

"I heard you. And yes, I will."

I don't think he believes me but at least he isn't willing to call me on it. Not today, anyway. Dad bends down to pick up the box. "I'll take this downstairs to the car."

"Thanks. But keep the clothes on top of it. Make it look like it's just old stuff I'm giving away."

"Why?"

"Just in case anyone sees you come downstairs with that box. I want it to be inconspicuous. I don't want anyone to suspect the painting is in there."

Dad's looking at me in that funny way again.

He thinks the beast is making me paranoid, and he might be right, but I don't care. I don't know if I'm still being followed. I told Vivaldi to leave me alone, but that doesn't mean he's going to. And if Vivaldi is still keeping an eye on me, I don't want to turn his eyes towards my dad.

"But why would . . ." Dad begins then stops and shakes his head, like he's too tired to argue again. "Whatever you say, honey. Look, I gotta head back. Dana's class should be ending soon."

He starts to carry the box across the living room.

"And don't open it until you're inside the house. When you do, put the painting in the safe right away!"

"Got it." He waves absently over his shoulder to me after I open my door.

I close it behind him and lock it, feeling a little better now that the portrait is tucked away. Someone more responsible than me is in charge of it.

CHAPTER 26

Two days later, I'm climbing the stairs leading to the D.C. library's Belmont Branch when my phone buzzes. I pause to dig it out of the pocket of my khakis.

We need to talk, the text message says on screen. It's from Jason.

He's called and texted me a few times since that night he showed up at my apartment. I have ignored all of his messages, but it hasn't seemed to deter him. He might not be stalking me in person, but he's certainly doing it electronically. I have no idea why he has such a newfound interest in me, especially considering he's the one who ended our relationship.

But when it comes to love and relationships, people don't act logically, Tati told me. *They make irrational decisions and do stupid things*, she said.

Maybe he's just jealous. I guess seeing me with Noah made him have second thoughts about the breakup. But it's too late. Now I've moved on. I have enough drama in my life. I don't need any more from Jason.

No we don't, I type back. We're done, J.

I see three blinking dots then the words, No we are not! You're going to regret ignoring me.

I've read enough. I type a few more buttons to block his number, drop my phone back into my pocket, and continue climbing the stairs. The canvas bag I'm carrying is so heavy that the straps dig into my shoulder. The bag thumps rhythmically against my hip as I walk through the sliding glass doors.

The bag is filled to the brim with old books that I'm returning, some of which I used for my research. I finished my essay last night and collapsed into bed soon after. Thankfully, it was a dreamless sleep. I guess removing the portrait from the apartment helped my psyche. I did some editing this morning and sent a draft to Priya to get her feedback.

"It's a little rough, but I like it," I wrote in my email to her, after explaining the story about Essie, her painting, and her relationship with the enigmatic Maude Bachmann. "Can you let me know what you think? And we should meet up for coffee. Let me know what day works for you!"

I'll do even more editing when I get back to my apartment, but for now, I just want to get away from the laptop screen and its blinking cursor. I want to give my sore fingers a break.

I expect to find Isabel but a young guy is standing behind the circulation desk instead.

At first, I wondered why I never heard back from her, but decided I needed to let it go, to focus on writing. Besides, Vivaldi was probably the guy whom she saw following me around the library that day, even if he insists he wasn't. I figured it out without her help.

There isn't a line so I sit my bag on the counter and start to unload my books. The guy widens his eyes at the growing pile.

"Oh, and I have a book in reserve that I'd like to check out," I say. He nods his dark, curly head and scans the books, sorting them into stacks.

"Sure." He turns to the nearby computer. "Under what name?"

I pull out my wallet from my purse to grab my library card. "Shanice Pierce."

"Shanice Pierce?" He stares at me. "Didn't you call here asking for Isabel?"

I nod again, now feeling awkward. "I had to ask her a question. I wanted to clarify something. Sorry, I kept leaving messages with you guys. I just wanted her to call me back."

"Did you know her? Were you friends?"

I notice that he's talking about her in the past tense. "Not really friends. She seemed nice and was helping me with my research, but . . . wait, did something happen to Isabel?"

His pale face goes about two shades paler. I know that's not a good sign.

"Is she okay?"

He takes a quick glance around the room then over his shoulder at the other librarians who are milling about behind the circulation desk, some having hushed conversations. He leans over the counter, beckoning me to do the same.

"I thought something was up when Isabel didn't show for her shift two days ago," he whispers. "She didn't call either. That's not like her. Then her mom called this morning to tell us the news. The police found Isabel's body last night. She was murdered."

PART III

CHAPTER 27

ESSIE

NEW YORK CITY

August 19, 1927

"TENTH FLOOR. PENTHOUSE," THE ELEVATOR OPERATOR ANNOUNCED.

Essie watched as the young man stepped forward to open the gate. She nodded her thanks and walked out of the compartment, feeling her heels sink into the penthouse floor's plush rug. She listened as the operator shut the elevator door behind her and then heard the soft chime as the compartment descended back to the floors below.

This would be her fourth time at Godmother's abode and she still couldn't stop the butterflies from fluttering in her stomach every time she saw the apartment's grand French doors. And today held even more significance: Godmother was taking her to the Knoedler & Company Art Gallery. She'd finagled Essie a meeting with the gallery's director to see about showcasing her work there. It was something Essie had wanted since she arrived in New York.

She eagerly reached for the door buzzer then stopped.

Get out while you still can, Doris's voice suddenly whispered into her ear, *or what happened to me could happen to you. Or it could be a helluva lot worse.*

Essie hesitated a beat longer then pressed the buzzer in front of her anyway and waited.

She didn't believe in haunts and curses—or at least that's what she told herself. Those superstitions were of the world she'd left behind in South Carolina. They were things to be feared as much as the night riders that burned down the sharecroppers cabins and hung Negroes from trees by moonlight. They were stories that the old folks told to scare the children into minding their mamas and daddies, or to pass the time while working in the fields.

But they weren't real. Neither were the allegations Doris made against Godmother, despite the other ill-spirited gossip Essie may have heard.

"So, you know about them too?" Langston Hughes had asked, all smug when she'd inquired about Godmother and her "friends" during one of his parties at the Manor. "I heard they commune with the dead, you know," Langston had said. "Or at least try. Who knows if anyone is actually listening."

Essie had never witnessed any seances herself—or had she? She thought back to the first night, that first party where she had seen the four people sitting around "in prayer." Is that what they were really doing?

"But it seems that every rich white woman in New York is holding séances nowadays or has a spiritualist friend," Langston had said dryly. "It's just what they do, like buying yachts or slapping their names on buildings."

Essie had eased closer to him, dropping her voice to a whisper. "Someone told me that they . . . that they do sacrifices to the devil at night in exchange for . . . well, for favors."

Langston had burst into laughter. "Is that what you heard?" He'd taken a sip from his drink. "Well, I can't speak to that, but I wouldn't put it past her. I'm sure Godmother could round up a billy goat or two. It would certainly explain how her friend Beau James became the mayor of New York City. You'd have to make a deal with the devil to pull that off."

Essie had left the party early, annoyed that Langston hadn't told her anything substantial and was only having fun with her.

For God's sake, stop being a fool, Essie, she now muttered to herself, ringing the doorbell again.

Finally, one of the French doors swung open.

"Yes?" the footman asked.

His blue eyes assessed her. His hand stayed firmly clasped around the door knob as if he could slam it shut at any moment.

Essie forced a smile. "Hello, I'm here to see Mrs. Bachmann."

She remembered the footman from the last time she'd visited, but he obviously didn't remember her.

"I'm . . . I'm Estelle Johnson," she added.

Still no sign of recognition crossed the footman's face. "Is Mrs. Bachmann expecting you?"

"Yes, we have an appointment scheduled at one o'clock."

He waited a beat, opened the door farther, and stepped back. "I'll let Mrs. Pickens know that you're here," he said before ushering her inside and closing the door behind her. He then did another curt nod and walked off, depositing Essie near the bottom of the staircase leading to the east and west wings.

Essie noticed that he hadn't offered her tea or a seat. Neither did any of the other servants as she waited for Godmother. One maid passed her, then another, not uttering a word. Essie might as well have been one of the potted ficus plants in the corner. But she wasn't surprised by the staff's rudeness.

Godmother had taken her under her wing, but Essie was still a Negro woman. Many white folks would rather eat a cockroach than wait on her. And the Negroes who worked for Godmother probably wondered what made her think she was any better than them. Why should they have to serve her when she had only landed in New York two years ago with thirty dollars and a cardboard suitcase? When her skin was just as brown as theirs?

Unsure what to do with herself, Essie began to pace around the great hall. Her eyes drifted to the black-and-white tile then the crystal chandelier overhead. She considered sitting on one of the velvet settees while she waited, but thought better of it. She began to hum softly to herself, running her fingers over the newel post adorned with fanged serpents, much like the one on the handle of Godmother's cane. But the hum abruptly stopped when, in the corner of her eye, she saw a skeletal figure standing at the top of the staircase.

He was naked, save for a red velvet robe that clung to one of his shoulders. The other side of the robe dragged behind him like a cape or the train of a wedding gown. His skin was so pale that it was almost translucent and it was knotted with a web of purple and blue veins that spanned from his head to his wrinkled feet. The veins seemed on the verge of erupting through his skin. His ribs were visible along with his knobby hips. She watched with alarm as he took one lurching step down the stairs, holding the railing to steady himself. He reached for Essie with his other hand.

"You came," he said, making Essie take a step back. "I knew you would come!"

She stared at him aghast, struck mute by his nakedness. By his flaccid penis bobbing in between his skinny thighs with each shaky step he took. His dark eyes seemed to bulge out of their sockets.

Essie looked frantically around her. Was anyone else seeing this? *Hearing* this? It couldn't be just her.

"Goddess, take me with you across the bridge. I'm ready!" he called to her hoarsely.

Essie instinctively reached for the medicine bag inside her purse, like it was a talisman. The medicine bag that she'd tried to throw away so many times but something had stopped her. She clutched it in her fist now, hoping to ward off this frightening vision. She took another step back, then another, finally colliding with the front door.

"I'm ready!" he said. "Please let me go with you!"

"Herr Bachmann!" a woman shouted. "Sir!"

Essie watched as the woman wearing a white nurse's uniform came rushing toward the stairs. She grabbed the old man's arm, all while hastily gathering his robe in an attempt to cover him.

"No! No, you can't keep me here! I want to go!" he shouted back. "She will take me!"

Whereas before, the great hall and staircase had been deserted—save for Essie, the nurse's shouts seemed to kick everyone into action, making servants flood from every corridor and room. A few of the footmen assisted the nurse, carefully guiding the old man back from whence he'd came. They disappeared to the east wing.

Essie guiltily pulled her hand out of her purse, releasing Doris's medicine bag.

What she'd just seen hadn't been some apparition. The nurse had called the elderly man Herr Bachmann. *Mr.* Bachmann.

Had that been Godmother's husband? Why did he look like that, and what on earth was he talking about? Who was keeping him here?

Godmother arrived less than five minutes later. She heard her before she saw her, hearing the rhythmic *click*, *click*, *thump* coming down the hall then the stairs.

"Hello, Estelle! Apologies for my tardiness, dearest. I hope I didn't keep you waiting long," Godmother said. She descended the staircase with her secretary, Mrs. Pickens, trailing silently behind her. She was wearing a fur coat and another one of those ostentatious ladies' hats—this time covered in a nest of gold ribbons, lace, and blue-and-green peacock feathers.

Essie was still trembling from earlier. Had they not heard the ruckus? Did Godmother not know what had just happened? Essie guessed not because the older woman was behaving so casually.

"No, I—I haven't been w-w-waiting long."

"Well, then," Godmother said, reaching the end of the stairs and linking her arm through Essie's. "Let us be off! An unfortunate change of plans today, I'm afraid. Mr. Russell at the Knoedler & Company Art Gallery called earlier and said he had to cancel."

"Oh," Essie said, still too shell-shocked to utter more than that or be disappointed.

"But never you mind, my dear. We will reschedule for another day. In the meantime, so our day will not be ruined, I shall treat you to lunch. How does the Russian Tea Room sound? It just opened and I heard it's quite exotic!"

Essie blankly nodded as Godmother turned to Mrs. Pickens. "Agatha, I will be back in a few hours."

"Yes, Mrs. Bachmann," her secretary said with a curt nod.

Godmother then headed toward the doors with a *click*, *click*, *thump*, *click*, *click*, *thump* as Essie stiffly followed her.

•

CHAPTER 28

"Ah, the atmosphere crackles, doesn't it?" Godmother said eagerly as they were led through the smoke-filled tea room to their table. "Full of so much revelry and creativity. I simply adore places like this."

Essie frowned. Godmother might be riveted but she was underwhelmed. There were several tea rooms back in Harlem that were a lot nicer and less crowded and weren't permeated with the scent of cigarettes and sickeningly sweet chocolate thanks to the chocolate factory next door.

"It's frequented by dancers from the Russian Imperial Ballet, writers, and actors. I heard sometimes they break into song and dance," Godmother said, waving her free arm in the air and doing a little jig. "They're merry and irreverent, just like your people, Estelle. You should feel right at home here."

Not quite, Essie thought as, once again, she noticed she was the only brown face in the room. They passed a table where a group of men pointed at them. One of the men said something in Russian and his companions burst into ruckus laughter.

Godmother lowered her raised arm and slowly turned to the men before leaning forward on her cane and speaking in furious, rapid-fire Russian.

The men instantly fell silent and went wide-eyed. Godmother then resumed walking.

"What did you say to them?" Essie whispered.

Godmother laughed. "Oh, I just told them not to shame their mothers and to be polite."

Essie glanced over her shoulder at the men who were still staring at them. One did the sign of the cross with a trembling hand.

"Here we are!" Godmother said as the host held out a chair for her and she took a seat.

Essie took the chair facing her. The table was so small, they were almost knee to knee.

"I must admit, I am famished," Godmother said, opening her table napkin. "I do hope they have a decent menu." Godmother nodded her thanks as a waiter brought two teacups filled to the brim. She held her cup aloft for a toast.

Essie set down her purse on the table and immediately did the same.

"To our friendship," Godmother said.

"To our friendship," Essie echoed before they both took a sip.

"And how are you feeling today?" Godmother asked. "Good, I hope."

"Yes, Godmother."

"You don't look it," Godmother said, eyeing her. "You look a bit weary, and you were so quiet during the automobile ride here. Something is bothering you. Tell me."

Essie opened her mouth, then closed it. She shook her head. "It's nothing."

"Really? I heard what happened today before I arrived downstairs," Godmother began gently. "What happened with my husband. I heard it frightened you."

Essie didn't respond. She simply lowered her eyes, unable to hold the older woman's gaze any longer.

"I'm sorry you saw him in such a state. I wish you would have met him *years* ago, Estelle," she said with a winsome smile. "Back when he still had his faculties about him. My husband was such a charming man. So handsome and brilliant! He had such a sharp mind. He'd done research in new fields of science. Telepathy. Hypnotherapy. He was quite respected among colleagues. But he has changed. It didn't happen overnight, but much more rapidly than I or his physician anticipated. His mind isn't what it used to be. Old age has . . . wilted it away. Now he can't remember anything some days, not even to eat." She sniffed. Her eyes became dewy. "He can't even remember me. He is nearing the end of his life, but I know someday he and I will be reunited."

"In heaven?" Essie asked timidly.

Godmother frowned. "Oh, no, my dear. In our next lives. We have done it many, many times over the millennia, and we will do it many times thereafter. That is the knowledge I keep in my heart. It's what helps me to see past what is happening to him now," Godmother said, blinking back tears. "I will see my love again. He will come back to me."

Essie had never seen Godmother cry before. She clumsily fumbled for her purse, opening the clasp and pulling out a handkerchief.

Godmother began to thank her and dab at the corners of her eyes with it, but paused to stare down at the table. Essie followed her gaze and saw Doris's medicine bag. It had tumbled out of her purse in her haste.

"What's that?" Godmother asked, pointing at it.

"Oh," Essie said, shoving the medicine bag back into her handbag and closing the gold clasp. "It's nothing. Just something . . . something someone gave me."

The older woman's gaze went from warm to more discerning in a matter of seconds. "It looks very familiar. Who gave it to you?"

"Just . . . just a friend, Godmother."

"A friend?"

"I—I only took it because she offered it. I—I . . ." Her voice faded.

"You can be honest with me, Estelle," Godmother pressed. "Have I not always been honest and forthcoming with you?"

Essie closed her eyes. "Doris Bingham. She gave it to me."

"You know Doris?"

Essie opened her eyes again, finding Godmother didn't seem surprised. She didn't seem angry either. She was expressionless.

"Well, I don't *know* her," Essie explained. "I only met her once. That's when she gave me this. She just . . . she just showed up at the brownstone. She barged in! I was too frightened to turn her away."

"But you kept it? What she gave you."

"I guess I—I put it in my purse and . . . and I'd forgotten about it," she lied again.

Godmother didn't reply. Instead, she drank more of her tea.

"Poor Doris," she began. "I wish I could've helped her, but she was too far gone when I realized what was going on with her. You know I am not one to frown upon merriment, but too many artists these days squander their talent in the frivolity of parties and drinking. Doris was one of them. She'd fallen prey to so many bad influences. To opium and other vices. I wanted so much for her, but she allowed herself to become distracted. Her art was no longer her focus, and it showed. Her writing had become inconsistent. Her work had become shoddy. And rather than accept the error of her ways, she blamed *me* for her failures.

"I loved her dearly and accepted this abuse. I took her blame. I continued to give her money, knowing full well what she would do with it. I continued to house her even though I saw what people she allowed into her home. But then, one day, she became indescribably angry with me. She threatened me with a knife, Estelle, and cut me. Here."

The older woman lifted her chin and pointed at a raised scar along her neck about an inch long. Estelle breathed in audibly, remembering the knife Doris had brandished that day at her apartment. Had she really used it on Godmother?

"Agatha told me to call the police. To have her arrested. I declined, but that's when I knew I couldn't engage in my relationship with Doris any longer, despite how much I cared. I barred her from my home. I told her she could no longer live in the apartment I provided her. Letting her go is one of the hardest things I've ever done, but I had no choice."

Godmother's eyes became dewy again. A tear tumbled onto her cheek and she wiped at it with Essie's handkerchief.

"I'm so sorry, Godmother," Essie whispered. She was ashamed that she had doubted the older woman. That she hadn't asked her about Doris and what had really happened. Instead, she had given into her fear and paranoia. "I didn't know that she hurt you."

"Why would you know?" Godmother reached across the table and began to pet her hand again. "But please, take this word of caution, Estelle: be careful of the company you keep. You are a bright light in this world. I knew it the very day we met, when I asked Herr Reiss at his studio who painted the portrait I was so taken with. 'Estelle Johnson,' he said. And I thought, of course! Estelle. *Estella.* The star. For you are a star, Estelle. You are meant for great things! Don't allow your light to be dimmed. Keep Doris Bingham and her like at a distance, and you will go far."

Essie felt like a fool for letting her imagination run away from her. Doris hadn't been deceived by Godmother; she was just a narcissistic addict who had allowed her dependencies to take over her life and ruin her literary career. Doris must have dreamed up a curse to explain it to herself in her bitterness over her own missed opportunities. Or she'd made up the story out of jealousy, to put a rift between Essie and Godmother just as Essie's career was gaining momentum. And poor Dr. Bachmann. He was just a sad, old man slowing going senile and behaving accordingly.

Essie nodded. "I will, Godmother. I'll keep my distance. I promise." She opened her purse and reached inside. She took out the medicine bag and handed it to Godmother. "And you can have this. I know . . . I know I don't need it. It was silly to accept it anyway."

"*Really?*" Godmother said, raising her brows. "You would give this to me?"

Essie nodded eagerly, holding it out to her. "Of course."

She wanted to offer it as a sign of faith, to show that she trusted Godmother.

"Thank you," Godmother said with a smile before accepting her medicine bag. "It is a fascinating object, is it not?"

The waiter appeared, placing soup bowls and spoons in front of them.

"Ah, borscht!" Godmother exclaimed before dropping the medicine bag into her purse. She clapped her hands gleefully. "I haven't had it in *ages*. Have you had it before, Essie? You simply must try it."

Essie watched as the older woman dug in. She slowly picked up her spoon and did the same.

CHAPTER 29
SHANICE

WASHINGTON, D.C.
Present day

I PACE IN FRONT OF THE BLUE METAL DESK WHERE A BORED-LOOKING security guard sits. I'm waiting for Priya in the lobby of an office building. It's where she works now.

These digs near Columbus Circle are very different from *The Intersector* magazine's offices. This building is modern; it's filled with natural light and made of glass and steel. Marble tiles are on the floor, and abstract art and sculptures hang on the walls and from the lobby's ceiling.

"Donated by the Whitmore Foundation," a plaque on one of the sculptures says.

A flatscreen TV is behind the lobby desk, showing promotional videos of the companies housed here, including the online media company where Priya works.

My eyes drift toward the bank of sleek, polished steel elevators almost twenty feet away. One of the elevators open and two women step out. I glance down at the time on my cell screen. Priya is running late. I hope she gets here soon because the waiting is making me anxious. It's allowing time for my mind to drift, and I know from experience that can be a dangerous thing. The beast likes moments like this, finds them downright delectable, and right now my mind can't help fixating on Isabel.

Isabel, the librarian, is dead and cops still don't know who murdered her. I confirmed it with Dwight, the other librarian, yesterday. It's been a full week since police discovered her body.

"It happened while she was walking home," Dwight whispered to me at the checkout desk. He seemed to relish the chance to share more gossip about the investigation. "Not too far away from her place. It's so crazy! I mean . . . she lived in a nice neighborhood. Maybe someone was trying to rob her and killed her instead."

"Maybe," I whispered.

Dwight shook his head. "It's so sad. I swear I hate this city sometimes."

Dwight told me her last name—Alvaro—so I looked her up online to find out more about what happened to her. I found a brief article on washingtonpost.com. Less than three hundred words.

Basic details about the murder: She'd been shot twice. Her body was left in an alleyway. There were no witnesses.

A quote from her mom: "Izzy was the light of my life. I don't know how I'm going to make it without her."

A number to call for Crime Solvers if someone had any tips to give to police.

I sifted through Isabel's social media accounts to learn more about her. There were no ominous posts that raised any alarm bells prior to her murder. In fact, Isabel seemed like a bit of a homebody. No boyfriend or girlfriend, as far as I could tell. Lots of photos on Instagram of her two cats, Wiggles and Tickle, and her baking projects. There were a couple photos of her with a few friends, but that was about it.

Her home address was listed online. I wanted to go there, to visit the nearby crime scene, but I resisted the urge. I can't go full Nancy Drew and conduct my own investigation. It doesn't seem like my place.

Especially if you're the reason why she's dead, the beast whispers.

No. It's just an unfortunate coincidence. Isabel's murder could've just been one of many that happen in D.C. A woman walking alone at night can be an easy target. I've had fears of what could happen to me walking alone many times.

Still, I shouldn't have told Vivaldi that she'd called me, that she'd warned me he'd been following me that day at the library and asking questions. Within days of saying it, she was dead. But what motivation would he have to kill her if she already told me that he'd been following me? What else could he possibly be hiding that she would've known?

One of the elevators opens again and Priya steps out. I'm relieved that I have an excuse to stop obsessing and beating myself up for what was probably a random crime.

Priya looks different from when I last saw her. She cut her long hair to chin length and added soft brown highlights. She's also wearing clothes a lot more stylish than what she wore at *The Intersector*; no more ill-fitting sweaters and jeans torn at the knee, but a brightly colored silk top and dark slacks. She strides toward me and waves, adjusting the satchel on her shoulder as she walks.

"Hi!" she says. "Sorry, I'm late. I had a call that went longer than I thought it would. Anyway, I'm so glad you came!" She gives me a quick hug. "I hope it wasn't a hassle coming down here."

"Of course it wasn't. Thanks for inviting me." I glance at the building's glass doors. "So are you ready? I wasn't sure which coffee shop you wanted to go to. It looks like there's like four in a two-block radius."

"Hmm, not coffee, but you know what I've been addicted to lately? Bubble tea," she says as we walk across the lobby to the doors leading outside. "There's this place down the street that makes the best mango green milk tea. It reminds me of the mango lassi at one of my favorite street vendors back home in India. Just without the cardamom. Would you mind if we go there instead?"

"No, I don't mind."

Ten minutes later, we're one of four patrons sitting outside of a bubble tea shop. It has a fat smiling cartoon cat on its window. I'm wearing sunglasses because it's so bright out here, but Priya doesn't seem to mind the sun. She closes her eyes, leans back her head, and basks in its rays. She then squints at me before taking a sip of the mango green milk tea she's been raving about.

"So, how have you been, Shanice?" she asks after lowering her jumbo plastic cup back to the bistro table.

Before I answer, I take a drink of my tea and try not to cringe. I got a matcha flavor but it has a weird aftertaste and is chalky on my tongue. "Umm, I've been fine. Busy! How about you?"

"I've been busy as well. Since my first day it's been meetings, meetings, meetings, and reviewing submissions from freelancers. I've had the chance to read and edit some not-so-good writing and some amazing stuff. Speaking of . . ." Her voice drifts off as she reaches behind her to open her satchel. She pulls out a stapled stack of paper. "I finally had a chance to read your essay. I wanted to make sure I did it before we met today so we could discuss."

"*Oh?*" I say, trying to sound casual even as I tense up when I see my words in print staring back at me from the center of our table. My heart begins to pound. The matcha in my mouth feels even chalkier. "So what did you think? Did you like the flow, because I was thinking about rearranging some of—"

"No, don't rearrange anything," she insists. "It's perfect the way it is."

"Perfect? Really?"

I was worried that she might not like it, that she'd say what Gary would say, "Nice try but it's not quite there yet. It would probably better in more experienced hands."

Priya wiggles her head. "Well, even the best writing could use a little editing. But I loved the story about your family and about Essie and her painting. Her background and her discovery by Bachmann. And Bachmann!" Priya throws back her head and laughs.

"She sounds so bizarre! All that cult stuff and her husband being the founder of a paranormal society. And her murder! I can't wait to read the next essay to see how her relationship with Essie develops. Chase, our executive editor, can't either."

My smile fades. "Your executive editor?"

"Yes, I had him read it too. I hope you don't mind, but it was so good that I thought . . . well, I thought that we might consider it for *The Miscreant.* We've been looking for this type of storytelling and nothing has come close to this. Nothing that we've read so far from our freelancers and staffers. I wanted to get Chase's feedback before I made an offer."

I blink at her in surprise. "Wait. You want to buy my essay?"

"We'd like to buy the series. You said there would be three essays, right? And you're working on the second now. When do you think you can have the entire series done?"

"Uh, a month. Two at most," I blurt out, though I have no idea if I can pull that off.

I'm still researching. There are plenty of missing puzzle pieces I need to write the final essay. But this opportunity is too good to pass up. I'll finally have my work out there and at *The Miscreant*, of all places.

Priya takes another drink of bubble tea. "That timeline works. I'll let Chase know and I'll have our team shoot you a writer's agreement for you to sign. We'll work out the word counts. Our rate is twenty cents per word, by the way."

I do the math in my head. Not a huge amount of money but enough so that I can afford my rent and bills for yet another month after the five thousand runs out. It buys me more time. It gives me more room to pivot. And the essays themselves can lead to more writing opportunities.

Mom would be proud of me.

Priya heads back to the office an hour later, and I'm walking to the metro when my cell phone buzzes.

I look down at the screen.

What are you up to? Want to meet for lunch? I thought maybe Brazilian, if you're interested, Noah's texts says.

I would but I can't, I type back as I walk. I'm still smiling from my meeting with Priya. I'm racing home to do some more research and writing. Someone wants to publish my work!!!

In less than a minute, my phone starts chiming. I see Noah's name on screen and raise the phone to my ear. "Hey!"

"Congratulations," he says. "That's big news, and even more of a reason for us to grab something to eat. Let's do dinner instead. We should celebrate. Fogo de Chão. My treat."

I should say no. I promised Priya I would have these essays done a lot sooner than I planned, which means I should get to work. But I haven't seen Noah in almost two weeks. I've been so preoccupied with writing, learning more about Essie, and trying to figure out what might have happened to Isabel. Hearing his voice makes me remember his laugh, his kiss, and how I miss them both. I miss *him*.

"Come on," he pleads, hearing my hesitation. "It's just a couple hours. Say yes."

I slow my steps as I draw closer to the metro station and gradually nod. "Okay."

"Okay?"

"Yeah, let's celebrate."

CHAPTER 30

I'M RUNNING THIRTY MINUTES LATE FOR MY DATE WITH NOAH AND mentally kicking myself for the reason behind it. I wasn't writing or researching but agonizing over what to wear. But we're going to eat skewered meat on a sword. Does it really matter whether I wear red pants or a pink skirt? Finally, I settle on jeans and a tank top, grab a sweater, and run out my door to the elevators.

I'm racing out the glass door of my apartment building and wobbling in my high heels when I see it. When I see *her.*

"You've gotta be kidding me," I mutter.

The black cat is sitting on the sidewalk near a sewer grate with one leg cocked, grooming itself. I almost trip over my own feet when my eyes land on it. It pauses, gives me a withering stare with its yellow eyes, then starts licking its tail again.

I don't know if it's the same cat I saw the day before Jason broke up with me, but it certainly looks like the same one. I haven't seen it in more than two months. Why is it here *today*? What does it mean that I've crossed its path?

"Nothing," I whisper as I run to the Chevy sedan that's pulling up to the curb. I called an Uber, hoping it would get me to the restaurant faster than the trains and walking.

There are thousands upon thousands of stray cats in the city. Even black ones. I was bound to cross paths with one eventually. And good things are happening to me. I've just got an offer to publish my essays. I'm on my way to my third date with a very sweet, very cute guy.

No bad luck is coming my way, I reassure myself.

"Hey!" Noah says when I arrive at the restaurant ten minutes later. He gives me a kiss on the cheek. "The woman of honor has arrived."

I slide into our booth. "Woman of honor?" I laugh. "Come on."

"Yes, *woman of honor*," he insists as he eases into the booth beside me. "Don't laugh. I meant what I said. We're here to celebrate your achievement, aren't we?" His eyes twinkle in the candlelight. "I know how important your writing is to you. Happy to hear you're making some progress. So tell me about the essays you're getting published. What are they about?"

The waitress arrives at our table before I can answer. She takes our orders, and when she disappears, I turn back to him.

"So, remember that artist I told you about, the painting, and the weird guy who was obsessed with it?"

"Yeah." He pauses. "Your essay isn't about the weird guy, is it?"

"Oh, hell no!" I wouldn't give Vivaldi the satisfaction. "It's about the Harlem Renaissance artist Estelle Johnson and her painting. I'm writing about her work and her life, about the big mystery of what happened to her in New York that made her end her art career. Essie will finally get the attention she deserves, I hope."

He cocks an eyebrow. "Are you sure *you* want more attention though? What if your essays attract even more people obsessed with the painting? What if that weird guy comes back?"

"He already has."

"What do you mean?"

I don't want to tell him about Isabel's murder and my suspicions that Vivaldi may be connected. I know how far-fetched it sounds. How paranoid I would seem.

"He showed up at my grandmother's house and offered to buy the painting for a half-million dollars," I say instead.

"Holy shit. A half mill? That is *a lot* of money. Are you gonna sell it to him?"

"Over my dead body."

I blanche as soon as the words come out of my mouth. It sounds prescient, almost like a curse.

"Are you not going to sell it at all? I mean . . . would you give it to a museum or is that out of the question too?"

I shrug. "I guess I haven't decided yet. I might consider it. I'd have to discuss it with Gram if another offer comes along. She gave it to me but it's been in the family for so long, I wouldn't feel comfortable making a big decision like that without her. But until there's another offer . . . *if* there even is one . . . the painting is safe for now. I'll try my very best not to worry about it. Though honestly with me that's almost impossible. I worry about everything."

"I know how to take care of that. My goal tonight will be to keep you from worrying about that painting or anything else for that matter."

"Oh, really?" I incline my head. I'm smiling again. "And how do you presume to do that?"

"I have something planned. It's a surprise though. We're going to eat dinner and have our drinks. I'll pay for our meals, and then you'll find out what's up next."

"I can't get a hint?"

"No," he says, leaning back and smirking at me.

"Well, okay," I say, amused and just a tad bit turned on by his "take charge" attitude.

What he planned next turned out to be bowling, which is a pleasant surprise. I was expecting some grand gesture, but I remind myself this is Noah, not Jason. Jason gave me rooftop dinners and scenic Ferris wheel rides overlooking the water, but he broke my heart in the end. Noah is a lot more subtle and turning out to be more fun. I'm interested in seeing where this goes.

"This place is cool!" I have to shout to be heard over the sound of balls knocking against bowling pins, cheers, and Top 40 pop music blaring on hidden speakers.

"Glad you like it. I figured we could bowl a few rounds, and if you're nice, I might even treat you to a beer or two," he says with an impish grin under the bowling alley's blue lights.

"Why wouldn't I be nice?"

I forgot how much I enjoy my time with Noah. I'm less anxious. Isabel, Vivaldi, and the painting of Essie hidden in Dad's home safe feel a lot farther away now.

"Because I was going to put a wager on a few games with you, and I want to make sure you're gonna play fair," he says as he saddles up to the counter to order our bowling shoes. He starts to unbutton his shirt cuffs and rolls his sleeves up to his forearms.

"I always play fair! But what's this about a wager? What are we betting on?"

"Best two out of three games, and if I win . . ." He turns to face me again. "If I win, I get to make one request that you can't say no to."

"What are you going to ask me to do? Something crazy like if I lose I have to hop on one of the bar tables and do the floss in front of everybody?"

He throws back his head and laughs. "Interesting proposition, but no. I'm not that cruel. I swear it won't be anything embarrassing."

"Fine, then if *I* win, I get to pick our next date. I want it to be a film I've been dying to see."

He winces. "Is it a romantic comedy?"

I give him a wink. "It's a three-hour romantic period drama."

"Oh, hell," Noah groans, making me cackle. He throws out his hand. "Okay, fine. It's a deal. We'll shake on it." We shake hands and he turns to face the guy waiting behind the counter. "Size eleven, men's, please, and she needs a . . . What size do you wear?"

"Size eight."

We arrive at our lane a few minutes later, and I grab a bright orange bowling ball to match my new shoes, which are hideous but more comfortable than my heels. I'm a little rusty. It's been years since I've bowled, but I used to go bowling on the weekends with Dad, who was a bowling champion in college. After Mom's death, it was one of the few things we still bonded over. He taught me the proper technique for how to hold the bowling ball and center it on the lane. How to do a wicked spin and a mean hook. But I don't tell Noah any of that. Better to let him find out for himself.

He wins the first round—just barely. I slaughter him in the second. The third round ends with me rolling a strike and soundly winning the bet.

Noah takes a slow drag from his beer as he looks at the digital scoreboard and shakes his head. "You set me up, didn't you? You knew I had no chance in hell of winning this."

I don't know if it's the beers and my mojito, but I spontaneously break into the floss victory dance anyway, making him fall over laughing in his chair. I'm laughing too when I collapse onto the seat beside him.

"I believe you owe me a date at the movies. And get your cash ready because you're about to buy me the biggest popcorn they have," I taunt, leaning toward him.

Noah's grin disappears. His laughter tapers off. Something changes in his eyes.

"What?" I ask just as he reaches out and snakes his hand around the back of my neck, drawing me so close that I can feel his breath against my lips. Then he kisses me.

The sound of the bowling alley fades. The strength and hunger behind his kiss catches me off guard. I feel like I'm swimming in a mix of sensations, then I'm drowning, like he's dragging me under some current. When I pull my mouth away from his, I'm gulping for air.

"Come home with me tonight," he whispers.

I gaze at him in surprise.

"Come home with me," he repeats, running a thumb across my cheek.

My heart is racing. I'm throbbing all over. Was this the request that if he'd won the bet, he didn't want me to say no to?

I want to say yes. I want to keep drowning and sink to the bottom of wherever Noah wants to take me, but the beast won't let me. It's starting to send out alarm signals. I'm sweating. My heart rate isn't slowing down; it's beating even faster.

Sometimes the beast doesn't know the difference between worry and anticipation, fear and excitement. It treats it all the same. So, when Noah eases forward to kiss me again, I lurch back, like he struck me. I tug his hands from neck and face. I frantically shake my head, making him frown.

"I'm . . . I'm sorry, Noah, but no. I can't."

"Why? What's wrong?"

"Nothing. It's just . . . I'm not ready for . . . that. Not now."

"Oh. Oh, it's okay. I'm the one who should apologize. I guess I read the moment wrong and came on too strong." He holds up his hands and eases back from me. Even under the blue lights, I see his cheeks have gone bright red with embarrassment. "I got carried away. Let's just . . . keep bowling. I'll buy you another mojito . . . or beer . . . whatever you want."

"No," I say, rising to my feet, grabbing my sweater. "I should call it a night."

"It really is okay, Shanice. I mean it's awkward, but I'm willing to pretend like it never happened if you are."

"I want to go home, Noah," I say firmly.

He purses his lips and gradually, he nods. "Okay, I'll . . . I'll get you an Uber."

CHAPTER 31

The instant Noah closes the car door behind me and the Uber pulls away from the curb, I'm kicking myself for saying no, for turning him down. I shift to look out the SUV's rear window to find him standing on the curb with his hands in his pockets. I wave goodbye but he doesn't return the wave. He tries to fake a smile but doesn't succeed; he still looks embarrassed.

The driver makes a left at the corner and the glowing sign of the bowling alley fades from view. I sink down into the backseat and close my eyes.

Twenty minutes later, I arrive at my apartment building, and I just want to climb into bed and burrow beneath the covers. I step out of the SUV, and my eyes dart to the sewer grate.

Of course the cat from earlier is long gone.

I tiredly tap the code to enter my building in the wall panel and tug the glass door open. The air-conditioned lobby causes goose-bumps to sprout on my bare arms as I walk toward the elevators. I reach for my sweater that I wrapped around my waist back at the bowling alley, and realize it's no longer there. I left it in the Uber.

"Shit," I mutter as I look over my shoulder across the lobby at the glass doors. The Uber is already gone. I turn back around and bump shoulders with someone walking in the opposite direction.

"Oh, sorry!" I say as I look up. "My bad. I wasn't paying attention."

He nods and keeps walking, barely giving me a glance.

I stare after him. He looks familiar for some reason.

He's tall, has a goatee, and is wearing a blue baseball cap. His long hair is tucked into a man bun underneath. As the glass door closes behind him, I stand near the elevators a few seconds longer, struggling to remember where I might have seen him before, but I can't.

I shrug and press the UP button. Maybe he's another resident who lives on one of the other floors and I've seen him around the building. Or maybe it's because he reminds me so much of Noah, with his blue eyes and blond hair.

Noah . . .

I step into the compartment as the elevator doors open.

I have to stop obsessing. I can't change what happened tonight. I have to quit beating myself up over making a decision that felt right at the time.

The elevator stops on my floor and the doors open again. I exit and dig my keys out of my purse as I make my way down the hall to my apartment. It's late and I really am exhausted. I let out a loud yawn, hoping to get some sleep soon.

When I round the corner and draw near my door, I halt in my steps. My door is open and a light is on inside. The beam shoots through the crack, creating a mini spotlight in the building's corridor.

Why the hell is my door open again?

I can think of only one reason.

"Jason!" I bellow as I charge toward my apartment.

I should have changed the locks like Tati told me. I shouldn't have trusted that Jason really gave me the last spare key. I took him at his word, like an idiot.

"Jason, just what do you think you're doing?" I shout, shoving my door open. "Who the hell do you think you are? Get out of my—"

My words evaporate when I see my living room and kitchen, when I see what's happened to my apartment.

It's been ransacked. All my drawers and cabinets have been thrown open. My pictures and books have been knocked off my shelves and walls. Essie's letters and broken glass litter the floor. My coffee table sits on its side along with my laptop. It was tossed across the room and now sits akimbo by the balcony door. The screen is cracked.

On shaky feet, I stumble down the hall to my bedroom, holding the wall for balance. In my periphery, I see my shower curtain and rod in my bathroom have been ripped down and now sit in my bathtub like a plastic banner.

My mattress is no longer on the bed frame but sits on its side on the floor. My drawers are all open and vomiting out my clothes and my underwear. Lotion and perfume bottles are everywhere and the smell now permeates my room, making my eyes burn. There's a splatter of some white substance on the wall near my armoire.

I look in my closet. It's even worse in there; it's like a bomb exploded. I take a step back from the closet doorway and hear something crunch underneath my heel.

I look down and see the picture of me and Mom from back when I was four years old. The frame is broken. The shattered glass is fractured, breaking her smile into a dozen pieces.

I look around my apartment again. It's my nightmare come true. Mom was right; a lock didn't keep them out. Nothing will.

My eyes begin to water. I can feel my throat closing up and a throbbing in my hip. I can feel an intense pressure in my rib cage, making me gulp for air. I have to get out of here. I have to call the police.

I reach for my purse but it's no longer on my shoulder. I must have dropped it somewhere in my apartment or maybe in the hallway. Now panicked, I scan my bedroom floor in search of it, in search of my cell phone, but I don't see it either.

My sight is blurring. My head is swimming. I have to get out of here. I'll die if I don't get out of here. They might come back and kill me.

I run down the hall of my apartment, through the foyer, and back into the apartment corridor.

Help. I need help.

I try to force the words to come out, but they don't. They're stuck in my throat. I can't do anything but cry. The most I can muster is strangled sobs.

I start pounding on my neighbors' doors. One finally answers. An older black woman stands in the doorway in her robe and curlers. She stares at me, looking both horrified and annoyed.

"What in the world!" She yells. "Why are you banging on my damn door? Do you know how late it is?"

That's when something finally comes out. That's when I scream.

CHAPTER 32

I WAKE UP AND RAISE MY HAND AGAINST THE BRIGHT SUNLIGHT COMING through the window blinds. I slowly sit up and look around me, confused.

I'm not in my bedroom. The walls are a pastel yellow, not slate gray, and the furniture is all wrong. There's a painting of a ship on the wall. A ceramic sailboat, a bowl of rope knots, and other knickknacks are on the dresser.

Where the hell am I?

"Oh, yeah," I whisper. Everything that happened last night all comes rushing back.

I'm in Dad and Dana's guest room, my old bedroom that they redecorated five years ago in a nautical theme. Dad must have brought me here last night after he picked me up from the ER.

"She's not up yet?" I hear Dad ask impatiently on the other side of the door. The floorboards creak as he walks past the guest room.

"I don't think so," Dana whispers back.

More footsteps. This time on the stairs. "It's almost two o'clock."

"I'm aware, Malcolm. We can always talk to her later. There's no rush. Let her rest for now."

More creaking and footsteps, then silence.

I try to throw my legs over the side of the bed, but my limbs feel heavy. So do my eyelids. The bed and pillow are calling me to come back, to go back to sleep. I know this sensation, though I haven't felt it in quite a while.

I'm back on benzos. That would explain the sluggishness and disorientation. But this time it's Xanax, not Klonopin. They gave it to me at the hospital when I arrived "hysterical and incoherent," according to my admission form. I guess the break-in was just too much. What little thread I had left to keep me stitched together, to keep me stable, was cut that night in my apartment, and I fell apart.

I heard one of my neighbors called 9-1-1, and the EMTs arrived before the cops did. Who knows what the police would have done with me—a woman screaming that she was going to die, that her mother had warned her in a dream that people were coming to kill her.

I guess I'm also lucky one of my neighbors found my purse and phone in my apartment and thought to grab it for me. I had Dad listed among my saved emergency numbers in my phone for times like these.

The car crash that killed Mom taught me to do those types of things, to always be prepared for the worst.

After a few tries, I finally manage to climb to my feet. I make my way around the four-poster bed. I open the door and step into the hall, gradually walk downstairs, and into their kitchen. I find Dad sitting at the kitchen table, gazing out the window with his arms crossed over his chest. Dana is standing at the granite island with a bottle of Clorox in one hand and a sponge in the other. She's wiping down the countertop.

"Hey, kiddo!" she calls out with a cheeriness that feels woefully out of place. She lowers the spray bottle as I enter the room. Dad looks up at me. "You're awake!" she says.

I nod and yawn. "Yeah. Sorry that I . . . uh . . . slept in."

"Oh, it's fine, hon," she assures. "We know you were really tired. Anyone would be, considering . . . well . . ." Her voice drifts off. "Your father stopped by your apartment early this morning to grab a bag for you of some clothes and a few things you might need. It's in the living room."

"Thanks," I murmur.

"It's not safe to stay there by yourself anymore," Dad says. "Not after that break-in. We want you to stay with us for a while, but we have to establish a few rules first. It's about time that—"

"Before we start in that direction, at least let her have some coffee to wake up a little," Dana pleads.

Dad's mouth clamps shut. He pushes his glasses up the bridge of his nose and looks away from me to stubbornly stare out the bay window again.

Even through my Xanax haze, I can sense an underlying tension here. They've been discussing me probably for most of the morning while I slept. Dad's sympathy for my episode is already wearing off. I guess I should brace myself for a lecture.

I told you that you should've gone back on your meds sooner, he'll say. *You should've listened to me! I told you this was going to happen. Why did you let this drag on for so long, Shanice?*

Dana goes to the Keurig machine near the fridge and makes me a cup of French roast. A minute later, with a steaming cup in hand, I pull out a chair at the kitchen table across from Dad. He looks at me again as I take a few sips, but he doesn't say anything. Dana continues to clean. The kitchen is silent, save for the sound of her spraying and scrubbing.

After a few minutes, the caffeine kicks in and my benzo fog begins to wane.

"Okay," I say, setting down my cup, "I've had my coffee. I'll start, since you're refusing to. You were right, Dad. I should've probably gone back on my medication, but there's no way that I could've predicted someone would break into my apartment and set me off like that."

Dad raises his brows. "That's what you think I want to do? Gloat that I was right?"

"That's not what I meant. I just meant that—"

"Do you realize that if I didn't do the fast talking that I did last night, you could still be at that hospital right now, sitting in some empty room on suicide watch?" Dad braces his elbow on the table. He narrows his eyes. "They wanted to keep you for further observation, but I told them you were no risk to yourself or anyone else. That I would get you help right away if you needed it."

I slump back in my chair, not knowing how to defend myself, especially since I'm back in the role of "ne'er-do-well" daughter and Dad is the martyr who's had to put up with me all these years.

"You told me that you wouldn't let it get this far again," he continues.

"And like *I* said, what happened last night couldn't have been predicted."

"But regular people don't react to these things the way you do."

"*Regular people?* What am I? An alien?"

"You know what I mean! You wouldn't have reacted the way you did if you were taking responsibility for yourself like you promised me you would! And what's this about Jason breaking into your apartment? Why didn't you tell me that?"

I loudly sigh.

I forgot that tidbit about Jason had come out during questioning by the cops at the hospital.

"Dad," I say, after taking another sip of coffee, "I didn't tell you about Jason because there was nothing to tell. He used a spare key to get in and . . ."

"*And?* And what?"

"We argued a little, but he left the key behind. He left that night and went home."

"You're sure he left the key?"

"I saw him put it on the kitchen counter."

More like throw it, but I don't say that part.

"And where is the key now?" Dad asks.

I open my mouth to answer, but pause, trying to remember the last time I saw the spare key to my apartment. "It's . . . it's still on the counter."

Or at least it was until the break-in. But I can't remember. *Was it there before the break-in?* Had I moved it?

"You said you argued, Shanice. Did Jason threaten you, hon?" Dana asks behind me, breaking into my thoughts, making me turn around at the table to look at her. Her peachy face is etched with worry now too. "*Has* he threatened you?"

I hesitate, remembering Jason's face the last time I saw him in person and his sheer rage when he told me how selfish I was and how I'd used him throughout our relationship. I remember when I believed he could be stalking me. I remember the last text message he sent me before I blocked him.

You're going to regret ignoring me.

"No, not . . . not really," I mutter.

"*Not really?*" Dad repeats. "What the hell does that mean?"

"It means he was . . . well, he was angry. People say things when they're angry that they don't mean."

But Dad wants to hear none of it. He starts shaking his head so hard that I think his glasses might fly off his face. "This is crazy. This is crazy! And I'm not going to entertain it anymore. That man threatened you, Shanice. It's obvious that he's the one who broke into your apartment and trashed the place."

"No, it isn't obvious, Dad. I told you that the person who broke into my apartment was looking for Gram's painting. The one that's in the safe downstairs. I'm being stalked because of it. I think a librarian was killed because—"

"Enough!" Dad shouts, pounding the kitchen table, startling both me and Dana. "Enough! I'm not listening to this! No more ranting. No more paranoia. I don't want to hear conspiracy theories about the damn painting. I'm going with Occam's razor on this one: the simplest explanation is almost always correct. The police said there were no signs of forced entry. Someone had to have had a key to get into your apartment. And that someone isn't a mysterious person. It was most likely your crazy ex-boyfriend! It's that simple."

Is it that simple?

I want to keep arguing with Dad, but I'm not so sure anymore.

Have I really created this whole scenario in my head about the break-in, Isabel's murder, and the painting when none of them are related? Maybe I'm not the victim of some elaborate scheme, but of a jealous ex-boyfriend who got angry, maybe a little drunk again, and decided to have a full-blown temper tantrum in my apartment when I was gone.

I was so convinced last night of what had happened, but now I'm not so sure anymore. I can't tell if I'm thinking more clearly because of the Xanax, or if the drugs and Dad's tirade are making me even more confused.

"And I hope the cops arrest his ass," Dad continues. "Until then, you're gonna stay right here with us, and you're finally going to get yourself . . . *your life* together."

I grit my teeth and hold my coffee cup so tightly it might crack in my hands. My skin feels hot. Despite the Xanax, my heart is racing; I'm that angry.

"You're gonna take your meds," he says, pointing at me. "You're gonna go to therapy. And after you get your head in the right place, you're gonna get a job and—"

"I'm *not* a child. You can't lay out rules and dictate what I do with my life. I'm twenty-nine years old."

"Then act like it!" Dad booms.

"Malcolm!" Dana says.

"No, I've had enough of this shit, Dana! She's damn near thirty, and I'm still running after her like she's some toddler, making sure she's okay," he says, like I'm not here. Like what I think and feel doesn't matter. "Year after year after year of worrying about her. Never knowing when she's going to fall apart. Hoping for the best and then seeing her crumble." He rounds on me again. "I can't change what happened to your mother. I can't bring her back, but I'll be damned if I just sit around and watch you do this to yourself."

"Well, you don't have to." I set down my cup and push away from the table. "Not anymore."

"Okay, everyone, let's just . . . let's just calm down," Dana says, stepping from around the island and holding up her hands. "Let's take a step back and—"

"No, Dana. This isn't going to work," I say.

It's my teen years all over again. Dad flying into a rage out of frustration and Dana coming in between us to try to defuse the situation. But she can't this time.

"I think it's best if I leave," I say, heading toward the living room. I spot a duffel bag filled with my things sitting on the floor next to their sectional. I grab it. "Where's my phone? I need my purse." I look around and find it sitting on one of the end tables. I open my purse and see my phone inside along with the pills from the doctor at the hospital who gave me instructions to use as needed. They sit next to my wallet.

"So now you're just leaving?" Dad follows me to the front door. "And where do you think you're going in your damn socks? Back to your apartment?"

"I'll figure it out," I mutter.

"Shanice, wait!" Dana calls out.

"Sure you will," he says, as I swing open the door. "But if you walk out this time, don't come back. The shop is closed. No more money from me, and don't expect me to come to your damn rescue anymore either. You hear me? Like you said, you're a grown woman. I wash my hands of all of it!"

"Malcolm, stop! You don't mean that." Dana sounds near tears. "Shanice! Shanice, come back! Let's talk about this."

But I don't answer her. I keep trudging down their walkway to the driveway then the sidewalk, trying to balance my heavy duffel bag and purse as I walk. I feel ridiculous in my socks and my oversized vintage Run-DMC Tee, but I refuse to go back.

Dana's pleas are cut short when I hear the front door slam.

I pull out my phone, flip through my contact list, and press a button.

"Hey, Gram," I say a few seconds later, "mind if I stop by?"

CHAPTER 33

GRAM SWINGS OPEN HER FRONT DOOR, GIVES ME A HUG, KISSES MY cheek, then stares down at my feet. She frowns.

"Where are your shoes? That bastard made you leave his house in your socks and your bed clothes?"

"Dad didn't *make* me leave. I left because I wanted to," I clarify as Gram steps aside to let me through the doorway.

I called Gram and gave her a rough overview of what's happened to me in the past twenty-four hours. She had a few choice words about my father, but before she could go on a full rant, I told her I needed to stay with her a few days since I didn't think I could face my apartment right now, even with my new Xanax prescription to fortify me.

"Don't try to defend that man to me, Shanice," Gram says with hands on hips after she shuts the front door behind me. "You've been through a lot. Yelling at you and giving you ultimatums ain't the way to handle it. I have half a mind to call him up and—"

"Please don't," I mumble, feeling tired all over again. "Is it okay if I go upstairs and take a quick shower? Maybe brush my teeth? I'd like to change my clothes too."

She gestures to the staircase. "Go right ahead. And grab a pair of my bedroom slippers too, while you're at it. They might be a little snug, but it's better than walking around in dirty socks."

I nod and trudge upstairs to the bathroom. I strip off my clothes and climb into Gram's cramped shower stall, scrubbing my skin with her lilac-scented bodywash and brushing my teeth and my hair in the foggy mirror. When I arrive back downstairs, I'm dressed in a T-shirt and shorts. I managed to find a pair of flip-flops buried in the bottom of the bag. I feel a little more human, less like a zombie. The smell of fried chicken and biscuits wafts from the kitchen. I find Gram hovering over the stove.

"Dinner will be ready in less than an hour," she says over the sound of crackling oil.

"Gram, it's not even five o'clock. Who eats dinner this early?" I pull out a chair at her dinette table and sit down. "And I'm not hungry anyway."

I'm not just saying that. The drugs may help smooth out my wrinkles, but they also take away my appetite. I lost fifteen pounds the last time I was on a similar medication.

"Nonsense," Gram says. "You're gonna eat. You've got to keep your strength up. Your daddy may not give a damn about you anymore, but I still do."

"Gram." I close my eyes and drop my head into my hands. "Are you going to talk trash about Dad the whole time I'm here?"

That's not why I came here. I came here to forget about what happened. I want to forget the argument and Dad's cutting words.

"*She's damn near thirty, and I'm still running after her like she's some toddler, making sure she's okay,*" he said.

I knew Dad felt I was a burden, but it's another thing to hear it out loud.

"And why shouldn't I trash-talk him? He deserves it." Gram shouts. "How dare he make *you* feel like trash when he knows damn well he ain't no saint! He's done his dirt. Trust me."

I open my eyes and lower my hand from my face. "What are you talking about?"

She sucks her teeth and turns over a drumstick with metal tongs. "Ask your Daddy."

"You know I can't. I'm asking you. What do you mean he's not a saint?"

Gram takes a deep breath and lowers the fire so the pan goes from a crackling boil to a bubbling simmer. She turns around to face me.

"Your daddy isn't who you think he is, Shanice. I knew the moment I set eyes on him that he was gonna break your mama's heart. When she brought him home for dinner that first time, he knocked over the saltshaker and sent it spilling all over the table. A bad sign. But she loved him because she thought he was smart and dependable. He was so practical, the opposite of your mother who had always been sweet, but . . . well, a little sensitive and flighty sometimes. 'He completes me, Mama. He won't ever let me down,' she said. Uh-hunh," Gram grunts. "So much for that! She told me before she died that she found out he was cheatin' on her."

My stomach drops. My mouth falls open. "Dad cheated on Mom?"

That doesn't sound like my father. Dad adored Mom. He almost idolized her.

Gram nods. "She didn't want to tell me at first. She was so damn ashamed, like she'd done something wrong. Like it was *her* fault, not his. She didn't know the woman's name, but she confronted him about it and your daddy confessed, though he swore up and down that it had just been a fling. Not anything serious." Gram slowly shakes her head. "It tore her up inside. She'd burst into tears at the drop of a hat. I told her, for her own peace of mind, to just *leave* him. No man is worth all this! He didn't deserve her anyway, but she wanted to stick it out. Because of their marriage vows. Because of *you*. 'I want Shanice to have the family that we didn't, Mama,' she told me. But she still wasn't the same. She wouldn't eat. Couldn't sleep. She was acting . . . different. I knew something was wrong with her. I wish she would've just left him. Maybe if she did, she would've been in her right mind and not gotten into the accident that day."

"*What?* What does that have to do with the accident? Are you saying that was the reason she was distracted?"

"Lord, forget I said that." Gram waves a dismissive hand. "She's dead and gone. Let's leave it be."

"No! No, Gram, you can't say something like that and then tell me to just 'leave it be.' You think Mom . . . caused the accident? Are you saying . . . are you saying she was distracted or . . . she did it *deliberately*?"

Gram hesitates then loudly exhales again. "The police weren't sure. Eyewitnesses said different things. No one knows if she purposely went through that red light or not. I want to believe that she didn't, but I don't know. I honestly don't know."

I stare at Gram, trying to absorb everything she told me.

I try to remember Mom and that time in my life. I thought my parents had been happy and in love. I remember her as bubbly and carefree. The type of mom who would leave work early and pull you out of school midday for a "girls' trip on the town," or make brownies for dinner rather than spaghetti just because she felt like it. But now, thinking back, her behavior seems erratic, not bubbly. Instead of just remembering her playing all those sad love songs and singing as she vacuumed the house on Saturdays, I also remember seeing her cry sometimes as she sang.

I remember the day of the car crash, all those details that I had pushed to the back of my mind because I didn't want to remember. Her coat had been buttoned wrong when I saw her standing in the principal's office waiting room and I told her, but she didn't fix it. I told her, too, that I had a history test that afternoon, and she said it didn't matter. I could take it another day.

I vaguely recall the moments before the crash. Me, seeing the Mazda speeding toward her passenger side. Me, screaming her name just as the other car frantically beeped its horn. Mom didn't turn to look at me, or the beeping car coming to T-bone us. She kept looking forward, like she couldn't hear us.

"Only your Mama knows the truth of what happened that day," Gram now says. I can see tears in her eyes now. She sniffs. "But I know what happened before it. I know what and who led her down that road if she did what I think she did . . . and I guess I'll never forgive him for it."

Gram blinks back her tears and turns to face the stove. She bends down to open the oven and checks on her biscuits.

She's back to the task at hand, stoically ignoring the emotional bombs she just dropped and ignoring her own emotions like she always does.

Meanwhile, I sit in silence for several more minutes before gradually rising to my feet. "I . . . I think I'm going to lie down for a bit," I whisper.

Gram nods as I walk out of the kitchen. "Okay, I'll call you when dinner is ready," she says over her shoulder.

I climb up the stairs and head to Mom's old room, the only bedroom on the top floor of the house besides Gram's room that we've started to clean, that isn't still filled wall-to-wall with junk. Many of Mom's things are still here though, waiting to be put in storage or given away. Her cheerleading trophies. Her yearbooks. Her old acoustic guitar that's missing one of its strings.

I close the door behind me, lie down on the bed, close my eyes, and start to cry. They aren't the screaming sobs like yesterday that left me breathless, but silent tears that wet my cheeks and dampen the old quilt underneath me.

I don't know what to think about Mom. About Dad. About my life and what all this means. I don't know anything anymore.

When I open my eyes again, it's dark outside the bedroom window. The streetlights along the block are on. I must have fallen asleep. I glance at the old digital alarm clock on the night table. It's 9:36.

I sit up, turn on the night table lamp, and open the bedroom door to find the house quiet. Gram is an early riser and an even earlier sleeper. I can hear her rhythmic snores through her closed bedroom door even from here in the hallway. I look around me in the dark, not wanting to go back to sleep *yet again*, but not knowing what to do with myself now that I'm awake with all the thoughts clamoring in my head.

I have to get out of here. I came here to escape . . . *what?* Dad? Memories of Mom? Myself? But everywhere I turn, they're all still here. *I'm* still here and more of a mess than I was before.

I go back into the bedroom and grab my duffel bag and purse. I step back into my flip-flops and walk down the hall, careful not to awaken Gram. I creep down the stairs and make my way out the front door, locking it behind me. I type Gram a quick text.

Sorry, Gram, I had to go. I will call you later.

I stand outside on her front porch, listening to the sound of the passing cars and the whir of the cicadas, unsure of where to go next. I refuse to slink back to Dad's house, especially now after the story Gram told me. I can't go back to my apartment. Should I call Tati and ask to stay with her? I scroll through my contact list in search of refuge, before finally settling on a name and number.

CHAPTER 34

I STEP OFF THE ELEVATOR AND FREEZE IN PLACE, NOT SURE WHETHER to turn to my right or left because I've never been here before. The industrial lights are too bright. There's a low, steady hum from the AC unit, and the air is so cold that I shiver and my arms sprout goosebumps.

Noah stands in a doorway down the hall. He leans out and waves. "Down here," he says.

He's bare-chested and barefoot and wearing blue sweatpants. His hair is flat on one side, like he's been lying in bed. His eyes are soft and full of concern.

"So you found your way here okay?" he asks.

I nod. "Yeah."

"It sounds like you've had a really rough couple days. Come in." He gestures over his shoulder, opening the door wider.

"Thanks for letting me stay here," I murmur.

"No problem. I set up the foldout in my living room." I follow him inside his apartment and he closes the door behind me. "I was gonna sleep there and you can have the bed, if you'd like."

I glance at the leather foldout sofa where a stack of pillows and a blanket sit on a mattress covered in white sheets. I only called him thirty minutes ago and he did all this without me even asking. Of course Noah would be this kind, this thoughtful. I start to tear up again. I don't trust what will come out if I try to respond, making Noah tilt his head.

"Or you can sleep out here if you prefer. You tell me."

I drop my bag and turn to him, no longer able to hold back the tears as they begin to spill over. "I . . . Thank you for . . . for all of this, Noah. Really."

He places a hand on my shoulder. "Hey, it's okay. It wasn't a problem."

"I'm sorry for crying, for just showing up on your doorstep a complete mess," I sniff.

"You don't have to apologize for crying. I get it. You're probably a little overwhelmed right now. The emotions have to come out."

I step forward and wrap my arms around him, dropping my head to his chest. He embraces me, holding me close. It feels good to be held, to be comforted. The warm touch of another human being feels like balm to all that's happened. After a minute, I lean back and climb to the balls of my feet. I close my eyes and kiss Noah, and the chaos of the world seems to momentarily disappear.

This is what I want. This is what I need, to drown in sensations. To feel anything other than desolation.

Noah doesn't flinch. He doesn't hesitate. He pulls me even closer, and, within minutes, we fall back onto the foldout sofa.

This time I say yes. I say it over and over again as he pulls me undertow.

CHAPTER 35
ESSIE

NEW YORK CITY
September 19, 1927

"Estelle, there you are, my dear!" Godmother shouted.

Essie stopped mid-yawn and lowered her gloved hand. She pushed back her shoulders and painted on a smile. "Yes, Godmother?"

Godmother was throwing yet another soiree. It was the fifth this month. Essie still hadn't gotten used to being on display at these things, at being guided around the room and introduced to guest after guest, subjected to a dizzying array of odd people and a long list of names she barely remembered. Mr. Harry *What's His Face.* Mrs. Silvia *Whomever.*

Essie found the whole exercise grueling, like she was a show pony expected to perform. But she also knew that whenever Godmother did it, it was only to spread news of her work.

"The world must know that Estelle Johnson exists," Godmother had said once while gently patting her hand. "That your art exists. We must shout it from the rooftops!"

So Essie put on a brave face and allowed herself to be led blindly around the room, even though the only place where her paintings hung for now was in her studio back in Harlem and Godmother's home. Still no galleries or art houses. They hadn't even rescheduled that meeting with Mr. Russell at Knoedler & Company.

"He's a busy man and he travels so much, dearest," Godmother had explained. "You know how it can be, but Godmother is working on it. I can promise you."

A few other gallery owners had offered to feature Essie's work, but Godmother had made her turn them all down.

"They aren't worthy, my dear. Better to wait for what's right for you than settle for the first opportunity that comes along," Godmother had assured her. "The right galleries will come with time. Just you wait! We must be ready when the moment comes."

Essie was still waiting for that moment.

"I want you to meet someone, Estelle. Madame Durand," Godmother now said as she *click-click-thump*ed her way across the ballroom, gesturing to the tall, gaunt woman beside her. "I was just telling her about you and the marvelous things I see in your future."

"Oh? Well, it's a pleasure to meet you, Madame Durand," Essie said eagerly.

Was Madame Durand the assistant of a gallery owner or maybe the owner of her own art salon? Essie readied herself to finally talk about her work.

"Show her your palms," Godmother said.

Essie did a double take. "My palms? Why?"

"To read your future, my dear," Godmother exclaimed with a laugh.

Essie's smile withered. She hesitated, wondering if this was the same woman who Doris claimed had read her palm, who had told Doris she had no future. Gradually, she unfurled her fingers and held out her hands. Madame Durand grabbed each, squeezed them within her bony fingers, leaned down, and inspected them.

"What do you *see*?" Godmother asked. "Have I chosen wisely this time, Madame Durand? Will this turn out as I hoped?"

Essie flinched. Was Godmother really asking a palm reader if she should still be Essie's patron? If Essie was worth the investment?

"I'm sorry," Essie said. She yanked her hands out of Madame Durand's grasp just as the old woman began to answer and clasped them protectively against her chest. "But I am feeling a bit under the weather. Or maybe I'm just tired. Perhaps we could do a reading another day."

"Oh, you do look positively exhausted," Lillian Oppenheimer exclaimed as she glided across the ballroom toward them.

Lillian, or "Lily" for short, was Godmother's *true* goddaughter and niece. Tonight, she wore a pale blue chiffon gown that floated around her like butterfly wings. A modest double string of pearls hung at the young woman's pale throat, accenting her long neck and almost birdlike, delicate features. She wore her dark hair in a page-boy cut that was all the rage now. Lily oozed effortless elegance and sophistication, traits that Essie envied.

"But Estelle isn't ready to leave yet, are you, pet?" Lily asked, eyeing Essie. "She's been wandering around like a lost little lamb looking for her shepherd, and I suspect I know who that shepherd is."

"Really?" Godmother turned back to Essie. "Who?"

"Go on, pet," Lily said. "Tell her."

Essie laughed nervously and shrugged. "I have no idea what you mean."

The truth was she'd been searching for Elias. Godmother said her son had returned from abroad more than a month ago and she expected him to attend tonight's party. Essie was especially interested in seeing him again after Lily mentioned that Elias had talked about her.

"My dear cousin spoke about you more than once when he visited mother and me in Paris," Lily had told her at Godmother's last party. "He said how charming and lovely you were. It became quite annoying. If I didn't know any better, I'd say Elias has become a bit infatuated with you. You two don't have anything going on, do you?"

"No," Essie had said a little too loudly. "Of course not!"

But it seemed that Essie would not be able to find out for herself if Elias truly was infatuated with her. It was well after midnight and there was no sign of him.

"Oh, look, she's being coy," Lily now chortled, making Essie's cheeks warm even more.

"That is *enough*, Lillian," Godmother said tightly. "She isn't being coy. She's obviously over fatigued. You poor, sweet creature." Godmother raised a hand to Essie's cheek and rubbed it tenderly. She then lowered her hand and sighed. "It is settled then. Off to bed with you. Agatha!" she called out to her assistant.

Essie grimaced, chafing at the idea of being sent to bed like a child but unwilling to argue and offend her patron. She took a step toward the ballroom doors, prepared to be given her coat and then directed to Godmother's driver who would take her home. So much for seeing Elias again. But her eyes widened when Godmother said instead, "Would you have one of the girls prepare a room for Estelle tonight? Oh, and sleeping attire."

Agatha promptly nodded. "Yes, ma'am. Of course."

Essie stared at Godmother in shock, making the older woman laugh. "We can't very well have you sleeping in your evening gown, can we?"

"N-n-no!" Essie stuttered with relief. Godmother wasn't tossing her aside after all. "I mean . . . thank you. Thank you so much, Godmother."

An hour later, Essie sat in one of the guest rooms wearing a white silk gown under a silk robe embroidered in lace. She felt like a princess dropped into a faraway palace. Her eyes scanned the grand oak furniture and velvet curtains, then the crystal chandelier overhead that twinkled in the light from her night table lamp. A Francisco Goya original hung on the wall in a gilded frame near the bank of windows facing the courtyard ten floors below. Essie ran her hands over the gold damask duvet and then one of the mahogany posts of the four-poster bed, using her fingertips to prove that she was there, that *all* of this was real. But even then, she still could not believe it.

She could already see the words she would write to Louise when she returned to her apartment tomorrow: *Last night, dear one, I slept in paradise . . .*

Essie yawned again before climbing to the top of the bed, removing her robe, and laying it beside her. She sank beneath the covers and rubbed her cheeks across the goose down pillows. She turned onto her back and gazed at the ceiling and saw a gold, blazing sun. She'd seen similar suns on the ceiling in Godmother's art gallery. It seemed to be Godmother's favorite motif in her Park Avenue home. Essie smiled at the sun, then turned off the lamp and closed her eyes.

CHAPTER 36

ESSIE HEARD IT BEFORE SHE SAW IT. THE SOFT CLICK AND THEN THE slow creak of a door. She blinked in the darkness of the bedroom to find a shaft of light coming from the hallway. The guest room door, which had been firmly closed when she fell asleep, now gaped open, making Essie shoot upright from her pillow in alarm.

"Hello?" she called into the dark.

No one answered.

Essie reached for the night table lamp, running her hands along the brass base and following it upward until she found the pull string. With only the night table lamp now on, much of the guest room was still cloaked in shadow, but at least she could see the doorway more clearly. No one was there, but Essie could swear she heard the faint sound of footsteps, of someone rushing down the hallway.

"*Hello?*" she called again as she threw her legs over the side of the mattress and climbed to her feet. Essie grabbed her robe, walked toward the door, and peered into the corridor. This time she *did* see the shadow of a figure at the end of the hall along one of the far walls.

"Is someone there?" she asked before stepping into the hall and shutting the guest room door behind her. She followed the shadow, watching as it grew smaller and smaller then disappeared completely.

Essie reached the end of the corridor and peered around the corner, expecting to find someone retreating. Instead, she found an empty hall.

But someone had been there. She was sure of it. Someone had opened the bedroom door as well.

Had it been one of the servants? Or maybe it was another guest of Godmother's who had mistakenly stumbled upon her room, thinking it was theirs. But why hadn't they answered her when she called out? Why had they fled?

Essie continued down the corridor, her stomach now roiling with unease. Most of the doors were closed but a lone door stood open. She heard music coming from inside—a rendition of the "Maple Leaf Rag" was playing on a phonograph. Were they in there? Essie leaned forward to peek through the doorway.

"What *are* you doing?"

Essie jumped back from the door to find Agatha glaring at her. Godmother's assistant was still wearing her gown from the party—another dowdy sack the color of dirty dishwater. Agatha's thin lips were pinched. Her nostrils flared angrily.

"I'm . . . I wasn't doing anything. I got lost on the way to the lavatory and . . . and . . ."

Her words drifted off, floating somewhere above her head and then dropping to the ground soundlessly.

She hadn't done anything wrong. She was simply trying to find who had opened her door, but under Agatha's critical gaze and after hearing the accusatory tone in her voice, Essie felt guilty. Like she had committed a crime.

"You have a lavatory adjacent to your room," Agatha said.

"Y-yes. Of course! My apologies. Thank you," Essie whispered, rushing in the direction of the guest room and turning the corner.

"Thank you *what*?" Agatha asked as she trailed behind her, making Essie halt in her steps.

"I'm sorry?" Essie asked, facing her again.

"Thank you, *Mrs. Pickens*. That is my name. That is how you should address me. You've yet to do so."

So that was it. That was why Agatha was always so stilted. She probably thought Essie was "too big for her britches" and maybe even didn't like the fact that Essie was being treated "above her race" by Godmother. And now that Godmother wasn't here, Agatha's mask was off, and she'd gone from stilted to outright hostile.

"I meant no harm. My deepest apologies," Essie said, forcing herself to sound contrite, using the same voice that she often used down home with white folks to show them the respect they thought they were owed merely because of the color of their skin. "Thank you, Mrs. Pickens."

She tried to walk away but stopped again when she heard "Mrs. Bachmann told me that you now have a mutual acquaintance. That you have befriended Doris Bingham."

"I didn't '*befriend*' her. She showed up at my apartment uninvited and told me lies about Godmother . . . about their relationship."

"Lies?" Agatha cocked her head. "I heard that you believed everything Doris said. That you thought Mrs. Bachmann had placed a curse on her."

"No, I didn't! I didn't mean to give that impression. I just . . ." She fumbled desperately for the right words. "I'm loyal to Godmother. I am! There's no question that—"

"But there *is* a question, Estelle. There is a question in my mind whether you are loyal. Whether you can be trusted."

Essie fell silent.

"I never liked Doris," Agatha went on. "I warned Mrs. Bachmann that she could be trouble. I could practically smell it on her. It emanated from every pore." She then gave Essie a slow assessing look. "I wonder if you will be troublesome as well."

"No," Essie whispered. "No, I won't."

"Mrs. Bachmann is a very kind, sympathetic woman. Sometimes to a fault. But I will not idly sit by and allow her to be taken advantage of or harmed again." Agatha took a step toward her. "Do you understand?"

Essie shakily began to nod but stopped when she heard a familiar voice say, “Agatha!”

Agatha’s shrewd expression suddenly changed. Her frozen smile was back. Essie turned to find Elias turning the corner and strolling toward them with his hands in his pockets, wearing a cardigan sweater and tan plus fours that billowed around his legs with each stride, like he’d just left the golf course even though it was after midnight. When Essie saw him, she grinned. She thought he wasn’t coming tonight. And here he was, arriving at what had to be the absolute perfect time.

“Mother’s looking for you,” Elias said.

“What?” Agatha took a step back. “Did she say what she needed? Is something wrong?”

Elias gave a shrug. “No idea. You’re her secretary, not me. I just know that she’s asking for you, and you don’t want to keep her waiting, do you?”

“No. No, I do not,” Agatha said, clearing her throat. “I shall see what Mrs. Bachmann requires.” She then turned to Essie. The smile didn’t disappear but her gaze was shrewd again. “I trust that you now know where to find your lavatory. There will be no more wandering the halls or stepping into random rooms or—”

“She’ll be fine,” Elias interrupted. “Don’t worry. I’ll make sure Essie goes where she’s supposed to go. You just worry about Mother.”

“Yes. Well . . . good night then.” Agatha gave a curt nod, turned, and left.

“You don’t know how happy I was to see you coming toward us,” Essie whispered breathlessly, leaning toward him. “I swear it was like seeing the angel Gabriel coming in with golden light and the blare of trumpets.”

“The Angel Gabriel?” Elias chuckled. “Well, well, well! With a compliment like that, I should walk out and walk back in again.”

She laughed.

“I’m afraid Agatha won’t be very happy with me though,” Elias murmured just as Agatha disappeared down another corridor.

“Why?”

"Because I lied. Mother isn't looking for her. She's in bed fast asleep."

Essie stared up at him in shock, then barked out another laugh. "You didn't!"

"Indeed, I did—and I'd do it again if I had to." He inclined his head. "You looked like you needed rescuing, and I *am* an angel, after all. You said so yourself."

That wasn't exactly what she'd said, but looking at Elias now with his twinkling eyes and his impish grin, she could see it.

He did look like an angel—like the fallen angel Lucifer himself who was here to tempt her with a handsome face and the promise of stolen moments and wicked delights. She knew she'd missed him all these months, but hadn't realized how much until now. Essie barely knew Elias and had only had snatches of time with him, but standing here under the magnetic power of his gaze, she was ravenous for more. More conversation. More flirting. More laughter. She did not want him to leave her side.

Elias raised an eyebrow. "Were you really looking for the lavatories?"

She lowered her eyes sheepishly and shook her head.

"So you *were* snooping." He chuckled again. "Well, my lovely Essie, if you're going to do that, you must do so correctly. Let me be your guide." He offered her his arm. "Come with me."

Essie looped her arm through his and her entire body warmed. She nearly melted.

As promised, he showed her each corridor and almost every room, from the gallery to the now-vacant kitchen where the staff had prepared tonight's meal. She watched with surprise when they entered the study and Elias crossed the room before pushing aside one of the towering bookcases, revealing a hidden passage.

"Why is this here?" she whispered in awe, gazing into a darkened corridor.

Elias reached inside and flicked a switch, revealing bare wooden walls and frame, plaster-covered floors and walls, and a line of single bulbs hanging from the ceiling with cobwebs dotting the corners. The end of the pathway was inky black. Essie sniffed the air. It smelled musty and felt dank against her skin.

"Father and Mother had it built in 1910 when they purchased the penthouse. They wanted a shortcut for the servants like the hidden corridors you find in homes in Europe. There are so many halls, you know. It takes forever to walk anywhere in this place. This takes you directly to all the bedrooms. Lily and I used to sneak away from the nanny and play hide-and-seek in the tunnel when we were children. I ran into one of the guest rooms and scared the dickens out of a maid who was turning the bed at the time," he said with a chuckle, making Essie laugh too.

She leaned into the darkness, feeling the cool, dank air blow against her face.

"Fascinating, isn't it?" Elias asked, but Essie didn't answer him; she wasn't listening anymore to Elias, but to music. It sounded like what she'd heard earlier that night. She began to step inside.

"Afraid not, luv," he said, grabbing her arm, making her leap back and run smack into him. "You can't go down there," he said.

She tried not to tremble at the sensation of his fingers on her bare skin. "Why not? I thought we were exploring."

"We are, but I told you: it's for servants only. It's been ages since I've been walking through there. We could get lost." He drew her toward him so that his torso was pressed against hers. He was grinning again. "Besides, if you're so eager to see the other bedrooms—mine, in particular—it's only right that you go through the front door." He paused for a beat. "I'm willing to offer you an invitation, if you'd like."

"*An invitation?* That sounds grand, but what makes your bedroom any different from any of the other rooms we've seen tonight?" she asked playfully.

"I'd be happy to show you," Elias said, snaking an arm around her waist. "I'm about five doors down."

"But that's so far. Why can't you just show me here?" she whispered, drawing her mouth close to his, no longer willing to resist him or play coy.

He pressed her back against one of the study shelves and kissed her. It started slow but quickly became rushed and greedy. All lips, mouth, and even teeth. Nips and bites. It was like they were trying to devour one another. She couldn't believe she had denied herself this for so long. The feel of him. The smell of him. He was a collector of actresses, singers, and dancers but tonight Elias Bachmann was hers. All hers.

The little undressing they did was just as frantic. She heard a seam rip and felt a few buttons pop. Essie inhaled sharply as he lifted her. She wrapped her legs around his waist and clung to his back, fisting the fabric of his sweater as he held her steady, never pulling his mouth away from hers. Soon, they were two conjoined bodies panting and moaning in the dark, handing themselves over to their desires.

Lost in the throws of passion, Essie didn't hear the footsteps this time. She didn't realize they were being watched, or notice when the door to the passageway silently slid closed.

CHAPTER 37
SHANICE

WASHINGTON, D.C.
Present day

"YOU'RE ALREADY PACKED?" NOAH ASKS.

I shove the last of my shirts into my duffel bag as I sit on the edge of his bed. I turn to find him standing in the bedroom doorway with a towel wrapped around his waist. He's using another towel to dry his hair that's still wet from the shower.

"Yeah, I have to be back at my apartment by nine so the guy can come to finally change my locks."

Noah nods, resigned.

I've been staying with him for the past few days. It's been like a vacation except without the sandy beach and blue ocean. In Noah's bed, in his arms, I've barely thought about Dad, Gram's revelations about Mom, Essie's painting, or the break-in.

But I can't stay here forever. Neither can he. Even if I'm not particularly eager to do so, we both have to get back to the world outside of these apartment walls in Brookland, a bustling neighborhood that sits near the Basilica of the National Shrine of Immaculate Conception. Even now, I can see the golden dome of the Basilica looming over us protectively from the view of his bedroom window. I don't want to leave its shadow, but I can't desert my apartment. I paid rent last week; I should at least get my money's worth.

"I feel like I should be there with you," Noah says as he walks farther into the bedroom. He sits on the edge of the bed beside me. "I shouldn't let you go back to your apartment by yourself. It doesn't seem right."

"You know you can't come with me; you have to go to work. You've taken off two days in a row already. *One* of us has to keep our job," I joke, but Noah doesn't laugh. He still looks edgy, so I lean over and give him a kiss to reassure him. "I'll be fine. I have my phone if anything happens, and—" I shove my hand into my purse and pull out a little red canister, holding it up for him to see, "I have my Mace. I'll use it if I have to." I drop it back into my purse and close the clasp.

But if Dad is right and Jason is the one who trashed my apartment, I doubt I'll have to use my pepper spray at all. Once he sobered up and realized what he did, I bet he regretted it. If he's anything close to the Jason that I remember, he'll be embarrassed that he got this obsessed, that he let things get so far out of hand that the police are now involved.

"Are you going to be okay staying alone there?" Noah asks. "I mean . . . with your anxiety?"

"I think I'll be fine. Before I went back on my meds, probably not so much, but I already took a pill today because I figured I'd need it. The Xanax helps. In fact, it helps *too* much, to be honest."

That was the problem before, but I'm hoping for better this time around.

I throw my purse strap on my shoulder, grab my bag, and rise to my feet. Noah stands too. We both walk out of his bedroom and down the hallway leading to his front door.

"Call me as soon as you get there," Noah says, "and keep me updated throughout the day. I'll text you, and I'm warning you that if you don't text me back, I might think something happened to you, so don't freak me out for no reason."

"I will, I promise! I'll just be cleaning up and writing most of the day anyway."

Priya sent the writer's agreement two days ago by email and I signed it electronically. I'm now contractually obligated to finish those three essays.

I have to go back to my apartment now at the very least to get my laptop, to try to salvage Essie's letters that weren't destroyed in the break-in, and continue my research and writing.

Noah and I reach the end of the hallway. He unlocks the door and opens it for me.

"I get off work at five. I'll stop by after," he says as I step out the front door. "I can bring some Schezuan for dinner."

I turn to look up at him and smile. I know Noah is making up an excuse to come by my apartment to check on me, but I'll pretend that I don't. "Takeout sounds good."

He cups my face and gives me a kiss that takes my breath away. I have to grab on to his bare shoulders to steady myself. "Keep kissing me like that and I might never leave."

"That's the point," he whispers, making me laugh.

Noah gazes down at me. His expression goes somber again. "You know, I really like you, Shanice Pierce."

I laugh again, caught off guard by his earnest admission, but it warms me up inside. "And I really like you, too, Noah Kelly."

"I'll see you tonight," he says, releasing me.

"Bye," I whisper back and let go of his shoulders. I then wave and head toward the elevators.

CHAPTER 38

INHALE, EXHALE.

Inhale, exhale.

Inhale, exhale.

I breathe deeply as I approach my front door, but my hand is trembling so much as I take out my keys and insert them into the lock that they jingle like sleigh bells. I push and the door opens with a loud creak. I step into my apartment and survey the damage.

It looks even worse now in the light of day. I shake my head and close the apartment door behind me. I lock it then grab one of the dining room table chairs that isn't broken and wedge it underneath the door handle.

I'm in my apartment, I text Noah.

Nothing looks strange? he texts back.

Define "strange."

I see your point. Are you sure your door is locked?

I send him a photo of my door and the chair. Locked and barricaded, I type under the pic.

He sends me the thumbs-up emoji.

I tuck my phone into one of my shorts pockets, turn back around to face my apartment, and set down my bags.

"It's gonna take days to clean up all this crap," I mutter, looking around me, now overwhelmed and unsure of where to start.

I finally settle on my kitchen, since it has the least amount of things broken and tossed around in there. I sweep up the shattered glass from an empty wine bottle that was knocked to the floor and dump the shards into the trash bin. I start slamming shut drawers then give my attention to the cluttered counter and suddenly, I hear Dad's voice in my head, "*You're sure he left the key? . . . And where is the key now?*"

I search through the debris. I reopen the drawers that I slammed shut only seconds ago, digging through the junk and piles of cooking utensils. But the spare key isn't here.

Once again, I try to remember the last time I saw it, but I can't. I feel panic tighten its grip around me like a dance partner eager to take the lead.

But someone is coming to change the locks. The key is missing but it doesn't matter anymore. Someone is coming to help.

At 9:07 a.m., the facilities guy arrives. He looks like he could be around eighty years old, and is so skinny that has to keep pulling up the waistband of his navy blue cargos to keep them from falling down. Not exactly reassuring. It's not like he could protect me if something else were to happen right now.

"How long do you think this will take, sir?" I ask him anxiously as he drops to his knees beside my door.

He shrugs and pulls out a screwdriver from his toolbox. "Probably thirty minutes. Can't imagine more than that."

I nod and get back to my cleaning. I start tackling the living room, and I see all the letters from Essie that Gram gave me. Their envelopes are scattered around my hardwood floor. Some of the pages are ripped. I see dirt smudges on others, like they've been stepped on. These letters survived an entire century and I couldn't keep them more than a month without them being damaged. It feels so irresponsible.

Just like Dad says I am, I think.

I pick up the letters and try to fold and stack them as carefully as I can without doing further harm to them, but I pause again when I spot one note on the floor that doesn't look like the rest.

It's handwritten in black marker and on white paper. The handwriting looks familiar. I bet if I compare it to the handwriting on the note that was taped to my door weeks ago with the five thousand dollars inside, it would be an exact match. When I read the words on the page, I go numb. My legs feel wobbly underneath me. Panic is gripping me again. It begins to dance.

"You took our gift but rejected our offer," the note says. "That was a mistake. Now YOU pay the price!"

CHAPTER 39

A WEEK LATER, I WALK OUT OF MY NEIGHBORHOOD GROCER'S AUTOMATIC doors with two canvas bags in tow, and look to my right and then my left. Just as I step onto the sidewalk, someone behind me bumps my shoulder, making me flinch.

"Pardon me. I'm *so* sorry," the woman says, chagrined. She then continues on her merry way toward the crosswalk.

I breathe deeply, telling the beast to pipe down. It takes me a few seconds to get myself back together, to get my racing heart under control. I start walking again.

It's been about a week since I found the note in my living room. I gave it to the police along with the original note that came with the five thousand dollars. I told the cop about Vivaldi and how I thought he was in some way connected to this.

"You think he wrote these notes to you?" the cop asked.

"Probably, though he'll deny it."

"But you mentioned at the hospital that your ex-boyfriend may have been the one who broke in. That he'd done something like that before. Frankly, that seems like a much better lead."

"No, that was my dad's theory. Jason wouldn't write this. He hasn't made me any offers I rejected. It doesn't make sense."

"Right." The cop gave a tentative nod. "Well, I'll follow up and see what I can find out."

But I could tell that he hadn't been listening; incredulity was written all over his face.

So, even though my locks have been changed, I feel more vulnerable than ever now because it seems like the person who actually did this won't be arrested.

I installed one of those home alarm systems with cameras around my apartment. It gives me an alert if any doors have been opened, and I can see videos of my foyer and bedroom on my phone now. But it doesn't mean I feel safe, especially after reading that note.

Now YOU pay the price.

In the past week, Noah has stayed with me a few nights so that I'm not as scared. But when he's not around, I wake up in the middle of the night at odd sounds, wondering if I heard footsteps.

Now as I glance over my shoulder and walk back to my apartment from the grocery store, I can't shake the feeling that someone is lurking behind me again. I think I'm being followed. I can see my building at the end of the block. It takes all my willpower not to run toward it, bags and all, and bolt for the glass door.

I'm less than fifteen feet away from the door when I hear pounding footsteps behind me.

"Shanice!" someone yells.

I turn, prepared to drop my bags and reach into my purse to grab my Mace, but my mouth goes slack when I realize who it is.

"*Jason?*" I say, squinting up at him. What is he doing here?

"Why the hell did you tell the cops I broke into your apartment?" he yells, coming to a stop in front of me. "Why did you tell them that I vandalized your place? We were together for five years! You know I wouldn't do that!"

"*What?* I—I never said that you—"

"Don't lie to me!" he shouts, cutting me off. "They called me at work, Shanice. Do you realize how bad that is? If I get charged with this, I could lose my security clearance. I could lose my job! Are you *trying* to ruin my life? Is this some sort of revenge thing?"

A few people walking by slow down to look at us. Some guy in a tank top holds up his cell phone. If Jason doesn't pipe down, a video of us could end up online, a viral post that could bring him more attention than I ever could. It could be the thing that would make him lose his job.

"First of all, calm the hell down, and second, no, I'm not trying to ruin your life," I say. "I told the cops it wasn't you. That it couldn't have been you. I even gave them evidence to prove it was someone else. They aren't listening to me."

He goes quiet. The furious expression on his face gradually disappears. "So . . . so, why do they think it's me?"

"Let's sit down over there," I say, tilting my head toward a nearby metal bench. "I swear I'll explain everything."

Jason looks reluctant but eventually he nods and follows me. Our audience loses interest. We both sit down and I tell him everything, from my first meeting with Vivaldi to Isabel's voicemail and murder to what I think really happened the night of the break-in and who may be behind it.

"Holy shit, that's a lot," he says, looking bewildered. "All this has happened in the past two months?"

I nod.

"So, you think this appraiser guy is behind it all?" Jason asks.

"Maybe, but I'm also starting to think there may be someone working with him."

I remember the note said "*our* offer" and "*our* gift," like the writer was referring to more than one person. Vivaldi also pointed out back at Gram's house that he spends most of his time in New York and wouldn't be able to stalk and terrorize me down here in D.C.

But he could get someone else to do it for him.

Jason looks at me apprehensively, making me frown.

"What?" I ask. "You think I'm wrong and just being paranoid?"

Jason shakes his head. "No, I don't think you're paranoid. It just makes me see differently something that happened a while ago. It puts it in . . . a new light."

"What do you mean?" My stomach starts to turn at the prospect of more bad news. "What happened?"

"After we broke up, I got a call out of the blue from this woman claiming she worked for some firm. She was calling about you."

"About me?"

He nods. "She said she was doing a background check for a job you'd applied for and wanted to verify some information about you. I mean, this is D.C. There are plenty of jobs with the feds and contractors that require background checks, so I didn't think the call was that out of the ordinary. I just wished you'd given me a heads-up."

My heart drops. "I didn't apply for any job, Jason. You should've called me to check."

"I would have, but like I said . . . we'd just broken up. It's not like we were on good terms. I thought it was presumptuous of you to use me as a reference but I answered her questions anyway. I thought, '*Shit, I'll do Shanice this last damn favor. Then I'm done.*'"

"Do you remember when you got the call?"

Jason thinks for a minute. "It was after I got back from my business trip but before I saw you at the coffee shop."

I do the math, figuring out that this phone call likely happened around the time I'd met Vivaldi at the gallery and he'd made his first offer for Essie's painting.

"The woman asked me where you worked before *The Intersector.* It was news to me that you had even *left.* She asked stuff about your family, about where you grew up." He grimaces. "Some of . . . some of the questions got really personal. She asked me about your strengths, your weaknesses. The challenges you've faced. I, uh . . . I told her about your anxiety disorder, about how you'd been battling it since your early teens, since your Mom died."

I close my eyes, dismayed that he had revealed so much about me to a complete stranger, providing them with plenty of information and ammunition that could be used against me.

"At the end of the conversation, the woman thanked me for my time and we hung up, but as soon as she did, something felt . . . off. I didn't know why. So, the next day, I tried to call her back to clarify some of the stuff I said. I left her a voicemail, but she . . . she never called me back. When I showed up at your apartment to return your spare key, I was going to tell you about the phone call, but then we started arguing, and well . . . you know what happened after that."

"You said it was a woman who called you." I open my eyes again. "But I distinctly remember Isabel, the librarian, said in her voicemail that there was a *guy* following me around the library."

"Maybe you have more than one stalker then," Jason ventures. "A group of people working together. I just know one of them isn't me, and I'd appreciate it if the cops knew that."

"I'll tell them again. I promise. I'll tell them everything that you told me."

"Thank you." He leans forward, braces his hands on his knees, and sighs. "Look, I know things have gotten really bad between us and part of that is my fault."

I raise an eyebrow. "*Part* of it?"

"Okay, *a lot* of it. I'll admit that I didn't handle our breakup and the aftermath well."

"The breakup that you said you wanted," I remind him.

"Yes, I realize that, Shanice. It doesn't mean I was prepared to work my way through it like the rational adult I thought I was. Shit, a lot of these misunderstandings, especially that stuff with the background check, could have been solved with just a phone call, but I wasn't ready. I'll own that." He turns to look at me. "And I . . . I apologize for it."

"I accept your apology." I tilt my head. "And if it makes you feel any better, you couldn't have called me anyway. I blocked you."

He bursts into laughter then falls silent. Jason stares at me a beat longer. "You know, despite all the drama, I really did love you, Shanice."

I nod. "I really did love you too."

"I just . . . I just didn't think we could ever make it work." He opens his mouth then closes it. "Take care of yourself, okay? Especially with all this . . . weird stuff happening. None of it sounds good. Be careful, Shanice."

"I will. Well, I'll *try*," I say with an awkward laugh before he rises to his feet and gives one last lingering, worried look at me. Jason then turns and walks away.

CHAPTER 40

ESSIE

NEW YORK CITY

November 16, 1927

THE MOMENT ESSIE AND ELIAS OPENED THE DOORS TO THE BACHmanns' Park Avenue abode, she knew something was off. And not slightly askew like a picture frame hanging cock-eyed on a wall in the great room, but full-tilt off kilter, like finding one of Godmother's rococo armchairs nailed to the coffered ceiling.

The song Essie had been lazily singing during the car ride there died on her lips. Elias's drunken laughter evaporated.

It was almost midnight, and Elias had invited her over for a nightcap and another clandestine overnight stay. Since that first night together, he'd been spending nights with her at her apartment on Sugar Hill, away from the prying eyes on the Upper East Side.

In Harlem, with the exception of a few "whites only" speakeasies and other venues, they could be themselves. They could eat together, dance together, and make love with no judgment. They'd been barely able to keep their hands off one another tonight at a smoke-filled basement club on 138th Street, necking as they slow danced to jazz music in the dark.

"We have to leave soon if we're going to make Godmother's party," Essie had moaned into Elias's ear.

"Damn the party," Elias had said, pulling her closer.

"We have to go, Elias. *I* have to go. You know I do."

Godmother was her patron, her benefactor, as she often repeated to herself like a mantra. She didn't want to disappoint her. She didn't want to prove Agatha right.

He'd groused even as he ran his fingertips along the soft skin of her bare back and shoulder, making her shiver. "Fine. One more drink, then we're off."

She'd expected to find the house abuzz with activity. Footmen carrying trays laden with wineglasses and tumblers. Rooms filled with men in tuxedos and women in evening gowns, reclining on sofas and chairs in conversation. A ragtime band playing music and couples swaying on the parquet floors. They'd planned to make a quick appearance at the party. Amid all the noise and bodies, they would make their way upstairs separately and meet in his bedroom.

But not tonight.

None of the servants had greeted them at the door. All the lights were out, save for the dimmed crystal chandelier over the center foyer table where a nest of purple gladiolus now sprung proudly from a crystal vase. No one was in sight. It seemed as if the entire household was slumbering.

"Did Godmother end the party early?" Essie whispered to Elias. "Where is everyone?"

"I don't know," he replied, yanking off his scarf before tossing it to the floor. "And I don't care."

He took her face in the palms of his hands and pulled her toward him. As their tongues danced, she tasted rum and inhaled the warm, heady scent of his cologne. He began to tug the straps of her gown off her shoulders, making Essie roughly pull her mouth away from his.

"Not here," she admonished. "Upstairs."

"Spoilsport," he said before reaching for her again. She dodged his grasp and ran upstairs, giggling. She was high and drunk and maybe a little bit in love.

He led her by the hand down the maze of corridors to his bedroom. As soon as he opened the door and softly shut it behind them, they were on the bed, undressing in the faint moonlight coming through the parted curtains. Essie never grew tired of his warm, nimble hands on her body, of his mouth on her skin.

Weeks ago, as Elias slumbered at her apartment, she'd crept next door to her studio and began a work inspired by their moments together. She'd painted the figures—all tangled limbs and bodies aglow. She'd showed it to Godmother and bit back a laugh as the old woman leaned toward the canvas, inspecting her progress.

"How delightfully lush and decadent," Godmother had said. "It's so . . . so *sensual*!"

"You think so?" Essie had asked with mock innocence, knowing very well that Godmother's own son had been the inspiration.

Now Essie felt as if she were in the painting, like her arms, legs, and chest were burning from the inside out or that she might combust into smoke and flames. She cried out and he quickly clamped his hand over her mouth to stifle her screams. The cries gradually subsided and her body went limp.

"Sorry," she said dreamily against his palm.

Elias pulled his hand away. "No apologies necessary," he said before lowering his mouth back to hers.

They began to kiss again but he halted when they heard a knock at the bedroom door, making them both go still.

"You think someone heard us?" she whispered up to him.

"Elias, it's Lily," his cousin called from the other side of his door. "Elias, are you in there?"

Elias held a finger to Essie's lips then raised himself to his elbows. "Coming!" he called back.

"I'll see what she wants," he whispered down to Essie. "Hide in the wardrobe."

Essie nodded.

As Elias turned on his night table lamp and put on his robe, Essie quickly gathered her clothes and scrambled to his wardrobe—a cherrywood armoire—on the other side of his bedroom. She climbed inside and he shut the door behind her just as Lily knocked again.

"Elias!" Lily shouted.

Essie stood naked in the stifling darkness, nestled between a wool sweater and pairs of trousers, trying not to make hangers rattle, hoping that Elias wouldn't be long and Lily would leave soon. She shifted and her foot knocked against something cool and made of glass. She heard footsteps then the click of a door being unlocked.

"Were you asleep?" she heard Lily ask.

"Of course I was. Whatever is the matter?" Elias replied. "What's wrong?"

A pause. "Do you have someone in there with you?"

"No. No, I don't."

"Don't lie to me, Elias."

"I said I don't! Now will you tell me what is wrong?"

"Godmother says it's time. Everyone is waiting."

Another pause. "Right. I'll . . . I'll be there in twenty minutes."

"Twenty minutes. No more than that. She will never forgive you if you miss this."

"I said I'd be there." Essie heard a door close.

A minute later, Elias opened the wardrobe door, flooding the interior with light. Essie blinked at the sudden brightness.

"I have to go," he whispered quickly as she hopped out of the wardrobe and back into his bedroom. She looked down and saw what she had accidentally kicked in the dark: a bottle of hooch. She watched as he walked to his dresser drawers, removing a shirt.

"Where are you going?" she asked.

"Just wait for me here," he said, not answering her question. He began to dress. Whereas Elias had been languid and carefree before Lily had knocked on his door, his body was now tense with nervous energy. His movements were frenzied, like he was operating under a stop clock. "I'll be back in an hour. Maybe two."

"*Two hours?* That long?" She stepped back into her gown. She knew she couldn't spend the night. Not in his bedroom, anyway.

"If that's the case, I can sneak out now. We can meet again in the morning or tomorrow night. I'll just—"

"No!" he shouted, making her flinch. He lowered his eyes and pursed his lips. "No," he said in a softer voice. "You can't leave, Essie. Someone might see you. I don't want anyone to know that you're here. Definitely not tonight."

"What do you mean? What's happening tonight?" she watched as he fastened the last button of his shirt waist.

Elias closed his eyes and grimaced. "Please, I'm begging you . . . just wait here. It's very important that you don't leave. Stay quiet. Let no one know you're here. I'll come back. I swear."

A few minutes later, he left the bedroom, closing the door behind him. Essie finished dressing and sat on the edge of the bed, staring at the mantel clock on his bookshelf.

Not too long ago, she had been all heat and throbbing. Now, in Elias's absence, she was left with a coldness and a dull ache. She climbed to her feet, walked back to the wardrobe, threw open the door, and removed the bottle of hooch. She sighed and took a swig, cringing and then coughing as the liquid made its way down her throat. It warmed her chest, giving back a modicum of heat that she'd lost.

I can wait an hour, she reassured herself. Elias had told her he wouldn't be long. Her eyes drifted to the closed door.

But where had he gone off to? And why had he and Lily made it sound so urgent?

She paced around the room, her steps measured by the constant tick of the mantle clock. One minute stretched to ten, from ten to thirty. As time passed, she drank more gin, finishing almost a third of the bottle. Essie was starting to feel addled by all the alcohol. She collapsed onto the bed to get the spins to stop. She closed her eyes, hoping that would help. She was soon fast asleep.

CHAPTER 41

For the second time that night, Essie screamed. She kicked and flailed at the phantom attacking her. It had no solid form, except for the eyes and talons. Its green eyes were bright and keen. Its claws were gnarled, ending in razor-sharp points. It grabbed her ankle and tugged, yanking her so hard that she thudded to the ground.

Her eyes flashed open as she sat up ramrod straight, now awake. She looked around with her heart still pounding at a rapid pace. She was trembling, ready to fight for her life, but no menacing phantom had latched onto her. Instead, she was alone in Elias's bedroom.

She took a deep breath. This often happened whenever she smoked marijuana, and she'd smoked her fair share tonight. It made her paranoid or gave her night terrors. She had to lay off the stuff; no high was worth this.

Gradually, her heart rate decreased and the trembling stopped. She looked at the clock again to see how much time had passed.

Four hours. She'd been sleeping for almost four hours? Elias had said he'd only be gone an hour, maybe two. Why hadn't he returned?

Essie climbed to her feet and slowly walked toward the door but hesitated before she reached for the handle. No one was supposed to know she was here. What if someone saw her? But then again, what if something serious was happening? Maybe something with

Godmother. And here she was, getting drunk and falling asleep in Elias's bedroom. It wouldn't hurt to peek her head through the door, to see if she heard or saw something. It would only take a matter of seconds.

Essie reached out again to turn the handle, but it didn't budge. She tried again, pulling harder but the door didn't open. She stared at it in shock.

Elias had locked her inside his bedroom. Why would he do that? Or had he done it? Maybe someone had locked her inside when she fell asleep. Maybe it was the same person who had opened her bedroom door the last time she'd stayed overnight at Godmother's. She hadn't found out who the culprit was. And now, here she was locked in a room with no idea when Elias would return.

Suddenly, Essie no longer cared if anyone heard her. She didn't care if anyone knew she was there. She started yanking, then pounding on the door.

"Elias! Elias!" she shouted. "Let me out! Let me out of here!"

She pressed her ears flat against the door. Silence. She heard nothing. No voices. No footsteps.

Essie thumped her forehead against the wooden slab and closed her eyes in defeat: she was stuck in this room, and with no idea for how long. She stood there for several minutes, waiting for the sound of footsteps, for Elias to return. But she continued to hear nothing. Abruptly, her eyes snapped open. She pushed herself away from the door, remembering something.

She remembered the bookcase in the Bachmann's library that Elias had pushed aside, revealing a long tunnel hidden behind the walls.

"This takes you directly to all the bedrooms," Elias had told her.

If it did, then there should be a path to the tunnel somewhere in Elias's bedroom that would lead her out of this room. She turned and looked around her. At the room. At the walls. The path had to be here.

Essie shoved aside grand velvet curtains as red and lush as blood, revealing not a secret door but just windows, an even brighter moonlight, and the New York City street ten stories below set in the ghostly glow of street lamps and fog. She shoved at his dresser, gritting her teeth. It moved one inch, then two. After a few more shoves, she managed to move it a whole foot. Gilded wallpaper sat behind it. She ran her hand along the wallpaper seams, using her fingertips to detect an opening or a faint breeze, using her eyes to detect a shaft of light—but she saw none. Essie's shoulders slumped in defeat.

She turned away from the dresser and gazed around the room again. Her eyes narrowed as she focused on a spot near his armoire. She traced the seam of the wainscoting, finding a gap in the wood. She pressed against it and felt the wall move. It was barely perceptible but she swore she felt it shift. She pressed again, even harder, and a door swung open with a loud squeak. And there it was again, the same musty-smelling corridor and the same wooden walls and frame and plaster-covered floors. She reached blindly into the darkness in search of a pull string or light switch but found none. Only cobwebs and dust.

Essie went back into Elias's bedroom, retrieving one of his lighters from his suit jacket pocket. She flicked it on, illuminating part of the tunnel. She hesitated only a few seconds before stepping inside, plunging herself into it, like diving into a pool of water.

Her hands shook as she walked, making the flame flitter in the dark. She followed the path of the tunnel, which seemed to go on forever. She listened for the sound of voices and sought another source of light that might reveal one of the other rooms but walked for a few minutes without seeing anything except the lighter's flame and hearing her own panting breath. Just when Essie was on the verge of turning back around, she heard it. A murmur. It was the muffled sound of voices. She held out her arm to guide her way as she followed the sound, drawing her to a spot in the tunnel wall.

In the orange glow, she noticed a wrought iron handle. Was another bookcase on the other side? She pressed her ear flat against the wall.

The voices were unintelligible. They were chanting something, but not in English. Now someone was speaking—a man, perhaps—but in another language. Italian, maybe? Or Latin.

She let the lighter flicker out. Now there was only the dim light coming from the far end of the tunnel more than fifty . . . maybe sixty feet away, back in Elias's bedroom. It couldn't help her see here, but she was still happy to have it out there. It was a lighthouse beacon to guide her back if she needed it.

She grabbed the iron handle and pulled, hoping that whatever was on the other side would move and do so softly. She felt it give less than an inch, then stop. Through the crack, Essie saw the room on the other side.

It was a bedroom, even larger than Elias's, and it was filled with almost two dozen people circling a towering four-poster bed. Essie squinted and stood on the balls of her feet, trying to see over the shoulder of a man standing two feet in front of her hiding place. She saw an old man sleeping in the center of a mattress. He was a skeletal figure surrounded by a sea of white.

She instantly recognized him as Herr Bachmann—Godmother's husband and Elias's father. He had been naked and shouting on the family's staircase only months ago. Now he looked even more feeble. The poor man.

To Herr Bachmann's right, nearest to the bed stood Godmother, clasping her husband's gnarled hand. Her cheeks and eyes were wet with tears. Beside her stood a man with a gray, pencil-thin mustache wearing a tuxedo and black robe, and a purple stole hung around his neck. A symbol was stitched on each side of his stole: an orange sun with two red-eyed, intertwined green serpents at its center. The symbol also hung over Herr Bachmann's headboard.

On the other side of the bed stood Elias with his head bowed. He also seemed to be wearing a black robe for some reason. Flanking him were Lily and Agatha.

Essie watched as the man wearing the stole began to speak again. His voice was deep and rumbling, bearing a gravity that made her skin prickle with goosebumps. But she still couldn't understand him. She felt like she was watching one of the silent movies at the Lafayette Theatre without subtitles, leaving her to decipher what was going on onscreen.

The man with the mustache stopped speaking and everyone in the room, including Elias and Godmother, responded in unison, "We send our brother, Klaus Bachmann, into the light."

Essie watched as Godmother let go of her husband's hand and tugged off a ring from his index finger. It had an oval-shaped, crimson stone that seemed to pulse in the glow of the bedroom. The older woman then placed his hand solemnly at his side. She leaned down to kiss Klaus's liver-spotted brow before handing the ring to the man in the mustache, standing upright again, and dabbing at her eyes with a handkerchief.

The man with the mustache spoke again, raising the ring to the bedroom ceiling. His booming voice had risen to almost a shout.

Essie looked around the room, realizing all the men wore the same ring—including Elias.

"We send him into the light. We send him into the light. We send him into the light," they all began to chant.

What the hell is going on? Essie wondered.

Had this been what Doris had tried to warn her about? The sacrifices by moonlight?

"She cursed me, Estelle," Doris had said. "They did this to me."

"So you heard about them too? . . . Godmother's friends," Langston had said with the smuggest of smiles.

The meeting in secret at night. The witchcraft. It was all true.

She was so transfixed by the scene that Essie nearly missed Agatha handing Elias a dagger with a gold hilt. She barely noticed when her lover took three steps closer to the edge of the bed. But she lurched back in horror after he raised the dagger over his head and plunged it into his father's chest, sending up a spray of blood that splattered Elias's shirt front and cheek.

The old man bellowed in pain. He let out a long, guttural groan. But no one helped him. They all just stood there.

Essie slapped her hand over her mouth in just enough time to stifle her scream as Elias pulled out the dagger and plunged it into his father again and again.

The groaning and strangled yells stopped. The old man's eyes went vacant.

Essie stumbled away from the crack, turned, and ran down the tunnel, dropping the lighter.

Hysterical. Frenzied with panic. She briefly considered going back the way she came, to Elias's bedroom, but decided she couldn't go there. Not after that. Not after what he'd done. What they'd all done. She had to escape, to find another way out of here, but where?

So she ran deeper into the tunnel, feeling her panic grow as what little light she had disappeared. She could no longer see her own hand in front of her face. The dark pressed in on her at all sides. She felt as if it were a growing thing, as if her fear was real and chasing her. Like the phantom in her dream had come to life and was drawing close, ready to attack the moment it got near enough to bring her down.

She was sobbing, calling out for help. For God. The air burned in her lungs. She felt a stab in her side from her labored breathing, telling her to slow down, but she kept running. She finally stopped when she collided with something solid. She fell backward, hitting the hard floor, falling headfirst into darkness.

CHAPTER 42
SHANICE

WASHINGTON, D.C.

Present day

I HEAR A KNOCK AT MY DOOR AND LOOK UP FROM MY NOTEPAD. Nowadays, I'm always wary of who or what could be waiting for me on the other side. I walk across my living room and gaze through the peephole to find Noah standing in the hallway. A row of my neighbors' doors flank him in the fishbowl lens. He's loaded down with takeout bags and staring off into space. With two taps, I turn off the alarm system I had installed—I keep it on even when I'm home—and quickly unlock the door and open it.

"Hey," I say, relieved to see him. "I wasn't expecting you for another couple of hours."

"I snuck out of the office a little early today."

I give him a quick peck and glance down at his bags. I can smell Indian food. "Thanks for getting dinner. You can set those on the kitchen counter. You know where the plates and glasses are, right?"

Noah nods as I rush back to the sofa to finish what I was writing. I don't want to lose my train of thought. He meanders into my foyer, juggling bags and kicking my front door closed behind him.

"Having a good writing day?" he asks as he walks into my kitchen, watching me as he starts to open bags and takeout containers.

I was right about the Indian food; I can see and smell tandoori chicken and basmati rice from here.

"Yeah," I say as I flip open another book, "I'm learning about cults."

"Cults?" Noah pauses from unloading, strolls to the sofa, and sits down beside me. He picks up one of the books piled on the coffee table and reads the cover: *Occult Explosion: Paranormalism in the Roaring Twenties.* "What does this have to do with your painting?"

"It's complicated," I mutter as I write more notes. "But I started to think about it after a conversation I had with Jason a few days ago. It might be even more important than I thought."

I've talked to Jason a few times since he stopped me on the sidewalk. He gave me the name and number of the woman who called him and pretended to do a background check about me. When I called her number, the phone rang over and over again like it did for him; no one answered. Unfortunately, that turned out to be a dead end. So, while the mystery of who's been stalking me continues to go unsolved for now, I've decided to refocus my energy on my essays about Essie's portrait, specifically an angle I want to explore in more detail: The Bridge of Light.

Were they involved in what happened to Essie? Could they be the reason why she suddenly left New York? Had they stalked her or harassed her until she fled?

Essie made a few passing references to "them" in her letters though she never calls out the cult by name. She wrote to Louise about "them," sharing rumors about Bachmann and her friends in The Bridge of Light, how her patron and those friends held rituals in Bachmann's home at night that were linked to the occult. Did Essie get pulled into that stuff as well? Is her painting connected?

"You had a conversation with Jason a few days ago?" Noah asks. "Jason, *your ex*?"

I look up from my notepad to find Noah staring at me. He looks horrified.

"I thought you said he was stalking you. That he threatened you, Shanice. Why would you have anything to do with him?"

"Because it turns out it just was a big misunderstanding between us." I set down my notepad. "We . . . we worked it out."

"You worked it out?" he repeats slowly, like my words weren't in English.

"Yeah. Surprising, I know. I guess we can both be adults about our breakup after all. He apologized for everything and now he's trying to help me figure out who's really been stalking me."

Noah doesn't say anything for a long time. Finally, he nods.

"Right. Okay." He rises to his feet. "I should eat. I skipped lunch and I'm starving."

He heads back to my kitchen. I watch from the sofa as he opens one of the overhead cabinets.

That was . . . awkward.

I hadn't thought to mention to Noah that Jason and I were talking again, but now I realize that I probably should have. Noah and I have just started to get serious, and now I'm reintroducing my ex into my life. I know there is no chance of me rekindling a romance with Jason, and the biggest reason why Jason and I are even talking is that he wants to help solve who was really behind my apartment break-in and get the cops off his back, but Noah doesn't know any of this. No wonder he's acting so strangely. I made him feel insecure. Not to mention that his last girlfriend cheated on him, sending him into a bout of depression. This is probably giving him bad flashbacks.

Shit.

"Noah," I say, walking into the kitchen, shoving my hands into the back pockets of my jeans, "I'm sorry. I should have told you about Jason. I handled that wrong."

He shrugs and keeps looking down at the plate he's assembling, not facing or even glancing at me. "You don't need approval from me to talk to your ex-boyfriend."

"No, but I don't want to give you the wrong impression. I don't want you to . . . to take it the wrong way."

His hands still. He finally turns away from the counter to face me. "And what impression would that be, Shanice? How exactly should I take it?"

His expression is just as flat as his voice now and just as glacial. I've never seen Noah like this before.

"Hey," I say gently, wrapping my arms around his waist and gazing up at him, "I'm not Laurie."

He squints down at me, like he has no idea what I'm talking about.

"I mean . . . I'm not shady. I'm not a cheater! I wouldn't cheat on you like your ex did. You don't have to worry. You're important to me. I like . . ." I take a deep breath. "I like having you in my life. I want to keep you around, Noah."

His face softens. He leans down and gives me a deep kiss. When it ends, he eases back. I can see he's smiling. Once again, he resembles the Noah I've been falling for.

"I like having you around too," he says.

"Well, I'm glad we agree." I give him a quick peck. "And again, I'm sorry if I made you think otherwise."

My phone buzzes. I suck my teeth and glance over his shoulder at the coffee table. It's where I left my cell. "Just one sec," I say, stepping away and holding up my finger to him.

I rush back into the living room and pick up my phone. I see Priya's name on screen and answer. "Hey, Priya. What's up?"

"I've got a bit of a situation that I need to talk to you about."

I frown. "Okay, what kind of situation?"

Whatever it is, it doesn't sound good. I brace myself for the worst case scenario: they've decided not to run my essays about Essie's painting. Priya is about to offer to pay the kill fee for my work and dash all my hopes.

"Before you freak out," she says, reading my mind. "It's not really bad news. Our executive editor Chase got an interesting call yesterday from Hanson Whitmore."

"Who's Hanson Whitmore?"

"He's the chairman of our parent company's biggest investor, the Whitmore Foundation. Apparently, he's a descendant of Maude Bachmann. I had no idea."

"Whitmore. Hmm." I grab my notepad and flip through a few pages. "He's probably a descendant of Lillian Whitmore. Though back then, I guess she was still Lillian Oppenheimer. She was Maude Bachmann's niece. What about him? Why'd he call you guys?"

"Now that is the interesting part. Somehow, he got wind of your piece. I'm not sure how it made it through the company grapevine, but it did. He asked to see a copy, and . . . well . . . Chase emailed it to him."

I slump back onto the sofa. "Let me guess. He didn't like what I wrote about Maude, and you guys want to kill the essay series now?"

"I haven't heard anything about him not liking the piece. For now, he just wants to talk to you about it. He said he thought he could enlighten you about her. Give you insight that the books can't. So, will you talk to him? I have his number."

My first instinct is to say no. I can only imagine what "insight" this Whitmore guy wants to give, and I have no interest in turning my essays about Essie into a puff piece for his dead relative, an eccentric rich woman who fetishized a group of black artists and ended up getting murdered probably either because she got involved in some crazy mystical stuff, *or* because she was an all-around awful person.

"Look, Shanice," Priya says with a gruff sigh on the other end of the line, "I don't like this any more than you do. I believe in freedom of the press and it's wrong to ask us to change our process or a story for this guy, but Chase wants to keep the overlords happy. The publication isn't even a year old and the Whitmore Foundation is very important to the company. Can you please give him a call? *And*," she adds, her voice going up a little, "you said you still have some unanswered questions that you need to finish your essays. Maybe he can answer them for you."

She does have a point.

"Okay, fine. I'll give him a call. Give me his number."

"Thank you! Thank you so much, Shanice. You're amazing."

"Yeah, yeah, yeah," I mutter with a laugh and an eye roll.

"What was that about?" Noah asks a minute later with a mouthful of food after I hang up with Priya.

I grab some naan, rip off a piece, and pop it into my mouth. I lean an elbow against the kitchen counter. "Nothing," I say between chews. "Priya just wants me to call a source. Some guy who read my article and wants to talk about it. She thinks he could help with my research."

Noah stops chewing. "So, are you going to call him?"

I take another bite of naan. "You mean *now*?"

"Yeah, I mean now." Noah glances down at his wristwatch. "It's a little after five. You might still catch him. You've been obsessing about this painting for months. You've written *thousands* of words about it. You said you had your home broken into because of it. Now you keep it hidden somewhere. You haven't even told *me* where it is."

"It's not that I don't trust you, Noah," I insist. "It's just—"

"I'm not offended," he says, cutting me off. "You're paranoid about the painting. I'd probably be too if I were in your situation. My point is, Shanice, that if this guy can give you the last missing puzzle pieces, maybe the painting won't have such a chokehold on you."

I screw up my face. "A chokehold?"

Has Essie's painting had a chokehold on me? Maybe.

To be honest, I've practically lived, eaten, and breathed Essie's life story since the day Gram gave me her painting. And the stuff that has been happening to me since that day all link back to it. Back to her.

"You can finish your essays and then . . . you know . . . finally take a breather. Focus on other things." Noah reaches out and rubs my shoulder again. "Don't you want that? Don't you want to move on?"

I don't know. If I don't have Essie and the mystery around her painting, what do I have?

The beast, which is being held at bay for now only because of my Xanax prescription, which will run out eventually.

Finding a new job or hustling as a freelancer so I can pay rent and my bills.

My fractured relationship with Dad.

Coming to terms with what might have really happened the day of Mom's car crash, the day that changed my life, and what it says about who my mother really was and her struggles.

Nothing on that list sounds appealing, but I can't avoid them forever.

"Go ahead and call, Shanice. Get it done." Noah kisses my cheek. "Dinner will be here waiting for you. Don't worry."

I groan. "Okay, fine!"

I grab my phone, the number that I wrote down, and dial it before sitting down on the sofa and pulling out my notepad.

"Hello," a woman answers, "Hanson Whitmore's office."

"Uh, hi. I'm Shanice Pierce. I'm a writer. My editor told me that—"

"Mr. Whitmore doesn't do interviews. I'll have to redirect you to the Foundation's Communications team."

She sounds curt and disinterested, pretty much what I would expect the assistant of a very rich man to sound like.

"I'm not asking for an interview. I wrote an essay for *The Miscreant* and I was told that Mr. Whitmore wanted to speak with me about it."

"Oh! Oh, yes, Miss Pierce. I am so, so sorry. Mr. Whitmore has been waiting for your call. I'll get him on the line right away."

I blink in surprise, shocked that she recognized my name or that this guy has been waiting for me to call him back. Within seconds, I hear a click.

"Shanice Pierce," a deep voice rumbles on the other end. "The author extraordinaire! Thanks for calling me. This is Hanson Whitmore."

"Hello, Mr. Whitmore, I—"

"Please, just call me Hanson."

"Sure . . . Hanson." I restlessly tap my pen on my notepad. "My editor, Priya, told me that I should call you. She said you had some issues with my essay."

"Issues? No, to the contrary, I thought your piece was wonderful. It was insightful and very well researched."

"Uh, really?" I ask, taken aback.

"Yes, I appreciated your honest portrayal of Maude. She was very forward thinking for her time in some ways, but less so in others. Chase told me there are more pieces to come. I just wondered if you would allow me the opportunity to provide more insight into Maude and her relationship with her artists which you so *vividly* portrayed in your work." He laughs. "Maybe it could help with your research."

I frown. This isn't at all what I expected. He isn't pissed?

"My great-aunt had a strong philanthropic bent, but she was very . . . eccentric, shall we say?" Hanson goes on. "That eccentricity brought a diverse group of people within her orbit. My father used to say that ol' Maude would give her money to every artist and crystal-wielding spiritualist on the island of Manhattan, if she could."

"And The Bridge of Light?" I blurt out. "She and Dr. Bachmann founded it. I'm sure she invested money in it as well."

"That *is* a titillating aspect of her story, is it not?" He laughs again. "Yes, my great-aunt was involved in The Bridge of Light. She was definitely a believer in the occult. But many were at that time. I wouldn't hold it against her."

"Oh, I don't, but I heard that it may have even been connected to her murder."

"Yes." He pauses. "That's *one* theory, but there are others. One of which involves your painter Estelle Johnson."

I sigh. "Yes, I've heard the rumor."

"It's not a rumor. I could show you a copy of the police report where she's mentioned along with all the incriminating details. I keep it in our family collection in the Hamptons. We practically have a museum worth of art there as well, including works by Johnson. Some of the pieces will head to the MoMA later this year where they're dedicating a wing to Great-Aunt Maude. You know what? I have a brilliant idea! Why don't you come to the Hamptons and see all of this yourself?"

I halt mid–pen stroke. "I'm sorry, what?"

"It works perfectly! My wife, daughter, and I are headed there this weekend. We'd love for you to join us."

Once again, I'm struck speechless. I had no idea he would offer such a thing.

"I'd pay for your transportation round-trip, if that's an issue," Hanson continues, noticing my hesitancy. "And you could stay on the estate. We have plenty of rooms to choose from."

I gnaw the inside of my cheek as I consider his offer.

Hanson has a copy of the police report. Maybe this is the final thing I need to finish my essays, to explain why Essie walked away from her art career and left New York. Maybe she was fleeing a murder scene. But I can't imagine going all the way to the Hamptons *alone* to hang out with the Whitmores. I look up at Noah, who's pouring himself a glass of white wine.

"Umm, can I bring a guest with me?" I ask Hanson.

"Of course! The more the merrier."

A couple of minutes later, I hang up and walk back into the kitchen. "How'd it go?" Noah asks.

"Okay, I think."

"Just okay? That was a long conversation for just '*okay.*'" Noah pours me a glass of wine and hands it to me.

"Thanks. Actually, it went better than okay. I got an offer for a free trip to his estate in the Hamptons to learn more about Bachmann and Essie, and he said I can bring a guest if I want." I take a sip from my wine glass. "Would you come with me?"

I hope Noah says yes. I hope the idea doesn't sound even crazier to him than it does to me.

He seems to consider my question for a bit then shrugs. "A free trip to the Hamptons?" he drawls. His smile is back. "Why not?"

CHAPTER 43

THERE WAS A BIG STORM TRAVELING UP THE EASTERN SEABOARD, SO our flight was delayed. For almost two hours, Noah and I have been parked in two of the blue chairs near our terminal gate. He's eating a toasted bagel with his arm draped around me while I lean my head against his shoulder and flip through my phone, perusing my newsfeed.

"Flight 1638 to LaGuardia will begin boarding in twenty minutes," the flight attendant smiles into her microphone. Her voice reverberates over the overhead speaker. A chorus of "It's about time!" and "Thank you, God!" erupts around us. "Customers who need assistance boarding, military personnel, and those with small children and car seats or strollers are asked to come to the flight attendant desk. Thank you."

"There you go. We're out of here," Noah says beside me.

I nod just as my phone buzzes. A text message pops up on my screen.

So it takes a trip out of town for you to talk to me?

It's Gram. I sent her a text yesterday telling her that I was flying to the Hamptons and would be back Sunday evening. She finally responded.

"I'm going to the men's room," Noah says, rising from his chair. "Don't worry. I'll make it back before we board."

"Okay," I murmur distractedly as I type my message to Gram. Out of the corner of my eye, I see Noah sit his carry-on in his chair and walk out of the waiting area.

I would've texted you sooner, I start to type back, but . . .

I stop typing.

I was going to make up an excuse for why I haven't reached out to Gram since that night she told me Mom's secret, since she shared what she thinks really happened that day of the accident. But she'll know I'm lying. So, instead, I dial her number. She picks up on the second ring.

"Hey, Gram. I should have called you sooner. I know. But I didn't know what to say to you after you dropped those bombs on me a couple of weeks ago," I blurt out. "It's just been knocking around in my head. It was . . . a lot."

"You told me to tell you the truth, chile. I was just doing what you asked. I even said I didn't want to do it and now you're blaming ol' Gram for everything."

"I told you to tell me the truth about *Dad*. I was not prepared for what you said about Mom, Gram. You never breathed a word of any of this for years and then you dumped all of it on me in *one night*. You told me Mom tried to kill me and herself in a car crash. Do you realize what that did to me?"

She goes silent. After a few seconds, she loudly sighs on the other end, filling the phone with static. "You're right," she murmurs. "I shouldn't have done that."

I stare down at my cell phone, wondering if there was some glitch in my service again. Did Gram actually admit she was wrong? This is a first.

"I thought I was going to take that to my grave. Maybe I should've. I was so angry at your father for what he did to you and I ended up doing something probably just as bad. But I meant it when I said it: *no one* will ever know for sure if that's what really happened that day," she goes on. "The only person who knows that is your mama, and she can't speak for herself. I shouldn't have tried to speak for her. But your mama loved you, Shanice. With all her heart. She told you herself. She told me all the time the dreams she had for you. How she wanted the best for you. That part ain't up for debate."

She clears her throat. "When I got word that your mama was dead, I cursed God for taking her away from me. I was even angry at your mama for not calling me that morning, not talking to me and telling me whatever might have been going on in her head. When I found out that you were hurt but you were going to survive, I switched from cursing to thanking God for sparing you. At least I had you left. And I couldn't focus on mourning her, even though I felt like I'd been ripped into a thousand pieces, because I knew that you would be mourning her too. Your mama would want me to be strong for you, stronger than I'd been for her. I had to be there for you so that what happened to her . . . how much she suffered on the inside . . . could never happen again."

"You were scared I might go 'crazy' like you think Mom did?" I ask softly.

So Gram doesn't think my anxiety disorder is all in my head and I just needed a long walk and "fresh air."

"I didn't know what would happen, Shanice. I just knew, no matter what, I'd be there if you needed me."

My sight blurs and I sniff. I lower my gaze to my lap.

"I love you, Shanice. I may not always say it, but I do. You know that, don't you?"

A solitary tear spills onto my cheek. "Yes, I know. And I love you too, Gram."

"Now you stop that cryin'."

"I'm not crying," I insist as I quickly wipe away my tear with my free hand and sniff again.

"Yes, you are. I can hear it in your voice over the phone," she says, making me laugh. "Have a good trip, and text me when you get home. I'm heading out myself. Going to Atlantic City with a couple of the ladies from the senior center for the weekend. And you better come back here next week and help me finish straightening up this house. We're at the finish line."

"I will, Gram. Enjoy Atlantic City. Don't gamble too much."

"You know me. The first sign of bad luck, I'm leavin' the craps table."

I laugh again.

"Bye, chile. Take care of yourself."

"Bye, Gram. I love you," I say before hanging up.

I wipe my nose with a napkin and look up to see that other passengers are forming a line already. I start to gather my things just as my phone buzzes again. Did Gram send another text?

I glance down at my screen and see the text is from Tati this time.

First weekend I'm off in more than three weeks, her text says. Want to meet up tonight for a margaritas, nachos, and a romcom?

I can't, I type back. Just about to board a plane for a trip to the Hamptons this weekend.

She sends a wide-eyed emoji. You're going TO THE HAMPTONS and didn't ask me to be your plus one?

I would've, I type. But I already have a plus one.

Within seconds, my phone starts ringing. It's Tati. I press the green button on screen to answer and immediately hear, "Who are you going to Hamptons with? Is it a guy?"

"Yes, it's a guy. His name is Noah. We're dating."

"What?" she squeals. "*When?* Why have you been holding out on me? Talk about a good rebound from a bad breakup. You meet a guy this quickly who wants to fly you to the Hamptons? Teach me your ways, sis!"

I laugh. Tati's playfulness is the perfect balm to the conversation I just had with Gram. My tears are replaced with a grin.

"He's not flying me to the Hamptons. I'm going there to learn more about the painting I told you about weeks ago. Noah agreed to go with me."

"So tell me more about Noah. What exactly does this fine brotha look like? What does he do?"

"Well, first off, he's not a brotha. But yes, he's very cute. He's a labor economist and he grew up in Texas like you."

"Really? Where 'bouts?"

I shrug. "I think near Galveston. Not exactly sure where. I know he went to Baylor though. He played for their soccer team."

"Oh, cool! My cousin went there. He's a die-hard Baylor Bear."

Noah walks up and tosses what's left of his breakfast into a nearby trash can. He throws the strap of his carry-on over his shoulder and grabs my suitcase. "Long line at the men's room. Sorry. But it looks like I made it back in just enough time." He leans his head toward the terminal gate. "I think they're boarding first class. We should head over there."

I nod and climb to my feet.

"Look, Tati, we're about to board, so I should go, but I'll try to set something up when we get back so you can meet him."

"Okay! Sounds like a plan," she says as Noah and I get in the line leading to the flight attendant desk. "Maybe we can watch a Baylor game together one day. Have a great trip and take pics."

"I will. Bye, Tati," I say before I hang up.

"Who was that?" Noah asks.

"My bestie, Tati. I was telling her that I was heading out of town with the hot new guy I'm dating," I say, nudging his elbow.

He laughs, leans down, and gives me a quick kiss.

"She was asking for details about you." We reach the front of the line. "You got instant approval when I told her you were from Texas too. That you and her cousin went to the same college."

"He went to Texas Tech?" he says as he hands his ticket to the flight attendant to scan.

I frown. "No," I say slowly, "he went to Baylor—like you did."

Noah casually shakes his head. "No, I didn't. I went to Texas Tech. I told you that."

I stare at him, confused.

"Ma'am," the flight attendant says. She glances down at my phone that hangs limply in my hand. "Would you like to scan your ticket?"

I nod and swipe the phone screen over the red beam and hear a loud beep. "Have a good flight," the attendant says with a smile.

As we walk down the jet bridge, I try to remember why I thought Noah went to Baylor University.

Our first date. That's when he said it, or at least I thought he did.

I gaze at Noah's back as we walk toward the plane. He's carrying his suitcase on his shoulder and dragging my rolling suitcase behind him. His stride is long and assured. His body language is relaxed. He doesn't seem like a guy who has anything to hide. He glances over his shoulder and gives me a reassuring wink.

We quickly find our seats in business class, and Noah puts our carry-on cases in the stowaway bin overhead. I sit down at the open window and he settles into the aisle seat beside me. I observe the baggage carriers in orange vests as they load luggage onto the plane while I try to slow down my racing thoughts.

Inhale, exhale.

Inhale, exhale.

"Anxious about flying?" Noah asks. "I notice you're doing your deep breathing."

I turn to him and nod. "A . . . a little," I say, and it's partially true.

"You'll be fine." He grabs my hand and squeezes it. "Don't worry, I'm here with you. The flight will be over faster than you think."

"Thanks for doing this, for traveling with me." I lean my head on his shoulder. "Maybe we can do it more in the future."

"That would be nice," he says, resting his head on top of mine.

I can feel the whiskers of his cheek on my forehead. I inhale his cologne and squeeze his hand too.

The airplane door slams shut and Noah and I put on our seat-belts. Soon, the male flight attendant begins to do our flight safety presentation, gesturing to the exit rows. I sink back into my chair, trying my best to stay relaxed, and tell myself yet again that I was mistaken about what Noah told me on our first date about where he went to school. I had to be. Because if not, the question would then be, why did Noah lie to me?

PART IV

CHAPTER 44
ESSIE

NEW YORK CITY
December 10, 1927

Essie sat at the table, staring listlessly into her teacup. Around her was a chorus of voices, the sound of silver clinking against porcelain, of diners eating and drinking. But Essie had no appetite. She could only nibble at the fluffy honey biscuits that the waitress had placed on her table in front of her while she waited for her guest. It looked like Louise was running late.

I should've met her at the train station, Essie muttered to herself.

But her friend had insisted in her last telegram that she wanted to freshen up at her hotel first after arriving in New York. She said that she would meet Essie for lunch instead at the Marguerite Tea Room, where they'd eaten the last time Louise had been in town, where Essie was a regular patron.

But what if Louise's train was delayed? What if she wasn't coming?

She has to come, Essie thought desperately.

Essie reached underneath the table and slowly rubbed her thumb over the rabbit's foot dangling from a chain looped around her wrist. She'd bought it from a street vendor two weeks ago for two pennies. She kept it with her at all times now—a replacement for the medicine bag Doris had given to her for protection that she'd stupidly handed over to Godmother.

"And this will keep away bad luck?" she'd asked the vendor. "Can it take care of curses too?"

Even the deadly kind, she'd wanted to add, but didn't.

He'd eagerly nodded and grinned, revealing missing and rotted teeth. "Oh, yeah! The evil eye. Any kinda' root or hoodoo anybody put on you. You ain't gotta worry about nothin'."

She didn't know if she believed the man, but she didn't feel like she had much of a choice. Not after what she'd seen at Godmother's Park Avenue apartment that night.

"There you are! You had me worried," Elias had said when she woke up in his bed the next morning with no recollection of how she'd gotten there. "I was wondering when you'd wake up. You were knocked out cold."

She'd woozily sat upright and looked around her, shoving off the wet rag he'd placed on her aching brow.

"I guess you'd gotten plastered," he'd explained, gesturing to the gin bottle sitting on one of his night tables, "wandered into the servants' tunnel, got lost in the dark, and lost your marbles. You must have hit your head. You've got a sizable strawberry growing there."

He'd raised his hand to touch her forehead, but she'd reared back from him like he'd struck her.

"What's wrong, Essie?"

"I saw you," she'd hissed, shaking all over.

"What?"

"I saw you!" she'd screamed, making him hold a finger to his lips to quiet her. "I saw w-w-what you did. You stabbed him! You stabbed him with all those people in the room, and n-n-none of them did anything. They just stood by and . . . and let you kill him! You killed your own father."

Elias had squinted and gradually shook his head. "I have no idea what you're talking about. You must have been very drunk."

"No, I *saw* you!"

"Essie, my father died in his sleep. That's why I left. That's why Lily came to get me. To sit with him and Mother. They didn't want me to miss the chance to say goodbye."

"N-n-no, you stabbed him! All of you were . . . were chanting. Godmother. Lily. Agatha. I saw it with my own eyes!"

He'd stared at her for a long time after that before sadly shaking his head. "It was a nightmare, luv. The worst kind, it sounds like. But I swear to you, it didn't happen. You have to know I would never do something like that."

She'd examined his face. The blood splatter was gone. It was no longer on his shirt either. She'd stared at his hand. He wasn't wearing the ring with the red stone anymore.

Had it all been a vivid nightmare fueled by gin, marijuana, and a haunting, dark tunnel? Had her imagination run wild in there?

And yet, three weeks later, Essie couldn't let those macabre images go. She still saw them in her dreams. She caught flashes of them as she painted, of the mustached man shouting as he raised Herr Bachmann's ring toward the ceiling, of Elias plunging the dagger into Herr Bachmann's chest over and over again. Every time, she'd throw down her paintbrush, repulsed by the images her hands were trying to create.

She saw them even now and had to force the visions to retreat as she stared into her teacup. She looked up and shifted her gaze to the tea room's entrance as several well-dressed women strolled out of the reception area. She finally spotted Louise's face and nearly burst into tears. She shot to her feet.

"Louise!" she shouted, waving frantically to get her attention.

Her friend turned to her, smiled, and waved.

Louise had put on a little weight since Essie had last seen her. For Essie, looking at her friend was like looking at a plumper, cheerier version of herself. They looked so much alike that they'd even been able to fool Aunt Idalene when they were younger, and that woman had practically raised Essie. They'd done it simply by switching dresses and wearing their hair a certain way. Aunt Idalene had wanted to whip their hides when she figured out the farce.

Louise now embraced Essie, rocking back and forth and laughing as she did it. Essie sank with relief into her best friend's arms now that she was finally here.

"Oh, honey, how I missed you," Louise gushed then stepped back. "Aren't you gussied up all smart like a high-class Park Avenue lady! And I love that hair. Would you look at them pearls?" she said, fingering the pearls at Essie's throat. "Doesn't my Essie look so lovely?"

Essie pursed her lips. She didn't look "lovely." She looked exhausted. She knew there were bags under eyes.

"I'm so glad you're here," Essie whispered, her voice trembling with emotion.

Louise sat down at their table in one of the tea room's rattan chairs. Essie took the chair facing her, not letting her friend's hand go, clinging to it like it was her last lifeline.

"I didn't know if I could make it. Chile, I had to do some fast talking with that new bossman of mine to get here. I told him my mama was at death's door and I had to go home to be with her. I thought the Lord was going to strike me dead for telling that lie. He still might," she said with a laugh and then went somber. "But I knew from your letters that you needed me. I knew I had to get here. It sounds like you've been going through something bad, Essie. Real bad."

"I'm scared, Louise. Godmother . . . her family . . . her friends . . ." Essie's voice drifted off.

"What happened?" Louise leaned over the table, now frowning. "It was going so well for so long. You seemed so excited. What changed?"

"Miss Johnson, I see your guest has arrived," their hostess exclaimed, making Essie jump in her chair and drop Louise's hand. The young woman poured Louise a cup of coffee. "Can I get you ladies anything to eat? We serve the best chicken and waffles in all of Harlem!"

"She hasn't had a chance to read the menu yet, Bertha," Essie said.

"Ah! Well, I'll let her do that and be right back. Let me know if you need anything else." She then walked off.

Essie turned back to Louise. "The Bachmanns . . . I saw what they did, and I can't forget it," she continued in a rasping whisper. "I'll never look at them the same way again."

"What did they do?"

In halting words, Essie recounted her story of what happened that night, from the moment she arrived at Godmother's home on Elias's arm to waking up in bed with Elias hovering over her. All the while, she watched as her friend's facial expression changed from surprise, to fear, and finally, to confusion.

"So, was it a dream like he said?" Louise asked.

"No!" She paused. "Well, I don't think so."

"But do you know for sure, Essie? You said you had that dream before you even went looking for him. Maybe you were sleepwalking."

"But I've never sleepwalked before."

"You're right," Louise conceded. "You're right, but you said that you had a whole lot to drink and smoke that night. I bet I'd see Jesus himself with all that corn liquor."

"Then why did it feel so real? Why am I still seeing it in my head?" Essie lamented, near tears. "And it's not just that. I started to remember other times. Other things that I witnessed at Godmother's home. The night months ago when I saw those people holding hands around candles. They were holding a séance, Louise. They were talking to the dead. The suns and serpents that are all over her penthouse. Those symbols were in the room that night when Elias killed his father. And then there was that night that I felt someone . . . someone watching me as I slept. Sometimes I feel like they're still watching me through my studio window. What if they're following me even now?"

As she said those words, she glanced over her shoulder and looked around the restaurant, the familiar sensation of watchful, unseen eyes returning to her.

Essie's frown deepened. "Honey, I don't think anyone's following you," she said, making Essie whip back around to glare at her. "That woman's Park Avenue friends would stand out like a sore thumb in this Negro restaurant. They'd stand out like sore thumbs just walkin' around 125th Street!"

"You think I'm lying? You think I'm making this all up?"

She was sweating now. She was starting to feel dizzy.

"No, I don't . . . I don't think you're lying. I think you really do believe it all happened, but . . ."

"But what?"

"Essie, I know what life has been like for you up here in Harlem. The parties. The drinking. Out until the wee hours of the morning. I ain't judging you for it. Sometimes, I read your letters and I wish I was having all the fun you do, but I know that kinda fun can mess with your head after a while. Maybe you just . . . just need some rest."

"Rest?"

"To clear your mind. Even if it means leaving Harlem for a while. Even if it means leaving that Godmother of yours. Because you gotta admit this all sounds . . . well . . ." Louise's words drifted off again.

Crazy, her friend wanted to say but wouldn't finish. Essie sounded crazy, like she was headed to the looney bin.

Essie closed her eyes, overcome with a wave of nausea.

"I'm sorry," Essie said, pushing herself away from the table, "but I have to excuse myself."

"Essie," Louise called after her. "What's wrong?"

Essie didn't answer her. Instead, she walked away, easing through the groups mingling in the reception area, hoping she made it outside before her stomach got the better of her.

"Essie!" Louise shouted again, following her friend through the tea room's glass doors to the busy sidewalk.

Essie made it to the street and beelined to an alleyway before she vomited, retching up the coffee and her breakfast. She leaned over and braced her hands against the brick wall as she did it, inhaling the smell of wet tar and garbage.

"Oh, Essie," Louise said, holding out a handkerchief to her when she finished. "I hate to see you like this. All this nonsense has you so upset that you can't even keep your food down."

Essie accepted Louise's handkerchief. She wiped her mouth as she stepped away from the wall and turned to face her friend. "That's not the reason why I'm sick. That's the other thing I had to tell you that I didn't want to put in a letter."

"What do you mean?"

Essie took a deep breath. Why was it harder to say this part than it had been to tell the gory tale of Herr Bachmann's demise? Probably because she felt like this part was all her fault. She should've known better, been wiser. She couldn't blame Godmother for this one.

Essie looked up to see if anyone was standing nearby, listening to them; Louise was sure that Essie wasn't being watched or followed, but she wasn't as convinced.

"I haven't . . . I haven't gotten my monthlies in weeks," she confessed to Louise. "And this is the third time I've thrown up in two days."

"Oh, Essie. Honey, that's not good."

"Don't you think I know that?" Essie said, unable to hold back the tears any longer. She sniffed. "The only man I've been with these past months is Elias, and—"

"So, get him to take care of it for you," Louise said, grabbing her hand. "He has money. I'm sure he can find a doctor to get rid of it."

Essie furiously shook her head. "I can't ask Elias for help with this."

"Why on earth not?"

"I told you what I saw him do!"

How could she possibly confide in him or trust him after that?

"Essie, do you wanna go to some butcher that could make you bleed to death? Are you gonna throw yourself down the stairs, or drink some nasty tea and just hope for the best?" She squeezed Essie's hand. "I know what you think you saw, and how it scared you but don't let it make you do somethin' you're gonna regret later. You got caught up. I did too with that son-of-a-bitch husband of mine. I knew I'd rather die than have his baby. You don't want this baby either. Do what needs to be done. And if you don't want anything to do with Elias or his mama after it's all over, that's fine. Walk away. Like I said, leave Harlem. You can come stay with me in Philly. Or you and me can find a new place to settle. Doesn't make a difference to me. You know I never stay still long enough in any place to let grass grow under my feet. I was thinkin' about movin' to Washington, D.C., next. See where the president lives."

Essie grimaced. What would she do in Philly or Washington? Harlem was her adopted home. New York City was the place of endless possibilities.

Some good, some bad, she now realized.

Nevertheless, she didn't want to leave it.

"Or stay here," Louise said, reading her mind. "But don't try to do this on your own, Essie. It's hard to be some fancy Park Avenue lady toting around a baby on your hip."

Essie considered her friend's words. She wiped her tears. "I'll ask some of my artist friends if they know anybody who can do it," she said, though she didn't know if her pride would allow her to ask. She felt so foolish.

"Then make Elias pay for it. That's the least he can do. The doctors . . . the *good* ones that do this type of thing ain't cheap." She then turned and looked back toward the tea room. "Let's head back inside. At least pay for the tea and coffee so they don't think we ran out on the bill."

Essie gradually nodded.

As they walked back to the Marguerite, Essie ran her thumb over the rabbit's foot in her pocket over and over again, praying that it would protect her, hoping it could help disentangle her from the spiderweb she now found herself caught in.

CHAPTER 45
SHANICE

EAST HAMPTON, NEW YORK
Present day

NOAH SHIFTS IN THE PADDED LEATHER SEAT BESIDE ME, STARING OUT the sedan's tinted rear window at the rolling hills of the vineyards, absently tapping his fingers on the armrest and nodding his head to the beat of whatever music is playing in his earbuds.

I never knew that the Hamptons had so many vineyards. I'd heard about the mansions, rich people, and the beaches, but not this. The vineyards seem to stretch on for acres and acres, maybe even a few miles.

The driver makes a right and we pass a barn with some of the slats painted an achingly bright white. Sunflowers sit in oversized pots near the door along with a sign that advertises fresh strawberries. It's all so picturesque, like a movie set.

I glance down at my phone. According to the GPS, we'll be passing into the next hamlet soon and then we'll arrive in Montauk and, after that, the Whitmore estate.

I've already traveled more than three hundred miles to meet the relatives of Maude Bachmann in the hope of getting the answers I need to finish my essay series about Essie. I should be thinking about what to look for in the police report on Maude's murder that Whitmore mentioned, what to ask him about The Bridge of Light, but I'm finding it hard to focus thanks to Noah. And it isn't because he's manspreading and taking up most of the backseat, which he is.

I nudge his knee with my own and he shifts over.

"Sorry," he murmurs.

Even though I've told myself to ignore it, to push it to the back of my mind, I can't help thinking about Baylor University. Did he say he went to Baylor? And if he lied about that, what else is he lying about?

I think back to that time in my kitchen when I mentioned his ex's name and he just stared at me blankly, like he had no idea who or what I was talking about. I excused it as him being angry or distracted at the time, but maybe he wasn't.

What else is Noah hiding from me?

I wanted some sign, *something* to show me that I'm just being paranoid and reading this all wrong. After we'd landed at LaGuardia and I'd excused myself to freshen up in the ladies' room and pop a Xanax, the first thing my eyes had landed on when I'd pushed open the bathroom door was a cracked mirror.

Serves me right.

I got exactly what I asked for. It certainly was a sign—just not a good one.

I look at Noah again now. He turns to me and smiles. I smile back.

Maybe I misunderstood him or misheard him. He could have said Texas Tech or maybe he went to Baylor for a year or two and graduated from Texas Tech, and now I'm making unfounded accusations.

Damnit, I'm going in circles.

Essie felt this way as well, but it was a lot worse for her. In one of the letters she sent to Great-Great-Grandma Louise—one of the last before she left New York—she begged her for help. She told Louise that she needed her, that she couldn't trust her own mind anymore. She claimed to have seen something disturbing at Maude's Park Avenue home, or at least she *thought* she saw it, though she couldn't be sure. It was so bad that even Essie refused to recount the details in the letter. She said she would tell Louise when she saw her in person.

I wonder what she saw—or what she thought she saw.

"Hey," Noah says. He reaches across the seat and grabs my hand. "Did you hear me?"

I shake my head. "No, I was daydreaming. Sorry."

"I asked, 'How are you feeling?' You've been quiet. You've been that way since we boarded the plane back in D.C."

"I just . . . I've just been thinking about Gram," I lie. "She's headed out of town too this weekend, but we talked before the flight. We talked about my mom . . . about us. It was a hard conversation. I'm glad we had it though . . . for the sake of closure."

"I'm glad you guys talked. Closure is always good," he says, bringing my palm to his lips and kissing it. "And hopefully while we're here, you can get some closure about that painting of yours."

"Hopefully," I mutter, gently pulling my hand out of his grasp.

Less than thirty minutes later, we arrive at the Whitmore estate.

I don't know what I expected. Maybe some huge mansion with a big portico and columns, or a brick castle with turrets and stained glass windows like the ones I'd seen years ago in the Hudson Valley. I'd imagined a long, black asphalt driveway in the front with imposing black, wrought iron gates leading to the property's interior. But it isn't that at all. The estate, with its expansive kelly green lawn, is jaw-dropping in a different way.

The Cape Cod–style house is charming though massive. I count ten dormers along its gabled roof and two dozen windows brimmed with overflowing flower boxes. As we slowly make our way up the gravel driveway and approach six-foot-tall white gates, pebbles crunch under the Mercedes's wheels. The gates slowly slide open and we drive inside, revealing another driveway, huge trees, and rosebushes.

The front door opens and a man walks out barefoot. He's wearing pink shorts and a white polo shirt with a pair of aviator sunglasses hooked into the collar. His skin is tan and weathered. His smile and body posture are relaxed and self-assured. I know from photos online that this is Hanson Whitmore.

Two women step out of the house behind him. One is tall with long dark hair that falls in waves around her shoulders. She looks breezy and casual in her sea green tank dress. Unlike Hanson, she's wearing shoes—ballet flats. Beside her is a much younger woman who looks to be in her early twenties. She's wearing a white T-shirt knotted at the waist and cutoff jean shorts that reveal long legs. Her blond hair is pulled back into a high ponytail. Even behind the oversized sunglasses perched on the tip of her nose, I can see she looks annoyed.

The car slows to a stop and Hanson strolls down the stone stairs and waves. Our driver climbs out of the Mercedes and opens my door. I step out first. Noah climbs out behind me.

"Welcome!" Hanson says. "Welcome to our home."

The woman with the dark hair grins. The blond continues to sulk while taking a sip from the glass of lemonade in her hand.

"Shanice, I presume," Hanson says, offering me his hand.

"You presume correctly," I reply, giving his large, warm hand a shake. "Nice to meet you."

His eyes shift to Noah. "And this is the guest you brought with you."

Noah nods. "Noah Kelly, pleased to meet you, sir."

Hanson shakes his hand too. "The pleasure is all mine."

The young woman lets out a snort and Hanson's smile tightens. He turns to the two women behind him. "This is my wife, Juliette, and our daughter, Skylar."

"Pleased to meet you both!" Juliette says.

Skylar gives a limp wave, leans against the doorframe, and drops her hand to her hip. She takes another drink from her glass.

I'm starting to suspect that there's more than lemonade in her glass. Maybe that's why she's acting so standoffish; there's a boozy clambake filled with other rich twenty-somethings someplace in Montauk where she'd rather be.

"Well." Hanson pauses to clap his hands. "Don't worry about getting your bags. We'll have them taken to your room. In the meantime, let us show you around the place. We want you to make yourselves comfortable. Unfortunately, because of travel delays, we had lunch without you. We tried to wait. But our chef can prepare something quick for you though if you're—"

"No, that's okay. We ate at the airport," I say.

I can still feel my overpriced tuna melt, chips, and bottled iced tea sloshing around in my stomach.

"Well, he has a wonderful dinner planned for us later. We'll eat at six," Hanson says. "In the meantime, you can freshen up or hop into the pool, if you'd like."

"Sounds good," Noah says before glancing down at me.

I nod in agreement. "It sounds great," I say, though as appealing as checking out our bedroom, sunning at the Whitmores' pool, and eating a four-star meal on their dime sounds, it isn't what I came here for.

"Don't worry, Shanice. I'm sure you're eager to see our artwork and our family library," Hanson says, reading my thoughts and giving me a wink. "You'll get the chance. But you're our guests, first and foremost. Relax and settle in. I promise you'll have as much time as you want with the research material."

"I'll hold you to that," I say, relieved to know that he really does want to help me finish my essays like he said. Hanson laughs.

"I know you will. I'm friends with a lot of journalists and you're the real deal. There will be more than enough to satisfy your curiosity. Trust me." He then leans his head toward the doorway. "Let's show you around."

CHAPTER 46

THE WHITMORES GIVE US THE GRAND TOUR. BESIDES THE SHEER SIZE of the house, there's nothing that screams over-the-top wealth. Lots of exposed beams, rustic wood, built-in shelving, and natural light. It actually feels welcoming here. I get why Hanson is so comfortable walking around barefoot. The house has a warmth and coziness I wasn't expecting to find in a place like this. But then I look at the paintings on the walls and remind myself they likely aren't reprints; they're originals that are probably worth six figures each. I bet the earthenware vase on the coffee table costs more than all the furniture in my apartment.

Between us strolling through the dining room and gazing at the sunroom's 270-degree views of the rocky beach and bay in the distance, we lose Skylar. I don't mind. It could be my imagination, but I swear she switched from sulking to glaring at me and Noah for most of the tour.

"And here is your room," Hanson announces as he opens a door and gestures inside one of the bedrooms.

Our luggage is already sitting at the foot of the king-size bed on top of an old-fashioned steamer trunk. The room is large and bright with pale green wallpaper and white bedding. The windows are open, creating a soft breeze that makes the linen curtains flutter. A vase filled with pink tea roses sits on the dresser.

"We'll let you unpack and freshen up. We'll be downstairs if you need us," Hanson says.

"See you at six," Juliette calls from over his shoulder.

They walk out, closing the door behind them.

"Nice," Noah says, before kicking off his shoes and flopping back onto the bed with a bounce. He closes his eyes and sinks into the mountain of pillows. "This bed feels amazing. Hotel quality. I swear."

I walk toward one of the windows. It faces the backyard that's divided by a large hedge. On one side, I can see an English garden with wooden benches and an ivy-covered arbor. On the other side is the Whitmores' swimming pool.

Skylar is lying on one of the deck chairs by the crystal blue water. She's put her ponytail into a topknot and is wearing a black string bikini. I watch as she takes off her sunglasses, tosses them onto the chair, and dives into the water.

"So, what do you think about the Whitmores?" I ask as I turn around to face Noah.

Noah pops open his eyes, shifts to sit up on his elbows, and leans back on the pillows to look at me. "They're fine. They seem to be going out of their way to be good hosts. Why?"

"Hanson and Juliette are, but not Skylar. I wonder what's up with her."

He frowns. "What do you mean?"

"You didn't notice how standoffish she was?"

He shrugs. "Yeah, but she's probably just some spoiled rich kid. I wouldn't take it seriously." Noah pats a spot on the comforter beside him. "Come here. Lie down with me."

I stroll back to the bed and flop beside him. Noah reaches out and pulls me close. Close enough so that I can count the pale freckles dusting his nose. His body heat warms my bare legs and belly where my shirt has ridden up.

"Don't worry about her," Noah says as he drapes an arm around me. "Focus on why you're here: to get what you need for your essays so you can finish writing them and move on and get your name out there in the literary world! Okay?"

I sigh and grudgingly nod.

"*Okay?*" he repeats. "I want to hear it." He gives me a series of quick pecks on my cheeks, nose, and neck.

"Okay!" I squeal as I laugh.

Noah kisses me again and I can feel anxiety loosen its hold. He turns onto his back and takes me with him. He snakes his hand up the back of my shirt and starts fiddling with my bra clasp.

This moment feels surreal, to be on an all-expenses-paid trip in the Hamptons, feeling the delicious anticipation of Noah's body on mine.

But he lied.

That nagging thought won't go away, no matter how much I want it to.

"What?" Noah asks, when I wrench my mouth away from his and tug his hand from under my shirt.

"Nothing," I say against his lips. "I just wonder if we should . . . you know . . . have sex in a stranger's guest room within thirty minutes of arriving. What if they hear us?"

"*And?*" he whispers hotly against the skin of my neck, giving me goosebumps. Noah then nibbles my earlobe. "What if they do?"

My eyes flutter close and my breathing deepens.

When Noah snakes his hand up my shirt again, I don't tug it away. When he kisses me, I kiss him back just as fervently, threading my fingers through his hair, pulling him closer. He undresses me and I undress him too. I fall under the spell of the kisses, the musk of his cologne, and his warmth.

I vaguely hear voices in the garden below. The splashing of water in the pool. If we can hear them, they can hear us. Once again, I suspect we're getting too loud. I try to keep the noise down, but with little success.

"Just give it up, babe," Noah says with an impish grin before tugging away the pillow I've been biting and tossing it to the floor. He then kisses me again.

We fall back on the bed minutes later, sweaty and spent. My heart is pounding. My arms and legs feel like they're made of jelly but I'm smiling. Noah spoons me and I stare at the fluttering curtains until my eyelids grow heavy. His chin rests on my shoulder as I fall asleep.

When I wake up, it's to the sound of raised voices.

"Where do you think you're going?" I hear Hanson ask. It's coming through the guest bedroom window.

"Out," a female voice snaps back. I dazedly realize its Skylar's. "I'm meeting Amy and Charlotte."

"No," Hanson says tightly, "you will stay here and have dinner with our guests. You can meet your friends later."

Skylar laughs. "This is your thing, Dad. *Not mine*, and you can't force me to stay."

A car door slams as I sit up on my elbows.

"Skylar! Skylar Whitmore, you come back here!" he shouts, followed by the rev of the engine.

"Make me!" she shouts. Seconds later, I hear a car driving away.

"Spoiled rich kid strikes again," I mutter then yawn. I look to my left to see that Noah is no longer in bed beside me.

I glance at the closed bathroom door. Maybe he's in there.

"Noah?" I call out.

He doesn't answer. I guess he's not in there either.

I stretch and pick up my cell, which is sitting on one of the night tables. I read the time and see that it's almost five o'clock. I was asleep for more than two hours. There's also a text from Noah.

Didn't want to wake you. You seemed exhausted, he wrote with a winking emoji. I went exploring. I'll be back before six.

I sigh, throw back the bedsheets,.and stroll into the bathroom to take a shower before dinner with the Whitmores.

When I return twenty minutes later, I see that Noah still isn't back yet, but for the first time, I notice that his suitcase is sitting open on the steamer trunk.

My eyes flick to the closed bedroom door, then back to the suitcase. It's like it's taunting me.

Take a peek inside, the beast whispers. *If you're so goddamned worried about what he might be hiding from you, look in there for yourself.*

And find what? Boxer briefs and sports socks? It's not like he'd be keeping his birth certificate in there.

But for now, it's my only option. Noah may have cyberstalked me after we met, but I'll never get the chance to do the same to him.

Noah told me that he took down all his social media accounts as soon as he got his job offer from the Department of Labor, before he moved from Texas.

"I scrubbed everything," he told me one night over wine and pizza. "I didn't want to tweet something stupid and give Big Brother a reason to fire me."

It seemed valid. Jason did something similar before he got his security clearance and his promotion for his current job. But now I wonder if it was valid—or just a convenient excuse for why I can't find any reference to Noah on the internet and fact-check anything he's said.

I creep to the suitcase and start to dig around, pushing aside T-shirts and underwear. I find a can of deodorant. A pair of cargo shorts. I begin to reach inside the interior side pockets. I find a pack of razors and an open box of condoms when the door suddenly swings open. Noah stands in the doorway, frowning. "What are you doing?"

Shit, shit, shit! I yank my hand out of the pocket guiltily, shoot upright, and place a hand to my chest where my heart is racing.

Inhale, exhale.

Inhale, exhale.

"What were you looking for?" he asks, raising his brows.

"Uh . . . umm . . ." I stammer.

It's on the tip of my tongue to just say it. To tell him what I'm really doing. To ask him why he made up the story that he went to Baylor and is denying it.

"I won't think any less of you if you tell me the truth," I want to say. "Why would you lie about something so stupid as where you went to college? It's not like I would care."

I want to tell him that he can be honest with me, that if we're going to make this budding thing between us work, we have to be able to trust one another. I've had to unravel so many secrets. I don't need any more, especially from him.

But I'm not ready for that conversation today. Not here in the Hamptons at the Whitmores' home. Not when we're supposed to be having dinner with them in less than an hour.

I don't know where it will lead Noah and me. So, instead, I lie. I force a laugh.

At least now, when I look embarrassed, I'm not pretending.

"Sorry, I couldn't find my phone charger and I was . . . uhh . . . I was wondering if maybe you had one in your suitcase," I say, tightening my towel around me. "My battery is low."

He walks to one of the night tables and opens the top drawer. He grabs a cord and hands it to me. "Here you go."

"Thanks," I mumble before climbing to the balls of my feet and giving him a kiss on the cheek. "I'm going to plug this in and start getting dressed so we won't be late for dinner. Okay?"

"Okay," he says.

He says it in a way that I can't read. His voice has gone flat again. Noah grabs his cell and sits down on the edge of the bed.

"Did you have fun exploring?" I ask.

"Yeah, it was cool," he answers absently but doesn't elaborate. I open my mouth then close it, knowing whatever I blurt out will only make the situation worse. I plug my phone in his charger and open my suitcase to find clothes for tonight's dinner.

CHAPTER 47

"Ah! Right on time! You both are in for a treat," Hanson announces as we enter the dining room. He already has a glass of white wine in hand. "Our chef, Frederik, was a sous chef at the Balthazar in Manhattan before we scooped him up for ourselves. He started in pastries, if you can believe it," Hanson continues, pulling out a chair at the head of the table. "Studied at the Le Cordon Bleu in Paris. He makes a tarte tatin to die for. Doesn't he, Juliette?"

"The best I've had outside France," Juliette agrees, taking one of the chairs closest to him.

"Please, have a seat." Hanson gestures with his glass to the empty chairs on the other side of the table facing his wife.

Noah pulls out a chair for me and I sit. He takes the seat beside me as I look around the dining room.

Hanson pours each of us a glass of wine before returning the bottle to the chilled wine bucket beside the table. "Unfortunately, Skylar won't be joining us. She had plans this evening. She sends her apologies though."

I bet she does.

Frederik, the chef, arrives a few minutes later with the first course and the meal begins.

"This is a nice place you guys have here," Noah says, breaking the silence.

"Why, thank you," Juliette says. "It's been in Hanson's family for several generations."

"We've done updates and additions over time," Hanson adds, "but we've kept many of the original features from when it was built in 1915."

"The stone stairs at the entrance are the same. So is the garden. But we got rid of those god-awful symbols that were everywhere," Juliette says with a flutter of her fingertips. "They were over all of the bedroom doors. We covered it with paint and changed out the molding. I don't know why anyone hadn't done it before we did."

I frown. "What symbols?"

Juliette wrinkles her nose. "There were all these snakes and suns. It was the most bizarre thing I had ever seen in my life."

"My wife doesn't have an appreciation for unique art deco design," Hanson says dryly before taking another sip of wine. "I'd seen it for most of my life, so I was pretty much used to it."

"Well, I wasn't. The interior designer was thrilled when I told her to tear it all down."

"Excuse me, but did you say snakes and suns?" I ask.

She nods. "I know, right? It freaked me out."

"It was probably the insignia of The Bridge of Light, the cult that Maude Bachmann and her husband belonged to," I say. "Did she build the house?"

"Good observation and yes," Hanson says with a nod, "Maude and Klaus were the ones who had it built. This used to be all farmland a hundred or so years ago."

"Noah and I saw some of the vineyards in the car ride here," I say, making Hanson nod again as he wipes his mouth with a napkin.

"So, you have an idea of what it probably looked like back then. I'll give it to Maude, despite her eccentricities," he says with a laugh and lofty roll of the eyes, "she saw the potential and knew what a good investment this would be. She wanted it to be the family summer getaway from the city. This was around the time that real wealth started to move into the Hamptons. She was one of the firsts. The Bachmanns even had an entry in the Blue Book of the Hamptons, first edition. After her death and the death of her son, Elias, my great-grandmother Lillian retained the estate. It was then passed down the line in our family to me—much like your painting was to you."

The dining room falls silent again as the chef brings in the next course.

"So, Shanice," Hanson begins a few minutes later, "I've been meaning to ask you . . . is there a reason why your family held on to your painting for so long? Was it merely for sentimental value?"

I shrug and finish chewing. "You could say that. Gram said that her mother gave it to her. She wanted to continue the tradition and give it me to . . . you know . . . keep it in the family. They didn't know who Essie was or the painting's backstory. We definitely didn't think it was worth anything."

He lowers his fork from his mouth. "And how much do you think it's worth now?"

"A lot to some, I guess."

"And how much is 'a lot'?" he asks. "Have you had it appraised?"

"I got an offer for a half-million dollars," I say and Juliette's eyes go wide.

"*Really?*" she asks. "A *half-million* dollars?"

Even though I was shocked by Vivaldi's offer, I'm a little offended on Essie's behalf that Juliette thinks the price of a half mil is too high. Essie's portrait is worlds better than some of the paintings Juliette has hanging around this place that probably cost just as much.

"I'm not surprised," Hanson says. "It could even be worth more than that."

"I told him that it wasn't for sale though," I say.

"Just to that buyer or not at all?" Hanson asks, leaning back in his chair. "Are you really going to sit on a half-million dollars? Are you hoping it's going to appreciate more?"

I shift in my chair and don't answer him, because I don't know how to answer. I hadn't really thought about it.

"She doesn't know yet if she wants to sell it," Noah answers for me with a smile, grabbing my free hand. He squeezes it reassuringly.

"I can understand your hesitancy," Hanson says between chews, eating again. "It's a very rare and important work. It should be treated that way."

For the rest of the meal, the conversation switches to lighter topics. The nice weather. The new art gallery on Lake Drive that opened this summer. After we finish dinner, the Whitmores offer to have drinks in the garden but I beg off and tell them I'm too tired from all the traveling today. Despite my midday nap, I'm exhausted for some reason.

Noah looks disappointed but he nods in agreement. "Yeah, we should probably get to bed."

"We understand," Hanson says. "We'll see you in the morning."

"You don't have to do this," I say a few minutes later over my shoulder as Noah and I climb the stairs to our room.

"Don't have to do what?"

"You don't have to come upstairs with me if you aren't tired yet. Go ahead and have a drink with them."

"You sure?" he asks, rubbing my back.

I nod and give him a kiss. "Yeah, I'll be fine."

Noah gazes at me for a bit longer then nods again. "Okay, but I don't think I'll get a drink. I'll just grab my swim trunks and go for a night swim instead."

By the time I've brushed my teeth and changed into an oversized T-shirt for bed, I can hear jazz music playing outside my window. I walk toward it and pull back the curtain. Juliette is swaying in the garden to the music while Hanson reclines in an Adirondack chair. He's holding a snifter instead of a wineglass now. The tealights hanging on a nearby arbor twinkle against his glass. Juliette leans down and reaches out her hand to her husband. He takes it and she tugs him to his feet. Juliette links her arms around his neck. The couple starts to slow dance and share a tender kiss.

Meanwhile, on the other side of the hedge, Noah is doing laps alone in their pool. I see the moon reflecting off the water as he cuts through waves.

I should be down there with him. Like Hanson and Juliette, Noah and I could be basking in one another's company and kissing in the moonlight, but the beast won't let me—being the cantankerous bitch that it is. Even now it's whispering in my ear, "*He lied to you. He's probably been lying this whole time and you—*"

"Shut up," I tell it before I turn away from the window, pull back the sheets, and climb into bed.

My eyes land on the guest room door, where the Bridge of Light insignia must have once decorated the trim over the doorway, until Juliette got weirded out and had it all removed. But I can still see the symbol in my mind—the red-eyed, intertwined serpents and the flaming sun in gold. I wonder what else I'll learn tomorrow in the Whitmore family library about this house, about Maude and Essie.

Finally, to the sound of crooning saxophones and lapping water, I drift off to sleep.

CHAPTER 48

ESSIE

NEW YORK CITY

January 29, 1928

Essie heard the door creak open, then the soft thump and click of heels on the hardwood floor. Even lying on the bed with her eyes closed and her back turned, she knew who had entered the room. The sound of Godmother's cane and her footfalls had a distinct rhythm as she walked.

Click, click, thump. Click, click, thump. Click, click, thump.

It sent Essie's heart racing like she was a scared rabbit hidden in a burrow, catching the whiff of a predator approaching. She slowly opened her eyes, not seeing much. Then she had the same thought she always had when she once again woke up to find herself in this room, in this gilded cage.

I never should have told Elias, she thought. *I never should have told him about the baby.*

"I heard that you are not eating, Estelle. Is that correct?" Godmother's voice echoed in the dark in her clipped New England accent.

"I'm not hungry," Essie whispered.

"Ridiculous," Godmother proclaimed, drawing closer. She grunted as she placed all of her weight on her cane to lean down and turn on the Tiffany lamp at Essie's bedside.

Essie squinted at the bright light suddenly flooding the guest room, revealing the grand oak furniture, velvet curtains, and the mahogany bed.

She'd been locked in here for weeks, since that day she was supposed to see the doctor.

Essie had quietly asked around for someone who could give her an abortion, and the best she could find was a woman in Harlem who could do it for thirty-five dollars—money she didn't have. Money that none of her artist friends had either. She knew she couldn't ask Godmother without making up some excuse, and she couldn't very well provide her with a receipt after. So, she caved and called Elias and told him that she was pregnant, that there was no way she could possibly have this baby, and she knew he didn't want it either.

He'd agreed to make the arrangements himself. He knew a doctor, he'd told her. A private physician with the utmost discretion who had done him a similar "favor" in the past. They would meet this doctor friend in secret at a tenement on the Lower East Side where he conducted his work for the right price.

But when Essie had arrived and the old woman at the door had pointed her to the long staircase leading to the doctor's office, she'd known something was wrong. She'd felt it in her bones but had just dismissed it as nerves or guilt. She'd reached the top of the staircase, pushed open the door, and saw Elias with his eyes downcast. On the other side of the dingy room had been Godmother sitting in a chair with two large men behind her that Essie had never seen before.

"I'm sorry, Essie," Elias had blurted out. "I had to tell her! She already knew everything. She threatened to cut me off. To toss me out and—"

"Quiet!" Godmother had boomed, making Elias instantly fall silent, making Essie wince. She had never heard Godmother sound like that before. "If there is anyone who deserves an apology, it is me." Godmother had then grabbed her cane and slowly pushed herself to her feet. "I told you to come to me if you needed anything, Estelle. To confide in me. And you do *this*? I consider it quite a betrayal."

Essie had opened and closed her mouth, unable to form words. She'd begun to tremble. "H-h-how . . . how . . ."

"How did I know?" Godmother had asked, inclining her head. "I know everything that goes on in my home, my dear," she'd said, echoing Agatha's words from months earlier. She'd then turned to the two men. "Please escort Estelle downstairs to the car. Be gentle. Remember, she is with child."

Estelle had watched in wide-eyed terror as they stalked toward her. She'd tried to back away, to flee. She'd let out a solitary scream and turned to run toward the stairs. She'd made it halfway down the stairwell but she could see the old crone from earlier, waiting for her, blocking her exit and slamming the door shut. One of the men had grabbed Essie from behind, lifted her off her feet, and clamped a handkerchief over her mouth. She'd twisted and kicked but within seconds, she'd inhaled the chloroform and blacked out. When Essie had woken up hours later, it had been in this very room. She'd discovered they'd taken everything away from her before throwing her in here. Her clothes. Even her rabbit's foot—depriving her of what little luck she had left.

The first few days, Essie had spent throwing herself against the bedroom door, screaming to be let out. She would have tried the windows, but the shutters had been nailed closed. She'd tried to fight her way out, only to be restrained and injected with something that made her so lethargic, she could barely hold up her head. She gave up fighting and screaming and searched the walls instead for a path to the servants' tunnel, moving furniture and stealthily peeling back the wallpaper. She'd finally found a panel leading her there—only to also find it nailed shut, as if they knew she would search for it.

"You *must* eat, Estelle, especially a woman in your condition," Godmother now said.

That may be the case, but with the exception of bread and water, Essie refused to let one bite of food pass her lips that had been prepared in this house, no matter how bad the hunger pangs got.

It could be laced with something to make her drowsy again. She couldn't take that risk. She had to keep her wits about her if she ever stood a chance of leaving this place. But each day that passed that she didn't eat, she grew weaker and more tired.

She was starting to give up hope of ever getting out of here.

"I don't want to have to instruct the staff to force-feed you, Estelle," the old woman said. "But I will if I have to. Won't I, Agatha?"

Agatha nodded from the doorway. "You most certainly will, ma'am."

Essie glared at the two women. Agatha was smiling while Godmother's face remained stern.

Essie could feel tears prick her eyes. "I don't want your food. I don't want a damn thing from you! I just . . . I just want to go home. I want to go home! You can't keep me here!"

Godmother blinked, looking surprised. "And you will go home, my dear." She took another step toward her. "In due time, you will. You've obviously misunderstood your situation. We are not your jailers. We never have been. We are your caretakers. We would never let anything untoward happen to you."

"Nothing untoward? You've *locked me* in here! My family . . . my friends . . . they don't know where I am," she sobbed. "Why are you keeping me here?"

She was sure Louise didn't know she had been in the Park Avenue penthouse all this time. She supposed anyone who visited her apartment or studio and found them both empty would have to come to their own conclusions of what had happened to her. Would they even look for her? Or would they just assume she was another wayward artist who disappeared? Maybe the Bachmanns had disseminated some story to explain her absence. Maybe they said she'd turned into just another junkie like Doris and was now wandering the streets of New York, looking for her next fix.

Godmother walked farther across the room to the blank canvas sitting on an easel in the corner. "I noticed you haven't been painting," she said, changing the subject, choosing not to answer her question, "even though you've had plenty of time on your hands. Why is that, Estelle?" Godmother asked casually, turning back around to face her.

She seemed oblivious to the young woman's tears.

"I haven't felt very inspired," she murmured sarcastically.

Godmother tilted her head. "I hope your mood improves, Estelle." The old woman glanced again at the canvas before staring pointedly at Essie. "When I come back tomorrow evening, I not only want to hear that you've eaten, but I also want to see something on that canvas, my dear, or I will be very disappointed. And you don't want to disappoint Godmother, do you?" Essie felt a cold chill go down her spine at those words.

"Do you, Estelle?" Godmother repeated, her voice hardening.

Essie quickly shook her head.

Godmother walked back across the room toward her. She reached out, making Essie flinch, even as the old woman's cool, wrinkled hand gently cupped her cheek.

"I told you that you've been chosen for great things, my child."

Essie squeezed her lids shut, shutting out the manic gleam in the older woman's eyes, wanting more than anything for Godmother to just go away.

"*Great* things. You think you're only here because of Elias. Because he told me your secret about what you had planned, don't you? My son *did* tell me you wanted to get rid of your precious baby. But the truth is, I knew this baby was coming." She paused. "Well, I suspected it, anyway. The spirits told me to keep my eyes and ears open, and I listened. I knew you and Elias had been sneaking off with one another for a few months now. He'd been spending the night at your apartment quite frequently, according to one of your neighbors."

So, Godmother had someone watching her, like she'd thought.

"And don't forget, I see the lists of all your purchases," Godmother went on. "I know what you buy every month, and I saw you hadn't bought Kotex the third week of the month like you usually do. Or the week after that. Or that week after that. Again, I suspected but I didn't know for sure. Then the doctor reached out to me. My son's doctor 'friend' is *my* friend as well. That's how Elias knows him. I pay the bills, after all. I've had him take care of my son's unfortunate mistakes over the years. And when the doctor told me that my son had asked for his expertise yet again, I put all the pieces together. I knew my darling husband was sending me a sign.

"Klaus has ascended into the light, and now he is coming back to tell the rest of us what he's seen. He's coming back as *your* baby, made by the fruit of his own loins in the womb of a mother from the dark continent—the most primal of places before it was tainted by the modern world. He couldn't have planned it better!"

Essie opened her eyes and stared at Godmother as if the old woman had suddenly morphed into one of the grotesque shrunken heads Godmother kept in her gallery. She shivered with revulsion. So, *that's* why Godmother was keeping her here?

She'd thought Godmother was ashamed of what Essie and Elias had done and was trying to hide it, to punish her for her misstep. Instead, the older woman had deluded herself into believing Essie's baby was her resurrected husband.

"You're insane," Essie whispered.

"I couldn't let you go through with it," Godmother argued. "I couldn't let you kill my Klaus, Estelle."

Essie eased back from her, bumping into the headboard when she could go no farther. Her shaking was getting worse. "You're crazy! You're all crazy!" she screamed.

"No, I am quite sane, my dear." Godmother gave an impatient sigh. "I know how strange this all sounds. I know you don't understand. You don't understand the gift that you've been given. That you were chosen for. And because of that, you're frightened. But you shouldn't be. You were *meant* for this, Estelle. Estelle, the star. And what is the sun but a star itself? The sun and the two intertwined serpents. Light and knowledge. That is what represents us . . . The

Bridge of Light. It's what my husband and I founded. It's what we believe in, and I believe in you too, Estelle. We *all* believe in you. You have disappointed me before, but I know you will redeem yourself. Show us that you are worthy of this faith."

She then kissed the young woman's matted head, lowered her hand from her cheek, and walked toward the guest room door with a *click, click, thump, click, click, thump, click, click, thump.*

"Eat, Estelle," she said, turning around at the door. Her face was gentle and calm. "Paint. I will check on you again tomorrow like I promised. And when you're done with your masterpiece, I shall put it in my gallery. I know the perfect spot."

She made her way into the hall. Agatha quietly shut and locked the door behind her.

Essie raised her reddened and swollen eyes to glare at the door and then the blank canvas. For the first time, she hated something that had once brought her so much joy.

"They can't make me. They can't make me," she whispered over and over again.

They couldn't make her paint. They couldn't force her to have this baby. But what was the alternative?

She no longer felt like anything she created was of her own free will or her own mind. She was just some vessel, some conduit for Godmother's delusions. But hadn't that always been the case? Hadn't Godmother always been steering her work, controlling her, and monitoring her secretly to make sure she did *exactly* what she'd wanted her to do?

She'd never allowed Essie's work to appear in any galleries, despite her numerous promises to do so. She would never give Essie a chance to be independent of her, to go off and make a career on her own. Essie now wondered if that had been Godmother's plan all along. Had Godmother become her patron because of her art, or because she had always seen Essie playing a part in a much, *much* grander picture for this Bridge of Light?

Essie climbed off her bed and stomped barefoot toward the easel. Beside it was a table where an assortment of paints, brushes, and palette knives were assembled. They had been waiting for her, neatly arranged according to color and size, taunting her for weeks.

Her eyes landed on one of the palette knives.

Could she use it to get out of this prison? Maybe hold it to the throat of one of the maids who would bring her breakfast tomorrow morning, or plunge it into Godmother's chest the next time the older woman entered her room?

Essie picked up the knife and ran her thumb across the edge of the blade, watching as it made an indentation in the skin. She ran it again. Deeper this time. Pricking her own blood.

Or maybe she could use it to cut her own throat. Then all of this would be over and Godmother and her friends couldn't get what they wanted.

"But I don't want to die," Essie whispered, her eyes flooding with tears again. She didn't want to disappear, for Louise to always wonder what happened to her.

She set down the knife, and grabbed one of the paintbrushes instead and then one of the tubes of indigo paint.

Minutes later, she did her first angry swipe at the canvas, stabbing at it in swift strokes. She didn't know yet what she would paint, but she would try her best to control the wielding of the brush, the shape of the image. She would try her very damndest to survive this, but if she didn't, she'd find a way to give her last message to the world.

In this painting would be the story of what had happened to her. She just hoped someone out there would see it.

CHAPTER 49
SHANICE

EAST HAMPTON, NEW YORK
Present day

I STARTLE FROM MY SLEEP WITH A SHARP INTAKE OF BREATH.

I was dreaming of Essie's portrait, except it wasn't at Dad's house or hanging in my living room. It was in its rightful place back in Gram's bedroom.

I was walking toward it, marveling at how lifelike and detailed it was, but I stopped when I realized the image in the portrait was moving. Essie was no longer looking at me from the corner of her eye, but turning to face me.

Her features weren't partially hidden in the shadows anymore. I could see them all clearly, and I realized for the first time that Gram and I had been mistaken. The portrait wasn't the image of a woman who was annoyed or angry. She didn't look like "she'd cut you if you looked at her sideways." She looked scared.

When Essie faced me head-on, her parted mouth slowly began to open wider and wider until it formed a full "O."

I wanted to leave the bedroom but I couldn't, now frozen in fascination. By my own fear. The portrait then began to scream.

"Help me! Help me, please!"

It thawed my limbs and sent me running. It made me flee even the dream.

After a nightmare like that, I know already it will be a struggle to get back to sleep. I turn onto my side, expecting to find Noah in bed beside me, snoring. But he isn't there. The bed is empty.

"Noah?" I call out.

He doesn't answer.

I climb out of bed and walk toward the bathroom. I gently knock on the door. "Noah, are you in here?"

Still no answer. I ease the door open to find the bathroom empty.

I glance at the clock on my night table. It's 1:28 a.m. *Where could he be?*

I stare at his empty pillow and decide to go looking for him. I grab a sweater I've tossed at the end of the bed, put it on, and walk out of the bedroom.

After I tiptoe my way downstairs, I notice that the Whitmores' home looks different at night. I didn't think it was possible but it seems even bigger in the dim light coming through all the open windows.

I squint when I think I hear something. The sound of a door opening and closing. I hear a faint voice in the dark. Is it Noah's? I walk toward their kitchen, following the sound. I walk around the kitchen's granite island and I'm about to round the corner that leads to a hallway and what I think is the mudroom when I hear something behind me.

"What are you doing?" a husky voice asks, startling me.

I whip around and spot a figure in the dark, but I can't make out who it is.

"I asked, '*What* are you doing?'" they repeat. Their voice has a harder edge this time.

The kitchen suddenly floods with light. I see that it's Skylar who's flicked a switch and is now standing on the other side of the kitchen. She's traded her cutoff jean shorts and tank top for a tight, sequined black dress. Her mascara is running and her red lipstick is smeared. Her brown eyes have a glassy look to them.

I point over my shoulder. "Umm, I was looking for some tea," I lie. "I couldn't sleep."

"Tea?"

I nod.

She regards me silently for a few seconds. "Pantry, third shelf."

I stare at her blankly. "Where is the pantry?"

"The door to your left," she enunciates slowly, like it was a stupid question.

"Thanks," I whisper before opening the pantry closet door.

In the light coming through the doorway, I immediately spot the dozen tin canisters of tea lined in a neat row on the third shelf. I grab one of them and step back into the kitchen where I find Skylar opening the fridge and removing a bottle of water. She twists off the bottle lid, drops the lid to the floor with a clatter, and closes her eyes. She throws back the bottle and drinks like she's taking a shot.

"Fun night?" I ask as she slumps onto one of the stools at the kitchen island.

"You could say that," she mumbles.

"Cute dress," I say while opening cabinets overhead in search of a cup.

She doesn't reply.

The kitchen falls silent again; the noises I heard from earlier have stopped. I thought Skylar might leave at this point, since she doesn't seem to want to talk, but she continues to drink her water while I make my tea.

"I can't figure you out," she says out of nowhere over the drone of the microwave. "You're either very smart or very stupid."

I turn away from the microwave to face her. *"Excuse me?"*

"Why'd you come here?" she asks in a louder voice. The microwave beeps. "What are you expecting to get out of this?"

"I was invited here by your father," I say, now irritated.

"But you didn't have to come. You didn't have to say yes. Why did you?"

"Because . . . because I wanted answers about my painting so that I could finish my article. Your father said he might be able to give them to me."

She braces her elbows on the island and cocks an eyebrow at me in disbelief. "And that's it? That's all?"

"Yeah," I say slowly. "Why else would I be here?"

Certainly not for her hospitality.

She stares at me for a long time before she nods. "Okay. You seem like you're telling the truth, but I can't say for sure." She pushes herself up from the stool and staggers to her feet. "I've been fooled before," she mutters cryptically.

Skylar turns and begins to walk out of the kitchen but she pauses. She tries to turn back around to face me but has to grab the wall to brace herself. She slumps near a shelf of fresh herbs.

"If you are telling the truth, I should warn you not to trust them," she says.

"Not to trust who?"

"*Any* of them. They're all assholes. My dad, especially. You may think he's doing you a favor, but believe me, he doesn't do anything unless there's something in it for him. Don't trust those motherfuckers." Her voice shakes with anger.

I stare at her. "Uh, care to elaborate?"

But her eyes are glazed over and she barely seems aware of me anymore. She shoves herself away from the wall and walks off.

"Good talk," I say to the empty kitchen.

When I arrive back in the guest room, I find Noah lying in bed with his eyes closed, like he'd been there the entire time. I roughly nudge his shoulder, waking him up.

"Where'd you go?" I ask him as I set down my tea. "I woke up and you were gone."

"I could ask you the same thing?" Noah answers sleepily, smacking his lips. "I came back and *you* were gone."

"Stop evading! Where did you go, Noah?" I repeat, smacking his shoulder.

"Oww," he says with a wince. "I got a phone call from my mom. She was visiting my grandpa at a hospital in Seattle and was giving me an update. She forgot how late it was here. I had to take the call, Shanice. I didn't want to wake you up, so I took it downstairs."

"I didn't know your grandpa was sick. You never told me that."

"We're not close." He eyes me. "What's with all the questions? What did you think I was doing?"

"I . . ." I shake my head in frustration. "Never mind. Let's just . . . just go to sleep," I say before taking off my sweater and climbing into bed beside him.

"That's what I was trying to do before someone woke me up," he grumbles. He then punches his pillow and turns onto his stomach.

I hear Noah's snores minutes later, but I can't fall back to sleep.

Did Noah really leave to take a phone call about his grandfather? Am I blowing this all out of proportion? Is he telling the truth, or is it another seemingly convenient excuse, another story to throw me off his tracks? I don't know if my suspicions are legitimate anymore, or if I'm just letting the beast have its way.

"*Don't trust those motherfuckers,*" Skylar said.

Little does she know there's already someone in this house I don't trust.

CHAPTER 50

"You don't have to hover at the door," Hanson says the next morning. "I thought you'd be eager to see this. Please come in."

I hesitate for a second longer before stepping inside his private study.

Noah has already left for the beach. I'm supposed to meet him later. Juliette said at breakfast that she was headed to town to meet friends for a shopping trip. I guess Skylar sobered up and recovered from last night; I saw her about a half hour ago, blasting music from her Mercedes convertible before sending pebbles flying in the driveway as she drove off.

I still can't decide if her warning not to trust her dad was just drunk, pre-dawn rambling, or if she really meant it. Looking at him now, sipping coffee and humming to himself, he doesn't seem bad; pretty normal, in fact.

I guess it was just a spoiled rich girl's drunken rant, another instance of the Hamptons' princess behaving badly just to spite her dad like what I overheard when I woke up in the guest room.

I look around me. There are wall-to-wall shelves filled with leather-bound books and framed photos. Many of the pictures are of Hanson, Juliette, and Skylar, but I spot a few black-and-white and sepia-toned photos as well. I instantly recognize Maude in one of them. In another photo, there is a dark-haired woman with birdlike features in a sparkling evening gown. She laughs with a cigarette in hand.

"That's my great-grandmother Lillian," Hanson says with a note of fondness as he sets down his coffee cup on one of the shelves and walks toward me. "She was quite the beauty in her day, wasn't she?"

My eyes drift to another picture of a guy with sinewy muscle and smoldering, movie star good looks. He stands on a beach in old-fashioned swim trunks with his arms crossed over his broad chest. He looks mildly annoyed at having his picture taken. "Who's that?" I ask.

Hanson leans over my shoulder. "That would be Lillian's cousin, Elias. Maude's son."

"*That's* Elias?"

He nods.

Essie mentioned him quite a few times in her letters. Seeing his photo, I now understand why. "Whatever happened to him?" I ask.

"It's a sad story, actually. He committed suicide in 1929, not long after his mother's murder. Some say it was because of the stock market crash. A lot of young men took their lives that year. Others say it was due to overwhelming grief from Maude's passing."

My eyes scan the next shelf and land on a small glass case where I see a gold ring with an oval-shaped red stone sitting on a velvet cushion. I've seen this ring before—on Vivaldi's hand.

"Red tiger's eye," I blurt out.

"What?" Hanson asks.

"The ring. That stone. It's called red tiger's eye. How . . . how did you get this?"

"It's a family heirloom. I believe it belonged to Elias. It's been passed down for decades."

"Can I see it . . . up close, I mean?"

"I don't see why not," Hanson says as he reaches for the glass case and lifts it. He removes the ring from its cushion and hands it to me.

I examine it carefully in the study's light. I'm sure of it now; it's identical to Vivaldi's ring. I tilt the gold band and notice an inscription.

"There's something written inside of it, but I can't quite make it out. Do you know what it says?"

"It's in Latin. It translates to 'Brothers of the light,'" he murmurs as I lower the ring. "'Keepers of the flame.'"

"So, this was the ring for The Bridge of Light? For its members?"

"Afraid so." He takes the ring from me and puts it back in the case. "I just see it as a family memento though. I try to ignore the sordid history around it."

"I've seen one just like it," I begin slowly. "The guy who wore it . . . his name's Mark Vivaldi. He's an art appraiser. He's the one who tried to buy my painting. Do you know him?"

Hanson gives a resigned sigh. "Yes, I know him, unfortunately." He shoves his hands into the pockets of his khakis. "He's quite the character."

"Oh, yes, he is," I mutter, making Hanson laugh.

"So you know him well, I see. Well, that *charming* gentleman sued me. Actually, he sued the foundation. He claimed that his family was owed a portion of the Bachmann estate. He said that Maude promised his great-grandmother, Agatha Pickens, who was her secretary, money and a portion of her art collection in some version of her will. Agatha and Maude were close for many years, that I will acknowledge, but they had a falling out and she was struck from the will. Maude was fickle," he says with a shrug. "Anyway, the will was quite clearly a forgery. He could never verify its authenticity. Nevertheless, we tried to reach an amicable settlement with him. I felt it only right out of respect for Maude and the relationship she and Agatha once had. But Vivaldi refused our lawyers' offers. The litigation dragged on for more than a year. It was quite costly. Lucky for us though, he wasn't successful."

So, Vivaldi's great-grandmother knew Maude. It would make sense that she was part of The Bridge of Light too. Maybe Lillian was as well and now their great-grandsons are walking around with cult paraphernalia like the objects are sweet family keepsakes.

"What artwork did Vivaldi claim rightfully belonged to his family?"

"Several pieces. Including a few by Johnson. I can show you one if you'd like. It's going to appear in the MoMA exhibit but we haven't shipped it off yet. I wanted to show it to you before we did."

I eagerly follow him across the study. On his desk sits a canvas with no frame. It shows two boys on a street corner. One sits on the sidewalk with two sticks in his hands, tapping away on an overturned bucket. The other boy seems to be dancing to whatever tune his friend is playing. A woman stands in the periphery, raising her arms with one hip cocked to the side, as if she's about to join the dance. I smile down at the painting, wondering if it's a scene Essie had observed one day while living in Harlem.

"I believe this is the second work that Johnson sold to Maude," Hanson says.

My smile fades. I step back from his desk. "She didn't sell it. She *gave* it to her. That was part of their agreement. With the exception of a few paintings Essie sold before Maude became her patron, she never made a dime from her work. She was beholden to her. Maude owned everything."

He grimaces. "You're right. And I agree the arrangement was disadvantageous to the artists. My great-aunt definitely had her faults, but—"

"Those weren't just 'faults,' Hanson. From what I've read and heard about her, Maude used her money and power to take advantage of people. She took advantage of Essie."

"And Maude paid the ultimate price for it. That's probably why Johnson killed her."

"We don't know that for sure."

He tilts his head. "No, but it all makes sense, doesn't it? She probably wanted to get out of their agreement . . . the contract she signed that bound her and her work to Maude for perpetuity, basically for Johnson's entire life and thereafter. It's why Johnson disappeared after the murder only to turn up dead in Philadelphia more than a year later. She had all the signs of someone on the lam . . . a murderer on the run. Let me show you something," Hanson says as he walks around his desk and opens a drawer, taking out a weathered sheet of paper sealed in plastic. "It's what I mentioned on our call when I invited you here. I suspect it's the final piece you'll need to finish your series. It's a copy of the police report. Near Maude's body, they found the murder weapon. It was a painting knife." He hands me the plastic-enclosed sheet.

I look down at the handwritten report and read the words "*victim stabbed several times*" and "*bloody painting knife found at foot of bed belonging to Estelle Johnson.*"

"Oh, Essie," I whisper.

I didn't want to believe she killed Maude, but reading this and knowing how Maude had financially trapped her—it seems like the most logical conclusion. Why else would she have run?

"Then why were there theories that Maude's murder could've been related to the occult?" I ask, now confused. "Where did those come from?"

He shrugs. "I think the obvious answer is Maude's involvement in The Bridge of Light. It all came out after she was murdered. The meetings in secret. The rituals. There was little understanding of non-Christian, spiritual beliefs at that time. The Bridge of Light . . . her and Klaus's belief in the occult seemed like a convenient boogeyman to blame her murder on."

"Well, thanks for letting me see this. I thought my research might lead me here. I want to tell the true story behind this painting, even if it isn't the story I thought . . . that I *hoped* I would tell," I say, my stomach turning at the image of Essie standing over Maude's body, blood dripping from her painting knife.

He gradually nods. "Speaking of the painting," Hanson begins, "as I said last night at dinner, it is very important. It's important to my family history, to Maude's . . . complicated story. You're looking for an ending for your articles, and I need something that pulls this exhibit together, that shows how Maude's story ended. This was the *last* painting she ever commissioned, perhaps the last piece she saw before she was murdered, and it's been virtually hidden from the public eye for almost a hundred years. I think it would be a travesty not to include Johnson's self portrait in the MoMA exhibit. I have to admit, as soon as I heard about your articles and the painting, the idea popped into my head. Do you know what a draw this could be?"

I eye him. So, was that the *real* reason why Hanson invited Noah and I to the Whitmores' Hampton estate and offered to help me with my essays? Because he wanted to ask me to donate my painting for the exhibit? Maybe that's what Skylar meant when she said her father would only do something if it benefited him. But still, I have to agree with him that showing the painting at the MoMA is a good idea. My article would help bring more attention to Essie's work, but that's nothing like being featured at the MoMA.

"I know you've rejected your previous offer. I understand why, especially if it came from Vivaldi. But please consider donating your painting to the exhibit. Temporarily, of course. My people could even help you work out the agreement with the MoMA," Hanson says. "You don't have to make the decision right away, but seriously give it some thought, please."

"I . . . I will." And I mean it.

Hanson suddenly looks up at the study window, at the sound of an approaching car.

"That sounds like our Range Rover. I guess Juliette is back from town. She and I have plans this afternoon. She'll probably want to head back out soon. I hope I have answered all your lingering questions, but don't hesitate to ask more if you have them. I can send you a copy of the police report if you'd like."

"Sure. I'd appreciate that."

He walks around his desk, smiles, and gestures toward the study door. "I'll show you out. You and Noah try to enjoy your last day in the Hamptons. See the harbor. Walk through town. Let me know if you need to use our driver. He can take you anywhere you want."

"Thanks, Hanson," I say as I walk back to our guest room, still seeing the words in my head "*bloody painting knife found at foot of bed.*"

Estelle's knife.

CHAPTER 51

"READY TO GO?" NOAH ASKS.

I nod, watching as the driver loads our suitcases into the trunk of the sedan. I then turn to find Hanson and Juliette standing in the doorway, just like they were when we arrived. Skylar isn't here this time, though honestly, I'm not surprised; she doesn't seem like one for goodbyes.

I wave to the Whitmores then climb inside the Mercedes. Noah climbs in after me. As the Whitmores' home recedes behind us and we start down the road, my phone buzzes. I look down at the screen and see that it's an email from Hanson with the subject header, Maude Bachmann murder / police report.

"Here's the report, as promised," Hanson's email says. "I hope you do seriously consider loaning the portrait to the MoMA. And, if you are ever willing to sell the painting, I'm willing to offer double what Vivaldi offered: $1 million. No pressure either way. Let me know if you need anything else."

I read the email again and force myself to blink because I'm so shocked. One million dollars? Is he serious?

"What?" Noah asks. "Why are looking like that? What's wrong?"

"Nothing. Just reading an email from Hanson," I mumble.

"About what? Did we leave something?"

"No, he made an offer for the painting."

Noah raises his brows. "He made you an offer too? For how much?"

I slump back into the seat. "One million dollars."

"*One million dollars?* What the . . ." Noah barks out a laugh. "Are you going to turn it down?"

"I don't know."

I was already seriously considering donating Essie's painting to the MoMA. It was one thing to not want to sell her painting to Vivaldi who, according to Hanson, probably wants it because he believes Essie's paintings should have been his all along. No wonder Vivaldi's been so persistent. But it's another thing to refuse allowing her last work to be shown at the MoMA. It feels like I'm being overly cautious, maybe even selfish. Essie wanted her work to be seen and appreciated, not hidden in Dad's safe. That's what she always dreamed of—and never got the chance. But this one-million-dollar offer from Hanson is definitely a curveball.

Noah and I ride the rest of the way to the airport in silence. He's wearing his earbuds and staring out the window. He's probably figured out that I'm lost in thought and in no mood for conversation.

By the time we get to LaGuardia, I'm ready to board the plane and go straight to Gram's house. I've called her a couple of times, but the phone just rang. I guess she isn't back from Atlantic City yet. I have so much to tell her and to ask her. I have no idea what to think anymore. She's the only opinion I trust right now.

The driver unloads our bags and we walk through the sliding glass doors. The stifling summer heat is now replaced with the frigid air of the airport terminal. My phone buzzes. I read the screen and I almost groan.

"It's Dad." I wave Noah toward the security checkpoint where a long queue awaits us. "Go ahead and get in line. I'll take this. It'll only be a couple of minutes."

Noah nods and walks off. I take a deep breath as my phone continues to buzz insistently in my hand.

You and Dad can have a civilized conversation, I tell myself. *Just keep it brief.*

I press the green button on screen and raise the phone to my ear. "Hey, Dad."

"Shanice, thank God you answered. Where are you?" Dad asks, sounding urgent.

"I'm in New York. I'm at the airport headed back to D.C. Why?" I ask, furrowing my brows.

"Why are you in New York? You know what . . . never mind. When you get back in town . . . as soon as you land, call me, then come straight here. Don't go to your grandmother's house. Okay?"

"Why?" I pause. "Did something happen?"

He hesitates on the other end.

"Dad?" My grip tightens around my phone. "What happened to Gram?"

As I wait for him to respond, the past and present bend and fold, overlapping one another. They become one. I'm standing in the airport but I'm also riding in the back of an ambulance, being driven away from the car accident that I had with my mother more than fifteen years ago.

I'm asking the EMTs about Mom. I'm asking if she's okay.

Dad clears his throat on the phone line. "I'm sorry, but they found your grandmother last night. The police called me this morning. Even after all these years, she still had me and your mama listed as her emergency contacts. She . . . oh, honey, I'm . . . I'm so sorry, but she's . . . gone. Your grandmother is dead."

After that, I no longer hear him. Everything goes silent and black.

CHAPTER 52

When the plane lands, Noah and I grab a taxi at Reagan National. I call Dad as we ride in the backseat.

"What happened?" I ask as soon as Dad picks up. "Was it a heart attack?"

I don't even bother to say hi or to tell him that I fainted back in New York, that the nurse at the first aid station at LaGuardia wanted to hold me for observation a bit longer and tried to keep me from boarding my flight. It all seems too trivial now.

"No, honey," Dad says. "There was a . . . a break-in. She was at home alone, and I guess she caught the intruder off guard. The son of a bitch killed her."

"What?"

Who would break into Gram's house and hurt her? Why would they do it? With all those tricked-out, renovated houses on her block, why would a burglar target her humble home?

"A neighbor saw him fleeing. That's what the cops told me," Dad continues as I blink back tears, as my mind reels at the news. "She heard your grandmother's screams and called the police. She saw him running from the house."

"Do you know what neighbor it was?"

"No, I . . . I don't, honey. Look, we can talk about this more when you get here. I'll answer all your questions, just—"

"I'm not coming there, Dad. I have to go to Gram's house. I have to find out what neighbor it was. What she saw. Maybe she could tell me what the man looked like."

Dad deeply exhales, causing static on the line. "Shanice, that is the *exact opposite* of what you should do. Let the cops do their jobs and find him. Stay out of their way."

"I should've been there, Dad."

I think about the night that I left her, and how I hadn't seen her since that day. I was so obsessed with saving a woman who is already dead, in solving her mystery that I lost my grandmother because of it. The tears I'd been trying to hold back, spill onto my cheeks.

"Gram shouldn't have been alone," I say.

"What are you talking about? You couldn't have stopped this. If you'd been there last night, *both* of you could be dead right now. Just come to our house and—"

I hang up, shove my phone into my purse, and wipe my eyes with the back of my hands.

"Are we really going to your grandmother's house?" Noah asks. "I thought we were going back to your apartment."

I glance up at him. He looks alarmed.

"I mean, isn't it a crime scene, Shanice? Will they even let us in there?"

"I'm not asking to see her body. You don't have to go with me. But I have to do this, Noah. I have to go."

He stares at me for a long time then nods. I lean forward and tell the driver that we're taking a detour and give him the address to Gram's house.

CHAPTER 53

When we arrive, I see that the front porch and fence are threaded with yellow police tape. A few neighbors linger along the sidewalk, pointing at her home. The police are gone but there's a news crew van sitting at the end of the block. A reporter with big blond hair is holding a mic and pointing it at Fawn, of all people. Fawn's son, Wesley, is clinging to Fawn's bare leg with his thumb stuck in his mouth as Fawn talks into the mic.

Was Fawn the neighbor who saw what happened?

I throw open the taxi door before the cab comes to a complete stop.

"Shanice!" Noah shouts just as I unlock my seatbelt, hop out, and race down the sidewalk to where Fawn stands.

"It was so awful," Fawn says, blinking her blue eyes rapidly. "She was such a wonderful woman. So kind. The grandmother of the block. I can't believe this happened to her."

"Fawn! Fawn!" I call out to her, making her turn away from the reporter and the camera.

"Shanice! Oh, my God!" She turns back to the reporter and gestures toward me. "This is Shanice. Her granddaughter."

The reporter's brown eyes light with interest. She turns to me and waves frantically for the cameraman to change his angle, to point the lens toward me. She holds out her mic. "Is that true? Are you really the victim's granddaughter? Can I get your full name?"

"I don't want to do any interviews," I say quickly before facing Fawn. "Did you see what happened? Did you see the guy who did it?"

"I can only imagine what you're going through," the reporter continues, easing closer. "I heard that Ms. Sumner—"

"I don't want to do any goddamn interviews!" I shout, making the reporter and Fawn step back, making Wesley stop sucking his thumb and stare up at me.

The reporter lowers her mic and whispers something to the cameraman.

I grab Fawn's shoulder. "Please, just tell me if you saw what happened? Were you the one who found her?"

Fawn purses her lips as the reporter and the cameraman walk away. She grimaces and looks down at Wesley. "Earmuffs, Wes," she chirps and the little boy instantly claps his hands over his ears.

"Yes, I found her," she whispers. "We . . . uh . . . we had the neighborhood barbecue last night and she . . . she didn't show up. I thought maybe she was ill since you said she got the invitation and wanted to attend."

"She decided to go out of town with friends instead. That's what she told me." I shake my head. "I guess her plans changed."

"When things were winding down at the barbecue, I decided I should be the good neighborhood block captain and check on her."

"I can still hear you," Wesley pipes.

"Then hold your ears tighter, honey," Fawn says through clenched teeth before returning her attention to me. "I made a plate and decided to take it to her. When I got near the house, that's when I heard it. I thought . . . I thought I heard shouting. Screaming. I heard a man's voice. And then when I got closer, the screaming just . . . it stopped. I heard this banging, thumping sound and then the front door swung open. And that guy came running out. I told him to . . .

to stop. We locked eyes. I swear to God, Shanice, my heart stopped." She brought her trembling hand to her freckled chest. "I'm sorry I didn't run after him."

I shake my head again and squeeze her shoulder. "It's okay. I wouldn't have expected you to."

"After . . . after he ran, I went to the house to check on your grandmother. To see if she needed my help. I . . . I climbed the porch stairs, and I looked through the opened front door. I—I—I saw her in the living room. And she was . . ." Fawn's voice fades like she can't finish. She lowers her eyes like she can no longer look at me. "I'm so sorry, Shanice."

"Did you see him? Do you remember what he looked like?"

"It was dark," she begins. "He was wearing a hoodie but it came off a little when he ran down the stairs. He was tall. I remember that he had blond hair," she says, pointing to her crown, "and—"

"Is everything okay?" Noah asks behind me. Both of us turn to look at him. "You just leaped out of there. The cab driver thought we were trying to skip out on the fare. I had to do some fast talking and give him a big tip to calm him down."

"I'm sorry, Noah. I just wanted to talk to Fawn. She was the neighbor who saw what happened." I gesture between them. "Noah, this is Fawn. Fawn, this is Noah, my boyfriend."

"Pleased to meet you." He holds out his hand. "Wish it was under better circumstances."

But Fawn doesn't take his hand. Her face has drained of all color, making her freckles stand out even more. She pulls Wesley close to her side and yanks his hands from his ears. "You can stop earmuffs now, honey. We're done."

I frown at her. "Is everything okay?"

"Everything is fine," she says quickly. "Fine. I'm sorry, but we . . . we have to go." She grabs Wesley's hand and leaves.

"What the hell was that?" I murmur as I watch her and Wesley walk away.

Noah shrugs. "I guess she just had to go, like she said."

But that excuse doesn't sit well with me. It sits so badly that I follow her again. She stops at the top of her brick stairs leading to a house with a neat lawn and immaculate wraparound porch. When she hears me approach, she glances over her shoulder.

"Fawn, did something happen back there? You just . . . you just walked off."

She smiles and unlocks her front door, pushing it open. "Nothing happened. It's Wesley's nap time. He just gets fussy when he doesn't have his nap. That's all. Don't you, Wes?"

The little boy nods.

Fawn looks over my shoulder. I follow her gaze to find Noah staring at us from the sidewalk.

"Again, I'm so sorry for your loss. For what happened to your grandmother. Let me know if you need anything. Anything at all," she says then abruptly pulls me into a hug.

I awkwardly hug her back. Just when I feel her loosening her hold and I'm about to pull away, she whispers, "He looks just like him, Shanice." Her words are hot and shrill against my ear. "He looks just like the man I saw last night."

She then lets go of me, grabs Wesley's hand, steps inside her home, and closes the door.

CHAPTER 54

"HE LOOKS JUST LIKE HIM."

"I know this is easier said than done," Noah begins as I open the door to my apartment and we step inside. "But try to get some rest, if you can. It's been an intense couple of days." He closes the door behind us. "Lie down. I'll make us dinner."

I drag my suitcase across the living room and place it by the sofa. "I don't want to rest. I still have a lot of writing to do."

Noah sighs. "I'm sure your editor will understand if you don't do any work today and take it easy, Shanice. For Christ's sake, your grandmother died," he says as he places his hands on my shoulders.

"She didn't die, Noah." I shove them off and glare up at him.

"*He looks just like him,*" Fawn's voice whispers in my ear again.

"She was murdered!" I shout. "Someone killed her."

He drops his hands to his sides. "I know that, Shanice, and I'm very sorry it happened."

"Are you?" I raise my brows and take a step toward him.

"What is that supposed to mean?"

Am I finally going to say it? I don't know if I can. For days, I kept hesitating when I wanted to accuse him of lying to me. Now I'm about to accuse him of . . . what? I don't know.

"She said . . . she said he looked like you."

"Who said . . . What the hell are you talking about?"

"Fawn said the guy who was fleeing Gram's house looked just like you! He looked just like you!"

His face changes. It goes slack and his eyes go flat. "What are you saying, Shanice?"

"The man who killed my grandmother. He—"

"So what? Lots of people look alike! And victims of crimes get that type of shit wrong every day. So, you think *I'm* the one who murdered your grandmother?" He points at his chest. "Are you seriously accusing me of that?"

"No!" I close my eyes and grit my teeth. I cradle my forehead where a pounding headache is forming between my brows. "I mean . . . I don't know."

"You don't know? *You don't know?*" he echoes, going up several octaves.

"I don't know what's going on! Gram is dead and—"

"And I had nothing to do with that! To even insinuate that I did is not only completely insane, it's also physically impossible. I was with you all weekend."

"I know that!" I yell, opening my eyes again. "Don't you think I know that? But all this weird shit has been happening. I don't know what to believe, Noah, because you've been lying to me! You've been lying to me this whole goddamn time."

"What are you talking about? Lying about what?"

"You told me that you went to Baylor University. You don't think I'd remember that? And . . . and you forgot your girlfriend's name when we were talking the other day."

"What?"

"What thirty-year-old guy isn't on Instagram? LinkedIn? Why don't you have a Twitter account? Why can't I find you anywhere on the web?"

"I told you why," he answers tightly. "We had this conversation already and I—"

"And you disappeared in the middle of the night in the Hamptons. I heard you whispering in another room. Were you really talking to your mom or was it just another convenient story?"

He doesn't answer me. He just stands there, frowning and shaking his head, looking bemused.

"You showed up the same day that the first letter did," I argue, balling my hands into fists. "It wasn't just a coincidence, was it? You showed up the same day I thought someone was stalking me. I can't trust you. I cannot trust you, Noah!"

Finally, he stops shaking his head. He opens his mouth then closes it. "Shanice, I have no idea what the hell you're talking about," he begins slowly. "I have no idea why you're saying these things. Look, I know . . . I know you've been going through a lot. I know a lot has happened and you're under stress. I know what your disorder does to you, but you can't just—"

"Don't bring up my disorder. It has nothing to do with this! I'm not crazy!"

"And I'm not a fucking murderer, or part of some conspiracy against you!" he bellows.

I blink at the sudden sound of his booming voice, at the veins raised along his neck and his temples. I go silent.

Noah takes a deep, shuddering breath, like he's trying to calm himself. He steps back. "You need time to yourself. I realize that now. Me being here isn't helping. It's obviously making things worse because if you were in your right mind, Shanice, you wouldn't accuse me of this stuff. I've been at your side this whole time. I was the one helping you and supporting you. I've been there when you needed me, haven't I? That's been the whole reason why I'm here."

I watch as he grabs his suitcase and walks out of my living room. I don't stop Noah from leaving, even though part of me wants him to stay. I collapse onto the sofa just as the door shuts behind him.

"I'm not crazy," I sob to the empty room. My vision blurs with tears so I close my eyes. "I'm not crazy."

CHAPTER 55

THE BLINDS ARE DRAWN AND MY BEDROOM IS DARK. IT'S BEEN THAT way for almost a week. I don't know whether it's night or day when I hear the knock at my front door.

I wonder if it's Dad. He's been calling and texting for the past week, asking me if I've started funeral plans for Gram, if I've even contacted the D.C. morgue to have her body transported to a funeral home.

"Look, I know this is a lot for you, especially at a time like this," Dad said in his last voicemail. I could tell he was struggling to be diplomatic. To not yell at me and tell me to just get out of the damn bed, take a shower, and get my shit together. "Honey, Dana and I are willing to help. But you can't leave your grandmother's body sitting down there. You *have* to bury her."

I've attempted several times to call him back, to tell him that I already know what funeral home to take her to. She mentioned the name of the place a few times over the years. I want to tell him that she probably wanted Reverend Heinz at Branch Avenue Baptist to officiate her funeral and she already paid for her burial plot. The paperwork is inside her house in her bedroom dresser. But I've yet to make the call.

My chest tightens at the thought of sitting in the funeral home office, discussing what casket to bury Gram in. I hyperventilate at the idea of watching her being lowered into the ground while a sea of mourners look on. And when all of it is over, I will add Gram's funeral bulletin to the pile of bulletins she already has amassed, including Mom's. In the bulletin, I'll be listed as her only surviving relative. Of our family, I'm the last one.

I raise my head from my pillow when the knocking at my door continues. If it is Dad, he's obviously not going away until I answer.

I drag myself out of bed and walk down the hall to my foyer. "Who is it?" I ask.

"Shanice?" I hear a woman answer timidly from the other side. "Shanice, it's me. Priya."

Why is Priya here?

Maybe because I haven't returned any of her emails either and haven't updated her on my work. The deadline for the final Essie essay was days ago.

I look down at myself. I'm wearing two-day-old PJs. I smooth my hands over my matted hair, an utterly useless gesture that only serves to remind me how bad I look right now. I take a deep breath and unlock the door, cracking it and peering into the hall.

"Hello," she says with a smile. "I just happened to be in the neighborhood and thought I'd stop by."

"Hey! Uh, hi." I smooth my hair again. "I know I owe you that essay. I've . . . I'll have it for you soon."

"Oh, no worries!" She holds up two oversized cups. "I bought some boba tea. I thought you might like it." She leans her head to gaze over my shoulder. "Can I come in? Are you busy?"

I hesitate. I'm not in any condition to accept visitors. Neither is my apartment, but she came all this way, and I've stayed hidden from the world for almost a week. I slowly open my door and usher her inside. "Sure."

Priya hands me one of the drinks and follows me into the living room after I shut the front door behind her. We sit down on the sofa and fall into awkward silence.

"Umm, thanks for the tea," I say when I can't take the quiet any longer.

"You're welcome. I hope you like it. It's a purple sweet potato milk tea. It's supposed to be good for you. Good for your health."

I nod down at the drink in my hand, swirling the concoction around and around.

"How are you, Shanice? I hadn't heard from you since your trip to the Hamptons to talk to Hanson. I was a little worried."

"I'm . . . fine," I lie.

She frowns. "Are you sure?"

I open my mouth to lie again and shake my head instead. "No, not really. My grandmother . . . died."

"Oh, I'm so sorry," Priya says.

"Actually, she was murdered. I found out when I got back and then I had a little . . . breakdown." I let out a breath that makes my shoulders slump. "It's the third breakdown I've had in the past three months. But I'll . . . I'll pull myself together, like . . . like I always do. I've battled this since I was a teenager. You just have your low points sometimes."

Though these low points seem to be happening more and more these days. The older I get, the worse it gets. Maybe I *am* just like Mom. I'm not sitting behind the wheel of a car, but I'm still barreling toward my own destruction.

Priya purses her lips. "The first time you had a breakdown . . . Do you mean that day at the office? That day we had the break-in?"

"Yeah." I sit my drink on the coffee table and interlock my fingers. "That wasn't one of my best moments."

"I'm so sorry that happened to you, that Gary blamed you for what happened."

"You don't have to apologize, Priya. None of it was your fault. In fact, you were the only one that spoke up for me. I really appreciated that."

"It's just I never intended it to . . ." Her voice drifts off. She turns away.

"You never intended to . . . what?"

She looks at me again. "Shanice, I did it."

"You did what?"

"I vandalized the office that night," she begins in a voice so quiet I can barely hear her. "I took the laptops and dumped them into the garbage. I—I did it."

I blink in surprise and shift back on the sofa. *"What?"*

"I remember what it was like being the intern. I did it even longer than you did—for two years. And Gary didn't make it easy. None of the staffers did. But I'd come from India to go to school here. To work here. I wanted to make a name for myself. I figured that being the office slave was just the price I had to pay. And if they hired me, the magazine could sponsor my green card application. I had to prove myself.

"Then Gary made me the editorial assistant. I was so happy. The job didn't pay much. It wasn't anywhere near the cost of living in the city. I was renting a room in a bug-infested house with five roommates. I could barely afford to buy food, but hey, at least I had my sponsor. Then one week, I noticed that there was about two hundred dollars less on my paycheck. Gary said it must have been a payroll glitch and it would be fixed. Then two weeks later, I was paid three hundred dollars less. Then one paycheck, I was paid only *fifty dollars*, Shanice. I realized it wasn't a glitch, despite what Gary was saying. I told Gary that I wanted my money. That I'd earned it and the magazine had no right not to pay me. I said it was illegal."

She finally sets down her tea and clasps her hands in her lap. "Gary told me that the magazine was in a 'rough period.' That it required some belt tightening and, in order for me to stay on, he had to greatly reduce my pay. If I couldn't accept that, I could quit." Priya closes her eyes. Her nostrils flare. "Shanice, Gary knew I couldn't quit. He knew I needed the magazine to sponsor my green card. I *needed* that job. I was hurt. I was angry. I didn't come to the US for this. But I knew there was no other option. So, I stayed there for another year, letting him . . . letting *them* take advantage of me and pay me a third of what the company was reporting to the IRS. I borrowed money from friends. I lived on my credit cards. I stayed long enough to get my green card. Then I applied for other jobs."

"Oh, Priya," I say, reaching out and grabbing her hand. "I'm so sorry that happened to you. I had no idea Gary did that. I knew he was an asshole but I had no idea he was that bad!"

She opens her eyes to look at me. "I wanted to tell you. I wanted to tell you what he was doing when he hired you. That this wasn't a good place. People like that bring in people like us because it makes them look good, Shanice. But it's just a facade. It's not that you aren't a strong writer or talented, but we're just show ponies to them. Mascots."

I think back to the day that I showed up for my interview. I remember talking to the other candidates while I waited, mostly trust fund, eighteen- and nineteen-year-olds who wore expensive clothes made to look inexpensive, who'd taken an Uber to their interview rather than the metro. I was the only one who'd gone to an HBCU. I was one of the oldest—a career-changer who was finally following her dream to become a serious journalist and write about things that mattered. A dream that I had confided in my mother back when I was twelve years old.

And out of all of those candidates, they chose me for the internship. I'd been so proud.

"*I just hope this isn't a way for them to get cheap labor,*" Jason had said. "*I don't want you to waste your time and end up at a dead-end job.*"

He'd read between the lines even then. I'd been so deluded.

"At the going-away party, Gary still kept pretending. He told me I was a 'good investment' and he hoped I would represent the magazine well, like I owed them something. He never apologized to me. He never offered the money he owed me. But I told him thank you in front of everyone because it felt like the right thing to do, and I *hated* myself for it, Shanice," she says, baring her teeth while balling her fists in her lap. "I hated myself for being the nice, Desi girl and playing this game, even to the end. So that night, I left the bar and

I came back to the office. I unlocked the door and I took out all my rage on those rooms. I just . . . I just couldn't stop."

Priya lowers her eyes again. She blinks back tears.

"When I sobered up the next morning, I realized the full extent of what I had done. I should have immediately told Gary I was the one who did it, but then he blamed you. I should have known he would do that. Of course, that bastard would. Then you ran out. After you left, after I saw what Gary did to you . . . what *I* had done to you, I pulled him aside and immediately confessed. He threatened to have me arrested, to call *The Miscreant* and tell them what I'd done. So, I threatened to tell the IRS he had lied about what he was paying me. I would go to the *Washington Post*, our competitors, and anyone else that would listen and tell them the truth. Gary agreed to let the issue drop."

I stare at her, now shell shocked.

"I will never forgive myself for not speaking up that day and for letting you get blamed," Priya says, looking at me again. "And I wish I would have been honest with you as soon as you started working there. I knew what you were walking into. I should have . . . I should've warned you. I'm sorry. I'm sorry a thousand times over."

"I don't know what to say," I mumble because I honestly don't.

I'm angry at Priya and hurt that she didn't tell me the truth and let things spiral out of control that day, but part of me sympathizes with her too. How can I not when she's been through so much? She felt trapped. Toyed with. That's when you make the worst decisions. I can speak from experience.

"I know. It's a lot to take in, but I didn't want to make you wonder anymore. I wanted you to know. I wish I would have told you sooner."

She slowly rises to her feet and I follow suit. She grabs her drink and walks back toward the door.

"So, the essays . . . Did you offer to buy them because you felt bad for me?" I say when we reach the foyer.

She turns to me. "Absolutely not. We acquired those essays because they were good. The best work I'd seen come across my desk since I started at *The Miscreant*. I didn't do it out of guilt."

I believe her. I unlock and open the door and watch her stroll down the hall.

"Priya!" I say to her after she presses the elevator button and the doors open. "I—I understand. I do and I forgive you."

She bites her lower lip, looking as if she's about to cry again. She then waves and steps onboard. I wave back as the elevator doors close behind her.

CHAPTER 56

"THAT BATHROOM IS SPARKLING CLEAN," DANA SAYS BEHIND ME AS she sits down the mop bucket by the stairs. I glance over my shoulder while she snaps off her rubber gloves. "I swear you could eat off those tile floors." She walks toward me and places her hands on her hips. "Okay, kiddo. What's next?"

I sigh and look around Gram's bedroom where I've just finished cleaning out her dresser drawers.

It's two days after Gram's funeral. I was in a daze for most of it, nodding blankly as mourners walked by, accepting their hugs and barely listening to their condolences and stories about my grandmother. My ears only perked up when one of her friends latched onto me, sobbing.

"I tried to get your grandmother on that bus, honey," the older woman wept onto my shoulder. "I promise you that I tried! She was so excited to go to Atlantic City until she saw that number on the bus: 0013. No matter what I said after that, she refused to get on. She said that number was bad luck. Now, come to find out, it was even worse luck that she stayed home!"

So that's what made her stay? A number on a bus.

Of course it did. Superstitions ruled Gram's whole life—and it may have sent her to her death.

Dad did most of the talking at the funeral and the days leading up to it, shaking hands with mourners at the wake and going over the program with the Reverend Heinz. I wonder if Gram was looking down from heaven the entire time, grunting and sucking her teeth in annoyance at Dad as he took charge. But for once, I was happy to let him do it. I don't know if I could have made it through that day without him and Dana, no matter how many Xanax I'd swallowed.

Now we're finishing up clearing out Gram's house. Gram did leave the property to me in the case of her death, like Dad said. But preparing the house for sale isn't something I want to do alone. Not with memories of both Mom and now Gram haunting me as I turn every corner.

Every time I think I hear footsteps, I expect to see her shuffling through the doorway in her bedroom slippers, holding a stack of family albums or telling me she just made us lunch.

"You can start cleaning the closet in the spare bedroom," I now say to Dana as I close one of Gram's dresser drawers. I've already removed all her clothes and put them in giveaway bags. "I've gotta warn you though. It'll be like excavating King Tut's tomb in there."

Dana glances at the open doorway. She purses her lips. "Maybe I'll save that room for later." She leans forward and lowers her voice to a whisper. "Your dad is in there right now."

"Oh? Did he want to clean it himself?"

"He's not really cleaning. He's just looking at your mom's old things for now. Sitting with them. I wanted to give him some time."

"Sitting with them?" I frown.

"Yes, Shanice. Sometimes you just have to sit with things."

"What do you mean?"

Dana sighs. "About three years ago, I was driving to D.C. and I had to take a detour because of construction. It took me past a skate park that Zach used to love to go to. Before I realized it, I was pulling into the parking lot and watching the kids laugh. I watched them do tricks on their skateboards. I just started crying. I couldn't stop. I stayed in that parking lot for two hours." She shrugs. "Grief catches you at odd times and in different ways. I just had to sit with it that day until the feelings subsided. I think with your grandmother's death . . . cleaning out this house is bringing back lots of memories for your dad. He just has to sit with it too. You know?"

I nod, though I wonder if it's really just grief that's plaguing Dad, and not guilt as well, especially after the story that Gram told me about what happened between him and Mom. I wonder if Dana knows what happened before Mom's death.

A couple of minutes later, Dana disappears to the first floor to give a more thorough cleaning to the kitchen. If anyone can make it sparkle, I'm sure it's her. While she works, I walk down the hall to the spare bedroom. I peek through a crack in the door and see Dad sitting on the edge of the bed, holding a dress to his nose. When I push the door open wider, he looks up and drops the dress guiltily, like I caught him trying to steal it from a department store.

"What are you doing?" I ask.

Dad gives an embarrassed smile. "It still smells like your mother. Even after all these years. I guess because it was encased in plastic so long, it never lost the scent of her perfume." He stares down at the fabric. "Some days, I swear I struggle to remember exactly what she looked like. How she laughed. Then some days it feels like she could come walking through the door at any moment, asking me if I picked up her favorite fried chicken and biscuits on the way home like she asked me to."

"I don't have a lot of memories of her anymore either," I say, leaning against the doorframe. "Just snatches. Her sitting in her favorite chair in your old bedroom reading one of her books. Her humming to music while she cooked."

Dad's smile broadens.

"Her crying as she vacuumed."

With that, Dad's smile abruptly disappears.

"Then I realize even those memories aren't real." I push myself away from the doorframe and walk into the bedroom. "What I was seeing wasn't what was really happening at the time, was it, Dad?"

"Honey," Dad begins, "I—"

"Why'd you cheat on Mom? How could you do that to her?"

Dad braces his elbows on his knees. His head sinks as he closes his eyes. "So your grandmother told you, huh?"

"I thought you guys were happy. I thought you loved her, Dad."

"I did love your mother." He rises to his feet. "Look, Shanice, I don't have to explain my marriage to you. Things between your mother and I were complicated. They always were."

"And you thought it would be a great idea to make it worse by cheating on her?"

"It only happened once," he says, dropping his voice to a raspy whisper. "*Just* once. And I regretted it the minute I did it. I never saw that woman again. Your mom and I were in a bad place. Your mother was . . . she was not doing well . . . mentally. It had happened before . . . her depressive episodes, but this was dragging on. No matter what I did, I couldn't get her out of it. I begged for her to talk to somebody. To get help. But she would just spout that mumbo jumbo about good luck and bad luck and how none of it mattered anymore because she'd missed all the signs and now . . . and now she was cursed. She said she had a curse hanging over her head. She said she was doomed—and so were you. I just couldn't . . . I just couldn't reach her, Shanice! She wasn't my Marissa anymore."

He takes a step toward me.

"That's why when you start in on that superstitious nonsense, I get so angry. I resented your grandmother for putting it in your head. For teaching it to Marissa. An unstable woman like her didn't need that. To be honest, for a while . . . I hated your grandmother for it."

"She didn't like you much either," I mumble and Dad gives a soft chuckle.

"Believe me, I knew it. But I tolerated her just like your grandmother tolerated me because of your mother. And I made sure your grandmother got a proper burial and I will help you and make sure all her estate will be taken care of because of Marissa . . . because of you. I'm doing all this because I loved Marissa and I love you too, honey."

I uncross my arms and drop them to my sides.

"I know I'm hard on you sometimes." He pauses. "Okay, *a lot* of times. It's just . . . when you spiral, it's like watching what happened to Marissa happen all over again. I get so damn scared. I just want to grab you and shake you, honey. I want to tell you to snap out of it. I don't want the same thing that happened to your mother to happen to you."

Dad reaches out and tugs me into a hug. I close my eyes and hug him back. I could be mistaken, but I do smell a hint of perfume in the air. It grows stronger with each passing second. It's like Mom has walked into the room. It's like she's sitting on the bed, watching us.

"You can't inherit luck, Shanice," Dad whispers into my ear. "But disorders can run in families. Trauma can be passed down. Don't let it rule you the way it ruled your mama and your grandmother. *Please?* I'm begging you, Shanice."

We hear a soft knock at the door and step apart as Dana pushes the door open. "Sorry, guys. I didn't mean to interrupt."

"You're not interrupting, honey," Dad says. "What's up?"

"Your phone, Malcolm." She holds out his cell. "You left it downstairs and it was ringing. I looked on the screen and saw someone from the DCPD called you."

Dad rushes across the room and I'm right at his heels. He takes the phone from Dana. "They left a voice message," he says and raises the phone to his ear.

Dana and I wait as he listens to the voicemail. We hold hands. The anxiety I feel as we wait for Dad to listen to the message is reflected on Dana's pale face. I hold my breath.

"They made an arrest," Dad finally announces, and I exhale. "They arrested the son of a bitch who killed your grandmother!"

CHAPTER 57

THEY FOUND HIM BECAUSE OF A ROUTINE TRAFFIC STOP. HE WAS speeding on Constitution Avenue and a cop pulled him over. They ran his ID and saw the guy sitting behind the wheel looked nothing like the photo. They ran his fingerprints and found out his real name: Thomas Jensen. He was wanted for other violent crimes in different parts of the country. They also figured out that he matched Fawn's description of Gram's murderer. Fawn later identified him in a lineup and his fingerprints matched those they found at the crime scene.

I saw his mugshot too. His resemblance to Noah was uncanny; I could see why Fawn had made the mistake, why the sight of Noah had scared her so much. I also could swear I remembered seeing him somewhere before, but I couldn't place where. In my building? On the way to work? But for Dad's sake . . . for my sake, I didn't indulge this time around.

I'm seeing a therapist now thanks to Dad and Dana's help. The therapist and I both agreed for my own mental health, I just have to let it all go.

So, instead, I called Noah and apologized for how out of line I was. I explained to him that he had been right. I was at a low and did a horrible thing by accusing him of something he was totally incapable of.

"It's . . . okay," he said hesitantly.

"No, it was not okay. And I understand if you don't want to forgive me for what I did to you, but—"

"I forgive you, Shanice. Of course I do. I know you were in a bad place. But are you better now? Are the conspiracy theories over?"

"Yes, but . . . but I also know I still have a lot of work to do. I realize that I should have been working on myself before I jumped into another relationship." Like I suspected in the beginning. "It wasn't fair to you."

He went quiet on the other end. "It sounds like you're breaking up with me, but I guess technically we already did that."

I gave a sad laugh. "I'm being honest with you, Noah." I tried to keep my tone even but it hurt to say goodbye to him. "I hope we can at least stay friends though."

"Yeah, I'm willing."

I wanted to hang up, to end it there, but I couldn't help saying, "Maybe we can even still get coffee sometime as . . . as friends?"

"That would be nice. Just tell me when you're ready."

I emailed Hanson Whitmore and told him that not only can Essie's final painting appear in the MoMA, I would also accept his offer in writing to purchase it.

"Good to hear! That's wonderful!" he wrote back within minutes. "I'll have my lawyers send you the contract soon."

I hope that signing it will release my obsession with Essie.

And two days ago, I finally finished my last essay and sent it off to Priya. In it, I told the twisted story of Essie's relationship with Maude Bachmann and the evidence that points to how it ended. I included the details from the police report about the palette knife found at the crime scene and how Essie was suspected of Maude's murder. Even the suggestion was painful, but I was careful to leave it open ended. Some mysteries have to remain unsolved.

Gram's house officially goes on sale at the end of the week. Today, I've decided to say goodbye to the little house in Anacostia that I've known my entire life. I'm in the sitting room. All the furniture is gone; it's been donated to Goodwill. Back at my apartment are a few boxes of her and Mom's things that I wanted to keep, but everything else is gone.

I do one final walkthrough of the house that's been in our family for generations and try to assure myself that it's fine to let it all go, including Essie's painting. But it feels like I'm letting go of Gram and Mom too. They may have passed on to me superstitions and trauma but also a complicated love. I force myself to step through the front door as my throat tightens and my vision blurs with tears. I shut it and lock it behind me. As I walk down the porch stairs, my phone begins to buzz.

I don't recognize the number on screen and press the button to send it to voicemail. When I reach my car, my phone buzzes again. It's the same number. I roll my eyes and press the button to answer.

"Hello?" I say with a sniff, blinking through my tears.

"Don't hang up," a familiar voice replies and I go still on the sidewalk. The blood drains from my head. "Please just listen."

It's Vivaldi. I blocked his number so he's obviously called from one I didn't recognize.

"Leave me alone or I swear to God, I will call the cops and tell them you're harassing me again. You're lucky you didn't go to jail for that break-in at my apartment. I—"

"*Break in?* Dear God," he whispers breathlessly, "how has this escalated so quickly?"

"What?" I snap.

"I . . . I heard about your grandmother," he continues. "I saw it on the news. I am so sorry, Shanice."

I'm caught off by his tone. Vivaldi actually sounds contrite. Even sad.

"But with your grandmother gone now," he continues, "I fear that the situation will only get worse. I suspect I'm being followed now too."

"What are you talking about?" Why is he speaking in riddles? "You know what. Never mind. Forget it. I'm hanging up now."

"No!" He shouts just as I begin to pull the phone away from the ear. "Please wait. You are selling Estelle Johnson's portrait to Hanson Whitmore. You haven't given it to him yet, have you? Have you signed a contract?"

"Are you serious?" I furrow my brows. "*This* is why you called me? Because of the fucking painting? My grandmother is dead!"

"Shanice, listen to me. I know I haven't been up front with you and that was a mistake. But Hanson isn't telling you the truth either. After all his machinations and conniving, he finally got it. Once again, he managed to cut me out of the deal, and now that he doesn't need me anymore, he holds all the cards," Vivaldi rambles, sounding more and more distraught.

"Look, I have no idea what you're talking about, but I am staying out of this drama between you and Whitmore about Essie's portrait."

"I told him about it," Vivaldi says. "I told him what was in it! That it could corroborate what was in Bachmann's will, what his lawyers kept denying. I told him I could secure it for him if he would give me what I was rightfully owed. But I had no idea that he was working behind the scenes . . . behind *my back* this entire time to get it himself. I should have known that a scheming shit like him would do it!"

"What the hell are you talking about?"

"*He's* the one who had you followed. *He's* the one who had you threatened."

"You mean Hanson?" I shake my head. "No, you're lying."

"He knew you would think it was me. That painting is worth a lot to him. It's worth a lot to his family. It's worth considerably more than you think. If the truth was known about Maude Bachmann, about Estelle Johnson's baby, how it all led Bachmann to change her will, well . . . Hanson's entire fortune could potentially be at stake."

"Essie had a baby?" This is the first I'm hearing about this.

"Yes. And Hanson doesn't want a chance of any of this to come to light, so he has to get rid of the painting. He has to destroy it.

There's no true record of it, correct? Some photos you took, but he could argue that they were doctored, just as he did with the will. The only other people who saw the painting . . . who really saw it up close, are you, me, and your grandmother. It would be our word against his, and you don't even know what you saw. What was right in front of your face!"

"Wait." My heart is racing. I'm starting to shake. "Back up! Did you say he was going to *destroy it*?"

Hanson said he was going to put it on display at the MoMA, to include it in the new Bachmann wing. Vivaldi has to be lying.

"I realize how all this sounds. I want to go into more detail, but I know you won't believe me if you don't see it for yourself. First, look at the painting again. Look at it *closely*, Shanice. Look at the bundle Estelle is holding. You'll see what I mean. Then call me back. I will show you the will myself. We can meet and I will explain everything. I'll tell you all that I know. But do not . . . I repeat . . . *do not* sell Hanson Whitmore that painting, or it will disappear."

After I hang up, I'm not sure if I should believe him. I don't want to get sucked down this rabbit hole again—but I can't help myself. I pull up my old photos on my phone of Essie's painting that I sent Vivaldi months ago. They are the only pictures I have. *The Miscreant* was supposed to send a photographer next week to take more-professional photos of the portrait for their website, but Hanson had insisted I send the painting to him and he'd make sure photos would be taken.

"Unfortunately, if we are going to include it in the collection unveiling, we need to get it to the MoMA right away," he'd said when I talked to him last. "Their specialists need to examine it and prepare it for display."

I now squint down at my phone screen. I zoom in and try to look at the bundle in Essie's arms, to see if I spot anything in the intricate pattern. I shake my head when I realize Vivaldi was right; thanks to my cheap phone, the pictures are of too poor quality to detect any details.

I race to the metro and arrive at Dad and Dana's house an hour later.

"Is the painting still in the safe?" I ask as Dad opens the front door. "Can I see it?"

"Well, hello to you too?" Dad quirks an eyebrow. "Yes, the painting is still downstairs in the safe. Why?"

"I need to see it, Dad. It's important."

He gestures for me to come inside. "You know you caught me in the middle of a basketball game, right?" he says as he shuts the door behind me and we walk across the foyer's hardwood to the door that leads to their basement. "Dana just gave me the remote back after watching one of her design shows. The Mavericks were up ten."

"Sorry, Dad," I mutter. "I swear that it won't take long."

He trudges downstairs in front of me, turning on light switches as we go. We arrive in the basement and walk down the hall to a rec room with a leather sectional and a home sports bar and barstools. Underneath a display of the Baltimore Ravens flags and jerseys sits a waist-high, slate gray safe. I watch as Dad leans down and punches in a series of numbers in the keypad. The door pops open.

The portrait is wrapped in protective cellophane. Dad pulls it out and hands it to me. I quickly begin to rip the cellophane off.

"It took me some time to wrap that, you know," he mumbles as I peel off the last piece. "You told me you wanted to ship it off tomorrow."

Essie's haunting eyes stare up at me. I examine the woven pattern again. I still can't see anything.

"Dad, do you have your cell? Can you take pictures of *this* part of the painting for me?" I ask, pointing to the bundle.

He tugs his phone out of his back jean pocket. Dad leans down and snaps a few quick photos before handing it to me. "Why are we doing this? What are you looking for?"

"I don't know," I say as I zoom in. "At least, not yet."

"Okay," he says slowly.

"I can't see it," I whisper. "Why can't I see it?"

I wish Vivaldi would've just told me exactly what I'm looking for. I rotate the image by 180 degrees and look at it again. I zoom in tighter.

That's when I see it. I see her words in the painting and my mouth falls open in shock:

BACHMANN IS HOLDING ME HERE AGAINST MY WILL
SHE IS FORCING ME TO HAVE ELIAS'S BABY
SHE AND BRIDGE OF LIGHT WANT TO TAKE IT
TO OWN IT LIKE SHE BELIEVES SHE OWNS ME
DO NOT LET THEM ERASE ME

CHAPTER 58

ESSIE

NEW YORK CITY

March 9, 1928

"I LOVE IT!" GODMOTHER EXCLAIMED WHEN SHE ENTERED THE GUEST room. She clapped gleefully as she admired the portrait on its easel. "It's your best yet. Wonderful! Just wonderful, Estelle."

Essie didn't respond. She only smiled tightly, not trusting herself to speak; she couldn't be sure if she would start babbling incoherently or laughing hysterically.

The longer she stayed here, the more she could feel her mind crumbling. Little pieces chipping away day by day.

Godmother leaned in close to the portrait, still grinning. Meanwhile, Essie barely resisted the urge to pick up the water basin on her night table and start bashing the old woman over the head with it.

"The contrast between the tribal and the modern," Godmother continued. "The dark and the light. I simply adore it!"

She continued raving for another ten minutes before finally leaving the guest room with promises to have one of the maids bring Essie's favorite dessert—peaches and cream—to celebrate the portrait's completion.

Essie had long ago given up her diet of just bread and water; the baby made her ravenous with hunger.

When Godmother closed the door behind her, Essie closed her eyes, walked to her bed, and screamed into her pillow.

For all her patron's talk of understanding the nuance and subtext in art, she hadn't understood why Essie had put herself in such ridiculous tribal dress in the portrait. She was The Bridge of Lights' African goddess, was she not? The cult's very own Mother Mary. And though Godmother had leaned in close, she hadn't noticed the message Essie had carefully written and hidden in small print, upside down in the multicolored cloth.

Days passed after the portrait's unveiling to Godmother. Essie bided her time, considering next steps. Today, she gazed at the painting while running her palm over her belly—the only thing that helped her keep track of time here. Her stomach hadn't swelled that much; it was barely noticeable in her nightgown. But it was now a hard mound, round and solid.

She'd felt the quickening three days ago. It was as if someone had run two little fingers along the inside of her stomach. Essie figured that put her at four-and-half-months pregnant now, maybe five. That meant she'd been stuck here for more than three months, though it felt a lot longer.

During that time, she'd walked around the bedroom at night, pacing her gilded cage, wondering what Godmother and her friends would do to her once the baby was born. Essie knew they would take the baby from her. They wouldn't entrust her with their little messiah. But would they kill her after the birth?

Yes, she'd decided. She didn't care what promises Godmother had made about protecting her. Maybe she would become some ritual sacrifice like Herr Bachmann.

But Essie didn't want to die. And now that she had accepted this baby was coming whether she liked it or not, she didn't want it taken from her either. She couldn't leave any child to be subjected to The Bridge of Light, to these demented, sadistic fools.

Essie glanced at the clock on the mantel. One of the maids would arrive within the hour to bring her dinner with a houseboy or footman bringing up the rear to make sure Essie didn't try anything.

Essie grunted as she dropped to her knees and reached under the guest bed. She removed a broken soup bowl that she'd dropped purposely earlier that week. The maid had removed some of the pieces but not all. In the bowl, Essie now mixed red and brown paint, adding her own saliva so that it resembled human blood in color and viscosity.

She took a palette knife and dipped it into the paint, before dragging the knife horizontally over her wrists over and over again, mimicking the jagged cuts of a blade, letting the paint ooze down her skin. She then sat on the hardwood floor at the foot of the bed and pooled the paint around her on each side. Even she marveled at how real it looked.

She tucked the broken bowl back underneath her bed, leaned back her head, closed her eyes, and waited.

The blood-curdling scream woke her up, along with the sound of shattering porcelain and glass and silverware clattering to the floor.

Essie was lucky that when she opened her eyes, she was facing away from the door and that the young woman had been so hysterical that she and her male companion hadn't noticed.

"She's dead! She's dead!" the maid screamed.

"What?" the footman replied as Essie closed her eyes again.

"Oh my God! She killed herself! We have to tell Mrs. Pickens!"

Essie then heard retreating footsteps.

She slowly opened her eyes again. She knew her window of opportunity was short. She had to leave now.

She hurriedly wiped off the oozing paint so she wouldn't leave a trail. Essie ran for the door and stepped into the hall, looking up and down the corridor, but she paused to glance over her shoulder at the painting. It was her last testament—in more ways than one. She couldn't leave it here.

Essie stepped back into the guest room, grabbed the portrait, and ran. Besides the maid's screams, she couldn't hear anything else yet.

She fled down the hall. When she reached the end of the corridor, she turned the corner and encountered another hall, but she wasn't sure where to go next. To her right or to her left?

After being locked in that room for so long, she struggled to remember the layout of the penthouse. Which corridor would lead her to one of the staircases and the first floor? She took her chances and headed right.

As she ran, she heard more footsteps and raised voices behind her. She darted inside one of the open doorways to hide, hoping the room was empty. She quietly shut the door behind her, listening to the sound of people approaching, holding her breath the entire time. She didn't release it until the thumping grew more distant, until she heard Agatha shout, "Call Dr. Philmore! Tell him to come at once!"

Then everything went quiet again.

Essie eased back from the door and jumped when she saw in the corner of her eye someone standing on the other side of the room. She clamped her hand over her mouth to stifle her scream. Within seconds, she realized it was her own reflection in a free-standing mirror.

She looked down at herself, at her flimsy silk and lace nightgown splattered with paint and her bare feet. If she somehow managed to make it outside of this apartment and to the street below, she would be fleeing in a blustery New York City winter. She wouldn't make it far in her current garb.

She set down her painting and quickly searched the room, looking around for something to wear. She went straight to double doors and opened them, revealing a walk-in closet. She could tell by the soft pastel colors, by the fur and silk, that she was in Lillian's room. The closet even smelled like the young debutante. Essie quickly reached for one of Lillian's mink floor-length coats. She grabbed a black cloche with a veil that would cover her face and a pair of Lillian's shoes from a shelf along the closet wall, but when she tried the shoes on, she discovered they wouldn't fit; they were too small.

"Damnit," she whispered. It looked like she would continue to run around barefoot.

Then, on the floor near the door, she spotted a pair of men's shoes. White buck oxfords. Why were Elias's shoes here?

She shook her head. It didn't matter. They were a bit large but they would work.

She exited the closet, grabbed her painting, and cracked open the bedroom door. Silence greeted her. She didn't see anyone either. Essie stepped into the hall, pulling the veil low over her face and clutching the fur coat tightly around her neck, and began walking down the corridor.

She finally spotted a staircase. It was one the servants used. She crept down the stairs, wincing with each echoing step, and arrived at another corridor. At the end, she could see the entrance to the great hall. That would take her to the front door.

Essie knew this part of her escape would be more perilous. Surely, they had realized her ruse and were searching for her. If she didn't get out in the next few minutes, she knew she would never escape.

She began to walk down the hall, forcing herself to keep her stride even, to not run and draw attention to herself. She could see servants in the rooms she passed. Most had their backs turned to her and did not look up when she walked by. She finally reached the great hall. The closer she drew to the oversized French doors, the faster her steps became.

In her periphery, she saw a footman pause as he walked down the staircase. He frowned at her.

She began to unlock the door as he walked down the stairs.

"Excuse me," he said, just as she pulled the door open.

She didn't answer him and, instead, slammed the door behind her and ran for the elevators. She frantically pressed the button over and over again. It had taken less than a minute but it felt like an eternity before the elevator car arrived.

She stepped past the operator into the compartment.

"F-f-first f-floor, please," she stuttered.

She didn't look up. She kept her head down while the elevator descended.

CHAPTER 59

SHE WAS CLOSE NOW.

Essie neared her block and took a cautious glance over her shoulder to make sure she wasn't being followed. That no one was watching her. She'd walked the entire way from Godmother's Park Avenue apartment to here, nearly one and half miles in the freezing cold and icy slush. She'd lost Lillian's hat along the way to the high, blustery winds.

A few times she thought she'd spotted Godmother's Rolls-Royce Phantom in the distance and she'd nearly jumped out of her skin, only to discover it was a white Ford Model A roadster or a black Rolls-Royce.

Essie had seen a few police officers during her journey. She'd wanted to go up to them, to tell them what had happened to her, but each time they turned her way with suspicious eyes or gave her a wary glance, she'd keep walking with her head down. She couldn't trust them, no more than she could trust Godmother or Elias.

They could be friends of the Bachmanns, she told herself. *They could be part of The Bridge of Light.*

Besides, she was just a poor Negro woman anyway. Why would the cops believe her?

Essie knew she could no longer stay in her apartment; they would come here looking for her soon. But she wanted to gather a few of her things and grab some money so she could take a train out of New York. She knew she had to leave; she and her baby wouldn't stand a chance in the same city as Godmother and her friends. But Essie's biggest challenge would be getting into her apartment with no keys.

She neared her brownstone and paused when she saw that the lights were on. They were blazing bright in her apartment.

Were the Bachmanns' henchmen already there?

She walked a little closer and stared through the parted curtains to find another young Negro woman sitting at a piano, writing notes on sheet music. The piano now sat where Essie's sofa used to be. And that wasn't the only thing that had changed inside the apartment. The steamer trunk where she kept her sketches was gone. So was the cabinet where she'd stored all her dishes.

Essie didn't know what had overcome her but she raced up the stairs of the brownstone, leaned over the railing, and started banging furiously on the window, startling the young woman inside. She watched as the woman whipped around from her piano to find Essie glaring at her through the glass.

"What do you want?" the woman asked as Essie continued banging. She looked frightened.

"That is my apartment! You're in *my* home!"

The young woman looked shocked then stepped away from the window. She appeared at the door a few seconds later, peering through the crack.

"I'm sorry, but I don't know what you're talking about," the woman said in a small voice. "This is my home. Maude Bachmann said I could stay here. When I came, it was already vacant."

"I used to live here. Godmoth—" Essie stopped herself. She couldn't stomach calling that woman "Godmother" anymore. "Maude let me live here. I had that apartment and the studio next to it. Did she keep any of my things? My clothes? My books? Did she keep *anything*?"

The young woman cracked open the door wider. She looked Essie up and down and slowly shook her head. "I told you. It was empty when I moved in."

Essie closed her eyes. The tears she had been holding back the entire night now came out in strangled sobs. "I have nothing! I have nothing. She took everything from me!"

"Wait," the young woman said. "Wait here."

She shut the door but Essie barely noticed, now overwhelmed with despair. She had no clothes. No money. She was wearing a nightgown, another woman's fur coat, and a man's shoes. Where should she go next? What friend could she go to for help? Could she trust them not to tell anyone they'd seen her?

She turned to face the staircase, to head back into the night, but stopped when she heard the door open again behind her. The young woman had returned like she promised. She held a fistful of dollar bills.

"It isn't much but she gave me extra this week. I get my allowance again tomorrow. You can have it." She held it out to Essie.

Essie wiped her eyes then her nose with the back of her hand. She hesitated only a second before taking the bills. "Thank you," she whispered.

The young woman nodded. "You're welcome."

Essie turned away then turned back around to face her. "You seem like a nice young lady."

The young woman's round face broke into a smile. "Why, thank—"

"Get away from here. Get as far away from Maude and all those crazy people as you can, and don't ever come back. I didn't listen to that advice when it was given to me. I hope you're smarter."

The young woman's smile faded. Essie turned again and fled.

CHAPTER 60
SHANICE

WASHINGTON, D.C.
Present day

THE SUN IS STARTING TO SET AND THE STREETLIGHTS ARE FLICKERING on by the time I arrive at the gallery on New York Avenue. I can see through the floor-to-ceiling windows that almost all of the overhead lights are out in the main showroom. It also looks like no one is inside. I hesitate at the glass door, pull my cell out of my purse, and check my old text messages and then the time on screen to make sure that I'm not too late.

Meet me at the gallery, Vivaldi wrote, at 6:30.

I'm on time, so where the hell is he?

I try the door handle and it opens. I step inside the darkened, cavernous space and look around me.

"Hello?" I call out. My voice echoes across the gallery.

Then, I hear the steady *clip, clop* of high heels over tiled floor. I turn to find the receptionist from months earlier walking out of the corridor leading to the back offices.

"Sorry, ma'am," she says with an apologetic smile, tucking her dark hair behind her ear. "But we've closed early today. I meant to put up the sign, but I hadn't—"

"Sonya," Vivaldi interrupts. He appears from the shadows as if he materialized out of thin air. He quickly walks toward us. "I've got this. Thank you. She is my guest."

"Oh," Sonya says. Her smile wavers. "Would you like me to stay to set the alarm for when you leave, Mr. Vivaldi? I can—"

"That won't be necessary," he says with an impatient shake of the head. "I'm perfectly capable of doing that myself. You can leave now. Enjoy the rest of your evening."

She demurely dips her head. "Yes, Mr. Vivaldi. Good night, sir," she says before turning to leave.

I watch as they both cross the gallery. She steps out of the door, letting it fall closed behind her as she strides down the sidewalk. He reaches up, does a little hop, and engages the door lock. He then turns to a nearby wall panel and presses a button, lowering venetian blinds that cover the floor-to-ceiling windows facing the street, darkening the showroom even more.

I wonder if Vivaldi realizes how much he sounds like an asshole when he speaks to people like that. It was one of the reasons why I didn't trust him the first time we met. It's why I wouldn't listen to him before, but I'm listening now thanks to the message hidden in Essie's painting.

"Do you still have the portrait?" he asks, walking back toward me. "Is it hidden in a secure place?"

I nod. "It's still safe."

I made up an excuse to Hanson, explaining that I needed to delay the pickup date for the paintings' shipment because I was finalizing the preparation of my grandmother's home for sale.

"Sure," Hanson said. "I completely understand. I suppose we can wait a few more days. Just be aware that we'll need enough time to prepare it for the museum as well. And you receive payment when I receive the painting."

"But I don't know how much longer I can hold Hanson off," I say now as I follow Vivaldi to his office. "He's going to start wondering why I haven't sent him the portrait."

"You won't have to do it much longer. I already know a journalist whom we can speak to," he says as he shoves open a door, revealing a large room filled with Baroque furniture, heavy, velvet curtains, and a mirrored shelf where Fabergé eggs are on display. I feel like I've been transported into a French palace except for the MacBook on his desk and the watercooler in his office corner.

"But I want to make sure we're on the same page before we speak to him," Vivaldi explains. "That you know everything I know about this."

"I'm already doing an article series about the portrait and Essie." I watch as Vivaldi opens one of his desk drawers and pulls out a manila folder. "I told my editor to hold it because I found something important that I wanted to include. Whatever you tell me today, I'll incorporate into the article."

Vivaldi pauses. "Does Hanson know about these articles?"

I nod. "He helped me with some of the research."

Vivaldi frowns. "Then your articles won't see the light of day if he has anything to do with it. Don't be fooled by any help he *claims* to offer." He flips open the manila folder and takes out a stack of papers. "Unfortunately, I did. I came to him and stupidly believed that he intended to be fair, that he wanted to do what was right. But I had no idea how manipulative and craven he is."

I look down at the stack and see typed on top of the first page, "LAST WILL AND TESTAMENT of MAUDE GERTRUDE BACHMANN."

"When I was cleaning out my father's attic, I stumbled upon Grannie Agatha's old files. For years, my great-grandmother had insisted that she was owed part of Bachmann's estate, but she had a stroke in 1933 and a few more thereafter. By the time I was born, her memory was already spotty . . . unreliable. No one believed her. It basically became family lore, until I found this." He points down at the will. "I simply could not believe my eyes. Bachmann *did* intend for several of her art pieces and some money to go to my great-grandmother, just like she said. It clearly says that here, but it also says that most of Bachmann's estate would go to her grandchild." He flips a few pages, gestures for me to come closer, and points down at a line of text for me to see.

"To the child born to my son Elias Bachmann and his lover, Estelle . . ." I read aloud then stop, shocked by the words on the page.

"You can have this copy of the will. I have my own," Vivaldi says as I pick up the papers and continue to read.

Maude willed nearly half of all her savings, trusts, and stocks to Elias and Estelle's child and joint ownership of all her properties to be shared between the child, Elias, and Lillian.

"Is . . . is this the baby that Essie was talking about in the painting? The one that she wrote that Maude and The Bridge of Light were trying to take away from her?"

Vivaldi nods. "I'm afraid so. There were . . . other things that Grannie Agatha said about Bachmann, about her days in New York, about The Bridge of Light that my family had dismissed as dementia, as a result of her strokes, because . . . well, because we didn't want to believe it, frankly," he says, lowering his eyes. "But now, after seeing your painting, I believe what she said was true."

"They kept Essie prisoner. They locked her up like some dog in a kennel, and were going to force her to give birth to this kid." I wince in disgust. "If she did kill Maude, hell . . . she'd be justified as far as I'm concerned! Who does this shit to another human being?"

Vivaldi loudly clears his throat. "I do not wish to presume to understand why Grannie Agatha and Bachmann did what they did to Johnson. Either way, Johnson somehow managed to escape. She made it all the way to Philadelphia."

"So, what happened to her baby?"

"That is the question." He steps from behind his desk. "And, if my suspicions and Hanson's assumptions based on research about your family are correct, your DNA may hold the answer."

I furrow my brows and squint at him. *"What?"*

"Johnson entrusted your great-great-grandmother Louise with her last painting, something that was so valuable to her that she took it with her when she fled New York. There's reason to believe that Johnson gave Louise a lot more before she died in that house fire. We believe she left the baby in Louise's care as well. Let me explain," he rushes out, because I'm even more confused now and showing it. "After I saw the message in the portrait, I told Hanson what I suspected. He wanted to confirm it before we took next steps, so he had his people . . . this legion of researchers look up your family's genealogical records using your grandmother's name and what other information we had. In a manner of days, they found a copy of the birth certificate for Estelle's child at a hospital in Philadelphia. It showed that in July 1928, Estelle gave birth to a girl she named Vivian Johnson. The father was listed as unknown. Then in the 1930 census, they found Louise living in Washington, D.C., with her two-year-old daughter, *Vivian* Mayhew. What are the chances that they both had daughters with the *same* name who would have been the *same* age in 1930 if Estelle's daughter had survived?"

He's right; the chances of something like that happening randomly are almost impossible.

I think back to Gram's funeral bulletin and the research I did about her mother's side of the family to write it. I'd found Gram's mother's . . . my great-grandmother's bulletin in her papers. I remember her: an elderly light-skinned woman with curly gray hair, wearing butterfly-shaped tinted glasses, smiling shyly in the photograph on the bulletin's cover.

Gram's mom's name was Vivian Idalene Lewis, fomerly Vivian Idalene Mayhew. As in *Aunt Idalene*. How had I not noticed that she had the same name as Essie's beloved aunt?

"Oh, my God! So, you think my great-grandmother was Essie and Elias's *baby*. Then, that would make me—"

"Bachmann's direct descendant . . . her *last* surviving direct descendant if you could prove it with a DNA test," he finishes for me. "You would have a right to the portion of the estate that was willed to your great-grandmother and perhaps her father's portion as well. An estate that's worth over six hundred million dollars today."

"Six hundred *million* dollars?"

"That is correct."

I'm starting to feel faint.

Inhale, exhale.

Inhale, exhale.

"I'm . . . I'm sorry . . . but . . . I have to sit down." I walk to one of the gold chairs near the water cooler and flop onto its velvet padded cushion. I drop the will to my lap and take slow, deep breaths.

"But it's all just conjecture at this point, Shanice," Vivaldi says. "Albeit conjecture with a *preponderance* of evidence, but nothing is proven. Be that as it may, Hanson didn't like the idea of it, the strong possibility that someone could challenge him for his estate. His lawyers were able to dismiss the will as a farce because there was nothing to corroborate it. No surviving witnesses. No evidence that any of what was written was true. But the painting shows that Johnson was pregnant. She was having a baby by Elias. Bachmann updated her will to include the child and Grannie Agatha. The will that he submitted in the lawsuit was the forgery, and he knows that."

"And that's why Hanson wants the painting," I murmur, making Vivaldi nod again.

"He and I agreed to work together to get it and, in exchange, he would give me what my family was owed. After that, I would destroy the will and we would never speak of it again. That was the deal. But I had no idea about the stalking and the harassment. That was not part of our agreement."

I glare up at him. "Why didn't you tell me any of this? That Hanson was behind it from the beginning? You keep talking about what *your* family was owed. What about mine? You said nothing about the will or Essie's baby . . . what it may have to do with my family. *Our* legacy. You were going to help him steal millions from us! All for what? Just to get some paintings?" I slowly shake my head in disgust. "You really are an asshole."

He grimaces. "I suppose I deserve that. And I deserve everything that has happened since." He gives a morose sigh. "You know what they say about making a deal with the devil. You only end up losing out in the—"

Vivaldi falls silent when we both hear a long, slow creak. It sounds like a door being opened.

"What was that?" I ease forward in my chair, staring at his office's opened doorway into the darkened hall. "I thought we were alone here."

"We are," he says, though he doesn't sound very convincing. "It's probably just an office door that was left open. Wait here," he says as he steps through the doorway. "I'm sure it's nothing, but I'll go check."

I shift back in my chair, fold the will, put it in my purse, and close the zipper for safekeeping. I listen to his receding footsteps as he walks down the hall. I grab one of the plastic cups next to the watercooler and pour myself a cup, drink, and pour myself another.

Vivaldi should be back by now. How long does it take to check a hallway?

I start to sip my second cup of water and walk to the office door to search for Vivaldi when I hear him shout, "No! Wait, please! You don't have to do this!"

Everything after that seems to happen in slow motion. I run into the hall and watch as Vivaldi crumples to the ground with a pained groan, making me drop my cup, cold water splattering all over the linoleum-tiled floor and the front of my sneakers.

Vivaldi clutches one hand over his stomach where a pumping wound spills blood onto the floor. The other hand falls to his side as his gasps and his body goes limp.

I look up and lock eyes with the shadowy figure in the ski mask, the person holding the bloody bowie knife. I'm frozen in terror as they stalk down the hall toward me.

CHAPTER 61

Run! Run now!

It feels like it takes forever for my legs to thaw, for my body to move, but it only takes seconds before I turn and try to run down the corridor to the showroom, to the glass doors and then outside. But the guy in the ski mask is faster. He sprints and lunges toward me with the knife, and I swear I can hear the blade zip through the air. I scream in anticipation of it sinking between my shoulder blades, of it cutting my back in two, but it catches the front of my purse instead as the guy slips in the pool of water I spilled. He falls to the ground, taking me with him.

I land on my knees. He lands on his ass and the knife slips from his fingers and goes spinning on its hilt toward the office door, knocking against the frame. I try to scramble back to my feet but he reaches for my belt, latches on, and tugs at my waist, pulling me toward him, yanking my feet from under me. Before I know it, he's on top of me, using his weight to pin me down.

I'm kicking, swinging, and screaming bloody murder. He tries to grip my wrists as I scratch at the mask and face, aiming for his eyes—the only vulnerable part of him that I can see. He shouts as my nails do their dirty work, nicking his right eye and ripping the front of the mask. I pull and the whole thing comes off. The light coming through the office doorway reveals the face that was hidden underneath. My eyes go wide.

"*Noah?*" I squeak.

At the sound of his name, he stills. His grip loosens on my wrist. He stares down at me blankly.

My face contorts again because I'm experiencing a different kind of pain this time. His betrayal feels like a stab from the knife.

"Noah, wh-why . . . why are you . . ."

His expression abruptly changes. His blue eyes go blank and his lips tighten into a thin, white line. The plains of his face harden into stone. His hold around my wrist tightens again like he's trying to crush the bone. Noah's gaze shifts toward the office floor where the bowie knife sits, and I know if there is any chance to escape him, I have to take it now.

I reach down to his crotch with my free hand and squeeze. I yank with all my might, making him release an ear-piercing squeal as the veins pop up along his brow and neck and his face goes beet red. He falls onto his side, cupping his crotch with his eyes squeezed shut, breathing sharply through his clenched teeth.

"Oh, you fucking bitch," he hisses.

I turn on my belly, climb to my knees, and run.

It's dark out here in the gallery. Darker than it was in the hallway now that the sun has completely set behind the blinds covering the floor-to-ceiling windows. I see a ghostly figure float past the glass, the silhouette of a pedestrian casually walking on the sidewalk past the gallery.

"Help me! Help me! He's trying to kill me!" I yell as I race toward the gallery's door and windows.

But the pedestrian doesn't pause; they keep walking. I realize the entire storefront must be soundproof glass.

I tug at the door handle, but it doesn't open. I pull again and again, but it doesn't budge.

It's locked, a voice in my head whispers. *Remember? Vivaldi locked the door.*

I begin to stand on the balls of my feet and reach up to disengage the door lock just as I hear Noah shout my name.

"Shanice! Shanice!" he bellows behind me.

I try to push the lock but my fingers are slippery. He's drawing closer. I can hear Noah's heavy footfalls now. I run back into the shadows and frantically look around me for a place to hide in the gallery filled with furniture and artwork. I finally settle on an antique secretary. I crouch behind it.

"You're gonna pull a move like that? Really, Shanice?" Noah calls to me in the dark. "But then again, you never made it easy for me, did you?" He limps farther into the gallery. "Where the fuck are you? I'm not in the mood for hide 'n' seek, babe."

I'm breathing so hard that I clamp my hand over my mouth to stifle the sound. I crouch even lower behind the secretary, praying that he won't find me.

"You know you brought this on yourself, don't you? You told me that you were better. That you were done with all this conspiracy shit, and I find out you set up a meeting with this asshole? You just couldn't leave well enough alone. You couldn't let go of that goddamn painting. Not even for a million dollars." He sighs gruffly. I can see his jean-clad legs and feet now less than thirty feet away. "Hanson sure as hell didn't offer Tommy and me a million bucks."

I look back toward the glass door that's halfway across the showroom. Could I make another run for it and unlock the door in enough time before Noah catches me? Probably not. I glance toward the hallway leading to the offices. There may be an exit door back there, which is probably how Noah got in, but I don't know where it is. I don't want Noah to box me in.

I look down at my purse that's still hanging around my neck. My phone is in there—along with my pepper spray. I slowly open my purse and reach inside, hoping I don't make a sound as I do it.

"It didn't have to be this way," Noah continues, drawing closer. "I tried to be good to you, to handle you with kid gloves. I tried *so* fucking hard, Shanice. We gave you chance after chance, but you wouldn't take it. Warning after warning."

When he says that, it all makes sense. *They* left those notes on my door and in my apartment. Tommy had been the one who ransacked my place that night, looking for the painting, while Noah and I were on our bowling date. Noah had tipped him off that I was on my way home so he would get out of there in enough time to go unseen. But he hadn't; I saw Tommy coming off the elevator. *That's* where I remember seeing him—*and* I saw him before that, back at the coffee shop on my first date with Noah.

Sneaking into my apartment building had been easy for them, as simple as slipping through the door behind another tenant. But getting into my apartment had required a key—the spare that Noah must have swiped off my kitchen counter when I wasn't looking.

"Your grandmother and that pain-in-the-ass librarian are dead because of you. You realize that, don't you?" he taunts, making me pause. "You fucking hear me, Shanice? The librarian was gonna ruin our plan, and your grandmother . . . well, we thought she was hiding the painting for you. Whoopsie!"

Noah chuckles, and I feel tears of rage prick my eyes at the memory of Gram's murder. I want to leap from behind the secretary and beat the hell out of him, but I know that's what he wants. He wants to trick me into revealing my hiding place, and I'll be damned if I let him manipulate me anymore.

My fingers finally grip onto my cell phone. I try to find the buttons on the side. I squeeze the buttons three times. The screen flickers on, creating a little spotlight in my corner of the gallery, illuminating my face and revealing the SOS Emergency button. I slide it to call 9-1-1.

Noah footsteps suddenly quicken. "But that's all water under the bridge now, isn't it? They're dead and now you're about to be dead too," he says as he nears the secretary.

"Help me!" I shout into my phone. "I'm at Dorian Gallery at

1100 New York Avenue. My ex-boyfriend is trying to kill me! He's already killed someone else. Please, send—"

I don't get to finish. Noah grabs my hair and yanks me to my feet, making me shout in pain and drop my phone. My hand latches onto my pepper spray as he swings. I feel the knife before I see it. Even as I twist and turn, it catches me in my left shoulder and I let out a scream I didn't think was humanly possible. I close my eyes and raise the pepper spray, sending a blast into his eyes.

He shouts out, lets me go, and goes careening into a wingback chair. He blinks over and over again, jabbing wildly into the air with his knife.

"That's it! I swear I will fucking kill you, Shanice!"

Despite the agonizing pain in my left shoulder, I run again for the door. I leap up once . . . twice and manage to undo the lock. When I push the door flies open and I sprint blindly into the night, hearing Noah scream my name behind me.

I'm on the sidewalk then asphalt. I can practically feel Noah's breath on my neck. His fingertips on the skin of my back. I keep running until I hear the car horn and see the glare of oncoming headlights, until the car barrels into us.

I open my eyes to find I'm no longer on New York Avenue. Instead, I'm back at Gram's house, standing at the threshold of the kitchen door. I can smell and hear the sound of crackling bacon.

The kitchen is the way it was before Dad, Dana, and I prepared the house for sale. There's disarray everywhere. Even a pile of mail and circulars sits on the counter. But all the disarray feels comforting somehow.

Mom sits in one of the kitchen dinette chairs. She's wearing one of her velvet tracksuits. She casually sips coffee from a green mug while gazing through all the potted plants at the view of the backyard. Gram stands at the stove, cooking breakfast.

"Hey, honey," Mom says with a grin before sliding out the facing kitchen chair. "Have a seat."

I slowly lower myself into the chair. "Am . . . am I dead?"

Gram laughs and glances over her shoulder at me as she flips a pancake. "No, chile, you are not dead."

I frown. "Then why am I here?"

Mom shrugs. "I guess you felt you needed to be."

I reach out and grab Mom's hand. It feels warm against my palm. "I miss you, Mom. I miss *both of you* so, so much."

She lowers her coffee cup and places her free hand on top of mine. "I know, honey. But we aren't far. Never were."

"Why can't I stay?" I ask, almost desperately. "It's been so hard without you. It feels even worse now that Gram is gone. So empty. I *need* you guys."

Mom shakes her head. "No, you don't, honey. We trust that you'll do just fine."

"But I don't know if I can—"

Mom raises a finger and presses it to my lips. I instantly go quiet. "Hush," she whispers.

"Don't even start up that nonsense," Gram says, using her spatula to make two plates of pancakes and bacon. She grabs both plates and brings them to the table. "You can't stay here. You've got too much to do. And like your mama said, we're not far." She sets the two plates on the table. "Okay, Marissa. Time for us to eat."

Mom lowers her finger, nods, and reaches for her knife and fork.

I glance at the stove. "Can't I get some food too?"

Now both of them are laughing. "Not here, honey," Mom says, before slicing into her pancake.

"Besides," Gram says, "you've been here long enough. Thanks for visiting. Your Mama and I missed you." She bends down and gives me a quick peck on the cheek like she used to whenever we said goodbye. "Now it's time to wake up."

PART V

CHAPTER 62
SHANICE

WASHINGTON, D.C.
Present day

When I opened my eyes again, it was inside a hospital room with Dad sleeping at my bedside. His large, warm hand was clasping mine and his head was cocked back. His mouth was hanging open as he snored. I heard a constant beep and realized it was a heart monitor.

I tried to shift, to turn toward Dad and speak, but I couldn't. My head felt like it weighed more than a ton. Someone had bound my left arm to my chest and there was an oxygen mask on my face.

"Malcolm. Malcolm!" Dana shouted as she rushed across the hospital room. She roughly shook Dad's shoulder. "She's awake! She's awake, honey!"

Dad snorted as his eyes fluttered open and he shot upright in his chair. He gazed at me, leaned forward, and grinned. "Hey, kid," he whispered. "Welcome back."

The accident didn't leave me with any long-term injuries. Just some bad cuts, a concussion, and a broken ankle, according to my doctors. But Noah wasn't as lucky.

The cops told me while interviewing me in my hospital room that Noah took the brunt of the impact from the Nissan Sentra that hit us. The paramedics couldn't save him. I also found out that day that the man I fell in love with, the same man who tried to murder me, wasn't Noah Kelly. His name was Cody Jensen.

Not only did I tell the cops that Noah . . . *Cody* murdered Vivaldi and tried to kill me that night too, but he'd done it under the orders of Hanson Whitmore.

"He and Thomas . . . they're brothers. They worked together for Hanson. They've been stalking me for months. Harassing me, all because Hanson wanted my painting. Thomas even killed my grandmother for it. Vivaldi told me everything before he was murdered. Cody confessed it too. Hanson Whitmore is responsible for all of this. He's the mastermind behind *everything*."

The cops gave me the same incredulous look that all the other cops had given me in the past. Of course, they didn't arrest Hanson. Besides what I told them and the words of two dead men, they didn't have much to go on. Thomas remained tight-lipped, refusing to corroborate any of my story. I suspect that Hanson had gotten to him, told him lies that he could get him out of jail if he continued to keep his secrets.

So, nothing happened—at first.

I told the story to the news crews who came to Dad's house days later while I was recovering from the car crash. With my ankle in a brace and my arm in a sling, I pointed out the message in Essie's painting. I showed them the copy of the will Vivaldi had given me. My story went from local D.C. evening news to primetime on the major networks.

If Hanson went after me or my family again, this time he couldn't do it in secret. *Everyone* would know he was likely behind it.

Hanson's lawyers threatened me with lawsuits, defamation for "attempting to destroy his character with false allegations," and breach of contract for not giving him the painting, as promised. He threatened to sue *The Miscreant* and no longer fund its parent company if the editors ran my essays about Essie, Maude, and the portrait. Priya had to kill the story, but not before sending me the email address and number for an editor at *The New Yorker* who was desperate to run the essays instead.

Make sure they pay you double what we offered, Priya texted.

I used the proceeds from the sale of Gram's house to get a lawyer of my own. It's surprisingly easy to find a legal team when there's six hundred million dollars at stake. We got a document authenticator to prove that the will wasn't a forgery. I got a DNA test and a genealogist to show that I was genetically related to the Bachmann family. And we reached out to the one person who probably hated Hanson just as much as I did.

"So," Skylar Whitmore said with an impish smile as she plopped her gold Gucci purse on the countertop at the bar in Georgetown where we agreed to meet, "you finally figured out my dad's the selfish bastard I told you he was. I tried to warn you," she said as the bartender handed her the citrus white wine spritzer she ordered. She sucked on the lime garnish and took a sip.

"You could've just told me what your dad was doing?" I said.

"Like I said that night, I didn't know if I could trust you . . . trust your intentions. My dad surrounds himself with some pretty messed-up people who would do just about anything to keep him happy. I didn't know if you were one of them." She swirled her straw around and around in her glass before eying me. "You know he conned me first, right? Cody?"

I did a double take. "What?"

"Yeah, he made me believe that he'd fallen in love with me too." Her smile disappeared. She lowered her eyes. "He was quite the charmer . . . and so full of shit," she spat.

"Oh, Skylar," I whispered.

No wonder she had been glaring at us when we arrived in the Hamptons.

"Cody and his brother stole over eighty thousand dollars from me. And he turned into a tremendous prick when I figured out what was going on. He threatened to release . . . well . . . pictures of me if I told the police what he'd done. I felt like an idiot going to Dad, telling him I'd been conned, and asking for help." I could see from the way her usually confidant facade faltered for a few seconds and she curled in on herself that she was still ashamed. "But instead of letting me press charges, he *hired* those bastards to work for him. He said it wasn't even that much money I'd lost and I needed to stop thinking about myself . . . to 'see the bigger picture.' So, yes, if that's what you're asking me: I can testify in your case, get recordings of my dad admitting how much of an asshole he is, whatever. I'll do it. I want him to suffer for what he's done too."

"Even if it means you'll have less money if I win?" I asked. I didn't want her to back out once she realized the full ramifications of her decision. "I'm suing for half the estate, Skylar, including the foundation."

"So we'll have more money than ninety-eight percent of the population instead of ninety-nine?" Skylar laughed. "If you knocked off fifty million from my trust fund, I'd still have plenty left. I'll survive."

She then held up her glass for a toast. I clinked mine against hers and watched as she brought her spritzer to her mouth, threw back the glass, and downed the rest of her drink.

She tilted her head, making her blond ponytail sway. "So, if you're related to the Bachmanns, are we like . . . cousins now?"

I paused, lowering my mojito. "Yeah, I guess. Distant cousins."

"Cool." She sucked on her lime again, nodded, and smiled. "So I read your articles in *The New Yorker.* They were really good."

"Thanks," I said before taking a drink.

"I'm sorry for what happened to Estelle. It sounds like she deserved better than what happened to her. A lot better."

I swallowed and stared into my glass. Gradually, I nodded and met her eyes again. "She did."

Skylar raised her wine spritzer. "To Estelle?"

I joined her in another toast. "To Estelle," I said, smiling as our glasses clinked.

CHAPTER 63

I PLOP ONTO THE SOFA IN THE LIVING ROOM OF MY NEW APARTMENT with my cell in hand to check my voicemail. I was in my home office, working on the outline and chapters of the book about Estelle, Maude, the tangled history they shared, and its far-reaching impact on my family and my life. Seven publishers made bids on it just based on *The New Yorker* essays and all the news coverage about what happened.

I've been staring at pages and my laptop screen for hours. I'm overdue for a break.

"Congratulations, Ms. Pierce." The voice I recognize is one of the lawyers at Wayne & Stanton, LLP, who have been representing me this past year in my lawsuit against Hanson and the Whitmore Foundation. "They have finally agreed to settle on the terms that we listed. You are now a fifty percent owner of the Whitmore trust and all the Whitmore Foundation's holdings. I'll have one of my assistants send you the paperwork soon. Oh, and Mr. Whitmore has agreed to drop the lawsuits regarding defamation and Estelle Johnson's portrait. You can proceed with your loan to the National Museum of African American History and Culture for its Harlem Renaissance exhibit as planned. Let me know if you have any additional questions. We'll be in touch."

I lower the phone from my ear and set it on the cushion beside me. After all that's happened, after all I've been through, it ends with one phone call. A voice message.

Gram would grunt and roll her eyes right now. "You telling me we went through all that drama just for this," she'd say.

But that's a lot of money I've inherited. I could start my own foundation under Essie's name to help fund inner-city, altruistic projects or give money to struggling artists and writers. There's a lot of good I can do. And Hanson may not be in jail, but his reputation has taken quite the hit. I heard several of his partners have pulled out of projects with him. He was kicked off two of his boards. A company he had funded that was going public announced it was changing plans just last week. And he knows I'm the reason why all this is happening to him, which is perfectly fine with me.

Just like Maude and Essie, it seems that Hanson and my name will now be inextricably linked.

I glance at the funeral bulletins that are splayed on my coffee table that I've been using in my research for my novel, to add even more color to this tangled story, if I can. Gram's bulletin sits on top. Not only are these bulletins full of people who were once important to Gram, like her mother . . . my great-grandmother Vivian, they hold the memories of our family. Memories I don't want forgotten.

I place Gram's funeral bulletin back in my ring binder, then Mom's. I sift through the pile and notice one for Louise Mayhew, Essie's dear friend and the woman who raised Essie's daughter, Vivian. I pick it up. It's been aged yellow by time. There's no photo and it was obviously made with a typewriter. I try to imagine some poor church secretary carefully tapping out the words on some ancient Remington portable. I read the bulletin's cover.

"Louise Mayhew, born November 19, 1903, died June 6, 1947," I read aloud then pause.

Wait a minute. That can't be right. I distinctly remember in her letters, Essie wishing Louise a happy birthday in April. *Essie* was the one with the birthday in November.

I sit down the bulletin and walk across my living room to the shoebox of Essie's letters. I quickly rifle through the stack and find the letter I was looking for. I was right. In a letter dated April 12, Essie writes, *I wish you a happy birthday, dear one. Sorry that I cannot be there with you!*

I look again at the bulletin. "That's weird," I murmur.

How could they have gotten the birth date so wrong? Why would she have Essie's birthday month and not her own?

I read more of the bulletin. It gives more of the details of Louise's life. How she grew up in Turnbridge, South Carolina. How she attended college as a young woman and never married.

"None of this is right," I murmur.

Louise didn't go to college; Essie was the one who graduated from Claflin University. And more than once in her letters, Essie referenced Louise's ex-husband. The one who never married before she died was Essie.

Suddenly, a thought springs to mind. I remember another passage from one of Essie's letters about how she and Louise used to dress alike when they were little girls and wear their hair a certain way to confuse others because they looked so much alike.

"Oh my God," I whisper.

The birth date on the funeral bulletin and the other biographical details . . . what if . . . Great-Great-Grandma Louise was not Louise Mayhew; what if she was Essie? Essie could have assumed the identity of her best friend and doppelganger, changing her name but not all the details of her life. It would be an easy thing to do back then. This is before the age of photo IDs and fingerprint tracking. Both women were transient; Essie could easily settle in a new place—just her and her baby, Vivian—with a new name and no one would be the wiser.

So, was Louise the one who died in the house fire and was misidentified?

I set down the bulletin and fall back against the sofa cushions, stunned.

Why would Essie assume Louise's identity?

For peace, maybe. To no longer have to look over her shoulder. She was on the run from The Bridge of Light, from cops and detectives who were on her trail and eager to charge her with Maude's murder. But it's impossible to charge someone with murder when they're already dead.

But I don't think Essie found the peace of mind she'd so longed for.

"*I think Grandma Louise was real sickly*," Gram had told me. *"In and out of hospitals most of her life, from what little I heard about her. Even went to a sanitarium once."*

I suspect what had happened to her forever changed her. It left an imprint on all of us in her line.

I close the bulletin and add it to the binder. I consider only briefly adding this to the book. But then, I decide against it. Essie wanted to disappear, for only her paintings to survive and tell her story.

Maude and the others had no respect for what she wanted; I will not do the same.

I glance at the portrait that now hangs on my living room wall. "Okay, Essie, I'll let this one go."

Some mysteries will just have to remain unsolved.

CHAPTER 64

LILLIAN

NEW YORK CITY

March 9, 1928

THEY STOOD AT THE DOOR, HOVERING CLOSE ENOUGH TO HEAR THE conversation between the two women on the other side. The voices were muffled but the emotions were clear.

"*How* could this have happened?" Aunt Maude asked.

"I don't know, ma'am," Agatha replied. "The maid left the door open when she found her in her room. She thought . . . she thought she had committed suicide so she—"

"Well, obviously she hadn't!"

"No, it was a foolish mistake. But I will take care of this. Estelle will be found. Perhaps she hasn't left. Perhaps she is still in the home now, hiding and—"

"You don't know that! She could be miles away and she has taken my Klaus with her, and now we have no idea where she is."

Lillian rolled her eyes and then locked gazes with Elias as he slumped back against the wood paneling.

Lillian and Elias had both been subjected to Aunt Maude and Uncle Klaus's "spiritualism" for more than a decade, since they were teenagers. What at first had been a quirk, a bemusing eccentricity had since morphed into an all-consuming obsession that had taken hold of them all.

Did Lillian or Elias believe in The Bridge of Light? As much as they believed Charlie Chaplin was their Lord and Savior.

It was one of many secrets they kept between them. Mocking Godmother privately, but indulging her publicly to stay in her good graces and make sure she didn't cut them off financially.

She claimed she knew everything that went on in her home—but she didn't know that.

The two cousins pantomimed the cult's rituals, even taking part in Uncle Klaus's ghastly murder, though honestly, Lillian had considered it more like putting the old simpleton out of his misery. A mercy killing of sorts.

They had even accepted Aunt Maude's imprisoning Essie, though Elias had done so reluctantly. Lillian figured in due time she would have to take care of Essie herself, since there was no way she could allow that baby to be born. But it seemed for now that Essie had escaped, throwing a monkey wrench in her plan. And now Aunt Maude was on a rampage.

"Making sure that she stayed here and her and the baby remained safe was *your* responsibility, Agatha," Aunt Maude went on. "And you assured me you could do it. You have greatly disappointed me."

"Again, I'm sorry, but I—"

"I want you to pack your things and leave here tonight. This very instant!"

Elias's mouth fell open, gobsmacked. "*What?*" he whispered just as Agatha said the same on the other side of the door.

Lillian raised a finger to her lips. Her gaze hardened into a glare. Elias instantly quieted.

"Ma'am, I have been your secretary for more than two decades," Agatha said, her normally confident voice now trembling. She hiccupped. Lillian could envision the woman's sad, wrinkled face now wet with tears. "I have served you well, doing everything that you've ever asked of me. I've followed your teachings. My husband and I are members of The Bridge of Light. We—"

"Which is *even more* of a reason why you should have understood why keeping Estelle here was important," Godmother replied.

"I've . . . I've left my family . . . my . . . my *children* to serve you. To be here and cater to you. To let this *one* thing eradicate all of—"

"I will hear no more, Agatha," Godmother said. "Please leave."

"But you promised me that you would—"

"Leave . . . *now*!"

The room fell silent. Someone cleared their throat.

"Yes, ma'am," Agatha said. They heard shuffling footsteps. Agatha would be at the door soon and both women would know they had been listening. Lillian quickly crept away and Elias followed.

"Can you believe it?" he asked with a snort when they neared the end of the corridor. "She gave Agatha her walking papers." Elias flinched when they heard a door slam behind them. A door that had probably been slammed by Godmother's former secretary. "I never thought that day would come."

"She's completely lost her marbles," Lillian said under her breath. "It'll be us next. You know that, don't you?"

As they turned the corner, nearing her bedroom, Elias frowned. "What do you mean?"

"I mean she already added your bastard to her will under some deranged belief that it's the reincarnation of her dead husband."

"Must you bring that up again? I had no idea she would—"

"*If* she does find Essie and that child is born, what's to stop her from disinheriting us and giving all the money to the child in the end? She could do it merely on a whim," Lillian said, pushing open her door. She walked across the room, heading straight to her dresser while Elias shut the door behind them and locked it. She yanked open the top drawer, removing a bottle of brandy and a tumbler.

Lillian watched in the corner of her eye as Elias kicked off his shoes, loosened his necktie, and fell back onto her bed, getting comfortable like he usually did.

"She won't find her." He adjusted the pillow behind his head before grabbing her cigarette case and lighter on her night table. "Essie could be as far away as New Jersey by now," he said as he lit a cigarette.

"Maude will go to the ends of the earth to find her." Lillian poured herself a drink. "She won't let her go. She's become her new obsession."

Elias blew out a puff of smoke. "Well, I for one hope that Essie gets away. I couldn't stomach her spending another week locked in that room. She didn't deserve that."

"No," she said before taking a drink, "*I* didn't deserve being subjected to your seemingly endless string of whores. One after another. Essie just happened to be one that Godmother decided to take under her wing."

Elias groaned. "Lily, we've always had an understanding. You know that. I've never objected to the men you've chosen to share your time with." Elias took another drag from his cigarette.

Lillian didn't respond, choosing instead to finish her glass of brandy.

Yes, they did have an understanding since they became lovers in their early teens. But they had remained close. Lillian always knew she had Elias wrapped around her little finger—that is until she heard about Aunt Maude's new pet . . . the up-and-coming Negro artist, Estelle Johnson.

Lillian had told Essie the truth when she said Elias couldn't stop talking about her while visiting in Europe (even while they lay naked in bed together) and how much it had annoyed her. When she finally met Essie, she was not only underwhelmed by the young woman, but confused by what Godmother and Elias saw in her. Why were they so taken with her? What was the appeal?

It plagued Lillian, keeping her up at night. She *had* to know. So, when Godmother invited Essie to spend the night, Lillian used the servants' tunnel to creep into her room as she slept. To watch her when she wasn't aware she was being watched. But then she woke up and Lillian was forced to flee.

Lillian then saw Essie again in the library—this time with Elias, torturing herself as she watched them make love.

Lillian now understood what Essie *really* meant to Aunt Maude, how she had become part of the old woman's fanatical delusions about The Bridge of Light, but she still could not understand why Elias had any interest in her. She just hoped it wouldn't mean that Elias would get in her way, that he wouldn't listen and obey like he used to. Because if they played their cards right, the events of the night—Essie's escape and the ever-vigilant Agatha now gone—could work in their favor.

"Never mind all that now." She lowered her empty glass back to her dresser, walked across the bedroom, and sat on bed beside him. "I have no desire to waste time arguing about who else you've shared your bed with, Elias. We have to fix this mess, and I have a plan."

She told him every detail and when they would do it. When she finished, Elias went quiet. He sat forward. "You want me to kill my mother?" he finally whispered, looking horrified.

"You killed your father. What difference does it make?"

"I didn't kill my father," he hissed. "It was part of the ceremony. I *had* to do it."

"Whatever you wish to tell yourself, darling. Either way, you're perfectly capable of doing it again."

He shook his head. "No, this is different. This is—"

"What needs to be done," she said, clasping his face, leaning in close. "And you will do it, because we have no other choice. She's pushed us to this, Elias."

She then kissed him, long and hard, and lowered her hand to his waistband, making him moan against her lips, ending their argument.

After the rest of the household had fallen asleep, she and Elias crept into the tunnel and headed to Aunt Maude's bedroom. "Use this," she said, holding the palette knife wrapped in cloth to him.

He squinted in the dim light from the candle she held. "Why?"

"Just trust me," she said, choosing not to explain this part of her plan.

She'd been inspired by Essie's fake suicide. She wanted to throw the police off their trail and what better way than using a weapon covered in Essie's fingerprints?

Elias reached for the knife but paused. He quickly shook his head. "I can't do it," he said. "She's my mother, Lily."

"You *have* to."

"No, I won't. I—I can't."

She could tell from the look in his eyes that he meant it. He was going to defy her. They were no longer connected; Elias was no longer hers. Had she lost him to Essie, or had it happened before that? Had murdering his own father been too much? She took only a few seconds to mourn the loss of the bond they once shared before pushing back her shoulders.

"Fine," she said through clenched teeth, "I'll do it then. Wait here."

Lillian then blew out the candle, plunging them both into darkness.

He didn't speak again. He didn't try to stop her either as she slowly pushed open the hidden door leading into Aunt Maude's bedroom and stepped inside.

AUTHOR'S NOTE

Nearly four years ago, I stumbled upon the story of Charlotte Osgood Mason—Harlem Renaissance patron and the inspiration for the character Maude Bachmann—while reading an article about Zora Neale Hurston's posthumously released work, *Barracoon*.

I'd been a fan of Hurston since my high school English teacher assigned her book, *Their Eyes Were Watching God*, as class reading. I loved not only Hurston's voice as a writer, but also how smart, vivacious, and opinionated she seemed. Though the world at that time went to great lengths to make Hurston feel inferior as a black woman and limit herself as an artist, she'd wanted no part of it. She seemed to live life on her terms—much like the character, Essie Johnson. So, I was surprised to read about the drama surrounding *Barracoon* eighty-seven years ago, and how the almost forgotten manuscript was a product of a battle of artistic visions and wills between Hurston and her patron, Mason.

For years, Mason had influenced and tried to outright control Hurston's life and art with her money. She'd done the same to several other Harlem Renaissance artists she patronized, from Langston Hughes to Alain Locke.

The more I read about Mason, or "Godmother," as she instructed many of her protégés to call her, the more I knew I had to write about this woman. Though I took several liberties with Bachmann's character in *Do What Godmother Says* (Mason was never in a cult and never abducted one of her artists), Mason's life still makes for a fascinating—if bizarre—tale.

Charlotte Osgood Mason was born Charlotte Louise Van der Veer Quick, to a family of farmers in New Jersey. She was a descendant of some of the first Dutch settlers in New York and would later inherit railroad fortune through her mother's side of the family. Charlotte Quick would marry Dr. Rufus Osgood Mason, a well-respected New York City surgeon almost twenty years her senior and family friend of the Rockefellers. Dr. Mason was one of the founding fathers of parapsychology and hypnotherapy. He conducted research and wrote papers about ESP, telepathy, out-of-body experiences, and remote viewing during his lifetime.

The Masons may not have had much in common, but they shared an interest in the supernatural. He introduced her to the concepts of "visions" and "divine energy." The Masons also believed in the spiritual superiority of the so-called "primitive cultures" of the Native Americans and Africans. Charlotte even claimed to have had visions of a "flaming pathway to Africa" that, if followed, could help cure the spiritually bereft white American society. She would become obsessed with creating this flaming pathway to Africa before she died.

After Dr. Mason's death, Charlotte with her sizable fortune had plenty of money to invest in her spiritual philosophy, funding the "primitive art" she so believed in. One of those investments was in the work by ethnomusicologist Natalie Curtis in her collection of traditional music of Native American tribes in the Southwest. Mason also gave what was estimated to be as much as one million dollars to fund the work of black artists like Hurston.

But the money Charlotte gave came with many conditions that her protégés could not have foreseen. Charlotte not only wanted to give feedback on their work, she also wanted to control the content and when and where her artists submitted. (There are some theories that Hurston's use of Southern African American dialect in her literary work and exploration of African American and Caribbean folklore was heavily influenced by Mason's own spiritual beliefs and artistic preferences.) Even Mason's contract with Hurston dictated that she owned Hurston's anthropological research material, from her documents to her recordings, while Mason was her patron. Mason kept Hurston's research in a locked safety deposit box to which Hurston did not have a key.

Mason's control also extended into her artists' personal lives. The detail I included about Essie having to write an itemized list of all her purchases and give it to Maude for review was based on a real-life example: Mason made Hurston do the same. Mason also expected detailed letters from her protégés about their lives and work, making some keep journals and read the journal entries to her.

If Mason disliked someone, she implicitly expected that the person would be excommunicated from her artists' lives as well. When Mason had a falling out with Langston Hughes, Hurston—his close friend and collaborator—distanced herself from the poet. She did it partly because of a disagreement she had with Hughes over the production and credit of their play, *Mule Bone*, and also out of fear of alienating Mason, according to one of her letters.

Unlike Maude Bachmann, Mason ended her years as a patron of the Harlem Renaissance through disenchantment with the movement rather than murder. She would eventually part ways with all of her protégés who chafed or outright rebelled against her control. Though Mason supposedly saw Africa and black culture as a "flaming pathway" to enlightenment in white American society, in the end, she would leave no money to any black causes, institutions, or artists after her death. She would only leave behind a complicated legacy and the strange tale of the "Godmother" of the Harlem Renaissance.

CITED WORKS

Booth, Melinda. "Charlotte Osgood Mason: Politics of Misrepresentation." *Oakland Journal* 10 (2006): 49–65.

Kaplan, Carla. *Miss Anne in Harlem: The White Women of the Black Renaissance.* New York: HarperCollins, 2013.

Marx, Edward. "Forgotten Jungle Songs: Primitivist Strategies of the Harlem Renaissance." *Langston Hughes Review* 15, no. 1/2 (Spring/Fall 1996): 79–93.

Pankova, Rebecca. "A Different Backstory for Zora Neale Hurston's 'Barracoon.'" *Los Angeles Review of Books*, July 7, 2018.

Story, Ralph D. "Patronage and the Harlem Renaissance: You Get What You Pay For." *CLA Journal* 32, no. 3 (March 1989): 284–295.

Van Atten, Susan. "A Literary Friendship and the Harlem Renaissance." *Atlanta-Journal Constitution*, March 26, 2019. https://www.ajc.com/entertainment/books—literature/literary-friendship-and-the-harlem-renaissance/a2ib4QzVZMk80FkyMMfRTN.

American Experience, "Zora Neale Hurston: Claiming a Space." Written and directed by Tracy Heather Strain. Aired January 17, 2023, on PBS.

ACKNOWLEDGMENTS

Though my pen name L.S. Stratton is still new to the literary world, I, as an author, am not. I've been writing fiction professionally since I was nineteen years old, and each book has been an adventure filled with both highs and lows. But I wouldn't trade any of it, and I'm honored to have people who have supported me and helped me facilitate my writing career all these years.

I want to thank my hubs, Andrew, for all his love and support. You've pep-talked me through my tears of frustration and joined me in celebration. Thanks for being my life partner, cheerleader, and sounding board. I also want to thank my parents for developing and encouraging my love of reading, and later writing. You always took my desire to write books seriously, even when my imposter syndrome didn't allow me to do the same.

I want to thank my rockstar agent, Barbara Poelle, for always making me feel important even though I know she has a long roster of clients and five million things to do any given day. We've been together for almost a decade now, and I still feel lucky that you saw something in my work and wanted to represent me.

Thanks to my editor, Laura Schreiber, for her wit, humor, and insight. You've made my writing so much stronger and made me see my stories in such unique ways. My books are my babies and you've handled them with care. And thanks to the rest of the team at Union Square & Co. for your tireless work and ideas.

I also want to say thanks to fellow writers who have shared words of wisdom and encouragement with me. You've been through this journey and know what it's like. Writing can be a lonely enterprise, but it feels less so when you've found your tribe.

Finally, I want to thank the readers who have reached out to me personally, written reviews, or even just purchased my books. You complete the circle and make this all worthwhile.